Every Wrong Reason

Rachel Higginson

Other Books Now Available by Rachel Higginson

<u>Love and Decay</u>
Love and Decay, Season One, Episodes One-Twelve
Love and Decay, Season Two, Episodes One-Twelve
Love and Decay, Season Three, Episodes One-Twelve

<u>Star-Crossed Series</u>
Reckless Magic
Hopeless Magic
Fearless Magic
Endless Magic
The Reluctant King
The Relentless Warrior
Breathless Magic
Fateful Magic
The Redeemable Prince

<u>The Starbright Series</u>
Heir of Skies
Heir of Darkness
Heir of Secrets

<u>The Siren Series</u>
The Rush
The Fall
The Heart

The Five Stages of Falling in Love, an Adult Contemporary Romance

Bet on Us, an NA Contemporary Romance

Magic and Decay, a Rachel Higginson Mashup

<u>The Forged in Fire Series</u>
Striking
Brazing

To my parents,
For teaching me the magnitude of forgiveness.

Prologue

<u>Reasons He's Wrong for Me</u>.
1. He's the most **selfish** person I know.
2. I would be **happier** without him.
3. He can't take a shower without leaving water **everywhere**.
4. If I have to clean up his toothpaste **one more time** I'm going to go insane.
5. How **hard** is it to put the milk away?
6. I don't **love** him anymore.
7. We were **never** right for each other.

How did we get here?

Again?

I just wanted to go to bed. I had the most obnoxious day of my freaking life and all I wanted to do was come home, take the longest, hottest shower in the history of showers and face plant into my pillows.

Instead, it's three o'clock in the morning and I have a migraine that's trying to murder my brain. Goddamn it.

"This isn't about the water all over the bathroom floor, Nick. God, honestly! It's about the principal of the water all over the bathroom floor!"

"Are you kidding me? What the hell does that even mean?" His handsome face contorted with frustration. He wouldn't even look at me.

I thought back and tried to remember the last time he looked at me, *really looked at me*, and couldn't remember. When was the last time he saw me? When was the last time we hadn't been fighting long enough for his clear blue eyes to look into mine and make a real connection?

It had been years.

Maybe he had never seen me.

"It means there's water all over the floor! Again! How many times have I asked you to clean up after your shower? I'm not asking for much! I

11

just want the full inch of water cleaned up off the floor so that when I go in there I don't soak my socks *every single time*!"

"You're going to take your socks off anyway! Why does it matter?" His long arms flew to his side as he paced the length of our bedroom.

I flopped back on the bed and the pillows depressed with the weight of my head. I felt like crying, but I wouldn't let something this stupid bring me to tears. I *wouldn't*.

Not again.

This whole argument wasn't really about the water. He was right; I had been planning to take my socks off. But I was so sick of asking him to do something so simple. Why couldn't he just listen to me? For once?

"Fine," I relented. "I don't care. Let's just go to bed."

"Typical," I heard him mutter.

I peeled my fingers away from my face and propped myself up on my elbows. His back was to me as he stared unseeingly at our closed blinds. I could see the tension taut through his broad shoulders. His thin t-shirt pulled on the sculpted muscle he was so proud of.

It was so late and both of us had to work in the morning, which only proved to fuel my frustration. His run had lasted forever tonight. He left shortly after dinner and hadn't come home until close to ten. I had started to think something had happened to him.

When I asked him where he was, he told me his running group had gone out for beers afterward. He'd gone out for beers and hadn't bothered to text or call or let me know he was alive and not dead in the ditch somewhere.

I'd had a terrible day and my husband got to go out for beers at the end of an excessively long run while I did the dishes, cleaned up the kitchen, started his laundry and graded papers.

And then at the end of all of it, I'd walked into an inch of standing water on our bathroom floor because he couldn't be bothered to clean up after himself.

And he wants to throw around the word "typical."

Okay, maybe it wasn't a *full* inch. That might have been a tiny exaggeration.

At least Nick was smart enough not to point that out.

Smart enough or he valued his life. And by life, I meant balls.

"What was that?" My voice pitched low and measured, in complete opposition to the pounding of my heart and rushing of blood in my ears.

This was not the first time we'd had such a lengthy blow-up. In fact, we fought more than we got along. If I were truly honest with myself, I couldn't remember the last time I'd enjoyed being around him.

"It's typical, Kate. Just when I finally get to the bottom of why you're so pissed off, you decide to shut down and turn yourself off. You're ready for bed and I just finally figured out what crawled up your ass. So what am I supposed to do with that now? Just forget it? Move on and pretend you didn't keep me up all hours of the night yelling about it? God knows, *you* will."

"I'm tired, Nick. It's three o'clock in the morning. We both have to work tomorrow! What do you *want* me to do? I guess we could sit here and talk in circles until the sun comes up, but like you said, you finally get it!"

"God, you can be a bitch."

His words hit me like a slap across the face. "And you can be a selfish asshole."

I watched his face fall. It was that perfect kind of hit that took all of the wind right out of his sails. His entire body deflated and I knew I hurt him as badly as he hurt me. Except instead of making me feel better about myself, I realized I had never felt worse.

He slumped down at the edge of our bed and buried his face in his hands. His tousled, light brown hair fell over the tips of his fingers and reminded me of the times I used to brush it back, out of his eyes.

Even now, after seven years of marriage, he was still one of the most gorgeous men I had ever seen. His tall frame was packed with lean muscle and long limbs. His face was blessed with sharp angles and deep, soulful blue eyes, a square jaw hidden behind a closely cropped beard like he'd forgotten to shave for a few days. His wild hair was a little longer on top than on the sides, but despite his unruly hair he had always been casually clean cut. No piercings. No tattoos. And his lips had always been dry, for as long as I could remember. But he had this way of dragging his tongue across them that used to make my mouth water.

I fell in love with him on our second date. We shared mutual friends that introduced us. My roommate Fiona was dating his track teammate, Austin, and one Saturday in October during our junior year of college, she finally hauled me along to one of their local meets.

We hit it off after he took first place in the thirty-two hundred and he was in a celebratory enough mood to not stop smiling. *I* couldn't stop staring at his lonely dimple or his bright blue eyes. He had the keen insight to know he'd charmed me.

Or maybe he just read the very obvious signs. I was not good at hiding my feelings.

Our first date was an absolute disaster, though. I was awkward and he was nervous. We didn't find much to talk about and when he dropped me back at my dorm, I swore to Fiona that he would never call me again.

I never understood why he asked me out for our second date, but it was that next time, when he took me to my favorite Italian restaurant and then out for a drive that ended with trespassing and a moonlit walk through random fields in the middle of the country, that made me realize I would never find another man like him.

He had something I decided I couldn't live without. His intentional questions and quick sense of humor held my attention and his big smile made my insides melty. I had never met anyone that made me feel that way… that made it seem as if I were the only person alive that had anything interesting to say.

If every night could be like that second date, I would never doubt what was between us, not even for a second. But after struggling to put up with each other for all of these years and knowing that whatever chemistry we had with each other fizzled a long time ago, I was exhausted.

I was starting to realize, I was also broken. Or if not broken, then breaking.

I couldn't keep doing this.

And while I was deciding these things I had started to collect reasons for why we weren't right for each other… why he wasn't right for me. I was organized by nature. I was a list-maker. I couldn't help but compile all of the reasons we were wrong for each other.

Even if they broke me.

Even if they destroyed us.

"What are we doing?" he mumbled into his hands.

Hot tears slipped from the corners of my eyes, but I wiped them away before he could see them. "I don't know," I whispered. My hands fell to rest against my flat stomach. "We hate each other."

He whipped his head around and glared at me over his shoulder. "Is that what you think? You think I hate you?"

"I think we've grown so far apart, we don't even know each other anymore."

It was his turn to look like I slapped him. "What do you want, Kate? Tell me what you want to do. Tell me how to fix this?"

I recognized the pleading in his voice. This was how it always happened. We would start fighting about something mundane that neither of us would give in to, inevitably it would reveal our bigger issues, the ones we usually tried to ignore, then finally we would round out the night by Nick promising to do whatever it took to make this work between us. Only, the next morning we would wake up and nothing would be changed or fixed or forgotten and we would start the delusional cycle all over again.

I was sick of it. I was sick of feeling like this and walking on eggshells every time we weren't fighting. I was sick of feeling bad for how I felt and the things that I said. And I was really sick of that look on his face right now, knowing I was the one that put it there.

I wanted to get off this crazy train. I wanted to wake up in the morning feeling good about myself and I wanted to go to bed at night knowing I wasn't a huge disappointment.

My hands clenched into tight fists on my belly and I squeezed my eyes shut before they tried to leak out more painful memories. I glanced to my left, taking in my appearance in the mirror on the door that led to our bathroom. My long hair looked black in the dim lighting and my skin was so pale it could have been see-through. I stared at my eyes, as equally dark and empty as a black hole, and wondered if they were reflecting my broken spirit.

"I don't think we can." My words were a shattered whisper, but they felt like clarity… like truth. They were hurtful, but they were freedom. "I think we're too broken, Nick. I think it's too late for us."

"What are you saying, Katie?"

I ignored the agonized rasp to his voice. If I started to feel bad for him now, I would never get this out. "This is over, Nick… *We're* over. I think it's time we were both honest with ourselves and admitted that."

His response was immediate, "You're for real? You really don't want to try at this anymore?"

My temper shot up again and my face reddened from the hot anger pumping through me. "I have been *trying*! What do you think I've been doing for the past seven years? I've been trying every single day! And it's not enough! It's *never* enough! I cannot keep doing this day in and day out. I can't keep pretending that things are okay and then falling apart every time we start arguing. Nick, I'm exhausted in my *bones*. You're a good person, but it's like… it's like I bring out the absolute worst in you. And the same is true about me! I'm fun. I'm a really fun person. People *like* me! All of the people except *you*. And I don't blame you! When we're together I'm a nag and I'm ungrateful and I'm just… ugly. And I hate that

15

person. I hate the person that I am with you. And I hate the person that you are…"

His head snapped up. I hadn't meant to go that far or finish that thought, but Nick was too perceptive to miss it. "You hate the person that I am with you. Is that what you were going to say?"

I shrugged one shoulder, ashamed that I'd let those words slip out. I shouldn't have said it, even if it was true. If nothing else, it drove my point home. I was a terrible person with Nick. *To Nick*. We'd made each other into horrible people.

Our relationship was toxic. He was slowly poisoning me.

I was slowly poisoning him.

"So what are you saying?" he demanded on a rasp. "You want a divorce? Is that what you want? You think we should get a divorce?"

I nodded, unable to get those precise words beyond my lips. "We aren't good together. We hate each other."

"Yeah, you've made that abundantly clear tonight."

"Can you think of any reason that we should stay together? Give me one good reason that we should keep doing this to ourselves and I will try. I swear to you, if you can come up with one reason to stay together, I'll keep doing this. But, Nick, *god*, this is ruining me. I don't know how much more I can take before I just fall apart."

This time when the tears started falling, I didn't wipe them away or try to stop them. My chin trembled from the force of my emotion and a devastating sob racked my chest. It was true. All of it. I hated myself and I hated him because he was the one that had turned me into this awful person.

I could not do this anymore.

If he came up with a valid reason, I didn't know what I would do. I knew I told him I would stick it out, but at this point, I couldn't do it. I would never really try again at this broken relationship. I had nothing left inside of me to give.

He watched me for a long time. I could see him processing everything behind his veiled eyes. I knew he thought he was hiding his emotions from me, but after seven years of marriage and ten years of being together, I could read him like an open book.

This was his analytical phase. He had to weigh each piece of information, emotion against truth, accusation against reality before he could come to a logical conclusion.

My husband, the cold-hearted thinker. Logic and reason outweighed everything else. If it wasn't a fact, then it didn't exist to him.

Or at least it didn't matter.

"If this is what you want, then fine. A divorce, legal separation... whatever will make you happy."

Whatever will make me happy. Is this it? Is this what I want? But I had already told him it was. Immediately I regretted everything about tonight, everything I had said and everything I'd accused him of. But I couldn't keep feeling this way. I couldn't go through this again, only to have it happen tomorrow and the next day and the day after that. It was time to stand up for myself and fight for my happiness. Nobody else was going to do it for me.

Not even Nick.

"Thank you," I whispered.

There was a long weighted silence as if he were waiting for me to take everything back, to make my final words disappear. Eventually, in a hoarse, tortured voice, he said, "I'll, uh, sleep on the couch tonight. I can move my things out tomorrow morning."

I sucked in a sharp breath. Was he serious? Were we really doing this? "Where will you go?"

"I'll stay with my brother until I can get a place of my own."

"Jared won't care? I mean... what will he think?"

"You can't have it both ways, Kate. You can't ask for a divorce and then hope to keep it a secret. Besides, it's better than staying at a hotel."

"No, you're right," I whispered. I rubbed my stomach and tried to ignore the sinking feeling in my gut. I asked for this. I practically demanded the divorce. So why did I feel such a horrific feeling of disappointment.

My body felt like it was being pulled apart in every direction. My heart felt trampled beneath a stampede of bulls. This was supposed to make me feel better. This was supposed to feel like freedom. I was finally digging myself out of the wreckage of our marriage and yet, I felt more wrecked at this moment than any moment leading up to this one.

"We're really doing this?" My words couldn't seem to come out stronger than a weak whisper.

"You tell me. You're the one that started throwing around divorce. It's not the first time you've asked for one, Kate. I'm frankly sick of trying to talk you out of it."

"I just... I don't know where else there is for us to go. Nick, we've tried. We gave it our best and now I think it's better if we move on... away from each other."

"Yeah," he breathed. "Tried and failed, I guess."

I wanted to argue with him. I wanted to tell him that he was wrong and that we hadn't failed, that there were as many good times between us as there were bad, but I couldn't bring myself to put up the effort. He was right. We failed.

We were failures at our marriage.

When I didn't say anything else, he grabbed his pillow and stomped downstairs to the living room. I rolled over in bed, pulled the duvet over my shoulders and cried until I passed out.

When I woke up in the morning, he was already gone.

Chapter One

8. My life will be **better** without him.

The bell rang and my stomach growled. I looked at my classroom, at the kids shoving papers and notebooks into their backpacks and the energetic chatter that warred with the high-pitched ringing of the fourth period bell, and wondered if I had some Pavlovian response to that sound.

I had been conditioned to know hunger, but I hadn't felt it in months.

I smiled at my students as they filtered from the room and reminded some of them about homework they owed me, but I barely heard the words that fell from my lips or acknowledged the concise instructions I was notorious for.

Behind my smiling mouth and teacher responsibilities, I was made of brittle glass and emptiness. I was nothing but paper-thin defenses and sifting sand.

I had never known this kind of depression before. I could hardly tolerate my soon to be ex-husband and yet his absence left me unexpectedly battered.

Once my English class filled with a mixture of juniors and seniors had left me behind, I let out a long sigh and turned back to my desk. I dropped into my rolling chair and dug out my lunch from the locked bottom drawer.

I set it on the cold metal and stared at the sad ham sandwich and bruised apple I'd thrown together last minute this morning. I couldn't find the energy to take a bite, let alone finish the whole thing. I'd lost seven pounds over the last four months, one for each year of my disastrous marriage. And while I appreciated the smaller size I could fit into, I knew this was the wrong way to go about it.

My friend, Kara, called this the Divorce Diet. But I knew the truth. This wasn't a diet. I'd lost myself somewhere in the ruins of my marriage and now that my relationship was over, my body had started to systematically shut down. First my heart broke. Then my spirit fragmented. Now my appetite was in jeopardy and I didn't know what to do about it. I didn't know if I would ever feel hungry again.

I didn't know if I would ever *feel* again.

I used to eat lunch in the teacher's lounge, but lately I couldn't bring myself in there to face other people, especially my nosey colleagues.

Everyone had heard about my failed marriage. They stopped me in the halls to offer their condolences or hit man services with empathetic expressions or playful smiles. They watched me with pitying eyes and sympathetic frowns. They whispered behind my back or asked invasive questions.

But none of them cared. Not really.

They liked having someone to talk about that wasn't them and a topic that didn't dive into their personal lives. I was the gossip martyr. As long as they could tear apart my bad decisions and argue whether it was my frigidness or Nick's playboy tendencies that hammered the last nail in our coffin they shared a macabre sense of community.

They didn't care that each callous comment shredded me apart just a little more or that I could hear them cackling from down the hall.

They didn't take into account their own divorces or unhappy marriages or faults or hypocrisy or shortcomings. They only saw mine.

And now so did I.

I should at least get a *thank you* for my efforts.

Or a spiked Starbucks.

Where was the gratitude?

The creaky door swung open and my best friend and fellow teacher/school guidance counselor, Kara Chase popped her pretty red head in the room. Her pert nose wrinkled at the sight of my untouched lunch and she smoothed down some of her wild frizz with a perfectly manicured hand. She had endless, luscious curls, but as the day went on and she dealt with more and more apathetic high school kids, her beautiful hair would expand with her impatience.

"That looks… yummy." Her stormy gray eyes lifted to meet mine and I couldn't help but smile.

I wrinkled my nose at her. "Don't judge! It's all I had."

She walked all the way into the room and leaned against the whitewashed cement wall with her hands tucked behind her back. "You used to be better at going to the grocery store."

The small dig cut deeper than it should have. "I've been busy."

Her lips turned down into a concerned frown that I mildly resented. "You can't wallow forever, Kate. Your marriage ended, not the world."

But he was my world. I kept that thought to myself. Now was not the time or the place to sift through my complicated feelings regarding Nick. I wanted this. *I wanted this divorce.* I had no right to be this upset or depressed.

Deep breath. "You're right," I told her. "I just haven't gotten the hang of cooking for one. Last time I went to the store, I ended up way over-shopping and then had to deal with rotten oranges and moldy cheese. Plus, I don't want the Chinese delivery guy to feel abandoned."

As gently as she could, she said, "You'll get the hang of it."

I pushed off in my chair until the back of it slammed against the whiteboard behind me. "I hope that's true."

Because if it wasn't...

Had I just made the most colossal mistake of my life?

No. This was right.

But then why did it feel so... wrong?

"Until then, let's sneak out and grab something better than... than whatever is on your desk now." Her expression brightened until I felt myself smiling at her. We had been friends since we started at Hamilton High School eight years ago. We had that kind of natural connection you only find once or twice your entire life. We were instantly inseparable. Even though Nick and I were already together, we were only engaged at the time. Kara had been my maid of honor at our wedding and my closest confidant over the years. She knew the lowest lows of my marriage and the hard adjustment I'd faced since I ended it.

I didn't want to think about where I would be without her.

I looked at my wrist and checked the time. "I have twenty minutes. Can we be back in time?"

"We'll hurry." Her kitten heels clicked against the polished floor as she moved to hold the door open for me.

She was the only teacher at this school that had any sense of style. Her expensive taste didn't mesh well with her public high school teacher's salary, but thankfully for her, her wealthy parents supplemented her meager income.

My parents questioned my choices and assumed I was a failure at life. They might not be wrong.

And yet we both knew what it was like to struggle to please impossible expectations and feel insignificant in the wake of our parents' cold assessments.

21

I might not have had a designer wardrobe, but at least my parents didn't try to buy my love.

I grabbed my purse out of the same locked drawer I'd tucked my lunch into and straightened my pencil skirt as I stood. I felt my spirits lift immediately.

Kara usually had that effect on me. And it helped that we were sneaking out of our jobs, to do something forbidden.

I loved breaking rules.

Just don't tell my students.

We were halfway down the hall and laughing with each other when we were caught.

"And where are you ladies off to today? I'm certain Ms. Carter has class in a few minutes." The deep voice made my skin feel too tight and my insides warm slowly.

I turned around and met Eli Cohen's rich brown eyes and tried not to smile too big. "Checking up on me?" I raised a challenging eyebrow.

Eli moved closer. "I was just in the lunchroom and heard a pair of junior boys discussing their hot English teacher."

That wiped the cocky expression off my face. "Gross. Don't tell me which ones. I don't want to know."

Eli's face split into a grin and a rich baritone rumble of a laugh fell from his full lips. "On one condition."

"This is blackmail!"

He laughed at me again, but when he raised his dark eyebrows and gave me an expectant look, I couldn't help but soften toward him. He was adorable. "Bring me back something from Garmans."

I couldn't believe him. "How do you know we're going to the deli? We could just be... just be... going to the bathroom together."

He shook his head slowly and grinned. "I see the determined look in Kara's eyes. I know that look. She's hungry. And she's enlisted you to help her sneak out."

"He's good," Kara mused. "I think our science teacher is a little too good."

"I'm starving," he admitted. "I've been watching the hall for five minutes hoping to catch a teacher on their way out." He held out his empty hands. "I forgot my lunch at home today and I have a meeting in three minutes."

I looked at Kara and tried to figure out what she was thinking. Eli had transferred to our school two years ago and over that time I had gotten to know him slowly. I could now say I counted him as my friend, but for a long time I had kept him at a distance. He was too good-looking, too perfect. His skin was nicely bronzed, his hair perfectly quaffed and for a science teacher, his body was surprisingly filled out. I had found him intimidating at first and then because I was married to a handsome man and supposedly in love with that man, I found it utterly ridiculous to be so affected.

I was a mess. Even back then.

But I had kept my distance until a few months ago. Until after Nick moved out.

"I suppose we can take pity on him," Kara sighed. "He does look famished."

I ran my eyes over his broad chest and flat stomach. "He's practically starving."

"Should I get you the cobb salad?" Kara asked innocently.

Eli pointed a playful finger at her. "Don't you dare. I wouldn't know what to do with something green. I'd probably make my students dissect it."

It was my turn to shake my head. "You're hilarious."

He smiled at me, wide and carefree. "I'll owe you one."

"Sure you will." Kara and I started walking again. "I'll be sure to collect."

"I'm counting on it." His low voice followed us down the hallway and I had to turn around before he saw an inflamed blush spread across my cheeks.

I pressed my cold hands against my face and tried to ignore the burn in my abdomen. It had been a long time since I flirted with someone, even longer since that someone wasn't Nick.

Kara's elbow found my side playfully. "What was that?"

"A favor?" I turned my wide eyes to her and silently begged her to tell me it wasn't as forward as I thought it was.

She pressed her lips together to hide her smile. "Sure it was."

"We're just friends."

"And now you're single."

A shuddering breath shook my lungs. "Not really. Not yet."

"Soon," she argued. "When the divorce is finalized, you'll officially be back on the market. Obviously, Eli knows that."

The flirty tingle turned sour in my stomach and suddenly I'd lost my appetite all over again. The blush drained from my cheeks and I felt myself turn pale and translucent.

Kara noticed immediately. "I'm sorry, Kate. I didn't mean to... to upset you. I just thought... It's been four months, babe. Nick hasn't even reached out to you. Not really, anyway. I thought you might be ready to move on."

Ready to move on after four months? Was that all it took to get over the last ten years of my life? To delete seven years of marriage? I had been with Nick in some form or capacity for a decade, but I was supposed to erase him completely from the important parts of my heart in four months?

How?

I wasn't against the idea. In fact, I would have loved to forget about him and the poisonous relationship we'd created. I would love for this pain in my chest to dissipate and the sickness that seemed constant and unrelenting to ebb.

But it wasn't that easy. I couldn't shake our relationship or the hold he had over my heart.

Not everything about him was bad. In fact, most of him was good and beautiful and right. But with me, he wasn't those things and I wasn't either.

But how was I supposed to let go of him? I loved him. I loved him for ten years and knew nothing else but loving him.

How could I walk away from him and even entertain the idea of another man after everything I had been through? I wasn't sure if I ever wanted to date again, let alone so quickly after my last relationship failed.

No. *Epically failed*.

Nick was supposed to be my forever. Nick was supposed to be my "until death do us part." And now that the rest of my life had taken a sharp, life-altering turn, I didn't know where I was headed anymore.

I was lost.

I was rudderless.

I was floating in a sea of confusion and hurt. I needed something to tether me, to pull me back to shore. But I knew, more than anybody else in my life that I wasn't going to find that with a new man.

"It's okay," I told Kara with a throaty whisper. "I just wasn't... I wasn't expecting that from him."

She squeezed my forearm and gathered her thoughts. "I know that what you're going through with Nick and everything is intense, but you're still young. You're still gorgeous. You still have a lot of life left to live. I don't want you to give up, just because the first try wasn't successful.

You're a catch, friend. You have to know that Eli isn't the only man lining up to take advantage of Nick's colossal mistake."

"The divorce was my idea," I reminded her. "I'm the reason we ended it." The words felt like stones on my tongue. I felt their gritty, dirty wrongness and I wanted to spit them out and wash my mouth out with something cleansing.

Something like bleach.

Or battery acid.

"Yeah, maybe," she sighed. "But he should never have let you get away with it."

Something sharp sliced against my chest. I felt the same way too. If he had really loved me, he wouldn't have let me go through with it. Right? If he really wanted things to work out between us, he wouldn't have moved out.

He wouldn't have stopped talking to me.

He wouldn't have left.

Desperate to change the topic, I pushed through a back door and blinked against the bright fall sunlight. "So, lunch?"

"Yes!" She smiled at me. I could see the concern floating all over her face, but she held her tongue in an effort to keep me together. "Garmans has the freaking best pastrami on the planet."

I would never understand how Kara could eat so much and stay so thin. She didn't have to do what the rest of us did, which was an insane amount of cardio and a universal ban on sugar. She could eat whatever she wanted.

I looked at a piece of chocolate and my thighs started jiggling.

It was like an alarm system for my flab.

Well, until recently.

We hurried across the lengthy parking lot and busy Chicago street until we reached the tiny corner deli that boasted whole pickles with every purchase and sandwiches the size of my head. It was a favorite spot for everyone that worked on this block, but especially for the teachers at Hamilton. When given the choice of bad cafeteria food, a quickly packed lunch from home or a thickly-meated, moist-breaded, delicious deli sandwich from Garmans, the choice was obvious.

But after an incident last spring, in which a group of students had left school to corner and threaten a teacher off school grounds, our administrator had banned teachers from leaving campus during the school day and so technically we were sneaking out and breaking rules.

Hamilton was located in one of the under-privileged sections of Chicago. We were firmly in the city proper, not skirting the affluent suburbs or near a wealthier area of downtown. No, Hamilton was directly in the middle of gang violence, low-income housing and race wars.

I'd been offered jobs at some of the more stable schools in the city and even one at a prestigious private school in a well-off suburb. But when I chose Hamilton, it was with my heart. I had examined all of my options, and I knew that taking this job was a risk professionally, but I couldn't deny that I felt something meaningful for these kids.

I wanted to make a difference. Not the kind that you see on TV or that moves you in a heart-warming movie, but a real difference. I wanted to empower these kids with knowledge that would never leave them and tools for a future that was beyond this neighborhood. I wanted to inspire something inside of these neglected teenagers that had all of the odds stacked against them and had to fight to just show up on a daily basis.

I fought a losing battle every day and I was exhausted. But it was worth it.

I could feel it in my bones.

Kara's heels clicked against the broken sidewalk as we hurried to Garmans, mingling with the sounds of angry traffic and city melee. The warm sun heated my exposed arms and face and I lifted my closed eyes to soak it in.

There was healing in this industrial chaos. There was a beautiful surrender to the noisy madness that felt cleansing and therapeutic. It wouldn't last. I would pay for my sandwich, go back to my desk and the reality of my broken life would come crashing down on me.

But for a few seconds, I had the flirtatious smile of an attractive man in my memory and a minute of reprieve from the demands of my life. I sucked in a full breath, taking in the exhaust and grit from the city. And yet, my lungs felt full for the first time in as long as I could remember.

"It's going to get better," Kara said so softly I barely heard her.

I opened my eyes to keep from tripping and they immediately fell to the cracked sidewalk and patchy grass on either side. "I'm not sure it is," I told her honestly.

She dropped her hand on my shoulder and squeezed, pulling me into a side hug. "There's more to life than Nick, babe. I promise you. And it won't take you long to figure it out. You just need to get the divorce finalized so you can move on." Her laugh vibrated through her. "And Eli would be a very good place to start."

"Maybe," fell from my lips, but I didn't feel any sentiment behind it. More sickness roiled through me and a cold sweat broke out on my neck. I swallowed against rising nausea and convinced myself not to throw up.

I was getting a divorce, but even the thought of another man still felt like adultery. Whatever our faults, Nick and I had always been faithful to each other. Moving on seemed impossible when I had dedicated my entire life to one man.

To the one man that had let me down and stomped on whatever remained of my happiness.

Nick and I were over, I promised myself.

I would move on eventually.

And Nick would too.

We grabbed our sandwiches, but I let Kara drop Eli's off. I had lost any desire to communicate with other people. I practically crawled back to my classroom and sunk into my chair. My deli sandwich went uneaten, just like my one from home, because I couldn't bring myself to feel good enough to eat.

Kara had meant to encourage me, but she'd done the opposite.

I realized that she was right. That one day I would move on.

But that I was right too. Nick would move on as well.

I knew I could find someone better for me. I knew my life would be better off without him.

I just couldn't swallow the hard pill that his life would be better off without me too.

That he would find someone better than me.

Chapter Two

9. He **hates** my mother.

Sunday rolled around with a crashing finality that made my legs lock up and my eyes instinctively roll of their own accord.

The apocalypse had arrived.

Also known as family dinner.

It had been a tradition in my household as long as I could remember. It was cemented into place when my older brother, Josh, left for college; written in blood from all members of my family when he got married twelve years ago; and cursed to damn those members of the family that did not show up straight to the fiery pits of hell when I got married seven years ago.

My mother was nothing if not intolerant of our absences. My father was the same way. He wasn't the most amorous man alive; in fact, some might take his stoic demeanor and lack of affection to mean that he didn't love us- or at least he didn't like us very much. But the opposite was true. He did love us. More than he cared to tell us. He just showed us his love with high expectations that were both everlasting and time-oriented.

Translation: Don't ever be late. Never ever.

Like I said, Sunday meant lunch with my parents. Neither of them could be bothered to pick up a phone during the week to check in with me, but by God, if I didn't show up on Sunday, I'd better be dead.

Nick had always found my family stand-offish at best. He loathed any time spent with them, but most of all Sunday lunches. My father, a successful plumber and notorious hard worker, didn't and wouldn't try to understand Nick's aspirations to be a professional musician. And my mother, who had been both emotionally neglected all of her marriage and also completely spoiled by my father who only expected her to cook, clean, iron his shirts and go to bed with him at nine pm every night, refused to respect a man that would choose an unstable career and could therefore impose upon his family to support him.

My mother always thought I could do better and she never kept that opinion to herself. My father didn't speak his mind openly, but he had never been Nick's number one fan, even if they could come together over the Bears and Blackhawks.

When I walked into my parent's dated, red brick row house five minutes before lunch began, I felt the dismal weight of failure settle on my shoulders.

As disappointed as my parents were when I chose Nick, they were even more disappointed in my pending divorce.

Love and happiness had never played a part in their marriage. They took vows, they made promises to each other and no matter how miserable they made the other, they kept their word.

It was embarrassing to them that they had a child who couldn't keep hers.

Especially since my perfect brother Josh had married such a nice Catholic girl and their marriage was never in jeopardy of dissolving and, consequently, their souls never at risk of being damned. To ice the cake, my brother's two kids were beautiful. Josh had a fantastic job and Emily, his wife, couldn't have been a better homemaker.

I, the baby of the family, was still acting like one. My dangerous job, my failed marriage and my lack of offspring spoke for me. I had disappointed my parents. In every way that mattered.

"There she is," my mother announced when I swept into the house, dropped my purse on the secretary desk near the front door and tripped into the dining room. My mother's dark brown hair, which had streaks of gray that she would never bother to cover with dye, was pulled severely from her face in a bun on the top of her head. Her high cheekbones and pursed lips made my stomach twist with dread. I felt like one of my students when I called them out for missing homework.

I should be nicer to them, I thought.

No, wait. I had momentarily forgotten that I loved torturing them.

Apparently my mother and I had more in common than I thought.

"I'm sorry I'm late," I huffed, even though I was early. "Traffic was a nightmare."

My father made an approving grunt. He hated traffic above everything else. If he could sell his soul for clear streets and green lights for the rest of his life, he would.

He wouldn't even ask to read the terms and conditions.

Sign here, Satan? Sure thing.

"We're just sitting down," my mother allowed. Her hazel eyes flicked across the table and took in my appearance with a shockingly quick assessment. "You're too thin. It's a good thing you come over here to eat."

I sunk onto my straight-backed oak chair and gripped the edges of the matching table that had been the centerpiece of my childhood. She said this to me every time she saw me during my divorce. Before that, it had been, "You're gaining too much weight. You need to exercise."

"She's under a lot of stress, Ma, give her a break."

I shot Josh a weak smile. He made life difficult for me because he did everything right the first time, but he always had my back. He really was a good guy, which was why it was so easy to hate him.

"She's under a lot of stress because she puts herself under a lot of stress." My mother thrust the bowl of green beans amandine at my sister-in-law, Emily, catching her off guard. She jumped a little in her seat and I had to press my lips together to keep from laughing.

I was thirty-years-old and hadn't lived at home since the year before I got married, but my mother could get under my skin like no one else.

She came equipped with internal radar of what buttons to push to piss me off the most. Zero to instant-rage in less than thirty seconds.

It was actually pretty impressive.

"Can I have the bread, please?" I kept my voice evenly upbeat and pasted on a fake smile. If I didn't provoke them, I could be out of here in two hours.

Nick would always come up with a code word before we walked in the house so that I would know when he'd reached his limit.

Rotten bananas.

Teriyaki chicken.

Winter is coming.

He would just blurt whatever safe word he'd prepped me with on the way over in the middle of a conversation and then jump to his feet as if he couldn't live through *another second* of my family. Sometimes it had been in the middle of the meal. Sometimes he made it to dessert.

Sometimes he started spouting code words before we'd made it through the front door.

During our marriage, I had been annoyed with his desperation to leave my family. I wanted him to somehow love spending time with them, even though I couldn't stand it.

Even though they were rude and unaccepting of him.

Over the last four months, I'd realized this was one thing I could have been nicer about. I missed his code words now. I missed his push to leave so we didn't get trapped in an endless marathon of bitter family and snide comments. I missed his intolerance for how my mom spoke to me.

He had always been respectful to her face, but after we got in the car, he had always reassured me that I was beautiful, that I was successful and that I didn't need her approval.

I hadn't done the same for him and now I wondered how her snarky digs must have cut him. I wondered if he had needed my encouragement as much as I needed his.

I wondered if I had enjoyed his code words and sarcastic tolerance of my family, if we would still be together. I wondered if those small things would have fixed us.

Or at least kept us from breaking.

But it was all pointless now. Nick was gone and I was left to face my family alone.

"Take two biscuits," she demanded. "You'll never find another man with those cheekbones."

"Cess," my dad warned with his rumble of a voice. "Let the girl eat. She doesn't need your instructions. I'm sure she's got the basics of it figured out by now."

My mother's disgruntled expression argued differently, but she let it drop. Cecily Simmons was a force to be reckoned with. I had never been under a different impression. My mother had intimidated the world from day one.

But I had been born with something wild and uncaring. My mom overwhelmed me easily. I knew better than to talk back. I knew better than to start something with her.

And yet, I could not keep my mouth shut.

It might be some kind of disease.

I should probably get it checked out.

I told my mashed potatoes, "I'm not sure I want to find another man."

My mom snorted a bitter laugh and I felt my father freeze from across the table. I didn't have to look at him to know I'd shocked the hell out of him and not in a good way.

"Of course you want to find another man," my mother insisted. "You think that now, but give it a few months or a year. You won't want to be alone. You'll get lonely and then you'll see. You'll know you need a man."

As if my mother's words weren't damaging enough, my father chimed in, "It's dangerous out there, Katie."

Ladies and gentlemen, my parents' opinion of me. Neither of them thought I was capable of taking care of myself. A man had to be part of my equation or I was destined to turn into a crazy cat lady that was raped and pillaged in her own home one night by the pizza delivery guy.

As if my future didn't feel bleak enough... Geez. *Thanks, Mom and Dad.*

And obviously my army of cats would protect me.

"Come on, guys," Josh interrupted again. "Enough already. She walked in the house five minutes ago and you're already giving her a hard time. Let her breathe a little, alright?"

Both of my parents looked put out this time. I wanted to cry.

One of my nieces piped up, wanting more mashed potatoes and the attention, thankfully, shifted off me.

Josh had two beautiful girls that were as well behaved as children could be and still be kids. They whined too loud and they screamed like banshees when they got mad, but they were beautiful and lovely and so precious they made my uterus ache.

Delaney and Adalyn had been easy for Josh and Emily. They had gotten pregnant exactly on schedule with their perfect lives, just like Josh had gotten the position he wanted and the raise he needed when they decided to start a family. Life worked out for Josh in a way that was completely unfamiliar to me.

Not that I didn't think he worked hard. I did. I knew he gave his hundred and ten percent and worked his ass off to be where he was today. But he shined brighter or something. The universe loved him more or maybe he had a head start toward perfection.

I worked hard too. I worked my ass off too. And yet... there was something missing.

I didn't have a gorgeous house in the suburbs or my two point five kids. I barely had a puppy and a job that paid less than tolerable wages.

I had a mountain of student loan debt and a husband that didn't fight for me.

And a pity party.

I had a massive pity party that made me sick of myself and of the constantly self-absorbed thoughts I couldn't shake. Ugh.

I needed a wakeup call.

Or a giant bottle of Grey Goose.

"So how's the school year going so far?" Emily asked while my parents drilled Josh about his newest promotion opportunity.

"Rough," I said honestly.

"Because of the divorce?" Her tone was gentle and nonjudgmental. I loved my sister-in-law, despite her serendipitous marriage to my brother. We weren't the closest friends, but Josh had chosen well.

I chewed a bit of pork chop while I decided how to answer her. "That's definitely part of the reason. But I have a few difficult classes this year. It's only the middle of September and they're already acting out. I feel like it's getting harder and harder to get through to them."

Her frown was both authentic and sympathetic. "I think what you're doing is amazing, Kate. Those students, *all* students, need teachers that genuinely care about them. You're doing something great. You need to remember that."

Emily was six years older than me and even if it was hard for us to connect sometimes, she gave really good advice. This was something worth listening to.

"Thanks, Emily. I needed to hear that."

She smiled softly at me. "And don't worry about rushing into another relationship either. I know the divorce is something you want, but I'm sure you're still struggling to move on."

I nodded, unable to form the words it would take to explain how very reluctant I was to even consider moving on.

"It's not like he was a bad guy..." My lame attempt at an explanation fell as flat as it tasted in my mouth. It was so much more complicated than two well-meaning people moving on with their lives. There were so many subtle nuances that would take days to explain. I needed complicated pie charts and colored graphs. I needed to watch a movie of my marriage and analyze exactly where things went wrong. Saying Nick was a great guy, though, usually caused people to question all of my motives.

Was I having an affair?

Was I a cold, heartless bitch?

Had I been abducted by aliens who sucked out my soul and left me vapid and broken?

I hadn't ruled out that last option yet. It might have happened.

Because why else would I have suggested that my husband leave me? For good.

Aliens were a legitimate possibility.

"Of course he's not a bad guy!" Emily rushed to agree. "But sometimes... sometimes it doesn't work out."

It wasn't her words that bothered me, but her lack of conviction. I hated that everything had become so personal to me lately. I couldn't have a conversation without a reminder of how great Nick was and what an idiot I was for leaving him. I was as obsessed with myself as everyone else.

Only, I was really, really getting sick and tired of me.

I cleared my throat to avoid commenting anymore.

"Divorce is hard," Emily went on. "When my parents divorced, my mom said it was like going through the death of a loved one. She struggled for a long time to stay out of depression."

I turned toward her and hoped to change the subject completely or at least get it off me. "That must have been really hard. How old were you?"

She nodded slowly, clearly struggling with hidden emotion. "I was eight," she admitted. "They thought they would be better off without each other."

Her words hit too close to home and I immediately wanted to change the subject to something else. The weather. Football. Aliens and anal probing. *Anything else.* Instead, I said, "Were they?"

She quickly shook her head. "I don't know, honestly. My dad never remarried. My mom did. She seems happy now. But we went through a lot of painful years afterward. It was really, really hard on my sisters and me."

"At least we don't have kids," I mumbled to myself.

If Emily heard me, she didn't respond. And for that I was grateful. I didn't need to talk about kids tonight or what it was like not to have them.

I knew what it was like. I knew that acutely.

I smiled at my youngest niece, Adalyn, as she tried to sneak long green beans back into the bowl. I shook my finger at her playfully and watched her five-year-old face turn red from embarrassment.

Even Nick thought my nieces were precious. He had one brother, but Jared was younger than us and not married yet, so Delaney and Adalyn were all we had. Both of us loved to have them over so we could spoil them or take them to fun things around the city.

They gave us the excuse to eat chicken nuggets shaped like dinosaurs and watch cartoons.

I might not have appreciated his attitude toward my mother, but he had always been the best uncle. He would have made a phenomenal father.

If only things had been different for us.

After Josh and I cleaned off the table and started on the dishes, a job that was still ours no matter how old we got, I felt his probing eyes on me. I could feel the serious conversation brewing between us, but I had hoped to avoid this awkward portion of the afternoon.

35

"I thought you would get back with him by now," he said out of the blue, with soap bubbles up to his elbows and a porcelain platter squeezed between his hands.

I nearly dropped the wet glass I was drying on the linoleum floor. "What?"

"I didn't think you were serious about the divorce," he explained. "I thought you guys might be having a rough patch, but I always expected you to work through it."

My stomach churned and my heart squeezed with racing panic. I tried to keep my voice steady when I replied, "It was worse than a rough patch."

"He didn't hit you or anything, did he?" Josh paused mid-rinse to look at me seriously.

I hated that people always jumped to that conclusion. Did all men have this hard of a time divorcing? Were they always silently questioned about spousal abuse?

"He never touched me like that, Josh. Don't ever think he did. We just... we don't get along. We're not right for each other."

"You haven't really tried," he countered immediately. "You guys are still newlyweds. Give it some time."

"We've been married for seven years."

My brother was nothing if not persistent. He got it from our mother. "It's nothing a couple kids won't fix. Try that. See what a baby can do for you guys. You could still save this."

I sucked in a sharp breath and kept my tumbling thoughts to myself. I could have told him that I hadn't talked to my husband in four months and that if he wanted to speak to me, he would have by now. If he had cared just a little bit about salvaging what we had, he would have reached out. I could have told Josh that we knew each other too well. That our faults had become walls that kept the other out and that our fights had scarred us so deeply we would never heal.

I should have told him that a baby wasn't a magical potion that made people stop fighting and every problem disappear.

But instead, I told him the reason that would shut him up for good, the one thing he couldn't argue with.

"We did try to have kids." My voice was a shaking whisper, reflecting all of the shattered emotions I couldn't reconcile. "We tried for two years."

He was silent for a long time. I had kept this to myself during our entire struggle. Only Nick knew how desperately I wanted a baby and how

36

impossible it seemed. We hadn't told our parents or our families because we wanted to avoid this moment. We wanted to avoid the questions and the pity and the attempts to understand something that devastated both of us- something we couldn't understand ourselves.

"Oh," Josh finally groaned. "I wondered-"

"It's me," I said quickly. "Or at least that's what our lab results say. I'm the one that stopped it from happening."

My brother had rolled up the sleeves to his oxford and looked out of place next to the sudsy water and pile of dirty dishes. He had the face of a corporate man. He was all clean angles and sharp edges.

But at this moment, he looked as lost as I felt.

"That's not a reason to get a divorce, Katie." His rasping rumble grated against my heart and I wanted to cry.

"That's not why we're getting divorced, Josh."

"It's a reason for something," he pushed.

"Then it's a reason that led up to the reason we're getting divorced. There's a lot to us that you never saw or heard about. A lot you will never hear about. Whatever my reasons for ending my marriage are mine alone. I don't expect you to understand."

"Does he know them?"

"Does he know what?"

"Your reasons for leaving him."

The wind rushed out of me and I thought I might pass out for a minute. The pain was too acute, too blinding. I couldn't breathe through this. I couldn't *live* through this. My brother had dealt the final blow, but the expression on Nick's face, when he had grabbed the pillow off our bed to take it downstairs all those months ago, annihilated whatever was left of my heart.

"Yes," I whispered. "And he has his own reasons for wanting to leave me too."

We finished the dishes in silence. I left my parent's house soon after that, using the valid excuse that I had a ton of papers to grade. My parents weren't happy to see me leave, but I wasn't sure they would have been happy to have me stay either.

I drove back to the small house I'd shared with Nick for the last five years. It was empty when I got there except for my puppy. Of course. I lived by myself now.

It was quiet too.

Too quiet.

It was dark and quiet and for the first time since we bought this damn house, I hated it. I hated it because it represented everything I couldn't have. Everything I lost.

I hated Nick too.

He wasn't supposed to let our marriage end like this. He wasn't supposed to let things get this bad.

And most of all.

I hated myself.

I couldn't help it. At the end of the day... after all of my explanations and logical choices, after my lists of his wrongdoings and all of the reasons we were wrong for each other, I hated myself and what I had done.

I hated myself for what I couldn't take back.

Chapter Three

10. He misses the **dog**.

I threw my keys down on the counter and looked at the leftover dishes from last night. I should have done them after dinner, but I couldn't find the energy. At the time, I told myself it was a reward for not picking up fast food on the way home from work again, but now I recognized my laziness for what it was.

It was funny how living by myself spotlighted all of these faults I hadn't noticed before. When Nick lived here, I always cleaned up after dinner. He hadn't asked me to or expected it, but I had always felt the drive to please him.

Okay, maybe not in every way. But he did things for me. He took out the trash without being asked. He changed lightbulbs when they burned out. He walked the dog when it rained. The dishes were part of my portion of housekeeping and whatever else you could say about me or about how I treated Nick, at least I kept that part of our bargain.

For better or worse, in sickness and in health, you mow the yard and I'll scrub the pans.

Now my vows were as empty and meaningless as my chores. What was the point of cleaning up if there was no one here to appreciate my effort?

I wanted gold stars and verbal affirmation.

The dog gave me neither of those things.

My feet ached and my head buzzed with the chaos of the day. I yawned so long and wide I half expected my jaw to unhinge.

I stood at the counter listening to the house. The ice machine kicked on and the refrigerator started buzzing. I could hear the hallway clock ticking its rhythmic tocks as it kept time. The most beautiful dog in the entire world plopped on the ground at my feet and let out a long puppy sigh.

I could see it in her big brown eyes. *Finally, you're home, woman. Now pay me attention and fetch my chewie.*

To be honest, she really wasn't the most beautiful dog in the world, but she was really close. And she was beyond spoiled, making her intolerably high maintenance and prissy. But she was mine. I loved her as much as I loved any human.

She was a petite beagle with big floppy ears that perked up when she was interested in something and huge chocolate eyes that conveyed more emotion than I thought a dog should be capable of. Her shiny coat was a mixture of caramel and white and was nice and silky because Nick insisted on the expensive dog food and weekly baths.

I named her Anne after my favorite teacher, Anne Shirley, from the Anne of Avonlea books. But Nick had started calling her Annie from the very beginning and the nickname stuck. She was my Annie-girl and when all other people failed me, she was my rock.

I swept down and rubbed her ears with my two hands. Immediately the stress of the day started to melt from my shoulders and the dishes, the bills left discarded on the table and my looming divorce didn't feel so impossible anymore.

"What did you do all day?" I asked her with a soft voice. "Did you miss me?"

A deep, masculine voice came out of her, answering my question, "I doubt that. She was too busy eating my socks."

I let out an ear-splitting scream and fell backward on my butt. After a few seconds of blind panic in which I contemplated the distance to my nearest butcher knife, sanity returned. I eventually recognized the voice and that it hadn't come from my dog.

It had come from my husband. My soon to be *ex*-husband.

I hadn't seen him in four months and now he was here. I had to brace myself before I could look at him.

"Nick! God!" My hand landed on my chest and I pushed down, trying to slow my racing heart. "You scared the *hell* out of me!"

He leaned over the white-tiled island and stared at me with listless eyes. "I thought you heard me come in."

I pressed my lips together and tried to ignore the pang of pain that hit me low in the gut. His eyes used to be his most expressive feature. They could glisten with humor or darken with lust in the span of three seconds.

They were what had pulled me so deeply into him so quickly. All he had to do was look at me and I had been his.

Until now. Now they stared at me as if I were the most uninteresting thing on the planet. They didn't light up when I walked into the room. They didn't dance with some sarcastic thought spinning around in his sharp mind. They didn't heat with desire or harden with frustration.

They just barely glanced at me, shuttered and apathetic.

"I didn't," I snapped. My heart hadn't found its normal beat yet and my voice sounded frustratingly breathless.

He moved around the island and held out his hand to me. I reluctantly took it and tried to be civil.

We had promised each other a peaceful divorce. This was something we both wanted. We had no reason to be anything but nice to each other.

Once I was standing, he looked me over again but refrained from speaking his opinion. I tried to swallow back my annoyance. After living with him for seven years and hearing every little insignificant thought that came out of his mouth, it bothered me that he had suddenly learned restraint.

What did he think about my outfit? Did he notice I'd lost weight? Could he see the dark bags beneath my eyes?

Did he think I was losing sleep because of him?

Habits, I reminded myself. These were just familiar patterns from our marriage. I was used to being able to ask him his thoughts, which he always gave freely.

Now we acted like strangers, even though we knew each other more intimately than I knew any other person.

"What are you doing here?" I finally asked when it didn't seem he wanted to explain his presence.

"I didn't think you were going to be here."

His casual words lit a fire inside of me that I couldn't ignore. My polite words tasted bitter and acrid in my mouth. "Teacher's meeting was canceled tonight. Mr. Kellar had a family emergency."

"Is everything alright?" Finally, some kind of sympathy flared in his blue eyes, but it wasn't meant for me.

My principal got his compassion, but not his wife.

"His eight-year-old broke his leg. It's nothing serious." My words came out clipped and short. Nick noticed immediately. His gaze sharpened and his lips parted as if to defend himself.

I braced myself for fighting words, the ones that would spiral us into a never-ending argument. He would set me off and I would retaliate with something blade-sharp and cutting. He would return by nagging me to death until I explained every last one of my emotions, at which point I would shut down and the barrier around my heart would thicken and expand.

Sometime in the last seven years, I had started to pay attention to our fights. We fought in phases, each argument trying to outdo the last. What was worse was that we had developed this toxic cycle that could not be broken.

"Huh," was Nick's intelligent reply.

"So why are you here?"

His gaze drifted to the dog. "I need to grab a few things of mine."

Righteous anger spread from the fire in my belly, snaking through my veins and reaching my fingertips and toes. "You should have called me first. You can't just walk in here unannounced. This isn't your house anymore."

Nick took an aggressive step forward. "This isn't my house? Are you kidding me? This is *our* house. As far as I know, my name is still on the mortgage. I can come and go as I please."

"I'm a single female, living alone. Don't you think I deserve privacy? I thought you were a murderer!"

"You're a single female, huh? Just like that? I'm gone for a couple months and suddenly you're living the high life?"

"That's not at all what I meant! And you know it!" I took another step forward and swallowed down the bitterness that bubbled up my throat. I wanted to claw at my itchy skin and burst into hysterical tears. How did we get like this?

Why couldn't we have just one decent conversation?

Nick's face heated with his matching anger. "I don't know *what* you mean, Kate. I'm starting to wonder if I ever knew what you meant. You kicked *me* out."

"Oh, that's nice. That's really lovely." I spun around and threw my hands out. "I love how I'm the bad guy in this thing. How it's all *my* fault." I turned back to face him and let my words punctuate the air with every ounce of resentment and exhaustion I felt. "We came to this decision together, Nick. Don't you dare put the blame on me. I've been the villain for seven goddamn years, but I refuse to this time. We did this together."

He rocked back on his heels and his shoulders deflated like the anger had leaked from his body. He was a puffed-up balloon with a quarter-sized hole. But he wasn't any less worked up. This was the quiet rage that cut deeper, sliced in jagged, unhealable ways.

"Sure, Kate. We both wanted this." His voice pitched low and firm when he launched his final assault. "At least it's what we both want now. You're not the only one that's been living in freedom lately. God, it feels good to get out from under…" I waited for the end of his sentence, knowing it would be about me, knowing it would be the agonizing reminder of what a terrible wife I was. But he shocked me when he finished with, "this roof."

It wasn't any less hurtful, but it didn't pack quite the punch I had been expecting.

My surprise quelled some of my fury and I found myself able to reply to him without goading him further. I ran my hands over my face and in a deflated voice, I asked, "What are you really doing here, Nick? I know you didn't stop by to fight with me."

He jerked his chin to the side so he didn't have to look at me. "I didn't think you were going to be here."

"Nick, *god*. Just come clean already." A wave of violent exhaustion knocked into me and I teetered backward. He did this to me. He wore me out completely. And he didn't even notice. He wouldn't even look at me anymore.

And somehow that was worse. Somehow I could take his harsh words and cruel accusations, but it was his neglect that pierced the hardest.

"I missed Annie," he mumbled.

I knew I misheard him. He hated the dog. He complained about her daily. "What?"

He lifted his chin as if he was prepared to defend his words and the damn dog to the grave. "I missed Annie, okay? I just wanted… needed to make sure she was okay."

A weird mixture of sorrow and affection twisted through me. I didn't know whether to scream at him or hug him. Confused and tired, I turned away from him and faced the sink. I needed to do something. I needed to use my hands and think about anything else but my husband and the dog.

"I thought you hated her," I accused weakly, my voice broken with hurt feelings and bewilderment.

His voice was lower to the ground when he responded. He'd bent over and started petting her in his rough, affectionate way. "I thought I did too."

A lump so big and intrusive clogged my throat that I had to gasp for air. I didn't bother to swipe at the tears leaking from my eyes. I didn't want to draw attention to them.

So while Nick petted the dog he had avoided, complained about and glared at for three years, I focused on scrubbing the dishes I left out last night. The water burned my hands, turning my skin bright red, but I welcomed the heat and the pain. I needed to focus on something else. I needed to redirect my mind from whatever dangerous place it wanted to go.

Nick murmured sweet things to Annie and I forbid my body to turn around. Listening to his familiar voice, with his low, gravelly baritone did funny things to my resolve. I started questioning everything I'd decided about him. I wanted to reconsider my decisions and accusations.

I wanted to fall on my knees next to him and beg for his forgiveness.

Which was so silly. *So completely ridiculous.*

If anything, his surprise visit should hammer down the point. We weren't right for each other. We couldn't even be in the same room together without wanting to strangle each other.

We might be good people separately, but we were monsters together.

I was doing the right thing. I wanted to be happy. I wanted to live a life without screaming and name-calling.

I wanted to breathe again.

"Have you taken her for a walk yet?" His question was asked with a soft pleading that I couldn't ignore, no matter how much the bitter part of me wanted to punish and torture him.

I shook my head, unable to speak the words that clawed at my throat. I kept my chin tucked to my chest so that my dark hair would fall in front of my face and cover the tears streaking my cheeks.

His voice grated when he asked, "Do you mind if... do you mind if I take her?"

I hoped he didn't notice my quiet sobbing. I couldn't stand the idea that he saw how weak I was acting. But the longer I thought about it, I decided the obvious emotion in his voice probably came from asking me permission.

Nick was nothing if not proud.

Instead of using this moment against him, I surprised myself by shrugging one shoulder and whispering in a thick voice, "Go ahead. She would love it."

He stood there silently for a long minute. I felt his eyes sear into my back. I sucked in slow breaths and tried not to fidget. The only sound in the kitchen was the sound of Annie's paws dancing on the tile and the splash of water as I worked on the dishes.

Finally, after endless moments, he asked, "Is her leash in the same spot?"

"Yeah."

"Come on, girl," he called in a friendly voice. "Let's go for a walk. Want to go for a walk?"

Annie pranced excitedly, her toenails clicking faster and faster. She let out an excited yelp and followed Nick into the hallway where the leash hung on the wall.

He fastened it quickly to her collar and they left out the front door.

"Traitor," I hissed when they were gone.

The new silence hit me harder than anything else. I had been living alone for a while, but I always had Annie with me. She was always here to greet me at the kitchen door when I got home from work or curl up with me on the couch.

Logically, I knew she was only going to be gone for a half hour or so. I knew Nick would bring her back to me safe and sound.

But the house felt immensely lonely now. It fell down on my shoulders with a crushing weight. My chest deflated and my lungs gave out.

I fell to my knees in a heap of loud sobbing and uncontrollable tears. My wet hands splashed water all over my work clothes, but I couldn't find the energy to care. I was too wrapped up in my own pain, too lost in the heartbreak inside my chest.

Unexpected grief crashed over me and I gasped for breath, stretched for the effort to continue living through this agony.

Why did it hurt so much? If this was what we both wanted, why did it feel like death instead of life?

I had loved this man once. I had loved him more than anything else in life. And now we treated each other like enemies. I hurt him every time I saw him. And I did it on purpose.

I was a good, decent person. I believed in my career. I wanted to change lives and give the kids I worked with a future they might not have otherwise. And yet, when I was with my husband, I turned into a vicious, crazed harpy that couldn't listen to reason or rationalize logically. Every nice, kind thing inside of me jumped out the window and I started flinging insults meant to wound, to harm permanently... to kill whatever good, decent person was left in him.

I hated who I was with Nick.

And I had to be honest with myself and admit that it wasn't Nick that made me this way. There was something ugly inside of me... something monstrous and vengeful.

I didn't want to keep talking to him like this; I didn't want to keep hurting him. What was even the point anymore? We were over. We were separated. The least I could do, after years and years and years of this, was treat him like a human being worthy of respect.

We weren't going to be man and wife anymore, but that didn't make us enemies.

Just because we didn't love each other, didn't mean our only option was to hate each other instead.

I grabbed the kitchen towel hanging from the cabinet next to my head and used it to dry my tears and my hands. I sat there while I tried to piece the shattered fragments of myself back together.

It wasn't easy and I wasn't entirely successful. But I managed to resolve something inside of me, something lasting and intentional. I didn't have to treat Nick badly to make myself feel better.

This was hard on both of us. And it didn't look like it would be getting any easier.

But if I could weather this storm, if I could walk this journey without inflicting any more lasting wounds, there might be healing at the end for me too.

I wanted this divorce because I was sick and tired of being miserable, of wishing I could be happy, of wanting a better life. On the floor of my kitchen, all alone and feeling my worst, I realized I didn't have to wait for Nick to go away before I could grab those things and make them realities in my life.

I didn't have to wait for the papers to be signed before I could stop being miserable... until I had a better life.

Those were things I had the power to change.

And I would change them. Starting now.

The front door opened and I jumped to my feet. I slammed the faucet down, so the water would stop running and give away my breakdown.

I threw the towel on the counter and wiped at my face one more time with my fingertips before moving quickly to meet Nick in the entryway. He unhooked the leash from Annie's collar and patted her on the head before standing up to his full, impressive height.

I knew by the way he looked at me that he could tell I'd been crying. Biting, defensive words immediately landed on the tip of my tongue, but I held them back, even if it cut into my pride.

"Thanks," I offered humbly. "I wasn't really up for walking her today."

His expression changed again. Storm clouds rolled in those starkly blue eyes of his and his face darkened with something I couldn't name. He rubbed his palm over the short scruff along his jaw, "Anytime."

"You too." The words surprised me as much as him. "I mean, if you want to walk her, just, maybe call first?"

He nodded. "I can do that."

We stared at each other awkwardly, shifting on our feet as the silence dragged out and neither of us could think of something to say. I didn't know if we'd somehow managed to reach a truce or if this was only a temporary treaty, but Nick seemed as tired of fighting as I did.

His gaze locked with mine, accidentally at first, but as he held it, I realized he was saying something to me in his silence. I couldn't read him, though. Either I'd forgotten how in the few months we'd been apart or maybe I never could to begin with.

Finally he said, "Well, I should go."

I couldn't bring myself to tell him goodbye. It didn't make any sense. But nothing I did made sense these days. He took my silence as a dismissal and left without another glance my way.

I was alone again, even if Annie was here this time. And even though we'd shared some hospitable moments, even though I'd managed to hold my tongue and not hurt him more, I felt more shredded than ever before.

Every time he left, I shattered apart.

Chapter Four

11. He doesn't **understand** me.

A week and a half had gone by since Nick stopped by to see Annie. For a couple days, I had anticipated his phone call. I'd caught myself glancing at my cell phone obnoxiously often or waiting to walk Annie just in case Nick stopped by and wanted to do it himself.

I couldn't explain my behavior.

This man didn't get to have access to my heart after everything we'd been through.

After everything we were going to go through.

When I realized what I was doing, how often I checked my cell and how far my heart sank each day he didn't call, I had temporarily contemplated checking myself into rehab.

Did they have rehab for bad relationships?

Was there an AA meeting for being addicted to the wrong men?

There should be.

"Ms. C, I need to go to the bathroom."

I whirled around from my position at the whiteboard, my marker held aloft. "You've already been, Jay. Twice."

Jay Allen's eyes narrowed and his lips curled with a knowing smirk. This was the second class I'd had with Jay. The first time I'd had him in class was two years ago as a freshman. He had been difficult to handle then, but nothing compared to the swagger he carried in his junior year.

He ran a hand over his shaved head and his eyes glinted with the promise of torture. "Bad Taco Bell." His large hand dropped to his stomach where he rubbed it dramatically. "I've got the shits."

I swallowed down pure, raw frustration as the rest of the class laughed and threw crass insults at him. This was what he did. Although it was very possible Taco Bell did give him the shits- we'd all been there. But this was

49

his regular MO. He wanted to rile up my classroom until it was complete chaos.

He didn't like me and I barely tolerated him. He had been a nuisance two years ago, but this year he had declared war on the first day when I asked him to be quiet and he had asked me if I was on my period. In front of the entire class.

His exact words were, "Damn, Teach, you on the rag? Why you so worked up? We just chillin'."

I had made him write "Excuse me, Mrs. Carter, are you feeling okay? You seem upset. I'm sorry for interrupting you," five hundred times as a graded essay.

He'd given me hell ever since.

"Fine, Mr. Allen, go to the restroom and take care of your... bowel issues." The class broke into hysterics again.

Jay flashed me a wide, toothy smile. He jumped from his seat and sauntered through the narrow aisles. He dropped two fingers on the edge of Keira Williams's desk and tapped twice. Keira sank down in her chair, a silly grin on her face.

I watched her while Jay grabbed the bathroom pass and left the room with as much noise and commotion as he was capable of. Keira glanced at the door, that happy smile still on her face.

She turned back to me and tentatively raised her hand.

Apparently, these kids thought I was an idiot.

"Yes, Keira?"

"I need to go to the bathroom too," she said shyly.

I resisted the urge to roll my eyes and give her a lecture on how love isn't real; it's only something our imaginations make up to make our libido feel better about itself in the morning.

Unfortunately, I didn't think the school board would appreciate that particular truth bomb.

"Let me guess, you had Taco Bell for lunch too?" I immediately regretted the snide tone to my voice when Keira's eyes went huge with embarrassment and she tried to melt into her chair.

I realized too late that even though her horny teenage hormones had no place at school, it wasn't my responsibility to warn her off men. I was only responsible until graduation.

"No," she answered quickly.

Damn high school girls and their low self-esteems. "I'm sorry, Keira," I told her with real remorse. "But you'll have to wait until Jay comes back."

She looked at the door longingly and I watched disappointment pull her features.

Had she really thought I'd let her leave for a mid-period hookup in the bathroom? I looked back at the whiteboard and contemplated giving up my lecture on dangling participles and replacing it with one on self-respect.

A skeezy tryst in the old boy's locker room wasn't going to do anything but give her athlete's foot and a reason to feel shame.

I hated that she wanted that for herself. I hated that Jay expected it from her.

Jay eventually came back looking impatient and aggravated. He shot Keira a look that I did not miss. She shrugged apologetically, but there was nothing she could do. The teacher had spoken.

The rest of class went by without incident, but I could feel Jay's angered glare as the minutes ticked by. As frustrated as I felt with him, his simmering anger got under my skin.

Fear fluttered in my chest and coiled in my stomach. This kid might be thirteen years younger than me, but he was bigger, taller, and he had more muscle than I could ever dream of.

I rationalized that he would retaliate in a way that drove me crazy, but wouldn't physically harm me. He wasn't stupid. He was too smart for his own good.

But rationalizing didn't help.

I breathed out slowly when the bell finally rang. Loud laughter and chatter filled up the once quiet space but faded as the students filtered into the hall.

Jay lingered behind. I could see Keira waiting for him in the hallway, but he wasn't in a hurry to catch up to her.

"You're ruining my game, Ms. C."

"You're ruining my class, Mr. Allen." I tilted my chin in a display of confidence I did not feel.

His deep brown eyes narrowed. "I didn't think you were this kind of teacher."

I leaned forward, emboldened by righteous anger. "And I didn't think you were that kind of an asshole, Jay. During class? Really? Have some respect for her."

He cocked his head back, shocked at my candidness. A slow grin pulled at his lips and my mouth went dry. Was he going to tell on me? Turn me into Mr. Kellar? I could get in a lot of trouble for speaking to a student like that.

51

"When she asks for it, I'll give it to her," he chuckled, the innuendo screaming through his words.

He turned away from me and strutted toward the door. I couldn't help but call after him, "Be better than that!"

He waved at me without turning back around, "Sure thing, Ms. C."

The door slammed shut behind him and I resisted the urge to puke. I placed my hands on my desk and leaned heavily on them. I dropped my head and focused on breathing. *Holy shit.*

Jay Allen wasn't the first difficult student I'd had. I'd called the cops more than once and I had been threatened at least once a semester since I started here.

The ego these boys carried around with them was incredible. They thought they owned the world and worse than that, they thought they *deserved* the world. They didn't appreciate a teacher that expected them to work hard and try at something other than sports or hitting on girls.

Sometimes the girls were even worse.

Entitled.

Cocky.

Neglected.

Underprivileged.

Apathetic.

These kids were a dangerous mixture of abandon and overpromise. I had to skate the fine line between realistic expectations and stern discipline.

Not one of them respected me for it.

A knock at my door and a deep voice pulled me from the turmoil of my thoughts. "Kate, are you okay?"

I looked up to find Eli Cohen standing in my doorway with a concerned expression on his face. His dark eyes swept over me, taking stock of everything that could be wrong.

"Rough day," I squeaked out. Fear still pounded in my chest and I wondered if I should go to Kellar. Nothing happened. Jay hadn't even threatened me. But years of experience taught me that I should trust my gut instinct.

"Your ex-husband?" Eli guessed.

I winced, unprepared for his question. A cynical smile tilted my lips and I stared at my shoes when I answered, "No, not Nick. I, uh, I had an altercation with a student."

Eli crossed the threshold and stood before me in three seconds. His large hands landed on my biceps, squeezing them compassionately.

I jumped at his touch. When was the last time a man had touched me? Even Nick?

Not for a very long time.

Eli's closeness immediately felt wrong. I had the strongest urge to smile politely and wiggle away from him. But I realized those were silly thoughts. I wasn't betraying Nick.

There was nothing left to betray.

"I'm so sorry," Eli apologized. "I shouldn't have assumed… I'm so sorry. Really. That was really stupid of me."

"It's okay," I promised him. In the end, I did shrug off his hands. They were too awkward and my head wasn't right. Plus, I started to worry about someone walking into the room and getting the wrong idea. "It could easily have been my divorce. It's been a weird few months."

Eli's concerned frown made me feel a little better. "I'm a jackass."

Surprised laughter bubbled out of me. "You're not."

"I am. What idiot walks in on a distraught woman and immediately brings up her divorce?"

My smile was soft and endearing. "It's really okay."

He gave me a sardonic look and shook his head. "I got divorced three years ago. I should know better."

His comment took my breath. I had never thought much about people in the midst of divorce before my own. I didn't even know that many that had gone through one. They seemed to be only stories my mother told me over Sunday dinners. *So-and-sos are getting divorced. I knew they wouldn't last. He was always lazy. She could never settle down.*

I never thought it would be me. I never thought I would be the restless girl or that Nick would be the deadbeat husband. Because according to my mother only worthless people got divorced.

"I'm so sorry," I told him quickly. This time it was me that put my hand on his shoulder. "I didn't know."

His deep chocolate eyes found mine and held them. "It was before I came here."

"How long were you married?" My curiosity couldn't be helped. Eli was gorgeous and an excellent teacher. He was a total catch. I couldn't imagine a woman not wanting to stay with him.

But I had once thought that about Nick too.

"Ten years," he answered with the slightest catch in his voice. "We were high school sweethearts."

We were quiet for a while as I heard all of the words he didn't say. The feelings that he didn't admit.

"Nick and I met in college," I admitted softly.

He turned around and sat down on the edge of my desk. His hands landed next to his hips and he leaned forward attentively.

I realized how strange it was to have this man's undivided attention. Nick didn't listen to me unless we were in the middle of an argument.

I couldn't count how many stories I'd told him only to have him lift his head and look at me like a lost puppy. "Huh?" he'd say. "Did you say something?"

I swallowed down the hurt of that memory and allowed myself to enjoy Eli's focus. I licked my dry lips and spoke beyond the fresh lump in my throat. "I thought we were perfect for each other."

"There's no such thing as perfect," Eli commiserated.

I groaned, "I know that now."

Eli stared at his scuffed brown loafers, so I took the opportunity to study the lines and planes of his face. His jaw was clean-shaven and smooth and his nose had small indents where his glasses rested. They were tucked into his pocket now, the end of one side poking out in the most adorable way.

He had great hair, great shoulders and great hands. He was so purely male that I knew half the female population of Hamilton High was deeply in love with him already and it was only September.

Not to mention I had heard really great things about his classes. He wasn't just a good guy, he was a good teacher.

And he understood what I was going through.

That was made evident when he confessed, "I remember getting to this point with Naomi and hating myself. It wasn't that I didn't love her anymore, it was that I couldn't stand to be around *me*." His eyes slowly lifted to meet mine. I felt his embarrassment behind his thick lashes. "Does that make me the most selfish man alive?"

I rushed to assure him that it didn't. "I know exactly what you mean." I pulled my thick hair over one shoulder and ran my fingers through the ends nervously. "I've actually been thinking about that a lot. It's like Nick and I are mostly good people... until you put us together. Then we're miserable and mean. I've never treated... I've said some horrible..." I let out a shaky breath. I barely knew Eli. These things were personal; I didn't need to share them with strangers.

"You're just not right for each other, isn't that it? You're good people, but better people apart."

I bravely met his gaze again. "That's exactly it. We are better friends than husband and wife." But even as I said the words they felt like a lie. I didn't know if we were better friends. We had never been friends. And I seriously doubted the probability that we would become friends now.

"Does it get easier?" My words trembled as they fell from my lips. I needed him to tell me yes. I needed him to offer hope.

"It does," he said solemnly. "It will."

Relief, sweet and strong, pulsed through me. I felt hot tears prick at my eyes. I held them back, frustrated that I could still cry at the drop of a hat. I needed to pull myself together. I needed to get a grip.

To my embarrassment, he noticed right away. "Hey," he soothed. His big arms wrapped around me and pulled me into a comforting hug.

I was so shocked at first that I didn't know what to do. But he didn't give up, he didn't let go. After a few more moments, I couldn't fight the warmth of his touch or the promise of his comfort. I let my arms encircle his hard torso and sank into him.

"Thank you."

He squeezed me tightly for another elongated moment before releasing me. "It's still fresh," he consoled. "Give it time. Remember what it's like to live alone and you'll be fine, Kate. You're a tough cookie."

I wrinkled my nose. "How would you know that?"

"You work here, don't you?" His playful smile put one on my lips too. "You have to be tough."

"Or stupid," I laughed.

His expression straightened, turning serious with his sentiment, "Well, you're definitely not that."

My stomach fluttered unexpectedly. I hadn't been anticipating such a sweet compliment. "Thank you," I told him. "Again."

He moved toward the door, offering me a small wave as he pulled his black-framed glasses from his pocket. "Any time. I mean that. Any time you need to talk, I'm just a few doors down."

I was too flustered to respond, so I nodded slowly and pressed my lips together to keep from smiling too big.

He disappeared through the doorframe and I stood there for a long time after, just staring at the blank space. I needed to prep for my next class, but I couldn't get over Eli and his surprising friendship.

I hadn't been open with anyone that wasn't Kara in a long time. And I hadn't had a man's opinion in my life for longer than that.

Nick didn't count since he rarely gave his.

Neither did my dad or brother since I never listened to theirs.

And not only had Eli been nice... but he'd understood too.

He hadn't judged me. He hadn't dismissed my feelings or made me feel bad for having them. He'd been through what I had and promised it would get better.

I held those words close to my broken heart. I let them take root in my chest and bloom with promise.

I needed it to get better. I needed to know I could survive this.

Because right now... right now leaving Nick... healing from our brokenness... moving on with my life...

It all felt impossible.

Chapter Five

12. We **never** talk anymore.

Friday night used to be the best night of the week. Once upon a time... before my age started skirting thirty and responsibility became more important than tequila shots and dancing the night away.

Also, since when did hangovers evolve into the bubonic plague? In our younger years, Nick and I could walk the thin line between alcohol poisoning and passing out in a friend's bushes, then wake up the next day refreshed and ready to do it all over again.

Now two beers were enough to land me on my ass for the rest of the weekend with a nasty headache and *Exorcist*-style puking.

Nick wasn't like me, though. He could still party unapologetically like he was at his bachelor party every single night. Which worked well for him.

He was in a band. A *band*.

But not the Backstreet Boys. Nick was the farthest thing from a Backstreet Boy. *Thank god.*

He had been named Nick Carter before the crooning boy band member had ever made the name famous.

Nick hated that he shared his name with someone else. I loved it. Not because I had a thing for boy bands. But because I could give him an endless hard time about it.

Come on. It never got old.

Plus, I could sing *I Want it That Way* and pretend like it was just to get under his skin.

At the age of thirty, my husband still hadn't given up his dreams of becoming the next big thing.

Our entire marriage had been centered around his big break, the big break that never came. Our weekends were booked with gigs and late nights at seedy venues. His college degree that he'd earned with honors was all but forgotten in his pursuit of happiness.

He was good at it. I would never claim otherwise. My husband could sing and play guitar and rock out on stage as if he belonged on the radio and in stadiums surrounded by hundreds of thousands of fans. He was something to see on stage. I was transfixed from the very first moment I saw him up there. He never failed to make me fall in love with him every time he took the stage and opened his mouth.

But the music industry was not a fair place. He knew that more than anyone else.

We had lost so much money to bad agents and self-recorded albums. I had watched my savings dwindle and my hard-earned paychecks disappear into new equipment and demos.

It had been amazing while we were dating. I used to love having the lead singer's complete attention. I loved that he wrote songs about how much he loved me. I loved that my husband *was in a band.*

Fast forward seven years, it wasn't as pretty. The shininess had worn off and the glitter had faded. I was tired of supporting us on my pathetic teacher's salary and begging him to get a real job, a job that paid something.

And I could tell *he* was tired. He was tired of failing. He was tired of not making it. With each passing year, he'd grown more cynical... more jaded.

His music was still great. His music would always be great. But at some point we had to grow up.

I supported him for as long as I could- both emotionally and financially. But I reached my limit and I couldn't hide it anymore.

I didn't even want to think about what that did to him... what it felt like to have the person that was supposed to love him most in the world give up on him.

Guilt swam in my stomach, erasing my hunger and determination to stock my empty refrigerator.

I pushed the cart forward and let go for a few seconds. Grocery shopping on a Friday night. This was about as grown up as it got.

But not in a good way.

I looked at the few items in my basket and tried not to roll my eyes. I had been wandering around the store for forty-five minutes and hadn't been able to find anything that sounded good.

I'd picked up lots of Nick's favorites before I realized that he didn't live with me anymore. Putting them back on the shelf made me feel so pathetic. I couldn't shake the feeling of failure when I acknowledged that taking care of Nick was a hard habit to shake.

Plus, it made me realize that I had been catering to his needs for so long, I didn't know how to take care of my own.

Why didn't I know what I liked to eat? Why couldn't I pick out groceries for *me*?

The embarrassing part was that I started to realize how much of a crutch Nick had been for me. When we were married, I felt completely fine buying junk food for us because it was all stuff that Nick liked. I realized I blamed him for bad eating habits, when really, when it came down to it, it was food I actually preferred.

Now my conscience wouldn't let me pick out the sugary cereals or the mountains of chocolate I craved. Now I had all of this obnoxious guilt for not buying organic produce and rice cakes.

Damn Nick and his obsession with processed foods.

And damn Dr. Oz for doing that special on weight gain and high fructose corn syrup.

I loved high fructose corn syrup.

I grabbed my wayward cart and dropped my head down to the cold metal handlebar. "It shouldn't be this hard." The chill from the freezer section pulled goose bumps from my arms and legs, but I didn't have the willpower to keep walking.

I just wanted to give up and go home. I could order Chinese. Again.

Or eat my weight in Wheat Thins.

My body jerked when someone banged their cart into mine. The scraping metal and squeaky wheels grated on my nerves and I snapped my head up, ready to rip someone's hair out.

Or at least give them a stern verbal lashing.

Okay, probably more likely it would have been a meaningful glare. But they would have felt shamed.

I would have totally shamed them with my evil eye.

Today was the wrong day to mess with me.

My lips parted and my eyebrows shot to my hairline when I saw Nick at the helm of the other cart. My eyes moved over his faded maroon t-shirt and low-slung jeans. In one second, I noted his hair that was just slightly too long and the thicker beard that roughened his jaw. I could close my eyes and picture this man perfectly naked. When he appeared out of nowhere, I saw the differences in him without trying. "What are you doing here?" The words fell out of my mouth before I could tame my reaction.

His lips twitched with an almost smile. "I think you forget that I'm still alive. It's like you don't expect me to keep on existing now that I'm not in your life every day."

His words were only barely playful. Mostly they held a sharp edge of bitterness.

"That's ridiculous," I countered immediately. Even though, maybe he was a little right. "You've just surprised me. Twice."

He leaned forward as if telling me a secret, "You're ridiculously easy to surprise."

The shock of seeing him here receded and I pressed my lips together when I felt laughter bubble up inside me. "Whatever." Memories of our relationship tumbled around in my head, but I suppressed them. I was already an emotional wreck. I didn't need him to witness my most recent damage.

Nick tugged at his earlobe, his nervous tell. "So, uh, really, you surprised me too. I didn't expect to see you here. On a Friday night."

"Ice cream," I suddenly decided. It was so much better than the truth. "I need ice cream."

He raised one eyebrow, a look I used to love on him. "Bad week?"

"Week from hell."

"Yeah, me too." His words were a forlorn mumble and I had the immediate urge to ask why.

Instead, I forced my lips to stay shut. We stared awkwardly at each other, neither of us knowing how to navigate our fragile peace treaty from last week. Long seconds ticked by while people moved around us and bad pop music drifted through the store.

"So, what are you in the mood for?" His gaze swung toward the frosted freezer doors, where cartons of ice cream sat hidden behind cloudy glass.

The million-dollar question. "I should probably get the staples first, right? If I pick out ice cream now it will melt by the time I get to the car."

"Yeah, me too."

I looked back at Nick and found him watching me. His fingers flexed and stretched while his palms rested on the metal bar. He was trying not to reach for his earlobe.

"What do you need to get?" I asked quietly.

It was weird talking to him. Even if it was just over groceries. Our relationship had always revolved around conversation, even if we were screaming at each other. But he'd been mostly out of my life over the last five months. We had nothing to fight about at the moment, but we couldn't exactly bare our souls in the middle of Meijer either.

We had never been good at small talk. Not even in the beginning.

What do you want most in life? That had been the first question he asked me on our fateful second date.

I remembered staring at him for longer than was comfortable. I remembered wanting to fidget, but wanting to figure him out more.

When I answered him, I hadn't known what I was going to say or if it would even be true. *I want a life, a real one. I want to know each day meant something profound and at the end of it, I want to know it was worth the journey.*

That doesn't sound easy, he'd said. His lips had tilted on one side with a crooked half-smile that had made butterflies take flight in my entire body.

I didn't say I wanted easy. I want beautiful.

He had met my eyes and I noticed for the first time how blue his were. They were electric with intensity, searing with focus. He had leaned forward and whispered, "*You* are *beautiful.*"

I cleared my throat and tried to erase the memory of our past. It was one of my favorites. It was the one that promised I would fall in love with him, the one that buried him beneath my skin and wrapped him around my heart.

"I don't know how to do this," he murmured.

His words hit me unexpectedly and like usual when he was around, I felt like crying. "Oh, sure," I said quickly. I tried to replace the defenses around my heart, but it was too late. He'd penetrated them too quickly. "It's not fair of me to ask you to small talk about... ice cream. I'm sure you have other things to do."

I yanked my cart back, ready to make a fast retreat when he stopped me with a chuckle. "Kate," he called. "I meant that I'm having a hard time grocery shopping. I don't know how to do *this*." He gestured around him with a lazy flick of his hand. "You used to... it used to be your thing. I'm completely out of my element."

As sharp and shocking as rejection hit me, the sweet pulse of relief was just as strong. I swayed with the dizzying notion and then immediately berated myself for letting him control my emotions like this.

Letting him *still* control my emotions like this.

"Want some help?" I offered gently.

He tugged on his earlobe while he weighed my question. I could see indecision flicker in his bright blue eyes. He wanted to know what this would cost him.

I immediately felt guilty. "I need help too," I said. "I can't remember anything I like. I only remember everything *you* like."

His lips kicked up in a small smile. "That's exactly my problem."

It was my turn to feel indecisive. What was I doing? Before I could talk myself out of my better instincts, I suggested, "We could... we could shop together. You remind me what I like and I'll do the same for you. That work?"

His Adam's apple bobbed as he swallowed thickly, "Sure. That works."

We turned our carts so that we could walk side-by-side. It worked well in the freezer department because the aisles were wider, but the rest of the store was more crowded so I took the lead.

"You like peanut butter," I offered.

"But what kind?" He stared at the shelves. His lips pressed into a frown and I watched his eyes move over the different kinds and sizes of jars with determined concentration.

It was my turn to smile. "You don't know what brand of peanut butter you like?"

He rubbed his hand along the side of his jaw, his dark scruff scratching his palm. "I know what I like, but that one's cheaper." He pointed to the store brand and my smile stayed in place. "Does it taste the same?"

When his eyebrows drew down and he looked at me with the helpless expression of a lost little boy I couldn't help but laugh. I shook my head slowly and said, "No, it doesn't. Don't be cheap with peanut butter."

"But the kind I like is three dollars more."

"And so worth it."

His forehead smoothed out and his lips twitched again. "Promise?"

"I promise."

"Okay, what about jelly?" He put his favorite brand of peanut butter in the cart and moved down a shelf.

"That you can be less picky about. I usually go for the one that's on sale and has a flavor I like."

His low chuckle followed him as he grabbed a jar of raspberry preserves. "Are we too old to eat peanut butter and jelly sandwiches?"

"Don't say that. We both know it's the breakfast of champions."

"So the cashier isn't going to judge me?"

"Just mention the kids you have waiting for you at home."

The jar fell out of his hands and crashed into the cart. He ignored the jelly and spun toward me. "You don't do that."

"Captain Crunch and corndogs are your favorites. Of course, I do that!"

His deep laughter warmed the air between us and I found myself smiling too. "You're an evil genius, Katherine Claire."

I ignored the way his teasing burned through me or the nostalgia that tickled my belly when he used my full name. I pushed my cart forward and led us to another aisle.

"Is it your students?" His deep voice chased after me.

I avoided running into another shopper when I turned the corner and processed his words. "My rough week?"

"Yeah, your rough week. Is it your kids this year? Or new management? What's going on at Hamilton?"

"Mostly the kids," I explained over my shoulder. "We're still establishing the pecking order. They're not ready to admit I'm in charge yet."

"Because high school kids are assholes," he added in my defense.

My lips turned up in another smile. "That they are." I rubbed my chin on my shoulder as I looked at him. "The beginning of the year is always the hardest."

He met my eyes with a steady gaze. "I remember."

My heart thumped painfully in my chest and I took a deep breath before I could tear my attention from him. "Pasta."

"What?" His voice was rougher than it had been a few seconds ago.

"You like pasta. And it's easy to make." I pointed at his favorite kind of noodles and sauce before adding some to my own cart. "Basically all you need to be able to do is boil water."

He reached for some noodles. "I think I can handle spaghetti. If I have to eat another cheeseburger this week, I might murder Jared."

I laughed. "Your brother doesn't cook?"

Nick threw me an annoyed look. "Jared eats McDonalds. For every meal."

I wrinkled my nose. I thought Nick and I had eaten badly, but that was above and beyond a bowl of ice cream every night. "He's going to die of a heart attack. He's twenty-six! He can't live like that forever."

Nick nodded, "I tell him that every day."

I smiled thinking of Nick's younger brother and how immature he could be. "He needs a woman to settle him down."

My smile died when Nick flinched. I realized my mistake, but I didn't know how to take it back. I just wanted to swallow every stupid word and run away.

Or throw a jar of marinara sauce on the ground to distract him.

I turned toward the shelves again and stared blindly at the sauces. I picked one up and tried to read the label, but I couldn't see anything beyond the tears swimming in my eyes.

Finally, Nick spoke and I wished more than anything I had just ordered Chinese. "A woman might save him from a heart attack, but she'll kill him in every other way." His voice dipped low and I felt the cruel bitterness in my bones.

It was a miracle I didn't throw the jar of sauce after all- only this time it would have been aimed at his head. I was too angry to look at him, too hurt to breathe. I felt suffocated by his presence, his bitter attitude, his razor sharp tongue. I wanted to abandon my cart and flee, but I couldn't convince my feet to move.

It was so silly. He hadn't said anything shocking. It wasn't like I'd never heard this before.

I was the dream-killer. I was the cold-hearted shrew blinded by rational thought and practicality. I was the reason Nick couldn't make it.

I was the reason Nick had to give up his dream.

And here we were again. Even though we were separated. Even though Nick was welcome to do whatever he wanted with his life. Even though I couldn't tell him what to do anymore.

It was still my fault.

"This was stupid," I spoke in a shaking whisper, one part tremulous tears, the other vibrating anger. "What are we doing?"

Nick leaned in and growled. "I ask myself that every damn day."

My head snapped up and I tried not to be sick. "I mean in the grocery store. I mean here, right now. What are we doing trying to navigate single life together? Are we stupid?"

His face flushed red and more emotions than I could name ping-ponged through me. I hated myself again. I hated him again.

I just wanted to stop feeling like this.

"We must be," he admitted. "There's obviously no other explanation for why we keep doing this to each other."

I nodded. Even though I felt the same way, it still killed to have him say it aloud. I lifted my chin and bravely told him, "I have a lawyer." I didn't. But I wanted one. It was time to stop being a coward.

He took a step back like I had physically hit him. The color immediately drained from his face and I thought for a second he was going to be sick. After an eternal minute where we stared each other down in front of noodles, he gritted out, "Good. That's good."

Immediately I felt guilty and tried to explain, "We can't stay separated forever. I figured you would want to move on with your life."

"Like you do."

I took a steadying breath and ignored the accusation. "I'm just trying to give us both peace."

"I've heard that about divorce. It's such a peaceful time for everyone involved."

Bile rose in my throat. "Why are you doing this?"

"Doing what, Kate? I'm not the one pushing for divorce."

"You're making it seem like it's all my fault. This is what we both want." I quickly swiped at a wayward tear and tried not to throw up.

He rocked back on his heels and swallowed thickly. "I keep forgetting that part."

"I need to go." Before I broke down in front of him. Before I admitted that this was so much harder than I thought it was going to be. Before I said anything to get that betrayed look off his face.

"Sure."

"Bye, Nick."

He stared at me without saying anything. I hadn't really expected a heartfelt farewell, but I couldn't stand the hurt in his eyes or the downward curve of his lips because I put them there. I hated the way his wrinkled clothes hung on his body because it meant I wasn't there to fold his laundry. I hated his empty cart because he didn't know what he liked to eat or his too-long hair because I hadn't reminded him to get it cut.

Our lives had once been separate. We had lived more than half of them apart. But over the last seven years they had been woven together, they had become one existence, one life. And now we were tearing everything we'd built to pieces. We were ripping apart at the seams. We were plunging forward in opposite directions.

I was losing half of myself.

And I wasn't sure there was enough of me to make a whole person again.

"Chocolate cherry," he suddenly called after me.

I almost tripped when my head whipped back to look at him. "Wh-what?"

"Ice cream. You like chocolate cherry the best."

I fled the store. I left my cart and groceries behind and I ran for my car. I broke down as soon as the door closed and I didn't quit until long after I was locked away safely in my house again.

I did make one stop on the way home, though. Even though my face was a mess of dripping mascara and big, fat tears, I couldn't go home until I had picked up a carton of chocolate cherry ice cream.

We might be different people now.

But he still knew me better than anyone else.

Chapter Six

13. He stopped **trying**.

"Kara, what are we doing here?" I put my hand up against an invisible wall and told my feet to stop walking.

They didn't listen.

Mainly because my best friend had a death grip on my bicep and I was afraid that if I stopped moving, she would rip my arm straight off my body.

"It's hump day," she tossed over her shoulder.

As if that explained everything.

"No, it's *Wednesday*. And we have to work in the morning." The neon lights over the bar flickered tellingly. They buzzed and blinked, clearly about to burn out. I stared up at them until I saw spots.

Kara made a disgruntled sound in the back of her throat. "*Noooo*, it's *hump* day and we deserve a reward for making it to the middle of the week!"

Her overly bright tone disguised the raw frustration she felt. It had been a rough couple of weeks for both of us. There must have been something in the drinking water this year because our students were some of the hardest we had ever had to deal with.

I couldn't do much more than fall face first on my couch after work most days. Grading papers only added to my stress, since most of my students thought they were either comedians or above the rules.

"Fine, let's reward ourselves someplace else." I stared at the rickety front door. The screen hung crooked on the hinges and loud music filtered through the murky screen. "*Any* place else."

Her Skeletor grip loosened. "At least it's not the alcohol you have a problem with."

"Of course not," I assured her. "In most every circumstance, I'm pro-alcohol."

She glanced up at the hot pink sign. "Then what do you have against Starla's?"

"Other than my first date with Nick was here? And that he sometimes still plays here? The bar is full of our co-workers."

She paused, her tall pointed shoes settling precariously in the gravel lot. "I forgot he used to come here." She didn't mention Nick's band because she rarely made it to a show. Kara tried very hard to be a free spirit, but the truth was her family had instilled high standards in her. Nick's lack of a full-time job and real-world aspirations bothered her. She might not have been pro-divorce, but she certainly didn't try to talk me out of it. "Are you afraid Nick is going to be in there?"

I chewed my bottom lip, struggling with the root of my fear. "Not really, no. It's more the memory of this place. And our co-workers. I hate our co-workers."

"Well, obviously. Everybody hates their co-workers."

I wasn't sure that was accurate, but it was true for me so I stayed silent. I shuffled my leather ankle boots and stared at the chalky gravel debris spread out at my feet. I wanted to be anywhere but here. But even the pissy people I worked with were better than going home to an empty house and the thoughts tumbling through my head. "I thought this would be easier," I admitted.

She leaned forward until we were just a few inches apart. "You keep saying that, babe. It's time to change your expectations. Then maybe it *will* get easier."

Ignoring the sting of pain, I suppressed a smile because she was right. "Okay."

"Okay to 'Kara you're brilliant and I should hire you as my life coach?' Or okay to the skeezy bar where our middle-aged fellow teachers are currently getting shit-faced enough to karaoke?" She flashed a huge, toothy grin and resumed her bruising grip on my arm so she could tug me into the bar.

"You didn't say anything about karaoke!" I choked on the thick musky air that smelled like stale beer and the remnants of burning cigarettes long extinguished. Smoking in restaurants and bars had been outlawed in Chicago, but places like this would forever hold the memories and lingering scent of when it had been legal.

The screen door slammed behind me and I felt it with a finality that reached my bones. I was here. And I was apparently staying.

And if Kara even hinted at the idea of karaoke, I would make her a fake Match.com account and set her up on dates with *World of Warcraft* gamers that still lived in their moms' basements. *So help me, god.*

When Kara and I first started teaching at Hamilton, the faculty preferred to let their hair down at an establishment closer to school. An equally desolate dive bar, O'Connor's had dollar drinks on Thursdays and STD's living on the toilet seats. But it caught fire four years ago and the owners had decided to retire instead of rebuild. Anxious to impress my new friends, I had offered up Starla's as an alternative. Nick and I had been coming here since college, Kara had been drafted in on non-live music nights and it was only a five-minute drive from school.

Walking in tonight, with Mr. Bunch, the art teacher, at the mic screaming out *Tainted Love*, I realized my mistake.

If we ever wondered why we had trouble relating to our students... this might be it.

The very reason.

"Let's get a drink!" Kara shouted over Mr. Bunch's shrieking warble. "Please!"

She smiled at me, laughter dancing in her eyes and led the way through the crush of sweaty bodies and rickety tables. The polished wooden bar took up the length of one side of the main room. Two bartenders worked relentlessly to fill pint glasses and mix cocktails. I breathed a sigh of anticipation and tried not to dwell on how much I was planning to use alcohol as an emotional crutch tonight.

It's Wednesday, I reminded myself.

I can't teach with a hangover, I lectured.

Gimme gimme gimme, my brain chanted, ignoring every good and well-intentioned reason to stay sober.

Kara leaned over the counter and ordered two whiskey and diets. I could have kissed her when she handed me the sweating tumbler filled with dark liquid. I took a sip and closed my eyes against the burning coolness as it slid down my throat.

The cheap whiskey went straight to my head. I took another sip and the burn spread from my throat to my limbs, searing through my blood and making my fingers tingle. I opened my eyes and licked my already wet lips.

Sucking in a deep breath, I waded through the tension that knotted in my neck and tied my stomach in tangles. I wouldn't really medicate with alcohol, but it was tempting. It was tempting to do anything to get rid of these feelings, these doubts and fears. This pain and self-involved misery.

"He's watching you," Kara announced in my ear.

I became instantly alert, my eyes scanning the crowd for Nick. "Who?"

"Eli," she answered happily. "He's near the stage!"

Eli. I shook my head. I wasn't expecting that. Or him. Or for Kara to notice. I found him across the room, sitting at a small table with one of our co-workers. His usually-tamed hair was tousled and wild, his glasses tucked away out of sight. He didn't bother to turn away. He kept his dark eyes trained right on me.

Something warm burst to life in my belly. I fidgeted uncomfortably on my low heels and tried not to give myself away.

"Let's go over there," Kara yelled.

I could hear the smile in her voice, but I didn't want to acknowledge it. "I don't think that's a good idea."

"God, you're such a party pooper tonight!"

I tore my gaze from Eli's and met my best friend's. "He's hot, Kara."

Her smile returned. "I know, right!"

I shook my head. I could feel the fear throw cold water all over the whiskey's delicious heat. "I don't know what to do with this."

Her shoulders rose with her deep breath, preparing her for battle. "Don't do anything with it, Kate. Just talk to him. Just be normal."

"I haven't admitted another guy's hot-"

She frantically waved her hands in front of my face. "And you're not going to now! I'm not asking you to go tell Eli what you think of him. I'm just asking you to have a conversation. I want you to try to relax. I want you to try to be Kate again."

"I should go home."

"You should have another drink and remember what it's like to be single."

If anyone else had said that to me, I would have turned around and left. I could be obnoxiously stubborn. Contrary just to be contrary.

But this wasn't anyone else. This was the person I trusted most in life. This was my friend that only wanted what was best for me.

And I knew I was making too big of a deal out of this. There wasn't any harm in a conversation. I could talk to Eli, just like I did at school the other day.

Just to be sure, I downed my drink and ordered another one. It was one thing to freak out in front of Kara. Eli didn't need to see my neurosis.

Er, any more of my neurosis.

We pushed through the crowded tables to the other side of the bar. It seemed like the entire faculty had come out tonight. Mrs. Patz, the school librarian, had made it on stage to perform a duet with Mrs. Chan, the geography teacher. I had never heard Cher sung quite like that before.

When I finally reached Eli's table, my eyes were wide and a smile danced in the corners of my mouth. It must have been a rough week for all of us.

That was the only explanation I could come up with for all of this... insanity.

This musical insanity.

Eli scooted down a chair so I could sit next to him. The gym teacher and assistant football coach, Kent Adams, made room for Kara. Kent was single and young and had a crush on Kara. They had been on a date before, but she claimed lack of chemistry.

I knew the truth. She was scared.

Kara was my opposite. I fell in love on the second date and got married the year after I graduated college. Kara refused to let anyone get that close to her. Her defenses were thicker than the Great Wall of China. She let very few people in.

I was one of the lucky ones.

Kent was cool though and he'd always been nice to me. I wished- silently, of course, because I valued not having my hair ripped out- that she'd give him a chance.

Eli leaned in with a crooked half-smile. "Hey."

I bit my bottom lip to keep from smiling wider. "Hey."

"Did you get your name on the list?" His head tilted toward the stage.

"It was the first thing I did when I walked in."

His smile widened and straight, white teeth winked at me from behind his full lips. "Liar," he teased. "You walked straight to the bar."

I took a sip of my new drink and felt a blush spread out on both of my cheeks. I blamed the alcohol. "And you didn't?"

"Of course I did," he chuckled. "This has been a shit week."

I nodded and took a deep breath. The cops had been called yesterday after two kids beat the shit out of each other during lunch. Today someone pulled the fire alarm and interrupted second period. That was on top of all of the other day-to-day drama this year seemed filled with.

"You are not wrong," I agreed.

We sat silently while new teachers took the stage. The beginning notes to Journey's *Don't Stop Believing* came on and I took a quick drink to hide my excitement.

Eli's breath brushed over my neck. "I saw that." His low voice rumbled in my ear.

I looked up at him from beneath my eyelashes and asked innocently, "Saw what?"

"You like this song," he accused.

"Everybody likes this song!" My defense was ruined with laughter. "It's maybe the most likable song in the history of songs."

His dark eyes lit up, glittering in the dim lights of the dingy bar. "Did you want to join them? I'm sure we could find you a mic."

"Just a small town girl," I mouthed to him. "Living in a lonely world." I held my tumbler to my lips, gripping it dramatically. "She took the midnight train goin' anywhere!"

Eli's head tipped back as he laughed out loud. "What will it take to get you to do that on stage?"

"A million dollars and your first born child."

"You drive a hard bargain, but it might be worth it." He leaned closer again and I inhaled his cologne. My stomach flipped and a shiver skittered down my back. "Would you like me to sign that contract with blood? Or will a regular old pen work."

"Blood, if you please."

I expected something witty and charming, but instead his laughter died and his expression turned serious. "It's nice to see you smiling again, Kate. It looks good on you."

My blush turned into a blanket of tomato-red and I wanted to press my ice-cold glass against my cheek. "Thank you," I whispered.

"Is there room?"

My head snapped up and I forced a smile on my face. Our private moment was interrupted by more co-workers. I could feel Kara's glare across the table, but I couldn't look at her or I would burst into laughter.

Andrea Turner and Meg Halston joined our group, dragging chairs with them. Eli and I were forced apart so they could squeeze between us.

I took a long drink and braced myself for two of the most annoying people I had ever met. Andrea and Meg worked in the office. Meg was the school nurse and Andrea worked at the front desk. They were both in their late thirties and the center of the gossip control tower at Hamilton.

I had never gotten along with Andrea. She had been snide with me from day one and I had no reason to try and get on her good side. I avoided her as much as I could, especially after I'd overheard her tell Meg that Nick left me because I was as frigid in the bedroom as I was in the classroom.

"Sure," Eli answered politely.

I had no idea if he genuinely liked these two or if he was just being polite, but I could barely restrain my cat claws. I focused on finishing my second drink and scrolling through my phone to see if I needed to download the Uber app to get home.

"I can't stand these bitches," Kara grumbled in my ear.

"Me either," I agreed.

"Where's your hubby?" The obnoxious voice grated on my nerves until I realized Andrea was talking to me. Then it went from grating to stabbing and I wanted to flee.

I lifted my chin and met her calculating gaze. "Me?" I asked pointlessly.

I tried not to hate Andrea just because she had perfect hair that fell in shiny, curled waves to her shoulders and a tiny nose and porcelain skin. She looked like a Barbie doll. Even her boobs were over proportioned.

I glanced down at my chest and tried not to wince. Boobs were not a legitimate reason to hate someone.

Right?

Sure. Right.

No, she had way worse qualities than perfect looks. Her personality was absolutely unforgivable.

"We're not together anymore," I answered lamely. "You know that."

She canted her head at me and laughed. "Do I?"

I cleared my throat and willed a waiter to come over by the sheer power of my desperate need for another drink.

Andrea let the awkward silence drag on for a few more painful moments before she cemented her place in hell and said, "That's too bad, Kate. He was a catch."

"Let's get more drinks!" Kara shouted.

Thank god for best friends.

I stood up so quickly, I almost knocked my chair backward. Kara caught it with her panther-like reflexes and then we escaped to the bar.

"Shots!" she shouted at the bartender. "We need shots!"

"Of what?" He raised his eyebrows at us, amused curiosity dancing in his expression.

"Something strong," Kara threw back.

"Something painful!" I added.

The young bartender's face lit with laughter. "You got it." He looked between us and clarified, "Two?"

"Two," I answered immediately. I saw Kara's eyes flicker back to the table and there was no way in hell I would let her take shots back to

Andrea to prove just how pathetic I was. No doubt, she already knew. I didn't need to advertise this shit.

The bartender poured two tiny glasses of gasoline, I mean, cheap tequila and handed them over. For a half second, I deliberated asking for a lime, but I couldn't waste any more time. I picked up the clear liquid and slammed it down, sputtering through the worst of the burn.

"Oh, god," I groaned.

"I might puke," Kara winced. "I'm not kidding. That was really bad."

"Another!" I shouted at the bartender.

He looked at me like I was absolutely crazy, the good fun draining away, replaced with concern. I wagged my finger between Kara and me and looked at him expectantly.

"Alright," he mumbled. This time he pulled out something a little smoother and handed us limes to go with them.

Kara and I slammed the second set of shots and bit down on our limes to ease the fire.

"I hate mean girls," Kara hissed after we'd acclimated to the new burn of alcohol.

"I hate divorce."

She laid her hand on my shoulder sympathetically, but there was nothing else to say.

The rest of the night went on like that. Eli and Kent came over to talk to us after a while and we laughed over another round of tequila shots. Worse karaoke and more gossip continued, but mostly there was relaxing.

I avoided Andrea and Meg as often as I could and let Eli entertain me with his funny stories and witty sarcasm.

I wasn't used to a man's focus. And I really wasn't used to a man like Eli, a man that paid attention to what I said. A man that paid attention to *me*.

"It's late," I said after blinking at my phone. Kent had convinced Kara to dance with him and Eli and I had been left alone. I leaned against the sticky bar, knowing I wouldn't be able to stand very long without its support. "I'm going to be worthless tomorrow."

Eli gave me his half smile, "Do you want a ride home?"

I hadn't seen him drink anything but water for the last two hours, so I hoped that meant he was sober. "Are you sure?"

He nodded. "It would be my pleasure."

"Let me grab Kara."

His gaze moved to the dance floor and when it came back to me, it was unreadable. But then again, that could have been the booze.

I retrieved my friend from the dance floor. She came willingly, but I could tell I took her from a good time. She was more relaxed than usual and I hated interrupting her. But we did have to be at school bright and early in the morning and our sanities were still salvageable if we left now.

Eli led the way out to his pickup truck. My eyesight was a little blurry, but I couldn't stop from smiling at the rusted wheel caps and faded paint. Eli's old Chevy just seemed to fit him in a way I couldn't explain. It was old, but it was also comfortable and full of character.

He held the door open for us and Kara nudged me in first. I tried not to fumble too much as I slid into the middle seat. Kara climbed up after me and Eli slammed the door shut. My ears rang in the new silence, damaged from the calamity of the bar. I slumped against the bench seat, the rough fabric scratching the backs of my knees and realized exactly how tired I was.

Eli climbed into the driver's seat, filling the cab with his cologne and the light tang of sweat. His warm thigh pressed into mine and I was too tipsy to feel self-conscious. I let my leg rest against his and felt the heat of his body to the tips of my toes.

That small touch kept me more alert than I should have been with the alcohol swimming in my blood. His touch did all kinds of things to my head, including keeping me silent. Eli and Kara talked on the way to her house, but I couldn't find the courage to open my mouth.

It was stupid. Completely stupid. That small connection should mean nothing. I shouldn't even be worried about Eli's leg pressed against mine. And yet, it was the most intimate I had ever been with someone else since I met Nick. I had never been this forward with another man. Ever. I didn't need to be.

And the entire ride to Kara's apartment I fought a war between excitement and shame. The thrill of my attraction to Eli fought seven years of loyalty to my husband. I didn't know whether to grin like an idiot or puke.

Finally, we dropped Kara off and I broke the contact between us, sliding to the passenger's side. I gave Eli my address with a shaking voice. I couldn't look at him anymore. I had crossed some invisible barrier tonight that I had set up myself.

I was too confused and too infused with alcohol to know if the buzzing in my veins was celebration or sorrow. And I was too tired to care.

"I had fun hanging out with you tonight, Kate," Eli's low rumble floated in the warm air of the cab.

This time my smile came easily and I stopped worrying about all of the rules I broke tonight or the consequences of my actions. "I had fun hanging out with you, too."

I felt his eyes on me, but I couldn't bring myself to look at him. "You going to be okay to get inside?" he asked gently.

"Yeah, I'll be fine."

We sat silently until it became a little awkward, until I knew I should move.

I had just touched the handle when Eli's voice stopped me. "Kate?"

This time I dragged my gaze to his. "Yeah?"

"I'll see you tomorrow, right?"

I smiled slowly. "I might not look this pretty, but yeah, I'll be there."

His lips tipped up into a flirtatious smile. "I'm looking forward to it, pretty or not."

I left his truck with a smile on my face, a smile that didn't leave until I had let myself into my dark house, a smile that stayed in place until after I'd brushed my teeth and climbed into my bed with Annie curled up next to me.

It was then that my smile slowly disappeared... that it turned into a frown as I stared up at the still ceiling fan and spread my body out on a bed I had shared with my husband in a house we bought together.

I expected to fall asleep quickly, but I tossed and turned until the alcohol wore off and my eyes hurt from unshed tears.

Eli was a distraction from the truth of my misery. Eli was fun to flirt with and divert my single-minded attention, but he didn't fix the problems inside me. He didn't solve my broken marriage or my heartbreaking divorce.

When I finally fell asleep, I thought I had done so sober. So when I woke up in the morning and found a new text message on my phone, nobody was more surprised than me.

Nick had texted: *Me too.*

I was confused until I saw the text sent directly before that one... the one sent from me at three in the morning. *This is killing me.*

Chapter Seven

14. He doesn't notice **the little things**.

The next morning was brutal. I didn't think I had ever felt this bad.

Besides the surprise text from Nick, my head had been squeezed in a vice grip and filled with a hundred dancing monkeys- the kind with the crashing cymbals- and my stomach threatened to upheave every time I moved or walked or talked or breathed or decided to keep living.

I crawled out of bed feeling like my mouth had been wrapped in cotton and dragged myself to a cold shower. The freezing water warred with my massive headache, but at least my body felt super-cooled.

I gingerly picked at a breakfast of Alka-Seltzer and Tylenol and washed it down with a huge glass of water, which did nothing to settle my upset stomach.

By the time I had dressed in my usual black pencil skirt and blouse, I only felt just this side of death. I glanced at the shoes in my closet and promptly stripped out of everything I had put on.

It was a flats and pants kind of day. I would not survive heels or skirts or anything but the most comfortable outfit I could manage. And since yoga pants were usually frowned upon by the administration, my tailored, wide-leg pants and a light pink sweater were going to have to cut it.

Thankfully, in the middle of October, the weather had cooled significantly.

Chicago falls could range from muggy heat that never wanted to leave to early winters that layered the ground with snow and ice. This autumn, thankfully, fell right in the middle. The breeze was crisp enough for light jackets and sweaters, the grass in my small front yard had begun to frost over in the mornings and the lone tree in front of my house had turned a brilliant rainbow of golds and reds.

It felt like football and Halloween and I loved every second of it.

By the time I parked my old Ford Focus in the teachers' lot, I felt like a living, breathing human being again. Granted, a living, breathing human being with a nasty hangover headache and the kind of nausea that turned my skin green, but still. It was an improvement.

I met Mrs. Chan at the mailboxes and noticed the equally sickly hue to her complexion. She stared at her box with the kind of abject vacancy I could appreciate this morning.

"It's going to be a long day," I grumbled.

She jumped, startled to find me standing next to her. Eventually, her expression settled back into miserable. "Ugh," she agreed.

I offered her a grim smile. "Starla's is a bad idea during the week."

She shook her head and said, "If any of those little bastards pull the fire alarm today, I will murder them."

My eyebrows shot to my hairline and I had to press my lips together to keep from gaping at her. Mrs. Chan was somewhere around fifty years old with a graying bob and a sweet smile. I had never heard her talk like that before.

Ever.

"Can I get you a cup of coffee?" I offered tranquilly.

She held up her travel mug and wiggled it gently. "My homeroom better hope this works."

"I think we're all hoping it works," I mumbled to myself as she trudged away.

I was shuffling through the various papers that had been stuffed in my box when Eli sidled up next to me. Our mailboxes were close together on the same column. Only Kara's and Mrs. Chan's separated us alphabetically.

When Nick and I married, my last name changed from Simmons to Carter. I got to upgrade from the end of the mailbox line next to Kara. It had been a great day for both of us. But especially for me. Every once in a while she showed up with Starbucks and a muffin. It was obvious why we were so inseparable.

The best kind of friendships were born and bonded over Starbucks. It happened every day.

"Morning, Ms. Carter," he said slyly.

I loved the deepness of his voice, the leftover scratchiness of the early morning and the rumble that seemed to hit me in the gut every time he spoke.

"Morning, Mr. Cohen."

I felt his sideways glance as he took in my appearance. "You lied to me last night."

His comment caught me so off guard I dropped some of my papers. I swooped down to scoop them up and he followed, squatting just a foot away from me.

"When?" I asked. Fear hit first. What had I said in my drunken stupor? Then disbelief. I didn't remember lying. I would remember if I lied to him, even if I was drunk.

Right?

"You told me you weren't going to be pretty this morning." He handed me some papers he picked up. "That was clearly a lie."

A blush crept up my neck at the same time my unhappy stomach turned unpleasantly. I didn't know whether to be flattered or call him out for being cheesy. I settled for wrinkling my nose at him.

His eyes twinkled with humor and he read my mind. "That was lame, huh?"

"It was sweet," I assured him. "Especially since I don't feel pretty."

We stood up and Eli looked around the quiet office. There were teachers near the coffee pot and slumped over in chairs, waiting for the morning to begin, but nobody was really interacting with anybody else. "At least you're not alone," he grinned.

"Whose idea was that anyway?"

Eli leaned in conspiratorially, "Tim."

"Mr. Bunch?" I laughed.

"He suggested it during the fire drill."

Well, I didn't blame him there. Fire drills were always a nightmare to survive. Keeping a tab on all of our kids was nearly impossible. Hamilton was built right on a busy street in a hub of business activity. Our protocol was to line up on the sidewalk as far from the building as we could, which usually turned into a giant exodus of students as they abandoned the day altogether. And there weren't enough of us teachers to keep everyone in line.

Shouting, "Make good choices!" while they walked away with their middle fingers waving proudly, never seemed to make much of an impact.

"I can see why there was such a great turnout then." I hugged my papers to my chest and looked around the room. "Do you think today will be any easier?"

Eli pursed his lips and shook his head. "I wish I could say yes."

"I wish you could too."

He turned to me so quickly I took a step back out of surprise. "Hey, can I bring you lunch today?"

Nerves fluttered through me and I hesitated. On one hand, whatever Eli brought me would be better than the granola bar and banana I packed for myself. On the other hand, I was so not feeling up to eating anything other than soda crackers. But maybe by lunch…?

"I promise it will be good," he coaxed after my hesitation turned into awkward silence. "I owe you one anyway. For Garmans that one time."

"Oh yeah," I smiled. "I forgot about that."

"I'll bring you something," he declared. "You'll love it."

"Thank you." I looked up and met his chocolate eyes, letting real gratitude shine through me. "Seriously, thank you. You might just save the day."

He paused midstride and smiled disarmingly at me. "That's the goal."

We parted ways and I headed off to my classroom. I noticed that it was easier to face the day after our pleasant exchange. My stomach didn't feel quite so violent and my headache had receded to a muted jackhammer.

Either the Tylenol had kicked in or Eli had healing powers on top of his superhero-lunch-bringing skills.

I thought about Eli the entire time I set up for the day. His interest in me was so unexpected. Sure, there had been mild flirting over the last couple years, but it had been harmless. He was just a good-looking guy that liked to have fun and I had been a married woman that liked the attention.

But I had never been serious, and I had never thought he was serious either.

My morning was a blur of unruly students and lectures on grammar. When I reached third period, which was a mixture of juniors and seniors, I was thankful for a class that didn't need to learn the basics of the English language. Even I knew my morning lectures were boring. I had been fighting yawns for hours.

Third period was my most challenging class of the day, but it turned out to be exactly what I needed. I finally woke up thanks to the livelier class and our discussion on the *Scarlet Letter*. It was one of my favorite books to read and to teach, because even if I couldn't get my students to actually read it, they all loved to share their opinions on adultery.

I mean, who didn't?

"These people are so stupid," Jay Allen declared, punctuating his opinion by slamming his book down on his desk. "It's just a baby. It's not like she was a serial killer or ate people or anything."

I tried not to smile. Ate people? Tried and failed. "But it's a different time period, Jay. The culture back then took sex, marriage, children outside of marriage and all other sins very seriously. It was their way of life."

"Well, it's a stupid way of life," he grumbled mutinously. "Leave the woman alone. She already had a kid to take care of by herself. She had enough problems. It's not like she had food stamps."

"That's true," I agreed, happy with the direction of his thoughts. "There was no system put in place to protect her from starvation or poverty."

Jay continued, shaking his head at Hester's tragic circumstances, "Being a single mom is hard anyway, but at least my moms has help. And nobody's making her stand in the middle of the city so they can yell bullshit at her."

Andre Gonzalez snickered from the other side of the classroom. "That's because ain't nobody wants to stare at yo' mom for longer than they have to. Hester was a hottie."

Jay half rose out of his seat to defend his mother's honor. A nervous twitch pulled at my gut and I wondered if I was going to have to call for help.

"Shut your mouth, Gonzalez," Jay hollered. "Talk about my mom like that again and we're going to have words."

"Alright, enough," I demanded with my most stern teacher voice. "Andre, if you talk about another student's mother in my class again, I'll send you to detention." Jay smirked proudly until I turned to him and said, "And you, Mr. Allen, if you threaten another student again, you'll find yourself in the same place."

Silence reigned once again so I tried to refocus them. "How do you know Hester Prynne was a hottie, Andre?" I doubted he had read his assignment so it took me by surprise that he was making judgment calls on her.

He stared at me for a long minute before finally deciding to answer. "She got the pastor to do the nasty with her, didn't she? That was like a... a... sin or whatever. He was probably a virgin and he knew he'd go to hell for it. It takes a certain kind of woman for a man to choose hell."

I rocked back on my heels, amazed at his insight. Andre was just as bad as Jay most days, at least when he chose to come to class. Some days he was worse.

"That's a good point," I said quietly. "Or maybe he was just desperate? Maybe he just wanted to get laid?"

The kids laughed at me, some of them threw out crass comments and escalated the conversation beyond appropriate school discussion, but at least they were engaging.

"Nah," Jay spoke up over the raucous. "He wasn't sleeping around. It was just her. Just this one girl."

"So he loved her?" I prompted.

"Sure," Jay agreed. "True love. It's not just the booty that would have made him stray from his vows. He needed something stronger than that."

"And did she love him?"

Jay nodded as if it was obvious. "I mean, her husband was a psycho, but she loved that Dimmesdale guy. She wanted to run away with him all those years later."

I let his words settle over the class and wondered if these kids knew anything about love. How could they? I didn't know anything about it and I was almost twice their age.

"So? What do you think about that?" I stared at them, but nobody was brave enough to answer. "Is true love enough? Was it enough for Hester and the way she was forced to live? Does it make their crimes forgivable? Does it redeem them?"

"No," Andre announced loudly. "It just made them stupid."

The bell rang and the kids jumped out of their seats before I could say anything more. Besides, there wasn't really anything else to say.

I was inclined to agree with him.

"Don't forget about your *Scarlet Letter* project! Now that we've finished the book, you need to be thinking about how you're going to represent it to the class." I hollered after them. "I want to hear your proposals on Monday!" They grumbled as they filed out of my room, but it didn't bother me.

I felt like we'd made a breakthrough today. Somehow, despite my hung-over brain and my students' usual lack of enthusiasm, we'd come together on social issues they could all relate to.

How many of them had single moms?

How many of them had been abandoned by people they loved?

Kara stepped into my classroom and I lunged for the trashcan. "Don't puke!"

After a series of mumbled curse words, she collapsed in my desk chair. "Don't say that word. God, don't ever say that word again."

I breathed a sigh of relief that she wasn't going to toss her cookies all over my desk and smiled. "Did you have fun last night, Kara? Are you super happy we went out for *hump day*?"

"I want to die," she mumbled. "Why *the hell* did I let you talk me into tequila shots?"

I tried not to laugh. Er, I tried not to laugh loud enough that she heard me.

"Am I interrupting?" Eli asked from the doorway.

I turned around and gave him a smile. "Nope, not at all. Kara is just dying."

"I can see that," he chuckled.

"Tequila," she winced.

Eli turned to me with his eyebrows raised and a playful smile on his lips. "Death by tequila, not a pleasant way to go."

"Eli, I hate you," she grumbled.

"At least you don't have to share your lunch with her," he said to me.

The heavenly scent of fried foods had made its way over to me and my stomach rumbled loudly. "What did you bring me?"

"Ruby's."

"Oh, my god. You're truly my hero!"

He set three Styrofoam containers on my desk and opened them slowly. My mouth started watering as soon as I saw the fried, crispy *lumpias* and spiced *tocilog*.

"This is my ultimate hangover cure," he explained. "Ruby's fixes everything."

Kara winced, "Not everything..." she slipped out of my chair and practically collapsed on the ground. She curled up into a ball and tucked her arm under her head. "Wake me up in ten minutes."

Eli and I shared a look. Then we dug into our lunch.

"So this is okay?"

"I *love* Ruby's," I said around a mouthful of *lumpia*. They were the perfect combination of crispy outside and spicy inside, like a spring roll only Filipino style. "Nick and I used to go on the weekends when we were first married because we could get so much food for so little."

Eli waited a beat before he responded. I realized I put him in an awkward conversation spot, but with his usual directness, he rolled with it. "Why did you guys stop?"

I glanced at Kara on the floor, but she seemed completely out of it. I didn't know why I didn't want her knowing I opened up to Eli about my divorce. It still felt weird to me and I didn't think I wanted Kara to look at it like a good thing.

I wasn't sure it was a good thing.

"Probably for the same reason we stopped doing most other things." I reached down to fiddle with one of the sauce containers, making my fingertips sticky. That wasn't exactly fair. "I don't know, actually. We always had fun at Ruby's. We just stopped going. Maybe we got too busy."

"Or maybe you stopped wanting to spend time with each other?"

I swallowed a large bite of rice and spiced meat and tried not to choke. Was he right? Instead of feeling the pain that I should or the insecurity in the truth of his words, I felt irritated.

My first thought was, *What did he know about me?*

What gave him the right to make judgments on my marriage?

But I swallowed again and tried to push those thoughts away. He was just being my friend. And he probably was *right*.

"Maybe," I said noncommittally. "Honestly, I'm still trying to figure out the majority of reasons our marriage didn't work out."

He leaned in and I felt the warmth of his body as his arm grazed mine. "You know, you don't have to torture yourself with all the whys and why nots. This is hard enough on you."

I looked up at him, noticing the shaved line of his jaw and the smooth skin over high cheekbones. He was wearing his glasses today and the fluorescent classroom lights glinted off his lenses, hiding his eyes from me.

"Does that work?" I asked quietly. "If I tell myself to stop analyzing everything, will I listen?"

His smile was filled with sorrow from his own past pain. "No," he said with a gruff rasp. "But you can try. Maybe you'll do better than me."

We finished up our lunches over small, easy talk. Surprisingly enough, I didn't lose my appetite. I ate as much of my lunch as I could until my stomach felt distended and I knew I would have to fight through a food coma to teach my afternoon classes.

We woke Kara up and Eli offered to walk her to her classroom since she still looked on the verge of puking her guts and every ounce of alcohol from last night up.

Once they were gone, I had about five minutes until the bell rang, so I dug out my phone from my locked drawer and stared at the screen for two minutes. I clicked my nails against the back of it as I cradled it in my palm. Curiosity and a masochistic sense of self-analysis buzzed through me in a way I couldn't ignore.

Finally, I texted Nick, asking, *I just had Ruby's for lunch today. It was so good. Why did we stop going there?*

A minute later he texted back, *They had an Ebola outbreak last year. Shut up!!!*

He sent back a smiley face and for another minute I thought that was the end of it. The bell rang, but I couldn't bring myself to stand up and greet my class. I kept staring at my phone, waiting for more.

Just as students started to filter into the room, my cell vibrated in my hand and I caught his one last text before I needed to put it away for the rest of the afternoon.

I wish we wouldn't have stopped.

Chapter Eight

15. We can **never** agree on anything.

"I can't believe you guys are getting a divorce." The high-pitched whine shrilled through the phone. I wanted to chuck it against the sidewalk.

"Fi, believe it."

I stepped out of my car and stumbled back a step when the force of the late afternoon wind smacked me in the face. For a minute, I couldn't hear anything on Fiona's end because of the static and interruption from the wind.

"Hold on!" I yelled to Fiona, my college roommate, as I fumbled with the keys to the side door.

Our tiny house only had an unattached garage, which made weather a real concern trying to get in and out of the house. Since Illinois only had about three good months of weather during the year before it turned either surface-of-the-sun hot or subarctic, it made leaving the house at any time obnoxious.

Except near Lake Michigan. Then it was only differing degrees of violently windy.

When we had looked at houses, Nick tried to convince me that the garage would be an issue, but I hadn't been willing to listen. I fell in love with this house from the street. I adored the cute coziness of it, the original but updated wood floors, the brand new kitchen that was small but modern. I loved the loft style bedroom upstairs and the office with French doors on the first floor.

We had always known we wouldn't live here forever. This was not a house you could raise a large family in and when we were house hunting, we assumed we would have a large family.

That was something we could both easily agree on.

But we had needed something to start with, something that was just the right size for the two of us and something we could easily afford with our tight budget.

This house had been perfect.

And despite everything that happened, I still thought it was perfect.

Except for the garage situation.

"Sorry," I huffed once I'd made it through the door. I dropped my tote bag filled with papers and notebooks that needed to be graded, my laptop, my purse and my lunch bag on the ground as soon as I stepped inside. My arm felt like it was going to break off. Annie danced around my feet, licking my legs and begging for attention. "I'm here now."

"I just can't believe it," she moaned. "You two are so perfect for each other."

My neck immediately started hurting. "I'm not sure that we are."

"But, K! What happened?" She asked the question then murmured something to her fussy baby.

Fiona and I didn't get to talk very often, but usually we could spend hours gabbing about nothing or everything or good times from our college years.

Today, though, I hoped her baby's cries meant she needed to get going. I really didn't want to have this conversation. I really wanted to talk about anything but my divorce or Nick or me.

The baby cried again and pain seared over my heart. "Shh," Fiona crooned. "That's a good boy." To me she said, "This has been my fussiest baby yet. He is just never satisfied."

I masked the brokenness in my voice by joking, "Because he's a man." I bent down to pet my own baby girl.

Fiona laughed at my joke and the baby settled down. "So tell me what happened. Last time we talked, you guys were doing great!"

We hadn't been great. We hadn't been great in a very long time. But I had never told her that.

I resigned myself to telling her the story. She wasn't going to let it go, so I might as well give her what she wanted as quickly as I could, then get her off the phone so I could wallow in my own pity. Except that when I turned the corner and walked into my kitchen the topic of our discussion was sitting at the kitchen island helping himself to my chocolate cherry ice cream.

"Holy shit!"

"Are you okay?" Fiona asked on the other end.

Nick gave me an apologetic wave but didn't make a move to stand up. "Uh, um, er, yeah."

Fiona's voice echoed through the kitchen as I pulled the phone away from my ear. "K, what's going on?"

I put the cell slowly back to my mouth. "I'll call you back, Fi. Something came up here."

"You'd better!" I heard her call, but I pushed end without saying goodbye.

"Was that Fiona?" Nick asked without preamble.

"Yeah." I took a solid minute to adjust to his presence, and then demanded, "What are you doing here?"

He took another bite of ice cream to hide his smile. "You literally say that every time you see me."

"You just... I'm just... Nick!"

He grinned at me and I was surprised to see his easy expression. His beard had been trimmed neatly, back to just barely there and his hair had been styled away from his face. I noticed his nice dark blue oxford and black dress pants and wondered what that was about. His sleeves were rolled up, exposing his forearms and I swallowed in a desperate attempt to stop staring at his tanned skin and lean muscle.

It was a shock to see him, but even more so to find him so attractive. It felt like I hadn't seen him in years or like maybe I'd never seen him before. My entire body reacted, took notice of every angular cut to his body and unique characteristic to his face.

When was the last time I had looked at him like this?

When was the last time I had seen *him*?

"Kate, you okay?"

I cleared my throat and nodded curtly. "I'm fine. Just, you know, surprised to see you."

He tilted his head toward the kitchen window. "Mr. Kirkpatrick asked to borrow my jack. I swung over to get it to him."

"You could have called me. I could have walked it next door." He raised one eyebrow and I found myself smiling. "Okay, point taken."

"It only took a minute anyway."

"And the ice cream?"

"I skipped lunch and somebody was taunting me yesterday with texts about Ruby's. I'm starving. I was actually looking for something more substantial."

I felt a blush stain my cheeks. "I've been meaning to go to the store."

He watched me for a minute. I didn't know what he was looking for or I would have tried to hide it from him. His silence grew awkward so I turned toward my discarded bags, deciding I should put everything away before I forgot.

"Do you have a gig tonight?" I kept my eyes on my task, hoping to avoid his forearms and the silly things they did to my insides.

He didn't answer right away and it was just on the tip of my tongue to ask him to leave if he wasn't going to talk to me when he said, "No, not tonight."

"Then what's with the clothes?"

"The what?"

I glanced over at him and our gazes locked for a moment before I tore mine away. "You look nice. I just thought... I thought you might have somewhere to be tonight. It's Friday."

I felt his smile from across the room, even though I wouldn't look at him. "I know it's Friday."

"Well, you usually have gigs on Fridays."

"Not every Friday."

Irritation bubbled through me. "You're *right*; sometimes they're on Saturdays instead."

He pushed back the stool and stood up. I heard him clattering around as he took his dish to the sink and washed it out. Leaning over, I noticed that he'd already washed the dishes I'd left in the sink. They sat on the drying rack perfectly clean. "I, uh, I'm taking a little break from the band. You know, while I figure shit out."

My heart tripped in my chest. That was something I had wanted to hear for a long time. I had never wanted him to quit music entirely. I knew he couldn't. And I also knew he shouldn't. He was too good. And it was too vital to who he was as a human.

I never wanted to crush his dreams.

But I had also wondered if maybe his dreams needed to change. He had been tired of constant shows that paid little and got him nowhere. He had been exhausted from feeling like a failure and never getting to the place he wanted to be.

When we first started dating his music gave him life, it made him come alive. After his shows, it was like he was riding a high, completely buzzing with the energy that performing gave him.

But lately he had come home angry and irritable. Gigs were more likely to suck the joy completely out of him than give him that same rush of adrenaline and fulfillment.

He hated it when I pointed that out. He hated that I didn't believe in him... that I didn't think he could make it.

What he didn't realize was that it wasn't that I didn't think he was good enough, I saw that *he* had started to think that he wasn't good enough.

And it killed me as much as it killed him.

I stopped fiddling with my bags and set them down on our kitchen table with a long sigh. "You really don't have a show?"

He turned around and leaned back against the counter, crossing his arms over his chest. "I really don't have a show."

"Oh." I tried not to stare at his clothes. He worked part time for a moving company, so he never would wear nice clothes to work.

Was it a date?

Oh, god. I thought I would be sick from the sudden, acrid burst of jealousy inside me.

He turned back around to wash his dish and so I went back to emptying my lunch bag into the trash, trying not to plot murder in the first degree for the unknown female. I heard him fiddling with the faucet but refused to turn around. I couldn't stare at him the entire time he was here. Maybe if I ignored him, he'd get the hint and go away.

"This is leaking," he announced gruffly.

Immediately I felt defensive. "I didn't break it."

His chuckle surprised me so I whirled back around. "I didn't say you did."

"Well, you don't live here anymore. I figured the accusation was implied."

Something dark flashed in his eyes and I had to look away. Suddenly, my heart was in my throat and I forgot how to breathe.

"I'm not blaming you, Kate. A leaky sink is hardly a sin anyway."

I nodded, still unable to look at him. *God, what was with this guilt?* When had I started worrying about his feelings or how I hurt them?

The silence between us became stilted and uncomfortable. I had just gathered up enough courage to ask him to leave so he could go on his stupid unconfirmed date, when he shocked the hell out of me by asking, "Do you want me to fix it? Most of my tools are still in the garage."

"If you don't fix it, will it like... break the house?"

His lips twitched and I noticed he had to look away from me too. But not because he felt bad. He was trying not to laugh. "It's better if I fix it," he said.

"That would be great. Thank you."

He pushed his sleeves up higher and then bent down so he could look under the sink. I hovered uncertainly. What was I supposed to do now? Should I keep him company? Did I need to watch him so he didn't try to steal the dog?

Did I have time to steal his phone and figure out who the other woman was? The one he planned to marry tonight and have ten babies with by tomorrow?

Should I check myself into a mental health facility because clearly I'd lost my damn mind?

"Go do whatever it is you need to do," he called out from under the sink, his voice slightly muffled with his head in the cabinet. "Don't worry about me."

I leaned over the island so I could see him better. "Are you sure? Can I get you something?"

"Go, Katie. I know you want to get out of those clothes."

I looked down at my outfit, wondering how he knew that. Er, how he remembered that. Obviously we'd lived together for seven years so he did know some of my habits.

My gaze traveled over his toned back and the nice shirt that hugged his runner's body. It was on the tip of my tongue to ask him about his date or the nice clothes he was wearing, but I changed my mind at the last minute. If he wanted to change, he would. Surely there was something in his closet he could dig out.

Instead of bothering him anymore, I escaped upstairs. I stared at my closet for longer than I should, debating what to wear.

My natural inclination was to throw on yoga pants and a sweatshirt, but there was part of me that wondered if I should look nicer while Nick was here. It wasn't that I wanted him to be attracted to me or anything; I just didn't want him to think I was a slob.

Not that he didn't know me better.

Not that he hadn't seen me in yoga pants and a sweatshirt a million times.

But I couldn't help wanting to show off a little bit for him. I wanted him to notice me like I noticed him. I wanted him to look at me and think, have I ever really seen this girl before? Do I realize what I lost?

Because maybe it was just me or maybe I was crazy, but those were the thoughts tumbling through *my* head.

Had I lost the best thing in my life? Had I lost the best I could do? The only man that would put up with me and love me for *me*?

Even if we had problems?

I swallowed down my remorse and changed into my black yoga pants and an old sweatshirt. I had cut the neck off of it in college, so it hung off my shoulder in a way that maximized comfort and cuteness.

Or at least I thought so.

I took my time upstairs, fiddling with my long dark hair. It was naturally curly, not like Kara's wild hair, but there were some definite volume issues I had to work out on a daily basis. I usually wore it down to work or partially back, but nothing felt better than at the end of the day when I could throw it up on top of my head in a messy bun.

I was pretty sure that would be what heaven felt like. Like a thousand years of messy buns.

I stared at myself in the mirror for long minutes after that. I looked at my dark brown eyes and the light smattering of freckles that dotted my nose and cheeks. I tried to rub away the barely there crow's feet that had started to crease next to my eyes and the smile lines I knew would only worsen.

Thirty.

I would be thirty-one soon.

And this was the moment in my life I had finally realized I was getting old. If not old, then older.

I thought back to when I first met Nick and how I had imagined my life at thirty.

This was not it.

I had not planned on getting divorced.

I had not planned to live in a tiny house on the edge of the city.

I had not planned to feel this much stress or this much emptiness.

Once upon a time, thirty had felt like I would finally have made it.

It had felt like a destination.

Like a *good* destination.

It wasn't fair of me to ask Nick to change his expectations if I wasn't willing to change mine. Was my life so bad?

Apart from the divorce, was it really such a terrible thing I didn't have the perfect house, the perfect job, the perfect two-point-five kids?

My hands settled on my abdomen and I felt a stinging pain lance across my soul.

Some things were okay. I loved this house. There were days that I even loved my job. And if I didn't love it, at least I felt fulfilled by it.

But there were things I wanted too, things that weren't terrible to want, things that were worth being disappointed with.

My marriage for instance.

My lack of kids.

This shattering of my heart and spirit.

I needed to do something. I needed to fix this hole inside of me and figure out what else I could have in life that would replace these things.

Or at least I needed to heal and move on.

I needed to change my expectations... my dreams. I needed to find new ones.

I needed to find something else to hope and wish for.

Unable to look at myself for a second longer, I turned away from the mirror and made my way back downstairs. My stomach grumbled loudly and I was happy to feel hunger again.

Ruby's had been the catalyst yesterday. I had been able to eat ever since and my body thanked me for finally getting some nourishment.

Nick was just finishing up with the sink when I walked into the kitchen. He'd removed his oxford and stripped down to the black undershirt he wore beneath it.

I swallowed convulsively.

That was just not fair.

I had to invest millions of dollars in antiaging creams and worry about my boobs trying to high five my bellybutton. And he turned thirty and looked like that. Like thirty was the best thing that ever happened to his face.

And womankind.

Men were the worst.

He turned around with a half-smile tilting his lips. "When I was out in the garage, I checked out your car. When's the last time you had the oil changed?"

I swallowed again, but for completely different reasons. "The oil?" Oops. He was going to be so pissed. "I think it was probably last month."

He raised his eyebrows in challenge. "Last month?"

"Maybe it was the month before that...?"

"Or maybe it was when I changed it last spring?"

I pressed my lips together and tried not to look guilty. "Is it bad?"

He let out a patient sigh. I expected him to lecture me or rip into me about how I break everything I touch, but he didn't. Instead, he put his wrench down and said, "Do you want me to change it while I'm here?"

"No, that's okay," I rushed to say. "I can take it in tomorrow."

"Take it in where?"

I hoped he didn't notice the weighted pause while I struggled to come up with, "The... oil change place."

94

"The oil change place?"

I cleared my throat. "Sure. The place... with all the oil."

"How about I just do it now, so you don't have to figure out where the place with all the oil is."

I blinked rapidly and tried to figure out how to get out of this. I couldn't let him change my oil. The sink was one thing. His name was on the mortgage so he had a vested interest in the house not falling apart. But my car was something else. It was my responsibility. He had forfeited his right to help when he moved out.

Why did we get married so young? I should know how to do these stupid things on my own!

Except I moved straight from a college dorm into an apartment with him and I had never learned how to be a grown up on my own. Nick had always taken care of everything.

He'd always taken care of me.

"Let me do it, Kate. I'll feel better and your car will feel better."

I looked at the counter where he'd set his ice cream bowl while he worked on the sink. "Then let me at least order dinner. As a thank you."

His blue eyes lit up with something I couldn't describe. Happiness? Satisfaction?

Hunger?

"Really?" He was hesitant, but I could tell he was interested.

"We're both hungry, right? Consider it a thank you for keeping me from falling into disrepair."

His mouth spread in a wide smile. "Alright, yeah. That sounds good."

"Pizza?

"You pick. I'll be happy with whatever."

"Okay, sure. You change my oil. I'll get us dinner."

"Sounds good."

"Sounds good."

He walked out of the kitchen and my stomach ignited with nerves. What had I just done?

Chapter Nine

16. He's a **bad habit** I can't shake.

I waited to order the pizza until Nick came in from the garage. In the meantime, I had cut up some cheese and laid it on a plate with crackers. I didn't have much for food, but I always had cheese and crackers.

I survived on cheese and crackers.

Good cheese, though, like white cheddar and smoked Gouda. Not Kraft Singles- much to Nick's dismay.

He grabbed a few slices from the plate and smiled at me. "This is nice."

"I figured you'd be starving by now."

He nodded his head and took another slice of pepper jack. "Do you mind if I shower before we eat?"

I ignored everything that buzzed through me. A thousand emotions mingled together and made me hot and cold all at the same time. I was frustrated with him for spending so much time over here, mad that he even stopped by, hurt from our past, heartbroken from our present, but something else too. Something I couldn't name.

Something I *wouldn't* name.

I swallowed thickly and jerked my chin. "Do you still have some clothes here?"

Nick's cerulean eyes swept over me, "I'm sure I can find something."

My thoughts continued to tangle together and suddenly my heart took off in a gallop. I cleared my dry throat and said, "I'll order the pizza."

He took a step closer to me, resting his hands on the kitchen island. We were only separated by the plate that held my silly little appetizer. His voice dipped low when he asked, "Know what you're getting?"

Was this a test? Nick and I could never agree on pizza. We liked different things. For instance, Nick loved olives more than anything and I could not stand them. I loved tomatoes on everything and Nick would not touch a tomato, raw or cooked. It had never made sense to me because he was fine with tomato sauce, just not tomatoes in their natural form. This was a quirk I had never had patience with. And in return, he couldn't stand my dislike of olives.

It seemed so childish now... now that we weren't in the heat of the moment or dealing with each other's obnoxious idiosyncrasies every day. But during our marriage these small things could cause hours of fighting and ruin entire evenings.

I lifted my gaze from where I'd been staring at my fidgeting hands and looked at Nick just a foot away from me. Had I really decided to torture him over tomatoes?

Had I really wanted to emotionally punish him because he wanted olives on our shared pizza?

Oh, my god, was I the most immature person in the entire universe???

He leaned in and I caught his familiar scent. He smelled like sweat from working outside, like the car grease and grime, like his cologne that I could pick out of a lineup and like him... like that rich, manly scent that was only him.

It was the smell that I had woken up to for seven years, the one that pulled me in when we were standing or sitting far apart, the one that still lingered in my closet and in my sheets, the one, that even now, could sink into my skin and make my body come alive with something hot and sweet.

"What are you thinking about, Kate?" His voice was nothing more than a gruff whisper. I felt the heat of his body as he stood close to me... closer than we had been in months.

"That fighting over tomatoes and olives is really stupid," I confessed. "I'm sorry I couldn't let that go."

He caught my gaze with eyes so intense I felt them blaze through me, felt their heat touch my skin and grip metaphysical pieces of me. "I'm sorry too."

And he meant it. I felt the depth of his feeling, the truth of his apology. I knew, without a doubt, that he saw what I saw too, that he realized his mistakes like I had realized mine.

It shouldn't have been a big deal. It was a stupid fight to begin with. Immature, petty, trivial... and yet his apology hit me like an earthquake. I took a step back and sucked in a steadying breath.

It was like his words had lifted me off my feet and moved me halfway around the world. Or maybe they took me to a different world entirely. A world that wasn't tied down to points that needed to be proved or stupid convictions that couldn't be swayed.

His small apology was *profound*.

And too late.

Why couldn't we have done this years ago? Or just one year ago? Even six months ago?

Nick's deep voice pulled me out of my whirling thoughts, "If you want tomatoes, Kate… get tomatoes."

I stood up straighter and made a decision. "I'm just going to get two mediums," I told him. "I'll get the one you like and I'll get the one I like, then we'll both be happy."

His smile was sad when he said, "Why didn't we think of this before?"

I didn't want to answer that. I didn't want to admit that I had been too stubborn to give into him, that I thought I had some philosophical point to prove by making him like tomatoes.

God, this was beyond a doubt, the dumbest thing we had ever fought over.

"Go take a shower," I told him. "I'll take care of the pizza."

He tapped the counter with his knuckles and then disappeared into the house. My house. I listened to his footsteps on the stairs and stood there silently while I tried to piece myself back together.

When I heard his footsteps again on the stairs, I jumped into action and pulled out my phone. I hadn't heard the shower yet, but he was going to think there was something wrong with me if I couldn't even make the call.

After I had made our order at our favorite pizza spot and hung up the phone, I realized Nick had started his shower in the guest bathroom.

I didn't know what to think about that. It shocked the hell out of me.

I had expected him to use our shower… er the master bedroom shower, because, well, because that was the obvious choice. But it was sort of endearing that he'd used the other one. It made me feel respected in a strange way… It made me feel like he took my privacy into consideration and our divorce with care.

Or maybe it was the opposite. Maybe he couldn't stomach being in the same place we had shared daily… laughed in… fought in… made love in.

He reappeared in the kitchen with wet hair and an old t-shirt that was nearly see-through from wear. His athletic shorts were from his college track days and they were a little short for his current style. They showed off his muscled thighs, his dark hair that curled from his hips to his ankles.

His body was insane. It had always been like this. From the first day I met him.

If attraction were everything, we never would have had a problem.

He caught me staring and warned, "Don't laugh at me. They're all I could dig up."

"I wouldn't laugh at *you*," I promised. "I might laugh at your shorty-shorts. But don't take it personally."

His bark of laughter was unexpected and I couldn't help but smile. "Did you call for the pizza?"

I nodded. "Yeah, it should be here in twenty minutes or so."

"Do you... do you want to watch something while we're waiting?"

I chewed on my bottom lip to keep from agreeing, but my head nodded anyway.

One corner of his mouth curled in a crooked smile, "Good. Jared doesn't have cable and I've missed our shows."

Before I could respond to that or remind him that they were no longer our shows, he turned around and headed for the living room. I picked up the plate of cheese and followed after him.

I felt surreal as we walked into the living room; it was almost an out of body experience. I was too nervous about the situation, too wired. This was my ex-husband. Or, soon to be anyway. Why were we hanging out?

Why were we being nice to each other?

Why were things finally coming together for us?

Maybe we really were better friends. Maybe we had to get out of our marriage in order to appreciate the other person for who he or she was.

Our living room wasn't large. Nick's huge TV hung on one wall with our entertainment console situated beneath. The TV was too big for the room and I had always told him that. But boys and their toys and all that. Especially electronics. There had been no talking him out of it.

I had been in charge of decorating the other half. We had a long, comfy gray couch against the opposite wall that was flanked by two mustard-colored wing-backed chairs. It looked really cute, but to be honest, the wing-backed chairs weren't really comfortable so we never used them.

A coffee table sat in front of the couch, low and practical. I had rescued it from Goodwill and Nick had refinished it for me and painted it gray. It was my favorite piece on the main floor.

Both of us settled on the couch, as far from each other as we could. Nick assumed control of the remote, which was fine with me because I was having trouble concentrating and I would have been useless to pick something out.

I still couldn't believe this was happening. I was spending my Friday night hanging out with my ex-husband.

Nick pushed buttons that took him to the DVR list and I held my breath. This was a secret I didn't want him to know. This was a part of our separation that was so silly and unexplainable that I actually felt ashamed.

"You haven't watched any of these?" The yellow cursor highlighted one of the shows we always watched together... one of the shows I couldn't bring myself to watch without him. "Or this one?" He continued to flip through the DVR while I shrunk into myself, unable to meet his eye or offer an explanation. Finally, I felt his gaze on me. The intensity of his stare burned into my skin, leaving permanent scars and disfigurement of my soul. "Kate, why didn't you watch any of these? What were you waiting for?"

For you to come back, my mind whispered.

"I haven't had time," I said instead. "I've been really busy. It's been a really hard school year. And I-" The doorbell rang, saving me from rambling more excuses.

I jumped up from the couch and practically ran for the door. I swung it open, surprising the poor delivery guy on the other side.

He laughed nervously and mumbled, "Whoa."

I closed my eyes for a brief second and desperately tried to pull myself together. "Hi. Sorry."

"You ordered pizza?" he asked needlessly. He opened his red warming case and showed me the two medium pizzas and order of breadsticks. "Twenty-three, thirty-eight."

"Oh, right." In my flight to get to the front door, I forgot to grab my purse. "Hold on a sec."

"I got it," Nick said from behind me. He reached around my waist, grazing my side as he went and handed the guy some cash. "That's all yours." I could hear the polite smile in Nick's voice as I stood there frozen and confused.

The guy held the pizzas out to me and I jerked forward, taking them awkwardly. "Thanks," I mumbled, but he was already headed back to his car.

I stepped back in the house and whirled around. "I thought I owed you dinner. You know, for helping me around the house."

He tugged on his earlobe and wouldn't quite meet my eyes when he said, "Yeah, well you can pay me back a different day. The pizza is my treat."

I couldn't think of anything to say. Nothing. There was nothing in my brain.

"It's just pizza, Kate."

"Thank you," I whispered.

He barely acknowledged it. "I'll grab plates. You take all that to the couch."

"Okay."

I moved robotically through the living room and set the pizzas on the coffee table. I'd ordered him his meat lovers with extra mushrooms and olives. I'd gotten a supreme pizza for myself- no olives or mushrooms, extra tomatoes. I set the breadsticks in the middle.

I had just sat down when he came back holding plates, napkins and two bottles of beer. "Is this okay?" He lifted the beer in my direction.

"It's fine." I didn't honestly know if drinking around Nick was the best idea tonight, but surely one beer wouldn't hurt. Maybe it would relax me. I desperately needed something to take this sharp edge off.

He handed me my beer and a plate with a smile, then plopped down in his seat, a little closer to me than the first time. I took a breath and ordered my mind to stop reading into every little thing. It was so stupid.

I was so stupid.

"Nice," he grinned at his pizza. "Why *didn't* we think of this forever ago?"

I scooted forward, a little closer to him too, but just so I could reach the food. "I think I was trying to make a point. It's dumb, right?"

He gave me a sideways look and a crooked smile. "I can't confirm that it's dumb because then I'd have to admit to being dumb too. I have too much ego for that."

I pressed my lips together to keep from smiling, but he elbowed me in the side and I let it go, grinning at him and shaking my head. "We can be idiots."

I thought he would laugh or smile or do anything but sober up completely and stare at me with that hot, penetrating emotion that seemed to follow him around everywhere tonight. "We can be," he said in a low voice.

I turned back to the TV and took a big bite of pizza. Why did he make me so nervous tonight? Why did his words feel so ominous?

He picked one of our shows to watch, one that we were super far behind in since we'd spent so many months not watching it and we dug into our pizza.

We didn't talk much as the show went on, just mostly ate in silence.

At some point I realized he didn't have a date with someone else tonight. My insane jealous was for nothing. I decided to ignore the intense relief that flooded my body from head to toe.

I tried to tamp my relief by reminding myself that he would eventually start dating.

I would have to face it *eventually*.

Eventually.

But not tonight.

"Another one?" he asked as that show ended and he grabbed another piece of pizza.

"Sure," I whispered.

Late evening turned into night as we spent another hour quiet and involved in our show. Occasionally he would make a comment or I would gasp in surprise, but mostly our interaction dealt with the pizza that was slowly disappearing in front of us.

After another show, he paused the TV to use the restroom and grab another beer. When he came back into the room, he flicked the lights off and settled in the middle of the couch without asking permission or checking to see if it was okay.

I didn't know why, but I didn't object or even make a comment.

After the next episode had ended, he said, "You know, if you're not watching this without me, we should probably watch another one. Just in case, we don't get to find out what happens."

"That's a good point," I conceded.

He turned his head toward me and captured my gaze. For a minute, we just stared at each other. Nothing was said. Nothing was thought. I wasn't even sure I took a breath.

I wasn't sure I could have taken a breath if I tried.

He leaned over, bringing his body closer to mine. We had somehow managed to scoot closer and closer during the night. Now, I could feel the warmth of his body. Sometimes if he moved, his leg would press into mine for just a brief moment or his elbow would graze my arm.

I could smell him again.

And it was intoxicating.

I licked my dry lips and tried to find sanity... rationalization. I tried to remember our divorce or what had led up to it. I tried to argue my way out of this craziness I'd walked into willingly.

"Kate," he whispered and his voice went straight to my heart, straight to my core.

Afraid of this moment, of our truce, of every single thing about him, I turned back to the TV and gave it my attention. Or at least pretended to.

I couldn't see anything in front of me or comprehend what was going on. But I couldn't face whatever it was that Nick wanted to say. I couldn't stare at him for a second longer and not lose myself completely.

He seemed to realize that I had shut down because he turned back to the show without another word.

In fact, we didn't speak to each other again for the rest of the night.

I had been planning to ask him to leave after the next show, but there was a cliffhanger and I was desperate to find out what happened. The show kept going and going, we hadn't watched it all summer and there were plenty of episodes to catch up on. Finally, I could focus on what was happening and not the man sitting next to me that I couldn't untangle myself from.

But my mind was never far from him.

And apparently my body wasn't either.

I must have fallen asleep at some point because one second I had been blinking slowly, trying to stay involved with the plot, the next I felt fingers threading through my hair, brushing gently behind my ear.

I inhaled a deep sigh at the caress, the luxurious feeling of being touched after not being touched for so long. Then I realized those fingers belonged to Nick. I realized I had stretched out on the couch and laid my head in his lap. I realized his other hand had settled on my waist and slipped beneath my shirt to press against the curve of my side.

I steadied out my breathing and tried not to move. I couldn't let him know I was awake. I couldn't let him know I didn't want to confront him about this.

I was a coward.

I was weak.

I was so frustratingly confused.

He shifted on the couch and I faked a sleepy stretch. His body stiffened beneath mine and I couldn't tell if it was because he knew I was faking or he was embarrassed at getting caught.

I kept my eyes closed and refused to open them. I would claim to be asleep until the end of my life. This was something I was willing to commit perjury over in front of a jury of my peers. You know, if I ever had to swear to this in court. I would never let him know I woke up.

Finally, after endless moments, after I realized the TV wasn't on anymore and we were sitting in the complete dark, he gently lifted me and stood up. I felt his presence as he hovered over me. I couldn't have guessed what he was thinking or doing or not doing.

He was, maybe for the first time since we first met, a complete and complex mystery to me.

Just when I thought he would finally leave, he bent over and pressed a warm, familiar kiss to my temple.

A whimper escaped my lips and my eyes squeezed tighter, giving me away, but still I refused to look at him, refused to acknowledge what had just happened between us.

He left a moment later. I heard his bare feet on the wood floor, his movements as he slipped into his shoes and gathered up his clothes, I heard the front door open, then close and his key as he locked the door behind him.

I didn't move the entire time.

I didn't move from the couch for the rest of the night.

Chapter Ten

17. We're **broken**.

I spent the rest of the weekend in a funk. I couldn't concentrate on grading papers and when I tried to clean my house, I spontaneously burst into an uncontrollable sob fest that lasted until my voice was hoarse, I felt sick to my stomach and I had no more tears to cry.

Officially, I was sick of myself.

By the time I walked into my mom's house Sunday afternoon, I couldn't wait to start school on Monday so I could get away from me.

That's how desperate I was.

I actually *wanted* to go back to work.

I was tired of thinking. Tired of overanalyzing everything. Tired of blaming my heartbreak and failed marriage on Nick.

I needed to take responsibility too.

But I also hoped he never found out. I would take responsibility silently. I would take it and never tell him about it.

Hopefully, one day, we would move on in separate directions. Hopefully, we could find the opportunity to heal.

Until then... I just needed to get this over with as quickly as possible.

I was early for Sunday luncheon. I hadn't been able to take another breath in the suffocating memories of my house, so I escaped to a different sort of hell- my family.

Josh and Emily weren't here yet. In the living room, my dad was watching a football game, not the Bears, though, feet up and laid back in his worn recliner. He was far too relaxed for a Bears game to be on. The sight of him like that made me smile. It was so familiar... so home-like that I couldn't help but pause in the doorway and grin at him.

He looked up at me with heavily lidded eyes, as if he were just on the brink of falling asleep. "Hey, Kiddo."

"Hi, Daddy."

"You're early."

"I thought I'd help out today."

He smiled lazily and turned his attention back to the TV, "Your Ma will appreciate it."

"Need anything? Iced tea? Beer?"

"Beer," he grunted. "But don't let your mother see."

I walked through the living room to the kitchen feeling more like myself than I had in months. Most of the time I couldn't stand my family, but it was irritation born from love. I loved them fiercely. I just also got irritated with them fiercely.

"Hi, Mom," I said softly. I walked straight to the refrigerator and pulled out a can of beer and the pitcher of iced tea, hiding one behind the other. I put the iced tea on the counter and walked back into the living room to hand the beer to my dad. I let my purse drop on the couch and returned to the kitchen.

Beer successfully delivered.

Mission accomplished.

"I saw that." My mother didn't lift her eyes from the sweet potatoes she was mashing.

"Saw what?"

She made a noise in the back of her throat but didn't argue further. My dad opened his can and the click of metal and his subsequent, "Ah," echoed through the house.

My mother made another disgruntled snort.

I couldn't help but smile.

"If it bothers you, you should say something," I teased her.

She threw me a look over her shoulder. "If I made it known every time your father did something that bothered me, we wouldn't have made it through our first year of marriage."

"But if you said something now, he would listen to you." For some reason, I couldn't let it go. I had to make her see that she needed to stand up for herself. My dad wasn't completely unreasonable. He would do what it took to keep the peace.

"Katherine, your father has known who he is and what he's wanted since the very first day I met him. If he wants to have a beer before lunch, by god, he is going to have one." I opened my mouth to argue, but she held up her spatula and silenced me. "I respect that. I respect *him*. I don't have to like it, but I do have to trust him. And I trust him to take care of me, this family, and himself. That's all I need."

Sufficiently chastised, all I could come up with was a soft, "Oh."

108

"But it would help if my children weren't accomplices to his every heathen whim."

This time I laughed. "I thought I was sneaky enough to get away with it."

She gave me a pointed look over her shoulder, "Child, I see all. I know all." My smile broke into a wide grin and I laughed until she said, "Now get over here and melt the butter so I can mix it with the marshmallows."

"Yes, ma'am." But inside I was doing a happy dance because we were having sweet potatoes.

Nick would have been so disappointed if he knew he missed my mother's famous sweet potato casserole. It was his absolute favorite and she made it for him at least once a month.

It was the only way we could convince him to keep coming back here for Sunday lunch.

I shook my head of thoughts of Nick. Clearly I was having issues letting go of my marriage.

Which was to be expected, right? We had been together for a long time. He had been engrained in my thoughts, tattooed on my soul, etched into my bones. Our relationship was the only adult relationship I knew. I was not used to making decisions without him. I had never spent so much time alone. And it had been a very long time since I had to deal with my family by myself.

He had been by my side through so much that I physically couldn't imagine my life without him.

At the same time, I couldn't imagine continuing to live with him or be with him or fight with him over every little thing.

I was doing the right thing, it just took adjustment.

I needed adjustment.

A few minutes later Josh and Emily arrived with the girls and it felt like a hundred more people had shown up. The girls were everywhere, running around to say hi to everyone, asking for bites of food and in general, just being their cute, crazy selves.

"Why don't you take them in the back yard, Kate," my mom suggested. "They've been dying to see you and that way I can get lunch on the table without stepping on them."

"Sure," I said. I had officially been kicked out of the kitchen. It was no secret that Emily was better at the domesticated woman stuff than me and I suspected my mother was tired of hovering over my shoulder to make sure I did everything just right.

"Laney, Addy! Come outside with me!"

I started walking toward the back door and they abandoned their plight to steal leftover marshmallows and followed me. I knew they would. I was an awesome aunt.

We stepped into the sunny but cool afternoon and I glanced at them to make sure they still had their jackets on.

My parents had a small back yard, longer than it was wide and sandwiched between two identical lawns on either side. The yard was bordered by a chain link fence that had been replicated down the line in either direction. There was a satellite that hung on the back of the fence and a garden my mother worked tirelessly on that stretched from one side of the yard to the other. They had a short deck that held their grill and on the patio beneath, a covered swing that would fit the three of us perfectly.

I grew up in this house. My parents were both born and bred Chicagoans and they made sure their children had the same fate.

It was one of the things I was most grateful for. I loved this city. I loved its pretty architecture and bustling downtown. I loved my parents' neighborhood and my neighborhood and the specific feel of it just being home. I loved Lake Michigan. I loved the tourist traps and the shopping. I loved the food scene. And the music scene. I loved everything about this city.

My parents' house hadn't changed much since I was a kid. They'd taken down the rickety metal swing set Josh and I grew up with, but only so they could replace it with safer outdoor toys for the girls. There was a sandbox now where I used to swing and a lone plastic slide that the girls barely played with anymore. They were getting too big.

Delaney was eight and Addison was five. I knew Josh and Emily were done having kids so I wondered if my parents planned to keep those toys or get rid of them. I obviously wasn't going to be fulfilling my portion of grandkids for them.

"Auntie Kate, push us!" Addy demanded sweetly.

I dug my toes into the cement and pushed off so hard the swing rocked back and forth on its legs. The girls giggled uncontrollably as we forced the swing as high and fast as it could go.

I was just convinced I was going to have to buy my mom a new swing, because we were on the verge of breaking hers, when Emily poked her head out the back door and called us in for lunch.

The girls jumped off and raced inside, acting as if they'd never been fed before. I moved more slowly. It had been such a breath of fresh air to play with my nieces, but they often left a gaping hole in the place that wanted kids of my own.

Emily waited for me at the door and I noticed her nervous smile as soon as I stepped onto the deck.

"What's wrong?" I asked carefully.

"Your parents did something really stupid," she whispered. "I'm so sorry. I would have warned you sooner if I had known."

"What did they do?" Panic and fear blinded me. I thought back on all of the other stupid things they'd done throughout the years and could only imagine how bad it was this time if Emily had come out to warn me.

"Nick is here," she whispered.

"What?" My voice was not a whisper. It was half shriek, half demonic growl. I couldn't even imagine why he would be over here. I couldn't imagine any scenario in which my parents would invite him over. "Oh, my god. The sweet potato casserole."

Emily placed a warm hand on my shoulder. "I'm so sorry. I don't know what they were thinking."

"They obviously weren't," I snapped, then immediately felt bad. "I'm sorry," I winced. "It's just... this is the very worst possible time for me to see him again."

I closed my eyes and remembered our Friday night together. I felt his lips on my temple, kissing me goodnight. I blinked and pictured us screaming at each other across the house, pissed and unforgiving and oh so broken. I pictured the last night we fought, as he picked up his pillow and left me on the bed... left me for months without a word.

I pictured him at the grocery store, lost... lost without me... lost in a new existence that neither of us anticipated.

I did not need to see Nick right now. I needed as much time and separation as I could get from him. The only thing lunch would do was confuse me more. And we would have to be so fake. It's not like we could hash out our years of issues in front of my parents and my brother and his perfect freaking family.

I looked at the backyard and contemplated my escape.

"Are you really going to run away?"

I could tell Emily was laughing at me, but this was so much more serious than she realized.

"I was thinking about it." I let out an aggravated sigh.

"Emily and Kate, the food is getting cold!" My mother's voice sounded shrill and irritated through the house.

I looked at Emily, hoping she would have a solution. "It's just one lunch," she shrugged. She held the door open wider and I stepped through it, knowing there was no way to avoid the impending train wreck.

I breathed deeply and made it to the dining room, where I stopped breathing altogether.

Sure enough, Nick was there.

Our eyes locked and I could feel his uncertainty pulsing off him in waves. He stood when he saw me, pushing back from the chair and making an awkward gesture of helplessness with his hands.

His smile was nervous and he looked as nice as he did the other day. Another oxford, this one a deep gray that brought out the blue in his eyes.

"What are you doing-" I had just about asked him why he was here, but he was right when he accused me of always being surprised to see him.

Even though this time I felt justified.

I started to wonder if I really did expect that he would stop living after I left him. Not that I wanted him to die, I just couldn't imagine his story apart from mine. I couldn't picture him in a life that didn't include me or a future that didn't revolve around me.

Did that make me the most self-absorbed person in the world?

Nick's lips twitched tellingly from obvious nerves. "I called your dad last week to see if I could pick up the amps we'd stored in his garage."

"I forgot about those." I cut a look to my dad, who was stalwartly avoiding eye contact with me.

"I knew we'd be home today," my dad told his roast chicken.

"I invited him to lunch," my mother declared. I looked at her, my eyes bugging out of my head. "What?" she gasped innocently. "Just because you no longer want the boy, doesn't mean we're ready to give him up. He's our son. We miss him."

Their son???

They missed him? They couldn't stand him!

I turned back to Nick with wide eyes, expecting him to be as skeptical of my parents as I was. But his gaze had narrowed and his smile had turned into a hard line.

"I'm sorry," I told him sincerely.

"You have nothing to be sorry about," he answered curtly.

"Sit down," my father demanded. "The food's getting cold."

I did as I was told, which meant I took the seat next to Nick. It was convenient how that was the only one left open.

We started to pass the food around the table and conversation began, but it was stilted and forced. My entire body prickled with unease. It was one thing to face Nick in my house, away from other people and prying eyes. But it was something else entirely to be on display in front of my family.

I felt their judgment skyrocket. I felt my own guilt triple. It was so stupid. I shouldn't have to deal with this!

When everyone but Nick and I was engaged in conversation, he leaned in and murmured, "You don't have to throw a temper tantrum. I won't bother you for long."

I gave him a fast glare and refocused on tearing my biscuit to shreds. "I'm not throwing a temper tantrum."

"Oh, really?" his chuckle was dark and without humor.

"Why do you need your amps? I thought you didn't like their sound?"

He stabbed at his chicken with his fork and knife, sawing them savagely. "Is it a crime to come over to your parents' house? To get *my* stuff?"

"Stop avoiding the question."

"Stop acting like a three-year-old."

That was it. The last straw. My chair scratched over the wood flooring as I pushed back and jumped up from my seat. I fled for the door, ignoring the protests and frustrated calls of my name. I had to get out of here.

I couldn't do this.

I couldn't be us again.

I grabbed my purse off the couch and let the screen door slam shut behind me. It snapped against the frame for a second time when Nick followed me outside.

"Kate, are you serious?"

I whirled around and tried to breathe through my anger. "Nick, are *you*?"

"What is your problem! I thought we were cool. Friday night we–"

My eyes flooded with tears and I wasn't sure why. "Don't," I whispered.

He took a step back. His hand had been reaching out to me and he dropped it. "You're serious," he said.

"I can't do this. I can't have you here with my parents, acting as if nothing's wrong. As if we're fine and normal and not in the middle of a divorce."

"We're not in the middle of a divorce," he bit out. "We're separated, Kate. Neither of us has filed. Neither of us has to file."

"What?" The breath whooshed out of me and for a second I didn't think I'd be able to stay standing.

"You heard me." He lifted his jaw defiantly and narrowed his gaze again.

For a hysterical second I thought he was going to dare me not to divorce him. As if all I needed was the challenge of making us work and I would forget about wanting to leave him.

As if I would take his dare.

As if it were that easy.

"Did you even need your amps?" I took a step toward him, not sure what I was going to do or say. Part of me wanted to shake him. The other part wanted to collapse in his arms and tell him he was right. So. Right. "Was this just an excuse to see me again?"

He returned my question with one of his own. "Why are you so hell bent on leaving me? Is this about having a baby? Kate, I-"

My heart jumped in my chest and then crashed back into place, only this time it was shattered into a million pieces. "Don't," I begged him with a broken, desperate voice. "Don't." A tearless, silent sob shook my entire body and I had to hold my hand to my face to keep from completely falling apart. "Nick, this," I flicked my finger between us, "is what this is about. Not kids, not my parents not any other reason than we cannot get along. When we're together, we're miserable. I'm tired of being miserable."

"We weren't the other night," he quickly reminded me. "We weren't miserable."

"That was one night! One! What about all of the other nights? What about all of the other days and fights and years of not getting along? I'm not trying to hurt you. Or, at least, not intentionally. I'm trying to give you a chance to find happiness somewhere else."

"Because you want to find happiness somewhere else."

I could have argued with him. I could have sworn that it wasn't entirely about me, that I wanted us both to be better off, that I was thinking of him as much as I was myself. But I didn't.

Instead, I let him believe it. I let him think the worst of me.

I let him decide that I wasn't worth fighting for.

"I have to go," I whispered.

He didn't say anything. He didn't argue and he didn't come after me again.

I got in my car and drove away. I didn't last one block before I started crying again, before the tears and pain became so much I had to pull over and cave into the pressure in my chest and the sobs that racked my entire body.

Eventually, I stopped crying. Eventually, I stopped shaking. But when I got home, I didn't feel any better. And when I crawled into my empty bed that night, it started all over again.

I didn't go to family dinner for the rest of the month.

Chapter Eleven

18. He can't let **go**.

I slumped against the doorframe to Kara's office and dropped my bag to my feet. She looked up at me from where she stood over her desk examining some papers and frowned at me.

Unlike the rest of the school, Kara's office was warmly lit and smelled like heaven. She burned candles all year round, despite the fact that they were against school policy. Mr. Kellar let her get away with it because she argued that her students needed to feel safe and comfortable. He apparently agreed, because he never said anything to her except when there was an inspection.

"You look like shit."

I glared at her. "Thank you."

"What happened?" Her voice softened to gentle concern.

"Don't ever get married. It's not worth it."

Her lips pursed and her shoulders straightened. "I wasn't planning on it, but thanks for the advice anyway."

I couldn't tell if I offended her or not. She wasn't married, she wasn't even dating, but that wasn't because there was something wrong with her. She was hot, successful in her own right and the best person I knew. She wasn't with someone because she chose not to be.

I had always thought of her as the quintessential empowered woman. But there was something in her expression just now... something I couldn't read.

I walked in and collapsed in one of her comfy chairs that sat in front of the desk. She hadn't invited me, but I was too miserable to care.

"You don't have a meeting or anything, do you?"

Her expression shifted to careful consideration and I wondered if she was going to bill me for my time. "Not for a few minutes. What's going on?" This time I heard real concern in her voice. She had gone home to visit her family over the weekend, so we hadn't spoken since after school on Friday. She didn't know about all of my Nick drama and I was finding myself reluctant to share it with her.

I didn't want to burden her with more of my depression, plus I was fairly certain she was as sick of hearing about my woes as I was. But I also couldn't get myself to speak the truth out loud. I didn't want to tell her about my Friday night with Nick because I wanted to keep that for me... I wanted to keep it special and untainted by snarky analysis.

I didn't want her to point out the possible obvious- that Nick didn't want to go through with the divorce. And I didn't want her asking questions to find out if maybe I didn't either.

There was too much past... too much history for us to ever be really happy moving forward. We just needed to cut this cord and move on.

"I saw the divorce lawyer this morning," I confessed.

I watched her shoulders sag and her mouth turn down in a frown. "Is that where you were?"

"I took the morning. I couldn't wait any longer." I picked at the frayed threads on the arm of the chair. "My parents invited Nick over to Sunday dinner yesterday. Things got a little out of control."

Her eyebrows shot up and her palms slapped the desk. "They did what?"

"Apparently they miss him."

"They hate him!"

"Apparently they only hate me."

She waved a dismissive hand. "Trust me, they don't. *My* parents hate me. Yours love you. Maybe too much, but they definitely love you."

I blinked at her, unsure if she was serious or not. Kara kept much of her home life to herself. She shared everything else, though, so I had never wanted to pry. I hadn't even met her parents before. It wasn't like college where most of my friends' parents either came to visit or hosted a group of us for a long weekend. Since I hadn't met Kara until our professional lives, there had been no reason to meet her family. I had never thought anything of it. She had only met mine a couple times over the years.

I tilted my chin mulishly, "If they loved me, they would not have invited my ex-husband to dinner. That's not love. That's torture."

"He's not your ex-husband yet," she said with an obvious amount of patience in her tone. "Maybe they were trying to get you back together? Maybe they don't hate him as much as you thought they did."

"They were part of the problem! They made things *so* difficult for us! We constantly fought about them. I had to drag Nick over there. He would put up such attitude every Sunday that I always felt like the bad guy. And then my mom! God, my mom can be such a brat. She would make me feel like the worst kind of human for marrying him. Now… *now* they want to play nice? It's not fair!"

She didn't say anything for a long time. I got the feeling she didn't know what to say.

"I'm just frustrated," I sighed. "It's not like I can say all of this to my mom. She'll take it like I'm blaming her for my divorce and I'm not. There were so many more issues besides that one. But they were a problem. A weekly problem. Sometimes more."

"If Nick hated it so much, and it sounds like you hated it too, then why did you guys keep going over there every single Sunday? That seems excessive."

I felt like a boulder dropped in my stomach and upset everything inside me, as if I was a puddle and the boulder threw up everything that made me in a fast, draining wave until I was nothing but emptiness and gritty earth. "Because that's what my parents expected us to do." But my explanation sounded so weak now.

"But, Kate, why didn't you guys just go once a month? Or every other week?"

I sat in stunned silence. Why didn't we? Why hadn't we set up better boundaries for our extended family? I didn't want to deal with my mom anymore than Nick did. So why had I tortured us week after week? Why had I let Nick be talked to like that every single Sunday? Why had I purposefully driven a wedge between us over my family?

Because that's what people do, my mind answered immediately. You spend time with your family because they're your family.

But my reply didn't hold the weight it once used to.

I didn't believe it quite so strongly.

It wasn't like Nick hadn't suggested this very thing on more than one occasion, but I had blamed him for being unwilling to try. I had blamed him like it was his fault. I had accused him of causing drama with my parents and being selfish with his time. It was our obligation, I told him. *This is what family does.*

But wasn't he my family? Shouldn't his needs and desires and wants come before my parents? He had never suggested cutting them out of our lives completely. He just wanted to spend less time with them.

It wasn't until Kara had pointed out the obvious that I finally saw things as they should have been.

Hell, at this moment in time, I didn't have plans to return for lunch ever again. And although I knew that would change eventually, I didn't have to force myself to go back every single Sunday. I could create my own boundaries. I could give myself a few Sundays off a month and actually feel rested when it was time to go to school on Monday.

Crazy.

Kara watched me for a long time before finally saying, "I'm surprised Nick showed up if he hates your parents so much."

"I am too," I breathed. "He needed to pick up some amps that my dad had been storing for him and then my mom invited him to lunch. Maybe he felt bad or guilty or something."

"Maybe." Her gentle gaze met mine over her desk. "Maybe he wanted to use your parents as an excuse to see you again."

I didn't know whether to laugh or to cry. "I thought you didn't like him either?"

She rolled her eyes and let out a short sigh. "I don't like that he's still trying to be a rock star. I want him to grow up and get a real job. Of course, I like Nick as a person. He's impossible not to like. I just hated that you were always so miserable, that you guys were always fighting. It had nothing to do with him. And I never suggested divorce. Honestly, I didn't know you guys had even considered it."

"He's really good, you know. I mean at the band stuff."

"Kate, I never said he wasn't. I just… you know what I mean."

"Yeah, I know."

"So? What if Nick isn't as pro-divorce as you first thought he was? What are you going to do then?"

"My lawyer asked me the exact same question. Along with a million others. And honestly I don't know. If Nick *is* pro-divorce, the actual procedure doesn't seem that difficult. It's mostly paperwork and legal fees. We will have to go to court to finalize it, but everything before then can be handled by our lawyers. We can file for divorce together and split everything equally. Hopefully, I'll take over the mortgage completely. I already pay it anyway. There are not that many bills to split outside of the house. He can take his things, I can take mine. Easy-peasy."

"And what if he doesn't want to do that?"

"Then it gets more complicated. I have to serve him the papers. They could show up at his work and deliver them like he's some sort of criminal. It sounds awful."

"So awful that you're not going to go through with it?"

I looked at Kara and saw hope flicker in her eyes. Did she really think this was a bad idea? Or was she just trying to save me the hassle?

"Do you really think I'm making a huge mistake?" I tried to keep the accusation out of my tone, but I couldn't hide it all. I felt suddenly betrayed.

She sucked in her bottom lip and then let it go, building herself up for whatever she needed to say. "Kate, the grass isn't always greener on the other side. It's not going to get magically better. You're not going to find the perfect person and live happily ever after. Happily ever after doesn't exist. It will never exist. Even if you go about this amicably, this divorce is going to be messy; it's going to hurt Nick and it's going to hurt you. It's honestly going to tear you apart. I love you. I don't want to see you go through all of that."

"And what about my marriage? What if I stay in a relationship with Nick and we just fight for the rest of our lives? What if he never wants to grow up and despises me forever because I'm asking him to? What if he thinks I'm nothing but a nag and a dream-killer and a rotten, heartless witch? How do I live with myself if my husband thinks *that*?" My voice grew louder and more hysterical with every word. I was on the verge of tears and screaming and drowning myself in cheap tequila by the end of it.

Kara, despite my hysterics, leveled me with a serious look and said, "I don't know, Kate. I don't know what happens then and I don't know what happens if you get a divorce. I just know that neither way is easy. And neither way is going to automatically make you feel better."

My breath came in short, violent bursts and tears swam in my eyes. I heard someone at the door and knew that was my cue to leave. I gathered up my bags and without saying goodbye to Kara, I fled her office.

I didn't have class for another fifteen minutes and the only thing I could think to do to fill the time was to call Nick.

Sure, I had papers to look at, lessons to plan for, I probably should have eaten something... but I needed to hear his voice. I needed to hear the certainty or uncertainty or whatever it was I was looking for.

I pulled out my phone and dialed his number. It rang for a long time and eventually kicked into voicemail. I let out an ugly curse that wasn't at all appropriate for school and tried again.

And then again and again and again until I had found my classroom and locked myself inside.

I finally gave up and just stared at my screen, wondering where he was and why he wasn't answering.

Had he gone to his own lawyer this morning? After yesterday's performance on my parents' lawn, I couldn't blame him. Maybe he just didn't want to talk to me. Maybe he wanted to avoid me for as long as he could.

I nearly screamed when my screen finally lit up and announced Nick's number across the front.

"*Finally*," I hissed. But I pushed the right button and brought the phone to my ear. "Hey," I said weakly.

"Kate?" He sounded confused and breathless. I could hear city noise and wind in the background as if he had just stepped outside.

Or maybe he was already outside. He could have been working for all I knew and I'd just interrupted one of his jobs.

"Kate?" he said again, louder this time.

"Hi. Sorry. I'm here."

More awkward moments spun by until he said, "Hey, Kate, I really want to talk to you, especially, uh, about yesterday. But I'm kind of in the middle of something. So if it's not urgent, then I should probably let you-"

"I saw a lawyer this morning." The words fell out of my mouth like poisonous snakes. I couldn't keep them inside me anymore. They were infecting me… killing me. I had to get them out. I had to poison someone else too.

He let out a sound that was half growl, half huff of surprise. "A lawyer."

"I needed to do something. I needed to get this in motion."

He was so silent that if I couldn't hear the background noise, I would have thought he hung up on me.

"You *needed* to-"

"I don't want to fight with you, Nick. I just wanted to let you know. It was a courtesy call." But had it been? Why had I needed to call him so desperately?

"It's only been six months," he shot back. His voice was firm this time, resolute. "Kate, give it some more time."

I ignored his plea. "If we file together… amicably then it makes the whole process easier and-"

"I'm not going to do that."

I was so shocked by the dominance in his voice I had to sit down. "Wh-what?"

"Go ahead and do what you want, but I'm not going to file amicably."

"Why not?"

"It doesn't matter why. You just need to know that I'm not going to."

I had no idea what to say to that. I was more confused than ever. Was he trying to be a pain in the ass? Was he trying to make this as difficult as possible?

Obviously.

But *why*? Just to piss me off? Or did he actually feel entitled to more than what fifty-fifty would get him?

Or was Kara right? Did he really not want to go through with this?

I fumbled, trying to think of something to say, "Well, you should probably get a lawyer then."

His reply was crisp and direct. "I have a lawyer."

After a long minute of silence I realized he hung up on me. I stared at my phone, dazed and completely shell-shocked until the bell rang and students started walking into class.

So Sunday had been lies? A last ditch attempt? If he had a lawyer, then he wanted a divorce.

He was going to make my life as difficult as possible, but the divorce was definitely happening.

With my mind spinning at a hundred miles per hour and my personal life in complete tatters, it was safe to say that the rest of the afternoon sucked.

Chapter Twelve

19. He's **purposefully** making my life difficult.

A couple weeks passed, but the most progress made on my divorce was the delivery of papers. I'd contemplated for longer than I should whether to have them dropped off at Nick's work. I had wanted to lash out against his refusal to make this easy.

If he wanted to play games, then public humiliation could go a long way.

But in the end I'd chickened out. I couldn't do it. I couldn't hurt him like that.

It seemed that no matter how difficult he made my life, I still cared about his feelings.

My lawyer thought these were particularly obnoxious obstacles, but there was nothing I could do about them. So he arranged to have the papers delivered to Nick's attorney- who turned out to be one of the better divorce lawyers in the city.

I honestly didn't know how Nick could afford his legal services. I had to scrimp, save and cut off my purse addiction to pay for mine. It wasn't easy.

When we'd separated, our finances were frighteningly easy to divide. We closed our joint account at the bank and each set up our own. We both agreed to leave our meager savings alone for the time being and I trusted him not to touch it.

Besides, the amount was so insignificant that if he used every penny, I really wouldn't have been that upset.

Although, I never would have told him that.

The only thing we still shared was our cell phone bill, which he'd offered to continue to pay for until our contract was up and we could go separate ways without paying astronomical fees.

I had been the breadwinner anyway and other than student loans, utilities and our mortgage, we didn't have many other bills. Our parents had helped furnish our house and we'd accumulated our possessions slowly enough that there was nothing to pay off. He had his credit card, I had mine.

I had always paid the majority of our bills, so I got to keep the house. He moved out. It only seemed fair that I keep paying the mortgage and utilities.

It was a little depressing how easy our finances had been to split. At the time, I expected more of a struggle... more of a fight. But we'd dealt with everything as cleanly as we'd ended our marriage.

As I packed up my classroom for the day, I wondered how he could afford his legal help. It was seriously bothering me.

Where was the money coming from?

His parents?

No way. They had plenty of money, but he would never ask them.

At least I didn't think he would.

Was he that desperate to screw me over in the divorce that he would go to his parents...?

I thought they liked me. Maybe our relationship had been strained and forced, but no more than their relationship with Nick. They'd never been close.

Nick had always been the wild rebel child that his successful parents couldn't take seriously. And they had always been the part of his life he politely tolerated. I thought I had created some kind of peaceful bridge between them.

Apparently not.

Apparently, they hated me as much as Nick did.

Sure, I hadn't heard from them once since Nick and I separated, but I didn't think they wanted to take all of my earthly possessions and leave me out in the cold.

They had always been nice. Distant, but nice.

Apparently distant-but-nice meant they had been harboring some kind of intense hatred for me. At least they had something in common with Nick now.

Kate Carter, bringing families together since 2008.

You're welcome.

If Nick was that desperate to ask his parents for money, then he really did want to make me suffer.

I dropped my coffee thermos on the floor as my entire world began to spin out of control. Nick couldn't hate me this much.

Sure, we'd had a rocky marriage, but did I deserve this? Was I that terrible of a person?

"You dropped this."

I nearly screamed at the intrusion. I snapped out of my internal breakdown and blinked Eli into focus.

"Oh, my god. You scared me." My hand landed on my fluttering heart and I sucked in enough oxygen so my brain could process his sudden appearance.

He gave me a playful smile. "You're kind of easy to sneak up on."

Nick's words bounced around in my head. *You're ridiculously easy to surprise.*

Was I?

"Sorry," I tried to smile. "I was lost in my head."

Eli's smile turned patient. "I gathered."

He held out my coffee cup and I took it from him. "Thanks."

"No problem." He shifted on his feet while I tried to collect my wits. "So, uh, you looked a little panic stricken when I walked in. Is everything okay?"

I nodded without thinking.

"You sure? You're a little pale. Do you want to sit down?"

I looked down at my desk self-consciously. It took me a few minutes to figure out what I wanted to say. I had trouble disentangling myself from my riotous thoughts. Finally, I lifted my gaze to bravely meet his and asked, "Am I a terrible person?"

Eli's eyebrows lifted with surprise. "Are you serious?"

"Yes," I whispered. "I just need to know if I'm a complete bitch. I can't tell."

"Well that should tell you something," he said with no small amount of amusement.

"I'm serious. You can be honest with me. I can take it."

"No," he said quickly. For a second I thought he was refusing to answer my question until he put a gentle hand on mine and continued, "You're not a terrible person. You're definitely not a complete bitch. You're none of those things. Why would you think otherwise?"

I felt better. Even if I didn't entirely believe him, my vanity was appeased. "I was just thinking about this divorce," I explained quietly. "Suddenly Nick is refusing to do this amicably. He's threatened to make this as difficult as possible. I just… I wondered if he was maybe punishing me for how awful I was to him during our marriage."

Eli's raised eyebrows dropped and scrunched together over the bridge of his nose. "I thought you said this was a decision you came to together?"

"We did. At least I thought we did. His behavior has been… confusing."

"Has he changed his mind?"

"What do you mean?"

Eli frowned. "Does he not want to get divorced anymore?"

I took a step back, feeling shaken up and unsteady. "Of course he wants the divorce."

"Then why is he being difficult?" Eli's question landed with all the gentleness of a tank running over me.

I shook my head helplessly, "I don't know."

He didn't say anything else about Nick. There wasn't really anything left to say.

"I'm sorry, Eli. I've been super self-absorbed since you walked in. Did you need something?"

He let out a nervous laugh and I immediately regretted how I'd phrased my question. He held my gaze though and asked, "I was wondering if you had plans tonight."

"Tonight?" I sounded like an idiot repeating him, but it was a school night. And by that, I meant a normal Tuesday…

Seeming to read my thoughts, he grinned and said, "I won't keep you out late. But I thought we could grab a cup of coffee?"

"Coffee?"

"Or a different beverage. I mean, you're not limited strictly to coffee. We could go for a soda instead. Or iced tea. Water even, if none of those, uh, sound good."

I realized that my parroting had made Eli nervous. And other than finding it completely adorable, it was not my intention to make him suffer. I laughed, hoping to diffuse the tension. "Actually, coffee sounds really good. I could use some caffeine." And then because I was still an idiot and didn't want him to think that the only reason I agreed to go out with him was because I was sleepy, I said, "It will be fun to spend some time with you!" And then because I wasn't sure if this was a date or not and I apparently had an addiction to sticking my foot in my mouth, I didn't stop talking and said, "We never get to hang out just the two of us!"

Oh, my god, somebody tackle me.

Stop talking.

Eli's expression told me clearly he had no idea what to think of me anymore, but he gifted me with a gentle smile and nodded once. "Good."

I put the last of my papers in my tote bag and fumbled around for my classroom keys in my purse. "Do you have a favorite spot?"

"Yes." His smile came more naturally as I shut off the lights and we moved to the quiet hallway so I could lock the door behind me. "It's not Starbucks though. Does that bother you?"

"What?" I shook my head at him. "There are other places that make coffee besides Starbucks? You're lying."

He laughed at my sarcasm. "I would not lie about something like this. I take my coffee very seriously."

"Well, I've never been much of a commercial coffee drinker." I waved my to-go cup in the air. "I bring it from home."

"I'm glad we share the same philosophy," Eli said seriously.

"I can't lie, mine's more about me being late every morning. I never have time to stop."

He threw his head back and laughed while I admired the strong column of his throat. God, I needed this. I needed to breathe a little and forget about the insanity of my divorce.

His gaze found mine again and with a sweetness I didn't think still existed in the male race, said, "Can I drive you? I'll swing you back by the school to pick up your car."

I paused for a second so I wouldn't trip over my tongue. "Yes."

We chatted about our days and the school year so far as we dropped off my bags at my car then walked to his. My heart started to beat triple time and I was feeling a little sweaty.

Eli and I had been friends for so long that I shouldn't feel this nervous. I only half paid attention to the small talk during our short car ride because inside I couldn't stop freaking out long enough to focus on any one thing.

The entire drive to the coffee shop, my stomach churned anxiously, my mouth dried out and my palms started to itch. I fidgeted in the high bench seat of his truck but tried desperately not to be obvious.

He had to think I was crazy already. I didn't need to fuel his opinion of me.

Yet, he'd asked me out.

And that was the problem, wasn't it?

I had a tendency to overthink everything. And so, during the few moments I wasn't obsessing over my own miserable life and divorce, I had thought about Eli and whether anything would progress with us. I hadn't really thought he'd ask me out so soon, but I knew there was chemistry between us. Kara had left enough hints that I had started to prepare myself mentally for the day that he would ask me out.

But I hadn't expected it *today*.

I thought he'd wait until my divorce was finalized and I'd had a little more separation from my husband than six measly months. I thought we'd continue to build a relationship slowly, enjoying friendship first and then, in the future, in the far, distant future, we'd naturally fall into something romantic.

Maybe.

If I ever got over the trauma of seven years of bad luck, er, my marriage.

And yet, he'd asked me today. Today, when I realized, that in all likelihood, I would have to spend the next several months in mediation with my not-yet-ex-husband. Today when all I wanted to do was go home, put my feet up and pour a bottle of wine into a fishbowl and drink it with a straw.

Maybe I didn't even need the fishbowl.

Maybe I would guzzle it straight from the bottle.

That sounded so much easier.

I was nothing if not practical.

"Are you listening?" Eli's dark gaze cut to mine.

I ruined any semblance of interest I had when I stupidly asked, "Huh?"

He looked down at his oversized cup of coffee and smiled into the black depths. Eli had brought me to a rustic, mountain-cabin-esque coffee house that was cute in the I-just-shot-a-twelve-point-buck kind of way. He drank his coffee bitter, dark as midnight and endlessly. I liked milk and sugar. I liked fru-fru and beverages that didn't give me heartburn. I wanted whipped cream. Lots of whipped cream. When I ordered my latte, the cashier looked at me like I'd just asked for liquid skunk. "You sure?" he said. As if I would reconsider my order and pick battery acid instead.

But in the end I did. I was too self-conscious to go through with it. "Just a regular coffee, then," I mumbled. "And some milk."

I shouldn't be that hard on the place, though. Despite my rough introduction, Eli had led me to oversized leather chairs that I could squish back in and tuck my feet beneath me. Now that we were leaned in close in our respective chairs, chatting over warm coffee while a light rain pelted the gloomy October afternoon, I felt more relaxed about the place- even if my bitter beverage was melting my insides.

Except I ruined the potentially romantic moment by letting my mind drift.

"I'm sorry," I told him honestly. "I just... I don't have an excuse."

I was too embarrassed to look at him, but I heard the forgiveness in his voice when he said, "Yes you do. You've got a lot going on."

I lifted my gaze shyly. "I hate that I always make our conversations about me and my problems."

"Don't be sorry. I like talking about you."

His words brought a fierce blush to my face, which I took as a good sign. See? I was interested in Eli. I liked his compliments. I liked his attention.

But then all of that was ruined when a rolling wave of nausea crashed through me and I thought I would be sick.

I swallowed back strong coffee and a hell of a lot of half-and-half and gave him a trembling smile. "Thank you for taking me out for coffee even if I've failed at conversation."

He watched me for long moments. Something flashed in his eyes, dimming them slightly. I didn't know him well enough to name every one of his emotions, but I was pretty sure this one could be called disappointment.

I nibbled on my lip self-consciously and tried to think of something to talk about.

"Has your school year improved?" he asked before I could say anything.

I threw myself into paying attention to him. "A little. I think the junior class is trying to get me to retire early. Really early. Possibly by Christmas break. But other than that it's mostly battling freshman to remember everything they need for class and going to war with seniors who think they're graduating tomorrow instead of in May."

"Your year sounds a lot like mine," he chuckled. "The juniors this year are something special."

"You would think I knew what to expect since I've had them for the last two years. But they are pulling out all the stops this quarter. Actually, I have one class with both juniors and seniors that is truly a challenge. I had to break up a fight yesterday over some HBO show. I thought they were going to send each other to the hospital."

"Who was it?"

"Jay Allen and Andre Gonzalez." He nodded at me sympathetically. "If those two boys were able to combine their egos, I think they would usher in Armageddon. I've never had such egotistical maniacs in class at the same time before. It's out of control."

Eli let out a bark of laughter and leaned forward. His fingers brushed mine, but I had to be honest with myself and say I didn't feel a single tingle or butterfly.

This was too soon for me.

That was abundantly clear.

"They really are something else," he agreed. "If they both make it to graduation, it will be a miracle."

That sobered me some. "I hope they do. Those two kids need high school diplomas. I don't want to think of what their futures hold if they drop out."

He canted his head and the corners of his lips drew down. "They might find a future like that anyway."

I took a deep breath and pressed my lips together to keep from agreeing with him. This was the price we paid as teachers. It didn't matter whether we worked in an inner-city school or a wealthy private one in the suburbs, we could invest everything we had in our students and they could still throw their lives away after graduation. We could give them every single thing in our educational arsenal, and they could still make poor decisions that ruined any chance of a successful future they had.

That was the problem with caring so deeply for the kids I taught. I wasn't really responsible for them. I had no control over their lives or the decisions they made. I gave and gave and gave and then hoped and hoped and hoped they learned something from me.

Eli downed the rest of his coffee and set his cup down on the small table that sat between us. "Thanks for hanging out with me."

I clutched my huge, gray mug with both hands. "Thanks for inviting me."

We were silent an awkward beat too long when he said, "You're not ready for this."

My eyes snapped up and widened at him. "What?"

His voice pitched low and soft, "I, uh, I thought you might be, you know, ready for something. You're not. That's okay. Obviously it's okay. I just read this wrong. I wanted to apologize."

"No, it's not that I'm not ready… Well, I wouldn't say that I *am* ready. But I'm not… *not* ready. I just… I don't know… What I'm trying to say is…" I stopped talking. That was getting neither of us anywhere. I took a deep breath and met his steady gaze again. "Okay, maybe I'm not ready."

He chuckled and I wanted to die, except that his eyes were twinkling again and his smile looked genuine. "You're not ready, Kate. I'm sorry I pushed you."

"If I'm honest, I didn't know you were pushing me. I thought I was… you know… ready to move on."

"It's okay." His hand landed on mine and he squeezed. "I had unrealistic expectations I suppose."

"Was it that easy for you to move on? I mean, it's only been six months. We were married for seven years. But I guess you were married for longer than that, huh?"

His warm eyes looked like melting chocolate when they filled with sympathy for me. "By the time Naomi and I separated both of us were more than ready to move on. We had spent so many years at each other's throats and wishing for change, that when we finally walked away from each other, both of us found peace we hadn't known in a very long time. I think that made moving on easier."

"Oh." My thoughts tumbled together. Hadn't the same been true for Nick and me? Was it just me that was having such a hard time moving on?

"That doesn't mean dating is easier than it was before. It's definitely as bad as I remember."

I smiled at him. "You still want to settle down with someone? Even after your first marriage?"

He didn't hesitate, "Definitely. Naomi and I weren't right for each other, but that doesn't mean I'm wrong for everyone or everyone's wrong for me. There's someone out there for me."

"There *is* someone out there for you," I told him honestly. "You're a good guy, Eli. I'm sorry this didn't work out."

He cleared his throat and murmured thoughtfully, "Me too."

I stood up after that. I didn't know what else to say. Unlike Eli, I didn't have the same perspective. My marriage wrecked me. I couldn't do that to myself again. I didn't want to.

The thought of going through that much pain again terrified me.

I was positive I wouldn't survive it.

And frankly, I couldn't hurt someone again like I'd hurt Nick.

Eli stood up too and his hand settled on my shoulder, but it was filled with nothing but friendly affection. At least on my part.

"I'll take you back to school so you can get your car," he offered.

"Thanks."

We parted ways on good terms. I didn't think there was enough interest on his part for him to be truly upset that I hadn't wanted more. And honestly, I hadn't known I didn't want more with him until we went out.

Eli was all the things that I thought I wanted. He was thoughtful. He was attentive. He *tried*. But even after all of that, if I was truly honest with myself, he was *everything* that I wanted and still not *what* I wanted.

I drove home wondering if things would have been different if he'd given me more time or if I had been more willing to let go of the marriage I thought I couldn't wait to get out of.

I wondered how long it would take for me to get over Nick. If I'd ever be ready to move on.

I wondered if I'd ever heal.

If I'd ever find myself again.

Chapter Thirteen

20. He won't **apologize**.

The next week hailed Halloween and I was in the worst funk of my life. The divorce hadn't moved forward. Nick was being difficult as ever and I hadn't had the energy to fight him. Eli hadn't just backed off pursuing me; he'd backed off everything. I felt like I lost a friend and that hurt worse than I was willing to admit.

In fact, loneliness had set in like concrete ankle blocks and I was worried that if just one more thing went wrong in my life, I'd tip off the end of a dock and sink to the bottom of an endless ocean.

Was that too dramatic?

Maybe. But I also knew that I had never felt this profoundly alone before.

I left home at eighteen and moved straight into a college dorm that I shared with Fiona for four years. I had spent summers in cheap apartments with friends. The year after graduation, while I planned my wedding, I lived with my parents. And then obviously I moved in with Nick. For better or worse, he'd been my constant roommate for my entire adult life.

I had never lived on my own. I had never really been on my own before.

I knew eventually I would grow used to it. At first it was even kind of fun, maybe a little weird, but mostly fun. I could do whatever I wanted without consulting another person. But it quickly stopped being shiny and new and the loneliness crept up on me. It coated the house that I loved and tainted my activities.

School became my life because when I left there, I knew I would have to go home to an empty house and have no one to tell about my day or share my struggles except Annie. And she rarely shared her opinion.

Sure, there was Kara, but even my best friend felt distanced by my issues. Besides, she had her own life to live. As close as we were, our entire relationship had revolved around my marriage. She always bent her schedule to meet my needs, to hang out when I didn't have any other plans.

Now I was on the other side of that.

Her life didn't revolve around me. I could understand that.

It was just hard when my life *had* revolved around someone else.

Now I felt lost. Adrift in a storm haunted sea.

A sunflower in a sunless sky. A flower that had no light to tilt my face to.

A year ago I had been so excited for Halloween. It really was one of the best holidays. It was all for fun. There were never family obligations to fulfill or gifts to buy or pies to bake. I could just celebrate something without extra stress.

Plus, I had always thought it was a great way to kick off the holiday season.

Until this year.

Halloween fell on a Saturday and I had no plans. Not even one.

Well, unless you counted the invitation from Kara to be a third wheel on her third date with the guy she met at her gym.

No, thanks.

They were headed to some super fun party and I couldn't even muster enough energy to put shoes on.

I adjusted my cat ear headband and slumped down on the bench in my entryway. A huge bowl of candy sat in my lap and it was taking every ounce of self-control I had left not to tear into the wrapped sugar and flood my house with wrappers.

Apparently I'd jumped from the Divorce Diet to the Divorce-Eat-My-Weight-In-Chocolate Plan.

Which sounded awesome at this point.

The doorbell rang and I jumped, even though I had been expecting it. I moved to the door and pulled it open, ready for the trick-or-treating brigade I knew would be flooding my doorstep.

"Trick or treat," Nick grinned at me.

I tried to hide my surprise while Annie danced around his feet and licked at his shins. "I'm supposed to give *you* candy." I eyed the bags he held in his arms and tried to decide if I should be furious or burst into tears.

He shrugged one shoulder casually, "I wanted to donate to the cause."

"You don't have to."

He took a step inside the house even though I hadn't invited him. "This used to be my house too. I guess I'm not quite ready to give up our neighbors yet."

I let out a weary sigh, "It's still your house. At least until you sign the papers."

I thought he would snap at me or start a fight. Instead, he cocked his head to the side and smiled. "Are you a mouse?"

"I'm a cat!" I adjusted the stupid headband I'd picked up at the gas station this morning and tried not to grimace.

"Oh."

"What does that mean? *Oh*? And what are you? A robber?"

He shook his head and grinned wider. "The Hamburglar. Obviously."

"The Hamburglar?"

"From McDonald's. Remember?"

"Oh, the mask. And the weird hat. I get it."

He took another step until he could close the door behind him. "You don't seem impressed."

I'm wondering how you make that costume look so good... "I'm confused."

"About?"

"Why are you here, Nick?"

"This conversation again? Honestly, Katie, did we talk about anything besides my location when we were married?"

I wanted to punch him. Instead, I stepped back, away from him and his cologne and that adorable costume and the bags of candy in his hands. If he could change topics without warning, so could I. "I thought you would have a gig tonight."

He shook his head. "I'm not in the band anymore, remember?"

"Like at all? I thought that was just a temporary thing?" Something warm bloomed inside of me. It grew hotter the longer I stared at him. Hotter and hotter until it was boiling inside of me, until it was lava and magma and the temperature of the sun.

The doorbell rang, interrupting our conversation. He opened it because he was closest and smiled down at the little kids dressed up as a robot and a dinosaur while simultaneously holding Annie back with his foot. She wanted to charge the kids. They looked like they wanted to run away screaming in terror.

My guard dog.

All twenty pounds of her.

Nick dropped his bags of unopened candy on the bench I had just been sitting on and grabbed handfuls of candy from my bowl.

I stood there dumbstruck. *What was happening?*

After they left, he closed the screen door but left the big door open. "I'm not in the band anymore, Kate. They found another lead singer."

"Oh my gosh, were you pissed?"

He threw a smile over his shoulder as he grabbed more candy for the next round of trick-or-treaters. "I sold them my old amps and gave them my blessing. I, uh, retired."

"You retired?" I hated that this divorce had turned me into a parrot. Was losing the ability to have original thoughts a side effect of divorce trauma?

He handed out more candy while I stood there blankly. More kids came to the door, dragging their parents with them.

While I stood there watching mutely, Nick talked to our neighbor for a little bit, shooting the shit and discussing the most mundane stuff ever. Neither of them acknowledged me. Chris, our neighbor, didn't even notice me at all. Or at least he pretended not to.

After we were alone again, I tried to form words. "You quit the band?"

"I prefer retired, but yeah, I guess that's what happened."

"But... but... *Why?*"

He shifted his shoulders and it was the first time I noticed tension in him since he arrived. His back had gone taut with some emotion that I wanted to believe was frustration or anger. But I couldn't make myself believe it.

I couldn't read him at all anymore. His eyes were hidden from me in the dim entryway and behind a black mask. I couldn't see them. All I had to read him by was his body language and his lean body didn't say much underneath a black and white stripped t-shirt and his familiar low-waist jeans. It wasn't that complicated of a costume, but for some reason it really got to me.

It bothered me that he'd dressed up and looked so good and on top of that, he'd showed up at my house with extra candy.

He wanted to make our divorce as difficult as possible and my life hell. And yet he was here. Like this.

It wasn't fair.

He wasn't playing fair.

The burn inside me became a searing force that actually hurt me.

"You were right, Kate. It was time."

"I was right?" My words sputtered from my lips with jolting disbelief. "So that's it? We decide to end things and *then* you quit the band? Are you serious?"

He turned around to face me. "I said you were right."

"I heard what you said! But why couldn't you have said that to me while we were still married?" I felt breathless with anger, blind with it.

"We *are* still married."

"*Nick!*"

He tilted his head arrogantly and clenched his jaw. "Would it have mattered?"

"Yes!" I couldn't put enough conviction in the word, though, so I amended to, "Maybe." I took a step back, gripping the huge plastic bowl of candy to my chest. "You could have tried! You could have at least tried!"

His words were soft, but not gentle. The hard tone buzzed over my skin, pulling at the hair on the back of my neck. "I did try."

I barely heard him. "What difference does it make now? Why quit *now*? For seven years, it was the most important thing in your life and now it's... it's not?" I sounded more than hysterical. I screeched at him like a lunatic, unable to control the volume of my voice or my crazed emotions.

"No. It's not. There are more important things than the band."

"But why did you wait to figure that out *now*? God, seriously! I can't believe this. I can't believe that I begged you for years to quit, to move on, to do something else and you didn't listen to me one time. Not one single time. And then we fall apart and suddenly you know *there are more important things*."

The doorbell rang, but neither of us moved to answer it. Instead, Nick pushed the main door so hard that it slammed shut, right in the bewildered faces of some little kids.

I glanced wildly at the door, wondering what neighbor I was going to have to apologize to tomorrow. Nick stepped right in front of me, pulling my attention back to him.

"Why do you care, Kate? You're going to divorce me no matter what, so what does it matter what I'm doing with my life? Huh? Why do you care so much?"

"Because!" A punch of air whooshed out of me and I struggled not to sway. My fury was too much for my mortal body. I felt like a force of nature, like a tornado that would destroy every single thing in the wake of my anger. "Because it's what I wanted from you! Because I worked so hard at our marriage, at making things work with you. And you didn't give me anything! You didn't try anything! And now… now it's too late and suddenly the decision is easy for you. It doesn't matter that we fought endlessly about it! It doesn't matter that I begged you, that I pleaded with you to try something different. It doesn't matter that I would have supported you anyway, against my will, against what I wanted, just because I loved you and wanted you to succeed." Hot tears fell from my eyes, landing on my cheeks and lips. I couldn't stop them. I couldn't fight them anymore.

Nick's wrath matched my own. He took another step forward and I forced myself not to retreat further. "Oh, really? You would have supported me no matter what?" He let out a bark of derisive laughter. "Then why are we here? Why did you file papers and kick me out of the house? Why, if all you wanted was for me to succeed, are you sleeping here alone and I'm living on my brother's couch?"

I took a step back anyway. I was a coward. Or maybe the pulse of his frustration was so strong it pushed me back. My shoulders bumped against the wall and one of my decorative pictures shook next to my head. "Why couldn't you try for *me*? Why couldn't you have decided this six months ago?"

His lips had pressed into a straight line before he gritted out, "I wasn't ready."

The sound I made was half-tortured, half-furious. "So why now?"

I waited for his answer while his shoulders jerked with the intensity of his emotion and his jaw clenched and unclenched. But he never said anything. Instead, he shocked the absolute hell out of me, by ripping the bowl of candy out of my hands and throwing it against the far wall.

Plastic collided against the drywall and candy flew everywhere. I had just enough time to let out a startled gasp before his lips crashed to mine with equal force.

He took my mouth in a punishing kiss. He knew me intimately, familiarly. He knew exactly how to kiss me. Exactly how to make my body respond. It only took one second for me to kiss him back.

I had so much emotion bubbling inside me. I had been through too much trauma over the last few months, spent too much time alone. I didn't have a prayer of denying Nick this kiss.

If only it would have stopped there.

But it didn't.

Our mouths warred with each other, his tongue chasing mine, his lips moving over mine with greedy need. I took his bottom lip in a sharp bite, pulling it between my teeth and truly tasting the soft fullness of his mouth.

His hands slammed on my waist before diving beneath my black sweater. His skin seared mine; my burning lungs stuttered with the effort to breath. I found my own hands clutching at his shirt, balling it up in my fists and holding him to me.

God, this was *too familiar.*

Too good.

It had been *too long.*

His body pressed against mine with a possessiveness I had never felt from him before. It was like he was declaring that I was still his, that I was still his wife.

Until every last paper was signed, I still belonged to this man.

And I knew it was a bad thing... that this made us completely dysfunctional and turned us into every embarrassing cliché out there, but I could not stop.

I could not get enough of him.

I *didn't want* to get enough of him.

His hands moved over my body, remembering every curve, every inch of me. My cat ears headband was pushed off, landing in a muffled thud on the wood floor. My shirt came next. He practically tore the sweater from my body in his effort to get to more of me.

I was equally desperate to get to his chest. I threw the hat somewhere on the staircase, the mask went next and finally the t-shirt.

As soon as his chest was bare, he pressed his body against mine and we both moaned into each other's mouth. The feel of him, with his skin against mine, his heart pounding against mine... it was too much. Too much sensation. Too much sweet anguish. Too much of everything good and right about our marriage.

There were so many reasons that we shouldn't be together.

But this wasn't one of them.

This was one of the reasons we had stayed together for so long.

"Kate," he groaned, tearing his lips from mine to explore my neck and chest. His tongue licked and his teeth nipped at the top of my breasts. I pushed my chest up for him, anxious to have more of him touch me and more of me touch him.

The high-pitched whimper I couldn't hold back pushed him over the edge. He was wild, savage, completely frenzied with lust and desire. He pushed his hips into mine and my eyes rolled to the back of my head. *God, this man.*

This man that I couldn't stand.

This man that I was divorcing.

He made quick work of my bra, flicking it open with his deft, practiced fingers. He yanked it from my arms without an ounce of gentleness or consideration. It was like he couldn't help himself. He had no self-control. No restraint.

And his wicked energy did nothing but make me hotter.

Our pants came next. We tore at buttons and kicked them frantically from our legs. My hands slipped into the waistband of his boxer briefs and I moaned again at the feel of this familiar area. My hands skated down his legs, taking his underwear with them, relishing in the delicious heat of his body.

My panties were next. But he did not worship my legs or touch me reverently. He tore at them; he shoved them down and desperately fought them off my ankles. He wasn't in the mood to be adoring or sweet. He was primal with his need, completely lost in this ferocious want.

For a short second reality flashed in my mind and I knew we were making a huge mistake. I tried to voice my objection. I tried to remind him that we weren't together anymore and that this would only set us back.

But it was like he could read my mind. As soon as I started to say something, his mouth took mine again in another consuming kiss.

Soon, I couldn't think of anything rational. There was no such thing as logic or good choices.

There was only him and me and our naked bodies.

There was only the familiar heat that had always been between us and the scorching intensity as we took each other in a new way.

We'd had makeup sex before. We'd had huge fights before today and used sex to get over them.

But this was something completely different. This wasn't an apology. This was war. A war of our bodies, of our wills... of our souls.

He took me right there. Right against the wall.

I wrapped my legs around him and he held me steady as he reminded me what it was like to have him as a husband. And at the same time, he revealed a side of him I had never known.

I clasped my arms around his head while he alternated between taking my mouth and taking my breasts. His short beard scraped against my skin in a familiar sting that I welcomed, that I *loved*. Our sweaty bodies moved together in a rhythm of something we had done countless times before, but it had never ever been like this.

Despite the newness, he still knew exactly what to do to get my body to respond to his. He knew how to touch me. He knew how to move inside me. He knew the moment I reached the brink of something shattering.

And then he knew how to push me over the edge and make my world explode.

I screamed out with the shock and intensity of an orgasm like none before this one. My fingers dug into his back and my thighs squeezed his waist, desperate to make this feeling last forever.

He followed after me, burying his face in my neck and sinking his teeth into the soft flesh there. The moment seemed to go on and on and on until he sagged against the wall and I collapsed in his arms.

When he set me on my feet, I was beyond dazed and more than confused. Not surprisingly, the anger had drained out of me and left me with a bizarre longing I couldn't explain.

Regret and disappointment with my own behavior followed shortly and I didn't know if I would be able to stand up against the force of these emotions.

I wanted to run and hide.

I wanted to cry again and never stop.

I expected that I would do both of those things.

Just as soon as I figured out what the hell Nick was thinking!

"Nick-"

"Don't," he growled and the depth of his tone made me shut my mouth immediately.

He jerked his pants up and buttoned them with furious movements. His gaze lifted to mine and the heat behind his eyes pierced me in place.

I was wrong. We didn't need to talk.

We definitely didn't need to talk.

We never needed to talk again.

We could just keep communicating like this.

Against the wall.

He grabbed his shirt and yanked it on. It was inside out and backward, but I was not going to be the one to point that out to him.

I stood there naked, awkwardly covering my breasts.

"Whatever you're thinking right now, Kate, stop."

"I'm not thinking anything," I whispered.

"Don't lie to me."

The command was too brutal for me to ignore, "Okay."

"I'll let you be now." His voice shook as if he were having a very hard time controlling himself right this second so all I did was nod. "I'll call you tomorrow."

I nodded again. Even though I mostly wanted to beg him not to. I wanted to beg him to forget this ever happened.

Even though I knew I never could.

Even though I knew I would remember the intensity, the soul-shattering connection... the profound desperation we'd taken each other with to my very last breath.

I would never forget this.

And I had a very disarming thought that this would be the time I compared every single other time to in my future.

But, damn.

Nick took a step forward and for one horrifying second I thought he was going to kiss me again. I couldn't take any more. If he kissed me again, I would shatter.

He seemed to realize this and stopped himself short. "I'll call you tomorrow," he repeated on his way out the door.

"Okay," I whispered.

But when he called the next day, I didn't answer.

And when he continued to call for the following three days, I continued to not answer. After that, he didn't call again.

144

Chapter Fourteen

21. He's completely **unpredictable**.

The next time I saw Nick was a week before Thanksgiving at our first round of mediation. My lawyer had suggested getting the help of a third party after Nick remained completely uncooperative. I hoped mediation was the answer. I didn't want to go to trial and I couldn't believe Nick did either. I truly believed we could work through everything civilly.

At least I hoped we could.

I had assured Mr. Cavanaugh that Nick and I could be polite and mature, but my lawyer was in his mid-fifties and had apparently seen his fair share of bitter wives and hateful husbands.

He didn't have the most positive attitude where the dissolution of marriage was concerned.

Then again, he had the kind of demeanor that generally expected the worst. Beneath his disheveled white hair was a face that could never be pleased. Deep wrinkles stretched across his forehead and gathered in the corners of his dull eyes. His mouth was perpetually turned down and his wide shoulders drooped beneath his crumpled cheap suits. He reminded me of a hound dog. An *old* hound dog.

But he knew divorce law and he'd promised to get me what I needed- which was a divorce. He just had no hope that the proceedings would be easy.

And he was probably right.

I stepped onto the elevator of the building that housed Whitney, Boggs and Stone and ignored the taste in my mouth that felt like vomit on my tongue and bile in my stomach. Our first meeting was set in Nick's lawyer's office. And it was immaculate.

I needed a minute to steady my nerves and prepare for the battle I was headed into, but the glass walls and busy lobby prevented solitude. I was on display the moment I walked into the building.

Not that I really thought all of these people were paying attention to little old me. But I felt like they were. My emotions manipulated my brain until I had to force myself not to hide my face in my hands.

It was silly. Especially when divorce was so common these days.

But I felt completely transparent for the world to see. I felt like there was a giant neon sign following me around, blinking an arrow at my back and declaring, "This one's getting a divorce! She couldn't make her marriage work! She's a failure! She's a failure! *She's a failure!*"

God, I needed a drink.

And maybe some therapy. With someone that wasn't Kara.

I stared at the climbing numbers as I moved upward and wondered what the statistic was on divorce driving people crazy. I had never been concerned about my mental health before.

Not until the last few months when it became an epic, life-ending struggle just to get through each day.

Now I felt brittle and breakable. I felt on the verge of losing every ounce of precarious sanity I had left.

The elevator opened on the eleventh floor and I stepped into the reception room. Mr. Cavanaugh waited for me near the door, glancing at his watch impatiently. Taking in his rumpled appearance I suddenly felt very self-conscious. I smoothed my hands over my brown, wide-leg trousers and tugged on my gold sweater.

A groan fell from my lips when I realized we were going to walk into the conference room looking equally ruffled. We were united in our disheveledness.

That didn't bode well for us.

Nick had been nice enough to schedule our mediation after school and I'd come straight here. I spent the entire day avoiding mustard and coffee stains. I had a close call when I snuck a Twix bar in the afternoon, but all in all I came out of school unscathed.

Still, I'd spent the entire day in these clothes. I hardly looked my best. And I hated how that bothered me.

I hated that it wasn't because I wanted to look professional or grown up. I hated that I wanted to look good so Nick could see what he was losing. I wanted him to regret this... to regret losing me.

And I wanted him to recognize the woman he couldn't keep his hands off three weeks ago.

I was sick.

There was something wrong with me.

"Ms. Carter," my lawyer greeted unhappily.

"Mr. Cavanaugh, I hope you haven't been waiting long."

He made a grunting noise I didn't know how to interpret. "They're waiting for us." His wrinkled arm swept toward a hallway. "This way."

I followed him around the corner and found Nick leaning against a doorframe I could see led to the conference room. A rush of nerves washed over my body. It started at the top of my head and deluged my entire being with sharp shivers and a cold sweat.

I shouldn't be here.

No, wait. This was exactly why I was here.

I had to face him.

I had to end this.

My heart clenched at the way his eyebrows scrunched together and the fierce concern in his blue eyes. Oh, god, why had I ever wanted them to come alive again? Why had I ever hoped that he would see me again? I should have wished for his gaze to stay lifeless.

At least around me.

It was too much.

He was too much.

"Are you all right, Ms. Carter?" Mr. Cavanaugh's hand landed with a tentative thump on my shoulder. "Ms. Carter? Kate?"

I blinked my lawyer into focus. "Huh?"

"Are you all right?" he repeated.

Courage, I demanded from my body. *Strength*, I whispered desperately. "Why wouldn't I be?"

His forehead wrinkle tripled with concern. "You stopped walking."

My brave façade crumpled, "I, uh, I... I thought I was ready for this, but..."

He leaned in and I tried not to wrinkle my nose against his pungent cologne. It was enough to wake me from my Nick-induced stupor, however. "He can't take anything from you unless you let him, Ms. Carter. We'll fight every last thing to the bone if we have to."

I let out a shaky breath and nodded my head even though I knew his words were a lie. Nick didn't have to wait for me to relinquish anything. He'd already taken enough.

He'd taken too much.

My happiness. My heart. My soul.

So why did the sight of him like this physically hurt me? Why did I have the almost undeniable compulsion to throw myself into his arms and never let go?

147

Mr. Cavanaugh's hand fell to my elbow where he nudged me forward. It didn't take long before we reached a clipped pace, hurrying toward the conference room as if we couldn't wait to be there.

I sucked in a sharp breath and held it as we passed Nick. Mr. Cavanaugh stepped aside to let me go first and I hoped to slip by Nick without incident.

His hand reached out and grabbed my wrist, "We need to talk," he said in a low, gravelly voice.

I shook my head once, letting him know I would not discuss anything other than our reasons for being here. "That's why we're here, isn't it? We're going to talk about this maturely. We're going to act like grownups."

"Two minutes," he demanded. "I want two minutes." He tugged on his earlobe with his free hand and my tenacity drained out of me. He wasn't playing fair.

It was on the tip of my tongue to agree. He wasn't the only one that wanted to say something about the other night. I needed to make sure he knew it was a one time deal.

I needed him to acknowledge that it was a mistake.

I'd been afraid of that very thing until this moment. Until I stood before him and started to question my own resolve.

"Kate?" my lawyer urged from behind me. "We need to get started."

Nick's sapphire eyes flashed up to glare at my lawyer. "She's paying you by the hour, isn't she? Bill her."

Bill me? Wait a second...

"Charming," Mr. Cavanaugh mumbled.

"Let's just get this over with, Nick. I don't want to be here any more than you do."

He stood up straighter and hit me with his steely gaze. "Yeah, but our reasons could not be more different."

My mouth felt suddenly like sandpaper. God, since when did he start talking in code? Why couldn't this be easy?

Or at least easier?

I walked into the conference room and closed my eyes against the sweet coolness that hit my face. This room was super cooled and even though the November chill had turned biting and ice-filled, I had been overly warm since I walked in this building.

Seriously, I was bordering on pit stains here. All this nervous energy gave me hot flashes straight from hell.

Nick's lawyer was young and attractive. He exuded an energy that made me feel like chum in shark infested waters- meaning, I could tell he was good at his job before he ever opened his mouth.

The conference room matched him. A huge, gleaming table sat in the middle of the room, surrounded by tall, comfortable leather chairs. Floor to ceiling windows took up one entire wall, boasting a beautiful view of the city and the busy traffic down below.

I glanced back at dear, old Mr. Cavanaugh and realized he hadn't given me his first name. I knew it from when I looked it up, but he'd asked me to specifically call him Mr. Cavanaugh.

Nick was without a doubt on a first name basis with his lawyer. They probably went golfing on Saturdays because that was the kind of client services this kid provided. Then Nick would get a bill in the mail for six thousand dollars and an invitation to do it all over again.

I hated the guy before he ever jutted out his hand and introduced himself as Ryan Templeton.

"Kate Carter," I said in return and gracefully extracted my hand.

"Normally I would say it's a pleasure to meet you, Kate, but..."

"It's not," I finished for him.

His smile told me he was used to this response. He waved at a chair for me to take and I did so I wouldn't have to small talk with him anymore.

"I'm just going to grab Marty and tell him we're ready."

Marty Furbish was the man we'd hired to mediate. He came highly recommended from Mr. Cavanaugh and apparently Nick's camp agreed. I hoped he was as nice as his name made him sound. I had a feeling I would need all the help I could get today.

Mr. Cavanaugh sat down next to me and opened his briefcase on the table to pull out the documents we would need. He handed me a legal pad and a pen and told me I could take my own notes if I wished.

I thought that was thoughtful of him. I immediately doodled my name and today's date in the right-hand corner. Teacherly habit.

Nick took the seat directly across from me and I breathed a little easier with the heavy, wide table between us. Ryan ushered Marty Furbish into the room, showed him to his seat at the head of the table, then took his seat next to Nick.

We were officially ready to begin.

The beginning of the proceedings was beyond tedious. There was a lot of legalese spoken and a long retelling of everything I already knew. I was the plaintiff, filing for divorce, or dissolution of marriage. Nick had decided to be a jackass and make every single thing as difficult as he could so forth and so on.

Ryan slid me an itemized list of all of the material possessions Nick considered his. "Among the items we have listed here, which my client claims are his," I began to peruse them slowly, ticking off everything with begrudging approval, "my client would also like full ownership of the house. Ms. Carter may willingly give up her portion or sell fifty percent of the appraised-"

"What?" My murderous glare found Nick's and if looks could kill, I wouldn't need to file for divorce, I'd be able to collect his life insurance.

Neither his stare nor his voice wavered. "I want the house, Katie."

"But you can't afford the house!"

"I can."

"You can't."

"I can."

"You forget that I know what you make, Nick. You can't afford it! Besides, you already agreed to give it to me!"

Mr. Cavanaugh tried to settle me down. "Ms. Carter, if you would-"

Nick spoke over him, "You have no idea how much I make, Kate. You don't even know where I work."

Ryan spoke over both of them, "If you look at this, I think you'll see that my client is perfectly capable of paying for the cost of the house and any costs related to it."

I looked at the next piece of paper that Ryan passed over. I rubbed at the numbers and figures laid out before me. I couldn't make sense of them. I stared at them senselessly, hating that I felt close to tears again... hating that I felt stupid and unintelligent because I couldn't comprehend them.

The room was silent as I absorbed Nick's new salary.

Finally, with a gentleness I didn't deserve, he explained. "I got a new job."

"I can see that." Hating that I snapped at him when he had been nice to me, I lifted my eyes and met his. "Where?"

"A record label."

"A record label?"

"Thrash and Sway," he continued softly. "They're kind of an up and coming-"

"I know who they are." And I did. I'd been married to Nick long enough to have an idea of who was who in the music industry in Chicago. Thrash and Sway Productions had been a dream for Nick. They produced the kind of music he played, they catered to the indie scene and they had a promising future. "So you work there?"

His smile was a little self-deprecating when he said, "I started as an intern. I fetched a lot of coffee. I mean a *lot* of coffee. I was promoted to an assistant shortly after I started and it was an actual paid position. I thought I would stay there for a while, but, recently I've been working with Mike Stanson; he's a producer and director and he does some other stuff... *anyway*, they promoted me to a scout position recently."

"It's a dream job for you." My words were nothing but a whisper. I couldn't breathe through the thickness in my throat, the tears welling up inside me threatening to flood this room. Maybe the whole office building.

I felt betrayed. I felt tricked. I felt... stepped on.

No, *trampled* on.

This was what I wanted for him. This was what I wanted for years for him. I had never wanted him to walk away from music completely. I just... I didn't want the late nights. The weekends that were wrapped up in shitty gigs that paid nothing. I was tired of the girls throwing themselves at him and the stench of smoke and booze. I was tired of the look on his face when he would come home... the one that said he knew better.

The one that cut me so deep I thought I would bleed out right there on the floor of our bedroom.

"It is," his voice was equally quiet.

My vision blurred as the tears pushed to the surface. I blinked rapidly, desperately trying to keep them at bay.

"Kate," he whispered. "I didn't do this to hurt you."

"But you did anyway."

"Can we continue?" Ryan's smooth voice penetrated the stifled air and I jerked in my seat.

I'd forgotten there were other people in the room. I swiped my cheek with the back of my hand and struggled to compose myself.

"Let's come back to the house," Nick suggested. "Give her some time to think about it."

"There's nothing to think about." My voice trembled, but there was steel behind it. Grit. I would not back down.

That was my house.

That was the only beautiful thing I would get to walk away with after this.

"Right, we'll come back to it," Ryan mumbled sardonically. "Next up, joint-custody." He slid more papers toward me.

"Joint custody of *what*?" I blinked at more papers that I didn't understand.

Ryan didn't seem as confused. "Of the child."

"*What child*?" My anger and hurt quickly swirled into out of control confusion. Honestly, what the hell was he talking about? Was it possible that Nick was also married to someone else? And they were also going through a divorce? And they'd had a child?

And that divorce had somehow gotten mixed up with my divorce???

Because that was the *only* explanation that would make sense here.

"The child you might potentially be pregnant with," Ryan explained concisely.

"The child... *What?!*" I slid forward in my chair, nearly falling out of it.

I felt Ryan's hard stare on me, but I couldn't see anything. His voice was harder when he asked, "Did you or did you not recently have sexual relations with my client? As recently as twenty days ago?"

"I... I... I..."

Ryan wasn't finished. "And did you or did you not forego the use of a contraceptive or take preventative measures?"

I slammed my eyes shut and rubbed my forehead with the heel of my palm. Oh, my god. This could not be happening. *This could not be happening*.

Keeping my eyes tightly closed because I could not look at any of these men right now, I started stuttering, "I mean, I guess..." That night flashed in my mind. Nick's body against mine. His naked body against my equally naked one. A flush suffused my body, boiling with its intensity. I felt every inch of my skin turn bright red. Nick's mouth on mine. His hands all over me, giving me what I wanted... what I needed. Nick inside me, making me his again... proving that I had never been anything but his. "Oh, god," I gasped and opened my eyes to escape the vivid images that were doing nothing to soften my blush. I found Nick immediately, a smug expression on his face and a wicked little smirk playing on his lips. That cocky bastard! "No, I'm not pregnant!" I practically shouted my verdict. Mr. Cavanaugh jerked next to me. I'd surprised him.

"Did you take any measures to prevent pregnancy?" Ryan asked steadily.

"No," I hissed. We hadn't taken measures to prevent pregnancy in over two years.

"So you can't be certain," Ryan concluded.

My eyes snapped up and I leveled him with my glare. "I *can* be certain. We didn't need to prevent pregnancy because I can't get pregnant."

Ryan raised one of his eyebrows and I knew this question was prompted by Nick. I mean, I couldn't prove that it was, but if I had to bet my life, I would say it came straight from him. "Is that a medical absolute?"

Losing my temper completely, I shoved back in my chair and jumped to standing, "It's a we-tried-for-more-than-two-years-to-conceive-and-never-did absolute! Yeah, it's a goddamn absolute. I'm not pregnant!" I was so angry my body started shaking. I ground my teeth together so forcefully I was convinced I was going to crack every last one of them. I turned my attention to Nick. "How dare you." He opened his mouth as if he wanted to respond, but I hit him with another, "How *dare* you."

He pushed to standing too, meeting me eye-to-eye. He leaned forward menacingly and rested both hands on the table. Marty Furbish, who had done absolute jackshit stood too, trying to pacify both of us by pumping his hands. I ignored him. I ignored everyone in the room but my very-soon-to-be ex-husband.

In a growling voice that packed quite the punch, Nick argued, "The truth is, Katie, we *didn't* use protection. And I'm not going to piss away rights to *my* child by ignoring the very real possibility that you are pregnant."

I leaned forward too, feeling as though I were about to spit venom. "Fine, Nick. If you want to believe I might be pregnant, then good for you. But other than humiliating me, I'm not sure why you felt the need to bring it up now before we could possibly know one way or the other! I would *never* keep a child from you! I would never take away your rights as a parent!"

Nick stared at me, his eyes piercing deeper than I thought possible. He raised one mocking eyebrow at me and issued a challenge. He didn't trust me. He didn't trust me to give him permission to see our child. If we had one.

Which we wouldn't.

It was impossible.

My hands landed on my stomach and I had to fight with everything I had left not to crumble in front of these people. They had no idea what this fight meant to me, how deep it cut.

They saw two people acting crazy, but they couldn't possibly understand how hurtful Nick's accusations were.

I wanted nothing more than a baby. I wanted nothing but for my nights to be interrupted by feedings and my arms to be filled with the likeness of

Nick or me. I ached with the need. My bones hurt and my spirit shattered with the frustration and disappointment of not being able to conceive.

This was the lowest he could go.

This was the very bottom.

I stood up straighter and sniffled. "We're finished." I started gathering up my papers. "I'm done for tonight. We'll have to reschedule."

Ryan tried to argue, "But we're not-"

Mr. Cavanaugh leaped to my defense. "That's an excellent idea, Ms. Carter." He turned his attention to Ryan. "We'll be in touch when we want to reschedule."

Ryan glanced wildly at Nick. "It's fine," Nick nodded. "This was a lot for one day."

My chin trembled with the effort to hold back my tears. I swallowed thickly and brushed at the corner of my eye.

I took a step back, the high back leather chair rolling smoothly out of my way.

"There's one last request that we didn't discuss," Ryan's cold voice caught me before I could leave the room. "I think it's in your best interest if we bring it up now. That way you'll have time to digest his demand."

My words tasted like sand and dirt, "What is it?"

"The dog, Ms. Carter," Ryan answered coolly. "My client would like ownership of the dog."

I saw red. My vision literally blanketed in crimson red and I thought for a second I would fly over the table and choke the life out of Nick. I couldn't even see his face when I responded. I couldn't see anything except red and violence and pure, unadulterated fury.

"Fuck you." And with that graceful, classy reply, I fled the conference room, the office building and if I had had anywhere to go outside of Chicago, I would have fled the state too.

Instead, I went back to my house and crawled into bed without changing clothes or even taking my coat off. Annie jumped up on the bed with me and with sweetness only she could show, licked my nose and laid her little head on my hand. That was when I finally lost it. Completely.

I held her close to my chest for as long as she would let me and cried, no, *sobbed* until the sun came up.

God, I hated divorce.

Chapter Fifteen

22. It's **too late** for us.

"Am I late?" Kara tossed her coat on the empty chair between us and
threw her purse down. Her pale cheeks were rosy from the blustery wind
outside and her hair was wild from the short walk to the coffee shop.

Starbucks. Not Eli's alternate reality coffee purgatory.

"No, I'm early." I smiled at her, but my face felt oddly stretched and
uncomfortable.

The barista at the end of the counter called her name and she left me
for a moment to pick up her giant macchiato. She sat back down a minute
later and held up her hand for me to stay quiet while she took the first sip
of her drink.

This time when I smiled it was small but natural.

"You look like hell," she murmured after she'd gotten her fix.

"I feel like hell."

"How was Thanksgiving?"

I thought back to the day spent at my parents' house. Josh and Emily
hadn't been there. They'd traveled to Emily's parents' in Minnesota for
the week. It had been an awkward six hours. My dad had spent the entire
day watching football and my mom had spent it trying to overfeed me and
grill me about Nick.

The turkey took two hours longer than it was supposed to and my pie
didn't turn out- a fact my mother couldn't help but point out. More than
once.

"Awful," I finally told Kara. "How was yours?"

"Equally awful. Next year let's have our own celebration. We'll start
new traditions, drink wine all day long and wear sweatpants."

I perked up a little bit. "That sounds amazing. We're adults after all.
We should be able to spend the day how we want."

She sat up straighter too. "Just because we don't have families of our own, doesn't mean we should be relegated to suffering with our parents for every holiday. Why not come up with our own thing?"

My rising spirits took a sharp plunge and I thought I would be sick. I didn't want to make this about me. I didn't want to spend our entire Black Friday psychoanalyzing my depression. But I couldn't form words.

I couldn't make anything come out of my mouth.

Kara noticed my change of mood immediately. "I'm sorry," she whispered. "I wasn't trying to insult you."

"You didn't," I rushed to assure her. "It's just... I used to have a family, you know? It wasn't much of one, but it was mine. And now... now I don't. It's just weird. It's, uh, surreal. I'm not sure that I've entirely grasped the concept of being alone again."

"Oh, babe," Kara sighed. "You don't have to grasp it yet. And I swear I wasn't trying to rub it in your face. I just wasn't thinking."

"I know. God, I'm sorry. I hate that I'm so self-absorbed. I feel like you're so sick of me, but I just can't seem to stop. I thought it would get easier... instead, it just seems to get harder and harder."

"I'm not sick of you," Kara assured me. She pushed her wild red hair out of her face and leaned toward me. "I actually understand more than you know."

"What do you mean?"

"I've never told you this before because, well, honestly, I haven't really told anyone in a very long time... It's hard for me to talk about. *Really hard*. I shouldn't have kept it from you. It's just... I couldn't make myself say the words." I watched her intently; afraid that any change in my expression would spook her. I had no idea what she was going to say, but I felt the heavy importance of it. Finally, after a long pause in which she seemed to need to pull herself together, she said quietly, "I, uh, I was married before."

"Wait, *what*?" I slid forward in my seat until I perched on the very edge. Kara had never even alluded to a previous marriage before. I knew she had some serious hang-ups with men, but I *never* could have imagined that they possibly stemmed from marriage! I took in a shuddering breath and had the worst feeling that I didn't really know my best friend, that she was just as much of a mystery as the rest of the world.

"Don't look at me like that," she growled. "It's not that I didn't trust you or wanted to keep it a secret, it's just that... well, it's embarrassing! I try not to ever think about it, let alone actually talk about it. Besides, it was a long time ago and has nothing to do with who I am today."

"It has something to do with who you are today," I argued.

Her expression crumpled and I realized all of her bravado had been exactly that... just a show of bravery to hide her past wounds... her past agony.

"You're right," she sighed. "It does. But I'm serious when I say it was a long time ago. I'm a different person today. I moved on with my life. Really, I built a new life for myself. I just, I just wanted to let you know that I really do understand what you're going through. And I also know that it gets better... that it won't always hurt like this."

"What happened? Tell me, please?"

She rolled her eyes at my soft tone but wiggled in a way that let me know she was gearing herself up for a conversation she didn't want to have, but would have for me. "You know I have a... precarious relationship with my parents?" She lifted her eyebrows waiting for my acknowledgment. I nodded once and she continued, "They've always been overbearing, completely impossible. Ever since I can remember, they've always wanted to... control me. It's always been difficult to live with their expectations, but especially during high school, and even more so when it came to my future and how I would live it out. They had a certain set of demands they wanted me to meet and I just wanted to, I don't know, be a kid... be free. I just wanted to live out from under their thumb."

She paused for a moment, seeming lost in the past. I reached out and squeezed her hand. It was a gentle move of sympathy on my part, but she jerked at the contact, jerked awake from whatever memories had momentarily imprisoned her.

"Naturally," she continued, "I jumped at the first opportunity to get away from them. That opportunity came in the form of Marcus Henry, my high school sweetheart. We were so in love. Seriously, Kate, you wouldn't have even recognized me. I was out of control. The world revolved around Marcus. The sun rose and set with him. And when he wanted to get married straight out of high school I didn't even think twice. I saw an opportunity to get away from my parents and bonus, I would be married to the man of my dreams."

"You got married at eighteen? I thought I married young! Holy shit, Kara!"

She dropped her face into her hand, "I know," she groaned. "It's embarrassing. I have no idea what I was thinking. And looking back now I realize how stupid I was. I wasn't in love, I was infatuated. And there just wasn't enough substance between us for anything to last."

"What happened?"

"Well, we got married without my parent's knowledge. We just snuck off to the courthouse and called it good. I didn't even change my name. I didn't know I had to! I thought it would be like an automatic thing."

I smiled at the eighteen-year-old version of my friend.

"Anyway, my parents were furious, as you can imagine. No, they were beyond furious. I have never in my life seen them so outraged. They cut me off completely, and for the first time in my life, I was introduced to the real world. Marcus was equally furious. Apparently his young and in love plan included living off my parents' wealth. His parents were a little more forgiving, and let us move into their basement, but they couldn't help us beyond that. All of our plans for college were abandoned as we went to work full-time at crap paying jobs and tried to navigate our lives as newlyweds. My parents are crazy, don't get me wrong. But I had a promising future, even if it wasn't the one I would have chosen. I was suddenly faced with a life I didn't want and a boy I didn't love... I wasn't even sure I liked him anymore.

"It took exactly eighteen months for us to decide that neither of us was willing to fight for happiness in a miserable marriage that was headed nowhere. And then... then he started cheating on me. He didn't even try to hide it. I think he wanted me to know or find out. I think he wanted out but didn't want to be the one responsible for ending it. Not that he didn't play his part. But he was like that. He never took responsibility for his mistakes. He couldn't keep a job for the same reason. I put up with the cheating longer than I should have. I don't know why. I knew my life had sunk about as low as it could go, but I was afraid of what else could happen if I left him. At least with Marcus I had a roof over my head."

My heart broke for my friend. I wanted to give her a hug, but I could sense that she did not want to be touched right now. Her back was stiff and her shoulders painfully held back. She was just barely holding herself together. If I did anything to spook her, she would lose it. "What did you do?" I asked carefully.

"The one thing I swore I would never do." She gave me a sad, defeated smile. "I went back to my parents. I begged them for their forgiveness and for their help."

"They gave it to you," I concluded. She spoke to them now and it seemed very much against her will.

"They did," she confirmed. "They helped me with the divorce, or I should say, *annulment*. They let me move back in with them. In fact, after I went to them I never saw Marcus again, except for the last time in court. They took care of removing my things from his house and all of the documents that needed to be signed or whatever. They saved me. And then they paid my way through school. They helped me move on with my life as if I never left them."

Sensing that their help cost her deeply, I whispered, "I'm so sorry."

She waved off my apology as if it wasn't necessary. "I got my way in the end, though. They thought they were giving me a practice with my degree, something they could brag to their country club friends about and recommend to all of the miserable trophy wives they know. They never saw the whole guidance counselor at an inner-city school thing coming. It still pisses them off."

We shared a victorious smile. "I wondered why you were so much older than me."

She stuck her tongue out. "Only three years. It's not like I have tenure."

"Thank you for telling me that."

She shrugged self-consciously, "I just wanted you to know that I mean it when I say it gets better. It hurts. God, it hurts. But it doesn't always."

"I need to hear that. Keep telling me. Don't stop."

She gave me a sad smile. "It's kind of nice, though."

All of my breath whooshed out of me and I thought for a second I would start choking. "What?"

"Nick. At least he's putting up a fight for you. Marcus didn't. Or at least I never heard about it if he did, but I'm almost one-hundred percent positive he just signed whatever papers my parents shoved in front of him and never thought about me again. We weren't right for each other, don't get me wrong. And what we did was so completely stupid. But looking back... I don't know... it would have been nice if he fought for me. It would have somehow soothed my ego after all of this time. I wouldn't feel so... discarded."

A million of my own thoughts tumbled around in my head, but I put them aside for now and said, "You're not discarded, Kara. He was an idiot. You guys were so young. *He* was too young and immature to realize how amazing he had it."

She tilted her head to stare out the window. "I haven't been able to look him up since. Not once. I know he's on Facebook because I see our mutual high school friends comment on his posts sometimes, but I'm too afraid of what I'll find. I know what I *want* to find. I want him to be alone and miserable and working a dead end job or still living in his parents' basement." Her pretty lips turned down in a frown. "But I'm too afraid that he'll be happily married with a yoga instructor for a wife and six perfect kids that model for Gap."

I let out a surprised laugh, "He's not married to a yoga instructor and if he has six kids then they're all from different moms."

She wrinkled her nose, "I like that."

"You're a catch, babe. Any guy would be lucky to have you."

Her gaze found mine again and her gray eyes sparkled like silver from unshed tears. "You too, Kate. Whatever happened with Nick does not define you. There's a better relationship out there. You'll find it."

"Maybe," I whispered. But what I really thought was *no*. There wasn't a better relationship out there. I'd been given a good one... a *great* one and I'd mismanaged it. I'd poisoned it.

I'd destroyed it.

I didn't deserve a better relationship after how I'd treated this one.

"Well, if it isn't the shrieking harpy effectively destroying my brother's life."

The harsh, guttural tone came from above me. Feeling the coffee I'd just finished swirl and churn in my belly, I slowly lifted my eyes to stare up at the very last person on earth I wanted to see.

Jared Carter. Nick's little brother.

"Hi, Jared," I smiled patiently, despite the rotten feeling inside me, despite the urge to run screaming from the coffee shop, waving my arms over my head like a lunatic.

Jared looked so much like Nick; it actually hurt to see him here. Although, where Nick's muscles had always been lean and lithe, Jared's were bulky and compacted. Nick had run college track, Jared had played football at a division two school, where he hit people so his teammates could score points. They had the same light brown hair, though, highlighted by streaks of the sun. Jared's eyes were a darker blue than Nick's too. Nick's eyes looked like blue flames and Jared's were so dark that you had to lean close just to be sure they really were blue. Jared was also younger by five years. Nick's body had filled out with manhood. Jared's, just like his attitude, was still working on it.

"Kate, wish I could say that it's nice to see you," he sneered.

"No, you don't."

His mouth spread in a cruel grin, "You're right. No, I don't."

"You know my friend, Kara." I tilted my head in her direction.

160

Jared nodded once, "Kara."

She clicked her manicured nails on the wooden tabletop. "Jared."

"Do you know what I'm doing here, Kate? Why I would choose this particular Starbucks in the middle of my busy Friday?"

"Because you don't have a job?" I leaned forward, uncharacteristically mean-spirited. "Or a life?"

His grin disappeared. "I'm picking up a coffee for my brother. He had to work today. They're letting him work on production. They like him there. They think he's a *natural*."

I struggled to swallow against my closing throat. "That's very thoughtful of you."

He loomed over us, not moving even after the barista called his name.

I let out a frustrated sigh. He was ruining my afternoon. "What do you want, Jared?"

His jaw flexed, just like Nick's would have. I licked my dry lips and tried not to slam my hands down on the table and demand that he leave.

"He's miserable," Jared finally ground out. "He… He's not over you."

My heart pounded against my chest cavity once, painfully, then stopped beating altogether. "I'm not over him either," I finally admitted. "That's not what this is about."

"You don't know what you're doing," Jared persisted.

Kara let out a sound of pure irritation and I snapped, "I know exactly what I'm doing. And Jared, so does he. I don't know what he told you, but he wanted this too. We came to this decision together."

"Then why is he doing everything in his power to stop it?"

My eyebrows shot to my hairline. "Is *that* what he's doing? He's trying to win me back by taking everything from me?"

"You wouldn't understand," he muttered.

"But isn't that the point? If he's trying to get me back, shouldn't I understand what he's doing? So far he's done nothing but make this more miserable than it needs to be and hurt me beyond repair. If Nick didn't want the divorce, he wouldn't have gotten the lawyer he did or write the list of demands that he did! If Nick didn't want the divorce, he would never have moved out of our house!"

Jared's upper lip curled back with distaste. "That shows you exactly how little you know him." I opened my mouth to launch into another argument, but before I could say anything he added, "And it shows how very little you realize the damage you've done."

He turned around and stalked out of the building, forgetting his coffee on the counter. I watched him go, wondering if I should chase after him with the abandoned cups or if I should leave before he came back in for them. In the end, I just sat there and he never came back.

The confused barista eventually threw the coffee away.

"God, he's an asshole," Kara declared.

"Such an asshole."

"How dare he!" she continued, then launched into a rant about his stupidity and how he had never done anything with his life and never would.

I only half-listened though. I couldn't get his words out of my head or write him off so completely.

It shows how little you know him.

It shows how very little you realize the damage you've done.

I told my students all the time that if they wanted to do anything with their lives, they had to take responsibility for their actions. That was why I chose the classics I did. *The Scarlet Letter… Romeo and Juliet… Ethan Frome.*

I practically preached responsibility.

And yet I had done nothing but blame and blame and blame Nick for destroying our marriage… for making our divorce as awful as possible.

I let him take all of the blame without ever owning up to my end.

Kara and I finished our coffee and then headed off to do some minor Black Friday shopping. But I never got over Jared's accusation.

And I couldn't shake off the bitter feeling that he was right.

Chapter Sixteen

23. He **doesn't think** things through.

Can we meet for dinner?
I want to talk.
Please, Kate. Just hear me out.

I slid my cell phone back and forth in my palm and looked at my last hour class. I had the strongest desire to ask their opinion on Nick's out of the blue invitation. Sure, they were freshman... young... immature... pimpled. But maybe if I explained the situation to them they would have some kind of genius insight and give me the advice I had been searching for.

Or maybe I had accidentally started taking LSD and I could no longer separate my hallucinations from reality.

Was that possible?

I looked down at my pink thermos.

Maybe these little bastards were slipping it to me when I wasn't looking.

"Mrs. Carter!" a gangly kid named Gabe shouted from the back of the classroom. I was so startled by his outburst that all I could do was look at him. He took that as permission to continue. "Do you want us to answer all of these questions? Or just the ones we know?"

I blinked at him. "This is a test."

"Yeah, but I didn't know if you wanted us to guess or not." He rubbed his nose with his palm and I could hear the slick slurping of snot from here.

"You're not supposed to have to guess, Gabe. You were supposed to study last night so that you would know all of the answers today." And honestly, had he never taken a test before? Did he really *not* understand the concept?

He canted his head to the side and looked as confused as ever. "So you *do* want us to guess?"

Some of his classmates snickered at his bewilderment and I shushed them. "Yes, Gabe. Answer all of them. You might even get some right."

"I'm not going to get them right," he mumbled.

I pressed my lips together to keep from commenting further. I squeezed my phone between my hands and decided it would be a very, very bad idea to ask these kids.

They couldn't possibly understand Nick's intentions any more than they could the *Canterbury Tales*. And that wasn't saying very much.

I held my phone under my desk and discreetly typed, *Where?*

If he said Starla's I would use this in court against him.

His response was immediate. *The Purple Pig.*

Ooh, fancy. I taunted.

My treat.

I hesitated for another minute. I lifted my eyes and watched the class for a few minutes, making sure they knew I would catch them if they tried to cheat.

Finally, when I was sure everyone was doing what they were supposed to, I turned back to my phone and typed, *I'll have to go home and change first.*

Two minutes ticked by before he responded. My heartbeat tripled in my chest and I wasn't sure of what to make of my nerves. I didn't know why my palms were suddenly sweaty or my legs so restless.

When his next text came, it was completely unexpected. *I could pick you up.* Followed by another one directly after it, *If you wanted.*

When I took a breath, it trembled in my lungs. *I can drive*, I told him quickly. *What time?*

7.

I stared at his simple reply and worried that I let him down. Then I worried about why I was so worried I let him down. Then I wanted to crawl under my desk and hide for the rest of the night.

The bell rang, followed by a collective groan from the struggling freshman still working on their test. I tried not to smile wickedly. If they had trouble with this one, just wait until I gave them the final.

Muahahaha.

Although, maybe I should incorporate some more in class review before I let them crash and burn in a couple weeks. Clearly they weren't going to take the lead and study on their own.

God, forbid they show a little initiative.

I collected their papers as they left the room and listened to their excuses and complaints with the patience of Gandhi.

I glanced at the clock in the room and calculated traffic, a shower and some time to down a bottle of wine. Maybe two. I needed to get moving if I was going to be on time for Nick.

Did I care if I was on time?

I decided not to answer that question.

I closed up my classroom in record time, threw the tests in my bag as I locked the door and skipped checking my mailbox. Whatever was in there could wait until tomorrow.

I passed Kara in the hall, but she was already involved in a conversation with our principal, Mr. Kellar, a balding middle-age man that was so tall, he made Kara look like a dwarf. But like a hot dwarf.

I waved to both of them, ignored Kara's penetrating curiosity and dove into the freezing December afternoon.

Scraping my windshield and waiting for my dated car to heat up had never been more irritating. But finally, I was on the road to my house.

By the time I pulled into the driveway, I was a jittery bundle of nerves and it had nothing to do with the fact that my heater hadn't gotten remotely warm on the commute.

I kept replaying our text conversation in my head and checking my phone every two minutes. Why had I agreed to dinner with Nick? I wanted to punch him in the face for what happened during mediation.

Or at least run him over with my car.

Wait, was that better or worse than punching him?

He had been so rude to me, so hurtful.

But maybe part of me thought if we could have a civil conversation, I could talk him out of wanting the house. I could reassure him that I wasn't pregnant and maybe that would ease his mind a little bit.

Maybe his unrealistic demands stemmed from a fear of losing a child?

His child.

Our child...

He had nothing to worry about, though. I was definitely *not* pregnant. And when my period had come four days after our failed mediation, I had hated him all over again.

As impossible as I knew it was, Nick's small flicker of concern about a potential child had ignited hope in me.

For those few days, I had wondered if maybe it was a possibility... if maybe my womb wasn't shriveled or wilted.

If maybe motherhood wasn't an unreachable pipe dream.

But then my period had come... stronger and more uncomfortable than ever- like it was on a rampage of righteous vengeance- and it was like fate was playing some kind of sick joke on me.

See? my mind whispered. *You'll never be pregnant. You'll never have a baby of your own.*

You'll never be a mother.

I had been furious with Nick all over again. I had written him a dozen hateful texts that never got sent. I'd even composed an email that vomited every vile thought I could think of.

But in the end I hadn't sent it. Not because I'd changed my mind, but because I didn't want him to feel as awful as I did. Even after everything we'd been through, even after his behavior during mediation, I couldn't deliver that news again.

I couldn't disappoint him again.

I assumed he'd figured it out by now.

I showered and dressed in a simple black wrap dress. It wasn't the nicest thing I owned, but it gave me the illusion of curves and I knew he liked it.

I would be freezing in this weather and I would hate myself for wearing heels when I would have to walk at least a block from the parking garage to the restaurant. But I couldn't *not* look nice tonight.

I didn't know if it was to impress him or punish him.

And I didn't examine my feelings long enough to figure it out.

When I walked into the trendy wine bar, the crush of people surprised me. I wasn't expecting this kind of crowd for a Wednesday night.

I pushed through bodies to find the hostess stand, but Nick caught my attention before I could ask her if he had arrived yet. He sat at the bar in stylish gray jeans and a black sweater that fit him well. His jaw had been trimmed and he'd recently had a haircut. His chestnut hair lay over his forehead just right, a little mussed and perfectly sun-kissed, even though it was the dead of winter.

He was gorgeous.

He was too gorgeous.

The corners of his mouth lifted when our gazes collided and he raised his hand in a small hello. I didn't smile back. Or wave.

I spent every ounce of energy composing myself before I had to speak to him.

When would it stop being such a lightning strike when I saw him? When would it stop feeling like the earth had come to a screeching halt and I had been pushed forward from momentum and propulsion and impetus and all other scientific terms until he became my entire world? Until he became everything I saw and heard and smelled and breathed?

When would this attraction to him die?

God, I was a mess.

He leaned in when I placed my hands on the high-backed bar chair. "Hey," he murmured. "Was parking a pain?"

I licked dry lips. "Parking is always a pain down here."

He shifted nervously and tugged on his damn earlobe. "Do you, uh, want to take a seat? I made a reservation earlier today, but they said it would be a while yet. I can ask them again if you'd rather-"

"This is fine," I interrupted. This was actually better. Sitting at the bar would feel infinitely less intimate than a table against the wall.

I hung my purse on a hook under the bar and slipped my coat off, hanging it on the back of my chair. After I'd climbed up and situated myself, Nick slid me a drink menu.

"What are you drinking?" I asked him while I studied wines.

"Manhattan."

I wrinkled my nose and saw him smile in my peripheral vision. "They have a cab franc," he murmured.

Instantly I perked up. My favorite.

I told that to the bartender who deadpanned, "We only sell that one in the bottle."

"Oh." My eyes fell back to the menu, perusing it for something different.

"We'll take the bottle," Nick announced.

The bartender immediately gave us his back and I swung my head to face my ex-husband.

Soon to be ex-husband.

"Are you trying to get me drunk? Do you think that I'll be easier to deal with after I'm three sheets to the wind?"

He chuckled lightly, "I know you won't be easier to deal with. I've seen you drunk." I glared at him because I didn't want to laugh. Seeing that he wasn't going to get a reaction out of me, he explained, "It's your favorite. Besides, they can cork it for you at the end of dinner and you can take it home with you. It's not a big deal."

Buying the wife you were separated from a bottle of her favorite wine just because it was her favorite wine was, in fact, a very big deal. But I decided not to point that out.

Instead, I nodded once and said, "Thank you."

He leaned in and I caught the tantalizing scent of his cologne and skin. "You're welcome."

The bartender reappeared with my wine. It took him a few minutes to uncork it in front of us and go through the tedious process of letting me taste it before pouring my full glass.

As if I was going to turn it down.

Clearly, he did not know me.

After he finally disappeared again, I examined the food menu.

"You can't stare at your menu the entire night," Nick teased. "This isn't just a free meal. You have to work for your dinner."

He was being nice to me and I had no idea what to do with it. Was he just trying to soften me up so he could get what he wanted? Or was he being genuine?

I set my menu down. "I didn't think it was a free meal."

"I was just teasing you, Kate."

"Oh."

"Do you know what you want?" His tone was less playful.

I hated that I'd chased it away. "I think so."

"Me too."

"Okay, good."

He fidgeted with the corners of his menu for a minute and I suddenly had a hard time swallowing. I could feel him building up to something, feel the energy inside him expand and contract until it pushed at mine... until it invaded every ounce of my space, every inch of my body.

The bartender came back before either of us could speak again and we put in our food order. He had a ridiculous amount of questions for us and by the time he turned around again I had decided that I should voice a formal complaint.

Except he wasn't doing anything more than what he was supposed to. My nerves had put me obnoxiously on edge. I took a shaky sip of my wine and savored the flavor, hoping to find center.

Hoping to find solid ground.

"I'm sorry for what happened during mediation. I didn't... I didn't expect you to take it so hard."

I stared at him, unable to form words for a full minute. Finally, I whispered, "Which part?"

"You have to know that if we had a baby... if you became pregnant, that I would do everything in my power to give that child the very best life."

"I'm not pregnant," I told him quickly. "You don't have anything to worry about."

He flinched. I watched pain fill his blue eyes and his shoulders tense with disappointment.

The wine churned in my stomach and I wanted to sob. Didn't he know what his disappointment with me did to me? Didn't he understand how much my inability to do this one thing right tore at me, shredded my soul to pieces... poisoned my thoughts of the future and turned all of my hopes and dreams to ash?

"I thought you'd be relieved." My voice was such a harsh rasp that I wasn't sure he could even hear it over the din of the restaurant.

He leaned in again, ignoring my comment completely. "I didn't realize how deeply affected you were until mediation. I should have. God, I should have known that it would kill you to even talk about it. But... before we separated you had seemed, I don't know... it was like you'd shut off all of your emotions about a baby. I thought you were... I thought maybe you were..."

"Callous? Heartless?" I lifted an eyebrow. "You thought I didn't care?"

"Yeah," he admitted sadly. "Yeah, I thought you didn't care."

"It started to hurt too much," I admitted. "I didn't... I couldn't keep hoping each month that that would be the one that was different. I couldn't keep waiting for each month to prove me wrong. It would have killed me."

He shook his head, struggling to swallow. "I'm so sorry, Kate. I'm sorry I didn't realize that. I'm sorry I was too blind to see how much you were hurting."

My chest felt pinched, my heart thumped painfully. "It's not something you have to worry about anymore, Nick. Like I said, I'm not pregnant. It's done. You can take it out of your demands."

His fingertips lifted my chin, "Hey, look at me." I obeyed, but he didn't give me much of a choice. His deep blue eyes pierced me, body and soul. I felt captivated... transfixed... imprisoned by the intensity of his expression. "I can't change the past, but I want you to know that I think you'll be a lovely mother. I think you'll be perfect. The *very* best." His voice roughened, deepened. "And one day, I know you'll get to be one. I know it will happen for you."

Tears welled in my eyes and I wanted to run from the room, but I couldn't move. I couldn't do anything but let him look at me and hold me in place with his sincerity. "You can't know that," I whispered.

"I can," he swore. "You're too beautiful a person not to have a child, not to be a mother. It *will* happen, Kate. I know it will."

A lone tear slipped beyond my control and slid down my cheek. He caught it with his thumb and brushed it away.

The bartender reappeared with our meals and I finally tore my eyes from his. I stared down at my elegantly prepared Osso Buco and wondered how I could possibly eat it. No matter how good it was, it would still taste like dust in my mouth. I would still have to fight to keep it down.

"Why did you really ask me here, Nick? Was it really just to apologize for that?"

He pushed his fork around his plate, stabbing his pork shoulder with a savage frustration. When he looked back at me the tenderness in his expression was gone, replaced by something fierce and primal.

"I'm not going to stop, Kate. I need you to know that."

"Stop what?"

He didn't answer specifically. Instead, his voice pitched low and his hand landed on my knee, his fingertips sliding beneath the hem of my dress. "I'm not going to back down."

"About the divorce?" I guessed. "You can't have the house. You can't have Annie."

"I want more than the house and Annie."

His words sent a shiver of fear slithering down my spine. "Why are you doing this?"

His eyes flashed with something dark and familiar. Lust, I thought at first. But then... but then maybe something more too.

"Because I can't stop." He sounded as pained and desperate as I felt. "I can't let this go."

I didn't know if he was talking about me or the divorce. I didn't know if he meant us or our things. But I couldn't speculate.

I couldn't ask him.

I jumped to my feet and he caught the bar stool before I could topple it.

"We shouldn't have done this."

"Don't be a coward now, Kate," he challenged. "Don't back down *now*."

I glared at him, even while my heart felt like it was splitting in two. "I'm leaving."

"Leave." His chin jerked toward the door. "Run if you have to. But this isn't over. I'm not going to stop just because you won't face me."

I shook my head, unable to come up with anything to say. I grabbed my purse and my coat and stumbled through the restaurant, pushing my way to the door.

The icy wind slapped me in the face as soon as I stepped outside, but it wasn't enough to shake off Nick's threats... or the electric heat that still sparked between us.

It was like I was addicted to him. Why couldn't I just move on? Get over him?

Why did I get sucked back into his gravity every single time?

It was finally obvious. This divorce was going to kill me.

I would die before I ever finalized the end of my marriage.

Chapter Seventeen

24. It's me. I'm beyond **damaged**.

Christmas break was within my reach. If I could make it through this day, I'd have three and a half blissful weeks of break.

Granted most of my plans included binge-watching Netflix shows... but the point was I wouldn't have to get out of my pajamas for days.

That was glorious.

Especially because this Chicago winter was unbearable and my pajamas were warm and fleece and heavenly.

Nick used to tease me that I turned into an Eskimo during winter break. He was right. Hamilton was frigid during the winter months. Our school building was painfully out of date and the heaters never worked properly.

Sentenced to look somewhat like a professional every day, I had to shiver through the majority of my classes and wonder if my health insurance covered frostbite.

Christmas break was the one reprieve I got between November and March. I could finally be warm for days on end. My teeth could stop chattering and my toes could regain feeling.

I just had to make it to the end of the day. Tonight I had a date with an entire pot of hot chocolate, cheesy potato soup that I was determined to make from scratch and old Christmas movies.

This was the first time I had something to look forward to in months and it was hard to contain my excitement.

I shuffled papers during my plan period and tried not to doodle on them. It was hard to explain hearts and stars bordering my students' essays. Usually, if I forgot myself and ended up drawing some stupid little doodle, I had to then come up with something positive to say next to it-like I'd meant to put it there.

But these particular essays were exceptionally bad. And I couldn't find the willpower to write "Great point!" or "Way to think outside the box."

These were, without a doubt, inside the box. Inside the cliff-notes-version-absolute-bare-minimum box.

Something slammed against the lockers outside my classroom and I squeaked in surprise. My heart immediately jumped into overdrive with the possibilities of what that sound meant.

No, I cringed. *Not on the last day.*

Please don't make me call the police.

I really didn't want to fill out paperwork today of all days. I just wanted to survive finals, go home and bundle up until only my eyes could be seen. And my fingers when I needed to push buttons on the remote.

Was that really so much to ask?

"I'll kill you, *motherfucker*." Another body or maybe it was the same body slammed into the locker again and I jumped to my feet.

They, whoever they were, sounded serious.

A surge of adrenaline pulsed through me and I fumbled with my locked drawer for a minute. When I finally wrenched it open, I grabbed my phone and left the drawer dangling there. I didn't have time to worry about someone stealing my wallet right now.

Besides, I didn't get paid until Friday. All they would get from me today was one, embarrassingly low credit limit and three hundred dollars in my checking account.

I sprinted into the hall and then slid to a stop. I should have looked first. *Goddamn it, I should have called for help first.*

Andre Gonzalez had Jay Allen pressed against the lockers on my side of the hallway with a knife balanced against his throat. A small bead of blood dripped from a tiny cut in Jay's neck and I swallowed against the panic that crimson dot pulled out of me.

"Wh-what are you doing?" I sounded as afraid as I felt and I hated my weakness.

Two of Andre's gangster friends flanked him. Neither had produced a weapon yet, but I wasn't stupid enough to think they didn't have one. They glared at me with a wildness that sent my stomach plummeting to my toes.

"Go back in your classroom, Ms. C," Andre instructed. "You don't want to get involved in this."

He was not wrong.

Jay pushed against Andre, pulling everyone's attention back to him. "You're dead, *puta*. You should *never* have put your hands on me."

"How-how did you get that past the metal detectors?" I squeezed my cellphone in my hand and wondered where the other teachers were. Where were the other students? Except that this wing of the school was mostly quiet during this period. I glanced up and down the hall, but most of the classrooms were dark.

Andre grinned and it sickened me. There was a calculated maliciousness there that didn't seem right. "Don't worry your pretty little head about that, teach."

"Andre, please let him go. You can't kill him at school. It's almost Christmas break. Can't you kill him during that?"

Andre cocked his head back in surprise. His grin spread and genuine laughter barked out of him. "He'll run. I'll never find him if I let him go now."

"Please don't kill him," I pleaded. Everything inside of me shook. I could barely stay standing. Tears pricked at my eyes and adrenaline surged through me, making everything feel extra bright, extra real.

Andre stood up suddenly and pressed his fingers against the dull side of the knife to close it. He slipped it back into his pocket and shrugged casually. "Ms. Carter, it's just a figure of speech. I wasn't really going to kill him."

I nodded to reassure him, but I didn't believe him. Not in any way. "I know," I whispered.

Andre's scary gaze swung back to Jay, "You'd better get my money."

Jay jerked his chin up, "I'll get it."

Andre took a step toward him again in an attempt to shield me from his next threat, "Better watch your back until it's in my pocket, *culo*."

Jay's jaw clenched dangerously, "I said I would get it."

Andre stepped back again and turned his attention to me. "You'll never find this knife."

I understood what he was saying. I didn't argue. "Okay."

"And you don't have any witnesses. Jay's not going to talk. Are you, Jay?"

Jay didn't say anything, but he didn't have to. I did, though. I needed to reassure Andre I wasn't going to turn him in. "Okay, Andre. I won't say anything either."

"It wouldn't matter if you did or not," Andre grinned. "There isn't anyone to back you up."

I nodded. I couldn't stop nodding. "I get it."

His smile died and he pinned me with a hard look. "Good."

Andre and his thugs walked down the hallway with the kind of swagger that told me they believed they were completely untouchable. They believed they could act like thugs and threaten teachers and hold knives to other people's throats and nothing bad would ever happen to them.

I watched them go and wondered if I would ever see Andre again. Sometimes things like this happened and the offending student never came back. As soon as their autonomy was questioned, they gave up school for good and left for the life they believed was inevitable. A life on the streets.

I couldn't decide if I wanted Andre to come back or not.

On one hand, he was smart. Too freaking smart. He could do something with his life. He could go places. Do things.

On the other hand, he had *threatened* me.

This school.

My legs finally gave out and I slid down the lockers until I was a messy heap on the floor. I felt like bursting into tears, but I held them back. I had to make it through the rest of the day. I couldn't breakdown now.

I'd wait until later... until I was locked safely in my home... until I was away from this place.

Jay slid down next to me and I jumped. I'd forgotten he was here.

He sat a foot away; his legs stretched out and crossed at the ankles. He crossed his arms over his chest too and stared at his shoes thoughtfully.

I didn't know what to say to him. I knew what I wanted to say. I wanted to yell at him for ever getting caught up in something so stupid. I wanted to hit him on the back of the head and ask what the hell he was thinking. I wanted to know why he owed Andre money and how he planned to get out of this mess.

I didn't say anything.

He wouldn't have answered any of my questions. And honestly, I was still trying to recover the ability to form words.

I was a trembling, terrified mess.

"Thanks, Ms. C.," Jay finally said in a low, sincere voice.

I looked up at him, jerking through an especially bad shiver and nodded my head. "Don't ever let that happen near me again."

He looked over at me with big eyes. "I wasn't planning on it."

My fierce conviction was evident when I said, "I mean it, Jay. Next time I'll call the cops before I ever step foot outside my classroom. Don't think I won't."

"You should have done that today!" The look in his dark eyes told me he meant it. "In fact, you should never have come out here! Damn, Ms. C., what were you thinking? Isn't there school policy or some shit? Next time call the police and lock your damn door."

I ignored all of his valid points and growled, "Goddamn, Jay! There better not be a next time."

His lips twitched like he was trying not to laugh and I wanted to smack him again. "There won't be. At least not at school anyway."

"You shouldn't be messed up with this." I dropped my face into my hands so that my words were muffled but still loud enough for him to hear. "You should know better. You're too smart for this shit."

"This shit?" This time I heard him chuckle but I chose to ignore it. "Besides, Ms. C., you have to say that. You're my teacher."

I let my hands fall to my lap, "Maybe I have to say it, but it's also true. You're brilliant, Jay. You could use that brain power for good."

"Not where I'm from."

"So move! Graduate from high school and move away. That neighborhood doesn't define you. This city doesn't define you. That's something you get to decide. That's *your* choice."

His jaw clenched again and I started to worry I was pushing him too hard. "You make it sound so easy."

"Because it is," I promised him. "Talk to Ms. Chase about the opportunities there are for you in school. Talk to her about the ways to pay for it, the financial aid that's available to you. *Especially* you, Jay."

He didn't say anything for a really long time and when he did, it wasn't exactly reassuring, but it was better than nothing. "Maybe."

"That's all I ask," I gave him a shaky smile. "And that you survive this year."

"I can say definitely to that," he grinned back. "What about you, though? You going to be all right?"

I looked down at my trembling hands. "I think so. I need a stiff drink, but I think I'll be okay." I looked up at him quickly. "I mean, coffee. I need a strong cup of coffee."

White teeth gleamed at me in the hallway. "I didn't mean after today. I mean are you going to survive whatever shit you're going through."

My eyes narrowed suspiciously, "How do you know I'm going through shit?"

He made a scoffing sound, "Anyone that sees you can tell you're going through something deep. You're always looking off into space and trying not to cry. You're a mess, Ms. C."

I smiled grimly against his honest assessment. "I'm going through a divorce."

"He beat you?"

"God, no." I started to ask him why he would think that but stopped myself. That abuse was his first guess said something about his home life I was positive he would never share with me. "We just... we don't get along."

"Boo hoo," Jay taunted. "I don't know one married couple that does get along." He bounced his heel on the gritty tile floor. "Come to think of it, though, I don't know many married couples."

"Your parents aren't married?"

"It's just me and my moms. Never met my dad."

I nodded to acknowledge that I'd heard him. When I put my life in perspective with Jay's, he was right. *Boo hoo.* He came from extreme poverty, had never met his dad and seemed awfully quick to recover from having his life threatened.

My problems were small.

Nick and my problems were small.

The bell rang and I stood up to my feet, brushing the back of my pants off. I speared Jay with my most serious glare. "Go talk to Ms. Chase, Jay. Ask about college. Be the one thing in my life that goes right."

He grinned up at me from the floor, looking more like a little boy than a soon-to-be man. "Okay, Carter. It's the least I can do for saving my life."

I turned around and threw over my shoulder, "He wouldn't have killed you on school property."

He didn't respond and that only made me more nervous. I stepped inside my classroom, blinking against the bright fluorescent lights. I raced for my chair so I could sit down again. A few tears slid down my cheeks, but I quickly wiped them away.

Students started to drift into the classroom and I had to hold myself together.

I had to.

Besides, all I had to do was administer a test. I could sit at my desk for the rest of the class and freak out as much as I needed to.

I knew I wouldn't keep this a secret. I would have to go to Kellar with it. But, I also knew that Andre hadn't been lying. We would never find that knife. I also knew that Jay was as likely to turn Andre in as Andre was. Nobody would back up my story.

Kellar would believe me, but there was nothing we could do.

And I wouldn't risk trying to punish Andre with a suspension because I was too afraid of how he would retaliate.

I settled my students down and passed out the final exam. This was my sophomore class and the only class I had this year that I felt confident they'd actually learned something.

As soon as they'd begun I sat back down, unable to support myself on legs made out of jelly. My hands still shook and my stomach felt very near the edge of upheaving itself.

I had wanted to go home earlier.

Now I was desperate for it.

Finally, I couldn't hold still. I picked up my cell that I'd dropped on my desk and stared at it.

I had to tell someone, if not every little detail, just enough so that I felt better. I needed someone to care.

I needed someone to be happy I wasn't bleeding out in the hallway.

I'm alive. After pressing send, I realized that was an odd text to send to someone.

After a minute, Nick texted back. *Was that in question?*

A powerful shiver jolted through me. *It kind of was...*

His response was instantaneous this time. *Do you need me? Tell me where you are.*

I'm okay. I'm at school. It was just scary for a minute.

Kate...

I sniffled back a fresh surge of tears. *Really, I'm okay. I just wanted to tell someone.*

If you need to talk, call me.

My chest flooded with something warm and sweet. *I'm in class. Maybe later tonight.*

I'm here if you need me. It doesn't matter what time.

Thank you.

I took a deep breath and it was steadier, evened out. My hands settled down. My legs stopped shaking. My head cleared and I felt like myself again.

See? I just needed to tell someone.

It didn't matter that the first person I went to was Nick.

It didn't matter that with only a few reassuring texts, he'd soothed me completely.

He had been there for me.

He would be there for me if I needed him later.

I knew that without a doubt.

Which was exactly why I didn't call him.

Chapter Eighteen

25. I just want to be **happy**.

The start of Christmas break was just as glorious as I'd hoped it would be. I was positive I had gained ten pounds on cookie dough alone, but I was warm, I was hopped up on Netflix and hot chocolate and I'd been able to sleep in for three days.

It didn't get much better than that.

Okay, honestly, my life wasn't exactly the picture of happiness and contentment... but I was on my way.

The doorbell rang and I set my Kindle down, pushed off my couch and tugged on the hem of my shirt. I begrudgingly put on real clothes for the first time since break started and I was having issues with not ripping them off.

I opened the door and was swarmed by munchkins. They ran circles around me, grabbing at clothes and body parts and whatever else they could reach. Annie jumped into the mix, torn between protecting me from the savages and trying to force their attention on her.

I knew I should have stayed in yoga pants and Nick's old tees.

"Look at you guys! You got so big! How did that happen?"

The middle munchkin stopped skipping to look up at me and say, "Veg-a-tubs."

I raised a curious eyebrow at my old college roommate, Fiona, and repeated, "Veg-a-tubs?"

She grinned at me, with her classic Fiona grin and said, "Veg-a-tub-les."

I stepped to the side so Fi could usher her gaggle inside with her full hands. She put the baby's car seat on the rug and closed the door behind her. After she'd systematically stripped each child out of their hat, gloves, coat and boots, she turned her attention to her newest one. I was anxious to see the little guy, but right now, he was buried beneath a zipper thing and a mountain of blankets.

"Can he breathe in there?"

She shot me a glare over her shoulder. "Yes. But these freaking winters. I swear we can hardly leave the house because I'm afraid one of my children is going to turn into a popsicle."

"I bet it's Gigi. She looks the most popsicle like." Gigi wrinkled her nose at me until her mom turned her attention back to the baby, then she stuck her tongue out. "Clever little girl." I leaned over and tweaked her nose. Standing back up, I announced to Gigi, the three-year-old and Jack, the six-year-old, "There's Legos on the table and coloring books for those who are interested." When neither of them moved immediately, I had to stoop to more desperate measures, "And snacks." They raced for the kitchen.

Fiona stood up with a gurgling baby in her arms and I felt myself start to glow. "Gimme gimme gimme."

She handed over baby Jonah and I cuddled him against my chest. Babies had the *best* smell. Annie licked my jean-clad leg, distraught that I had something else to snuggle with.

Fiona looked a little lost with nothing to hold or scold. Her eyes moved around my entryway and living room, looking for something new or breakable she should put up, out of her children's reach.

She had always been remarkably beautiful. Her long hair was a soft, supple brown that fell in the kind of glossy waves that belonged in a shampoo commercial. And her eyes were the same rich, coffee-with-cream hue. She'd put on some weight since having her kids, but it looked good on her. It gave her that curvy, pin-up girl figure. She was one of the lucky human beings that could gain weight in all the right places. Like her boobs. I could never gain weight in my boobs. But you'd better be damn sure that was always the first place I lost it. My body hated me.

Satisfied with my preventative measures, she turned back around and asked, "But what are we going to do in five minutes when they've eaten you out of house and home and they're bored with the new toys?"

"Then I have Netflix."

"God, you're good."

I grinned at her. "Anything to spend time with you! Do you want a drink? Or a snack?" I started walking toward the kitchen. "I made cookies!"

"What kind?" She followed after me. "And are they burnt?"

"Chocolate chip. And half of them."

"Give the burned ones to the kids."

I laughed at her. "Won't they notice?"

"As long as they taste sugar, they will literally eat anything. They're like locusts."

I whirled around and pulled her into a hug, gently keeping the baby out of the way. "I've missed you so much."

"I've missed *you*!" We released each other and she took a seat at the table, immediately pulling a few Legos to her so she could fiddle. "But I was hoping you'd put on a bunch of weight. Like at least a hundred pounds. I hate how skinny you are."

Knowing she was just being snarky, I ignored her sassy comment. "Yeah, well, divorce will do that to you."

"I still can't believe you and Nick are getting a divorce! It doesn't seem possible. You guys have always been perfect for each other!"

Her words stung. There was a silent accusation there that I only picked up because I knew her so well. I focused on doling out the cookies. "Obviously not. We fought *all* the time. I couldn't make him happy and he couldn't make me happy. You haven't been around us much in the last couple years, Fi. It's been bad."

She let out a patient sigh and reached for more Legos. "Come on, Kate. You know better than that. You guys weren't perfect for each other because you never fought. You were perfect for each other because you can still love each other even if you're fighting."

"But I'm *so* tired of it. I'm so tired of disagreeing about everything, of always being on the defensive. I'm sick and tired of hating myself."

Her gaze snapped up to catch mine and her eyes glittered with the gravity of the moment. "Then stop."

"That's what I'm trying-"

"No, I don't mean get a divorce so you don't have to deal with him anymore. I mean stop fighting with him. Stop being defensive. Stop disagreeing and disrespecting him."

I tilted my chin stubbornly. "It's not that easy and you know it."

"It is, Kate. Be in control. Be in control of your words and actions. Take control if it doesn't come naturally to you. Do something other than throw away a perfectly good man and a perfectly good marriage because you're tired of going through what every other married couple on the planet goes through."

Her words landed with the subtlety of an atom bomb and I wanted to dive into my cabinets for cover. How dare she. "That's easy for you to say. You have Austin."

Her gaze that had been firm yet gentle narrowed dangerously. "You think we don't fight? Kate, everybody fights. Just wait until you throw a couple kids in the mix."

Her words were like a kick in the gut and I physically recoiled. Annie danced around my legs, sensing trouble.

Fiona pushed to her feet, the chair scraping back against the floor. "Kate, I'm sorry."

I shook my head, desperate to keep the tears at bay.

"I didn't mean that," she whispered. "I didn't mean... Damn."

Gigi and Jack giggled and scolded their mom for using a bad word, but she ignored them. She took a few careful steps toward me. Her empty hands looked emptier than usual and the anguish on her face was clear.

I held Jonah against my chest as if he could rub some baby germs off on me. Maybe if I snuggled with him long enough, held him in my arms long enough, maybe then my body would know what to do.

Maybe my uterus would wake the hell up.

"Kate, please," she pleaded. "I'm sorry."

Fiona and I had known each other for a long time and we'd always been straight with each other. We weren't as close as Kara and I were, but only because we didn't see each other every day. And Kara and I were childless; we could get together almost whenever we wanted. Fiona didn't have that kind of freedom. So even if she didn't know the minutia of my life, she knew all of the big stuff.

She always knew the big stuff.

Like how long Nick and I had been trying to have a baby. She was the first person and only person I told when we started trying. I hadn't been able to hold in my excitement.

I'd thought it would be easy.

Fiona had been with me the whole time. Encouraging me. Crying out of frustration with me. Giving advice and suggesting tricks she'd looked up on the internet. And getting furious when I couldn't stand the failure anymore.

Because that was what it came down to. Failure.

What was wrong with *my* body?

Why could every other woman in the world get pregnant except *me*?

Was this the universe trying to tell me I shouldn't be a mother? That I was somehow unfit?

That I was somehow unworthy?

"God, Kate, don't look like that." Fiona stood at my side, her arms wrapped around my shoulders, her chin pressed to my temple.

She wasn't much taller than me, but at some point I'd bowed my head and tried to curl into myself. I held Jonah against my chest and let the sorrow fill me.

I didn't cry. I couldn't cry over this anymore. I'd spilled too many tears and dealt with too much heartbreak.

It wasn't that I didn't want to cry. It was just that it didn't fix anything. If crying helped my infertility, I would have had hundreds of kids by now.

"It's not fair, Fi," I sniffled.

With the tone that only a mother can carry, she whispered, "Life rarely is." We stood there until Jack needed his mom's help and Gigi got restless.

Eventually, we moved into the living room where the kids could curl up with us and watch a movie. Fiona took Jonah back so she could nurse him. I exchanged a real baby for my fur baby. Annie crawled up on my lap and nudged my hand with her cold, wet nose until I stroked her back and scratched behind her ears.

Gigi eventually fell asleep against my side and Jack wandered back into the kitchen to play Legos again. My friend's kids were amazing. Well behaved and adventurous. They could be handfuls of chaos, but they were sweet and respectful too.

In college, Fiona had been a little wild. Even at the beginning of their marriage, she and Austin had loved to go out and party. But as soon as she found out she was pregnant with Jack, she changed. It was like she found her purpose in life, her meaning.

I watched her grow from sorority girl to super mom overnight and I could not have been prouder.

I wondered if that was the difference. I wanted to be a mom, but I also loved my career. Nothing hurt more than not being able to have a child, but at the same time I couldn't imagine giving up teaching.

I couldn't imagine not going to work every day or making a paycheck.

Was that the difference? Was that why Fiona could get pregnant just by ovulating and I couldn't manage to conceive once, no matter how many books I read or weird oils I rubbed on my stomach or how many times I tilted my hips in the right position and tracked my cycles like an obsessive maniac?

Halloween had been the first time Nick and I had spontaneous sex in over two years. We were slaves to the cycle… to the ovulation.

No wonder Halloween had been so hot.

"I'm sorry I got mad at you," I said quietly.

Fi's sly smile told me she had already forgiven me. "I'm sorry I was so bossy. I should know when to keep my mouth shut by now."

I wrinkled my nose at her. "Babe, if you haven't learned how to keep quiet by now, I doubt it's ever going to happen."

Her laughter stirred Jonah, who was sleeping against her chest. She stared down at him, rocking him gently to coax him back to sleep. "This will happen for you, Kate. I know it will."

My heart dropped to my stomach. "I'm not sure it will." She opened her mouth to protest, but I held up my hand to stop her. "I'm thirty, Fi. And I'm in the middle of a divorce. Who knows when or if I'll ever meet another guy. And let me just be clear that I am not ready to jump into another relationship. My biological clock is ticking. No, not ticking. It's on a countdown timer. One that's attached to a bomb and hidden in the underground parking garage of a mall. The chances of diffusing that thing are slim to none."

"So what you're telling me is you need John McClane."

"Or Jack Bauer."

"Tom Cruise?" When I gave her a funny look, she clarified, "*Mission Impossible* Tom Cruise."

I laughed, "Yes, that's what I need. I need *Mission Impossible* Tom Cruise without the weird religion and couch jumping."

"What does it say about you that you knew who John McClane was but didn't get the Tom Cruise reference?"

"Nick loved the *Die Hard* movies."

"So does Austin."

"It used to be our Christmas movie. Not *It's a Wonderful Life* or *A Christmas Story*. No, we watched *Die Hard*."

She grinned at me. "That's adorable."

"Then he'd quote the movie for weeks. 'Now I have a machine gun, ho ho ho.'" I picked at the seam of my couch. "I've actually missed it this year. I can't make myself watch any of the other stupid movies. I just want Bruce Willis with hair."

In a soft, caring voice, she said, "Maybe you just want Nick."

Now the tears came. I held them back, but I felt them hot and broken against my eyes. "It's too late for us, Fi. I promise it is. I know you're all about rainbows and unicorns, but there is no fixing us. We are beyond broken."

I could tell she wanted to say more, but this time she didn't. She reached out and squeezed my hand and discussion moved to gossiping about everyone we went to school with.

It amazed me how she was able to keep up with everyone. She was like an internet detective.

It was actually kind of scary.

An hour later, Gigi woke up and our quiet afternoon turned to mayhem. Gigi had not woken up happy and Jack was bored with Legos now that his sister was around to bother him. Fiona bundled them all up again and herded them toward the door. We said goodbye and promised to do this again soon.

It wouldn't happen for months, but the promise was enough to keep us optimistic.

"I'll come to you next time," I told her. "That way you don't have to do this again." I waved at the coats, hats, mittens, boots and other little odds and ends that had taken us twenty minutes, even working together.

"Don't you dare," she huffed. "You would be horrified by the mess. Besides, it's good for us to get out of the house. I swear to god, sometimes it feels like I'm a prisoner there."

"Stop," I laughed. "You're so dramatic."

"It must be why we're such good friends. We understand each other."

I gasped, surprised by her dig. "What does that mean?"

She just winked at me. She picked up the baby in his car seat and wobbled. "Geez, this thing is heavy."

"The thing being your baby?"

Her eyes went big and defensive, "Yes! He's huge!"

"Love you, Fi."

"Love you too, K." She kissed my cheek and gave me a quick squeeze. "I'm not giving up on Nick," she whispered. "Or you."

Then she turned around and yelled at her kids to get in the car before they *froze to death*. I didn't have a chance to ask her what she meant by that or why she couldn't just let us go. She disappeared out the door before I could even formulate a sentence.

I watched her go with a swirling sense of dizziness. My hands landed on my abdomen and I couldn't help but feel the fresh, sharp disappointment that nothing had come of my one-night stand with Nick.

I hadn't even thought a child was a possibility until he said something in our mediation. I had stopped letting myself entertain the idea a long time ago.

But I also wondered about my motive for having a baby. What Fiona and Austin had was incredible. They loved each other like nobody I had ever known. They loved having babies too. Their children were born out of love and mutual respect for each other. They were born into a home filled with laughter and affection. They were raised by parents who adored each other.

When Nick and I first started talking about having a baby, it seemed more a way to fix our splintering marriage than anything else. I had thought a child would force him to grow up... to get a real job. And I was ninety percent sure he'd assumed that if I had a child, I would get off his case.

But the longer we tried without results, the more I realized I wanted one. I had this hole inside of me... this baby-sized emptiness. I *wanted* to be a mother. I wanted to see the result that would be an even mixture of Nick and me.

Would he have Nick's eyes?

Would she have my good skin?

I wanted to grow our small household and become something more than just a couple. I wanted to become a family.

I didn't know if Nick had felt the same way at the end. Our efforts became tedious and about as unromantic as possible by the end of it. Sex had been nothing more than a chore... a tiresome activity that we were both disappointed with before we ever began.

And it was really a tragedy. Nick and I had always had amazing sex before we tried to have kids. It was what fueled the first couple years of our marriage. I had been as wrapped up in lust with my husband as I was love.

But that had dwindled, then died completely when it became about charting and ovulating and doing everything just right.

I hadn't realized it until now. Which seemed silly, but maybe I was too caught up in the moment to see the bigger picture.

God, I hated that we'd lost that heat... that spark that made us want to touch each other all the time.

But maybe that wasn't just the infertility?

Maybe all married couples eventually fell out of lust. My parents had. Not that I wanted to think about that, but I couldn't remember the last time they'd touched each other.

Kara and her first husband had. And really fast.

Fiona and Austin hadn't... but they had to be some kind of anomaly. They weren't normal. Sex became boring for most couples. It became a chore whether they had kids, were trying for kids or never had any.

It was just impossible to stay sexually attracted to one person for the rest of your life.

I glanced back at the wall in the entryway.

No, that was wrong. That was a lie. I had never been more attracted to Nick than that night. My skin flushed and heated as I thought about how

188

his body pressed against mine or how his lips felt as he tasted my skin and urged me to give him everything I had. Everything I was.

But it didn't matter anyway because it had been a mistake.

A crazy mistake.

Even though it was impossible to regret it completely. Mostly because I knew I would never have sex like that again.

I would never feel that hot again… like my skin was on fire… like his lips would turn me into unquenchable flames and his touch would incinerate every inch of me.

By the time I'd cleaned up the kitchen, the table filled with Legos and the living room, I had almost convinced myself that our sex life would have become dull and boring no matter what. It wasn't the baby. It was life. It wasn't the frustration of not conceiving. It was marriage and the years passing us by and everything that came between us.

And I had almost convinced myself to stop thinking about Halloween.

Almost.

But not quite.

Chapter Nineteen

26. I **deserve** someone who loves me for me.

When I walked through the door Christmas night, I had never felt lower. Christmas with my parents had been beyond draining. Even though Josh and Emily had been there with the girls, my mom had been in rare form.

It was like she went out of her way to remind me how alone I was. Not that she needed to try very hard. My single status had never been clearer.

On top of Josh and Emily and their undying love for each other, I had been forced to watch my parents dote on each other.

Christmas did that to people. I knew that. Even Nick and I had been able to get along on Christmas. But I always thought my parents survived by never touching each other.

Not this year.

I set my opened presents down on the kitchen table so I could bend over and greet Annie. "I'm sorry I left you alone all day," I cooed to her. "I should have brought you with me." She danced on her cute little paws and licked my palms.

I picked her up, unable to keep from holding her against my hurting heart. A single tear slid from the corner of my eye and I couldn't figure out why I suddenly felt the urge to cry.

My parents usually grated against every one of my nerves, but rarely did they reduce me to tears.

Swiping the back of my hand against the silly show of emotion I didn't understand, I decided that I was just overemotional. This was the first Christmas I had ever spent alone.

I was bound to be upset. And confused. And nostalgic. And heartbroken.

Those were completely normal feelings to have after walking into a dark, empty house with no one to greet me but my dog.

I scratched at Annie's neck and my fingers bumped up against something unfamiliar. I pulled back to find a brand new, pretty pink collar on her. "What is this?" My heart rate picked up, even as I realized it must have been Nick.

She licked at my chin, anxious for me to get back to petting. "Did Nick stop by?" I asked the dog. She just kept licking me. "What else did he get you?"

She didn't answer.

I flicked on more lights. I wasn't afraid of Nick by any means, but knowing someone had been in my house while I was gone still freaked me out. I seriously needed to get his key from him.

I walked into the living room, needing to make sure he locked the front door after he left when I tripped over the new dog bed nestled up next to the couch.

"What in the world?"

Annie dove from my arms for her new bed. She turned in circles as if showing off for me before settling down with a big doggie sigh. Her cute little nose rested on her outstretched front paws and I found myself smiling.

"He spoiled you." There was a big rawhide bone tucked in the corner and a new chew toy under the coffee table. "I suppose you love him more now. I only got you a new brush."

She let out another big sigh and I took that as a yes.

"Well, listen, if his lawyer puts you on the stand, would you please pick me? I can spoil you too."

Her brown puppy eyes lifted to stare at me with an indolent, "Yeah, right."

I stuck my tongue out at her and walked to the front door. "He's not going to get you. Get that thought out of your head right now."

It still made me sick that he would even consider taking Annie from me. She was *my* dog. I was happy that he didn't hate her like I thought he did. But that didn't mean he should win her in our divorce.

And I hated him for trying to.

The door was at least locked. That should have soothed some of my anger, but by the time I reached it, I was really starting to get worked up.

What had started as melancholy remorse quickly turned into outraged fury. How dare he try to take Annie from me! How dare he try to take my house and get partial custody of a kid that didn't even exist!

If he wanted this divorce as much as I did, then why did he have to make it so difficult?

192

Why couldn't he just let me go?

Why couldn't he just walk away and leave me to the embarrassing remnants of my shattered life?

When I turned around and saw Annie happily lounging in the new bed he bought her I saw red. It was even gray to match the living room as if he thought he wasn't just going to win the house, but everything inside the house too!

I pulled out my phone and jabbed my finger at it. He had officially ruined Christmas for me.

Okay, maybe it hadn't been that great to begin with, but this was the last straw. He had pushed me over the edge and he was going to get a piece of my mind.

"Did you find it?" his rough, low voice asked. There was no hello, no merry Christmas, only the slightly nervous question that stripped all the wind from my sails.

"The dog bed?"

"The picture."

"What picture?"

"Were you calling about the dog bed?"

"I was… I was calling… What picture?"

"Where are you?"

"At home."

His low chuckle carried through the phone and I felt my anger begin to disintegrate. "I mean, where are you in the house?"

"Oh." I took a needed breath. "In the living room. By the dog bed."

"Look up."

I did. I looked at the far wall and at the new picture hanging there. It had an ornately golden frame. *Antique*, I thought immediately. The picture wasn't of people, but words. I couldn't read them from here. They were written with curly black letters on a soft gray background.

Even though I didn't know what it said, I could tell that it matched everything perfectly. It looked amazing on the wall. It brought everything together and added a bit of flare.

But why would there be a picture on the wall?

"What is it?" I whispered.

"You should go read it?" His voice pitched lower, trying to disguise his nerves. If I hadn't known him so well, I wouldn't have noticed. But I did know him. I knew him so well.

I didn't move.

"Kate," he whispered as if he could see my feet stuck in place and the way my hands trembled. "Go read it."

I shook my head, but he couldn't see me.

"Please."

It was the broken plea that scratched from his throat that made me finally move. I couldn't say no to that. No matter how much I wanted to. No matter how much I wanted to believe I could move on from this man, I couldn't. Not if he said please like that.

Not if he sounded like he needed me to look at this picture more than he needed to breathe.

I had only turned on the lamp in the living room, so it was still fairly dark as I walked over to the wall. I bumped into the coffee table and clipped my shin because I couldn't be bothered to pay attention to where I was going.

I found it harder and harder to swallow as I made my way to the wall. It took seconds, but I had myself so worked up by the time I reached the picture that I was worried I would pass out.

I propped one knee on a chair and leaned in.

Love that is enough.

Love that is big enough for two.

Love that is endless enough for more.

Love that is just between me and you.

My voice trembled as I asked, "What is it?"

I had heard his breath quiver before he asked, "Do you like it?"

"Nick, *what is it?*"

His sigh told me everything he didn't say. He didn't want to tell me what it was. He didn't want to explain his actions or motives or anything. He just wanted me to like it.

But I couldn't do that. I had to know. I had to know where it came from.

What made him do it?

"Do you remember Jared's old girlfriend? The weird artist one?" I sucked in a sharp breath while he paused. Finally, he admitted, "Last year. I had it made for you last Christmas."

"Why didn't you give it to me?" I closed my eyes to stop the tears that threatened to spill over. Last year he'd gotten me a new Kindle. Mine had stopped turning on and I asked him for one. He'd gotten the exact one I'd picked out.

It had been a great gift. It had been exactly what I wanted.

But this... This was something... else.

194

His laugh was bitter. "Do you remember last Christmas?"

"Yes," I whispered. "No... I mean, I don't know."

"We were not in a good place." His voice was a roughened rasp against the phone. "Jared had asked to borrow money and we argued about it. I had to work Christmas Eve and you were mad and... and I chickened out. I didn't want to upset you again. I didn't want to fight with you on Christmas. It was easier to get you what you wanted."

My heart thumped painfully against my chest. "Why did you think this would upset me?" Even though I knew why he would think that. Even though I knew, I could be mean.

More than mean.

I could be house-falling-on-me-because-I'm-the-wicked-witch-of-the-east kind of mean.

"I was afraid to remind you about... about having a baby. You were so confident it couldn't happen. You still are."

"Nick," I hiccupped. I didn't want to fight with him about this again. "It's..." *Too late*. "Lovely."

"We're a mess, Kate." His voice sounded stronger. It was absolutely silent on his end of the phone, so when he shifted I could tell that he was in bed. I pictured him in athletic shorts and a t-shirt, his long runner's legs stretched out in front of him, his hair tousled from his fingers running through it all day.

"I wish you would have given this to me last Christmas." I licked dry lips and stopped fighting the tears.

His voice was infinitely sad when he whispered, "I do too." There was silence between us for a full minute, but I didn't feel compelled to hang up with him.

Despite the pain of this moment, the poignant sense of loss, I needed to be near him in some way. It was like we were both acknowledging the magnitude of what we'd lost. We were both admitting how things could have been different between us.

When the heavy moment passed, Nick let out a long sigh and asked, "How was your Christmas?"

"Ugh," I sighed. "My mother was extra special today."

I swear I could hear his smile through the phone. "She's usually super special."

"Whatever," I grumbled. "She's like your new best friend. All I ever hear about anymore is how great you are, how I'm the biggest idiot ever for letting you go."

"Well, that's clear to everyone," he teased.

I should have been irritated, but I smiled instead. "At least your ego is still intact."

"You have your mom to thank for that."

I laughed at his sarcasm. "I'm pretty sure your ego was just fine before my mom decided she approved of you."

"It's weird, though." When I didn't immediately agree, he added. "That she suddenly wants to be my friend. I went through years of hell with that woman and now she decides to like me."

"Oh, my god, I've thought the exact same thing!" I plopped down in the chair I'd been kneeling on, unable to look at the picture anymore. "Do you think it's your new job?"

"No," he answered immediately, "she doesn't know about it. Unless you told her."

"Oh." I had, but not until recently. When she invited him over for lunch that one Sunday, she didn't know.

"I'm pretty sure she had a partial lobotomy. That's the only reason I can come up with."

"I don't think you're wrong." I felt myself smile even though I felt as if I were spinning out of control. I forced myself to form words and ask, "How was your Christmas?"

"It was fine," he sighed. "Jared and I went to our parents. We played Super Nintendo all day and ate too much. I felt thirteen again."

I smiled again at the picture. Jared could be an absolute asshole, but I had always appreciated Nick's relationship with him. They were good brothers to each other.

"He told me about when he saw you in Starbucks by the way," Nick added. "He won't talk to you like that again, Kate. I promise you that."

My heart thumped in my chest. I believed him. "Thank you." After another minute of silence, I asked, "How are your parents handling the divorce?"

He coughed suddenly and I could tell he didn't want to answer the question. "Not as well as yours."

"They blame me."

"They blame both of us."

I didn't know what to say after that. I looked back at the art he'd made for me and felt a brand new sense of loss. "Did you write it?"

He knew exactly what I was talking about. "I did."

"For me?"

"It's not the first song I've written for you."

"It's a song?"

196

He didn't say anything for a minute. I wasn't sure he took a breath. There was only silence on his end, so much so that I had to check to make sure he didn't hang up on me.

"It is a song," he finally breathed.

Something I couldn't name buzzed through me and made me breathless. "Have I heard it?"

"Nobody's heard it."

"Sing it." I had to hear it. I had to know. I had to listen to these words he wrote for me a year ago, these words he had been too afraid to share with me while our marriage dissolved.

"Kate…"

"Please," I whispered.

And just like me, he couldn't say no. "I, uh, hold on a sec."

I heard movement on his side of the phone while he moved around his room. The entire time I waited for him, I found myself chanting, *don't hang up don't hang up don't hang up.*

But I didn't know if it was for him or for me.

I sat frozen in place, too afraid to move, too afraid to make a sound in case I frightened him off. When the first plucks of guitar strings reached me, I realized what he had been doing.

"This is going to be rough," he warned. Then, under his breath, he mumbled, "I can't believe I'm doing this."

I pressed my lips together in anticipation. I felt near tears again, but I didn't know why.

When he started singing, my knees went weak and I would have collapsed if I hadn't already been sitting. His voice, so familiar and achingly sweet, wrapped around my skin and sunk into my bones. I closed my eyes and listened to him sing about two people so in love they breathed each other. He sang about the world coming between them and tearing them apart. He sang about their love being wide enough to reach around the entire world and find each other again. He sang about love and loss, hope and sorrow, he sang about a girl that wanted more but a boy that had enough. And then he sang the chorus.

Love that is enough.

Love that is big enough for two.

Love that is endless enough for more.

Love that is just between me and you.

He didn't finish it. He trailed off somewhere in the second verse and claimed he couldn't remember the rest.

"That was beautiful," I whispered. Emotion clogged my throat and silent tears tracked down my tears. "Nick, that was…"

He cleared his throat uncomfortably. I could picture him tugging on his earlobe. "I should have sung it for you last year."

I couldn't respond to that. I had no words. No ability to speak. We sat there silently for another minute. Then suddenly I had to get off the phone with him right then. I couldn't spend another second talking to him.

Besides, what was I doing? We were getting a divorce! Why was I reminiscing with him about a past neither of us could change?

I wanted to throw my phone against the wall in frustration.

I forced polite words out, "Merry Christmas, Nick."

After another beat of silence, he repeated. "Merry Christmas, Kate."

I hung up the phone before I could say another word. I dropped my cell into the chair like it could burn me or turn into acid and eat away my skin. I jumped out of the chair so quickly Annie yelped in surprise.

I stumbled back from the wall and then toward it. I had to do something. I couldn't feel like this anymore. I couldn't even describe what I was feeling. It was just… everywhere. My skin crawled, my blood felt itchy and wrong. My head started pounding with a fresh headache.

God, I was a mess.

I looked at the picture he hung for me and had the strongest urge to tear it off the wall and throw it outside. I had to get rid of it. I had to get it away from me.

Instead of shredding it to pieces, I carefully lifted it from its place and carried it to the hall closet. It was heavier than I'd anticipated it to be. It wasn't very big, but the frame was nice and sturdy.

It wasn't just poster board slapped haphazardly together. Nick had put it together with care… made to last.

Unlike our marriage.

I set it in the hall closet next to the vacuum and closed the door behind it. I let out an agonized breath and let myself feel a little bit better.

There.

I couldn't see it.

It wouldn't haunt me if I couldn't see it.

I looked around at my house and felt loneliness stir inside me. The dark corners seemed to press in on me, eating up the dim light and the happy memories that once belonged here.

Unable to take it or myself for a second longer, I called Annie to my side and dragged my tired body to bed. My mind whirled and whirled while I got ready for bed and hours later while I stared up at the ceiling fan rotating in lazing circles.

Unable to find sleep or peace, I crawled out of bed and braved the chill of night. I crept downstairs like I was a burglar in my own house. I knew no one else was there, but I couldn't help feeling like I was doing something wrong.

Or maybe I was doing something right for the first time in a long time.

I pulled the picture from the closet and with shaking hands and trembling limbs, I rehung it on the wall.

I stepped back and stared at it.

It wasn't a solution, but I felt a little better.

At least when I lay back down in bed, I could finally fall asleep.

Chapter Twenty

27. **Second chances** are a myth.

By the middle of January, school had started back up again and Nick and I had been through our second round of mediation.

We'd gotten nowhere.

Neither of us was willing to give up the house or the dog.

Mr. Cavanaugh had been exhausted by the end of it and Ryan Templeton had been contemplating murder of the first degree in his head. I wasn't sure for whom, but if I had to guess, I would have picked me.

He probably wanted to run me over in his expensive sports car. I bet it was something beyond pretentious.

Poor Marty, the mediator, was beyond exhausted. He had wanted to speak with us both separately. Neither Nick nor I would comply.

It wasn't that I didn't trust Nick. I mostly didn't trust his slimy lawyer.

I had begun to hate Nick's lawyer with the fire of a thousand suns. He wasn't the only one contemplating homicide during mediation.

Every time Nick looked close to breaking, Ryan would whisper something in his ear that would make Nick clench his jaw tight and turn him completely unreasonable.

Ryan Templeton was like the devil on Nick's shoulder, whispering all kinds of evil things.

Nick needed an angel telling him to do good, nice things. Things that ended mediation with giving the dog and the house to me.

Okay, so maybe Ryan wasn't the devil on his shoulder. Maybe I was.

I had tried to look at this rationally or from his point of view. But I couldn't. My pain was too blinding. My need to keep the things I loved and that still loved me was consuming. I couldn't let Nick have any of it.

I didn't mind if he took the TV or the furniture or even my car. But I needed the house.

And I needed the dog.

I wouldn't be able to live without those things.

I shook my head and tried to focus on the day. My second and third-hour classes were trading places. Students pushed through the door and chatted animatedly.

I continued to get ready for class while students took their seats. The second bell finally rang and I was happy to see that the majority of my students were in their places. A few stragglers raced in just as the bell stopped ringing and I waved my hand at their pleading faces.

"Be on time tomorrow," I warned them.

They promised that they would be, even though we both knew they were lying. Tomorrow I would have to write them up. But it was only Monday.

I gave grace on Monday because Monday was the definition of awful.

I glanced around the room and noticed a few empty desks. Two of the kids had been excused from school today for a debate team meet, but one hadn't been shared with me.

"Does anyone know where Andre Gonzalez is?" A chilled silence crept through the room and I immediately looked at Jay Allen. "He's not marked as absent today. Is he skipping?"

I hadn't been out of my classroom yet today. If there was gossip about his whereabouts, I hadn't heard it yet.

My class was silent so I pressed them. "It's better if you tell me." When they continued to stare at me, I felt familiar fear. "Is he hurt? Sick? Did something happen to him?"

"Arrested," someone called from the back of the room. "He got arrested last night."

It wasn't the most surprising news in the world, but it still dealt a painful blow. "Damn," I whispered. I looked up and saw fear reflected in my students' eyes. Fear and resignation. "How old is he?"

It was quiet for a long time before someone said, "Eighteen."

Grief swirled through me and for a moment I thought I would be sick. I hated that he was an adult. I hated that he hadn't been smart enough to get out of trouble on his own. But I hated more that I felt relief that he was off the streets.

And then I felt intense regret.

He had terrified me before Christmas break. And I had never gone to Mr. Kellar with what happened. I had been too afraid that Kellar would expel him.

It had been stupid of me. Dangerous even. But I wanted to give Andre a chance to finish school. I wanted to help him.

But I hadn't. I hadn't helped anything. I'd let him continue his wayward journey and now he'd gotten himself arrested.

My gaze tracked to Jay Allen, who sat with his head down, stabbing his notebook with a short pencil. He didn't look up at me. It was like he knew what I was thinking.

Only I doubted Jay felt the same sense of loss.

It took me several minutes to pull myself together enough to teach. I struggled and stumbled until I found my rhythm. The class never fully engaged with me. They all felt the loss of one of their peers.

Unfortunately, it happened too often in this school. They weren't always arrested. Sometimes they just dropped out.

Sometimes they were killed.

A chill slithered down my spine as I remembered how smart Andre could be... how far he could have gone.

When the bell finally rang, I knew I could have done so much better. Those were not my finest moments as a teacher.

I slumped back in my desk chair and tried to pull myself together for the rest of the day. The next hour was my plan period, so I had a little time, but it still felt like an impossible feat.

Long fingers tapped at the edge of my desk and I lifted my gaze to find Jay standing there with a determined expression on his face.

"Can I help you, Jay?"

"I know you never said anything to Kellar."

His accusation felt strange like he wanted to call me out on it, but there was something more. I lifted my eyebrow, daring him to say whatever it was that he wanted to say.

"Why?" he finally asked. "Why didn't you say anything? He threatened you. He threatened *me*!"

"Are you mad I didn't turn him in because you felt threatened?"

He rolled his eyes at me and rubbed his hand over his shaved head. "Don't be stupid." He cut me a sideways glance that I interpreted as an apology for being rude. "But isn't it your job to say something?"

"Yes," I admitted. "I should have said something. He could have threatened another student. He could have brought another weapon to school. He could have truly hurt someone. I *should* have said something."

"So why didn't you?" His deep brown eyes searched mine intently, flickering back and forth, waiting for the truth.

So I gave it to him. "If I had said something, he would have gotten expelled."

Jay let out a bark of mocking laughter. "So what! He ended up in *jail*, Carter. That's way worse than getting expelled."

I swallowed around the golf ball lodged in my throat. "Yeah, and if he would have gotten expelled? Would that have changed anything?"

Jay snorted, "No, he just would have ended up there sooner."

"Exactly. I wanted him to avoid jail or prison or the lifestyle that he was so bent on having. I wanted him to have a chance at something better. I want the same thing for you and everyone else that comes into this classroom. I gave Andre a second chance and he squandered it. Nobody is more upset about that than me."

"You don't know the kind of neighborhood Gonzalez is from. They don't give college scholarships to kids like him. They get their prison cells nice and ready because they know it's only a matter of time."

I expected Jay to be gloating over Andre's fate, but I only saw an interesting mixture of regret and fear in his expression. Wondering if this was my chance to finally break through to him, I said, "They give scholarships to kids of every kind. It doesn't matter what neighborhood, social class or family you come from. If you try hard enough. If you *work* hard enough, you can find a school that will want to take you."

"So you're saying Andre actually had a chance at college?"

"Andre was brilliant, Jay. So are you. Every student that comes into this school building and shows up day after day has a chance. But we can't make you take it. You have to decide that you want it... that you want to do something bigger than prison or jail or whatever."

He rocked back on his heels while he thought about it.

"College isn't easy, Jay. And maybe it's too late for a scholarship. But there's financial aid. There are options for you. Have you talked to Ms. Chase?" He shook his head. "Talk to her. Please. She can walk you through this better than I can."

"Maybe."

"What are you afraid of?"

His gaze snapped back to mine and it was lethal. "I'm not afraid of anything. You saw me with a fu- with a knife to my throat. Did I look scared then?"

I breathed through the rapid beating of my heart. "Then why won't you try at this?"

"It's not that I don't want to try."

I stood up and placed both hands on my desk, my attempt at looking intimidating. "It is. You have to do something with your life, Jay, or you're going to end up just like Andre."

He stepped back, ready to run. "You don't know me."

"I know that life is hard work. I know that growing up is the hardest thing you'll ever do and if you don't try at something, if you don't make yourself into something, then you won't become anything. What Andre did? That's the easy way out. Getting yourself out of your neighborhood and through college? That's going to be a lot of goddamn work. But it will be *worth it*. I swear to you, it will be worth it. The best things in life come with a price. Work hard for those things. Work so hard that you don't know how to be lazy."

Jay's lips twitched and I held my breath, hoping to God I got through to him. "You swear more than any other teacher I know."

"That's because I'm the coolest teacher you know."

The look on his face told me he didn't believe me. "Is this my second chance, Ms. C?"

I smiled at him. "I knew you were smart."

He looked around us dramatically. "Shh, you'll ruin my street cred."

I rolled my eyes and pulled out a pass pad. "Do you need one of these? Are you late for class?"

"Yeah, but I just got Mr. Bunch and he doesn't give a shit." He started walking backward, out of my classroom. "Unlike you."

"That sounds like an insult."

"It might be. I haven't decided yet."

I laughed, despite myself. "Go to class, Jay."

He gave me a sarcastic salute and disappeared out the doorway.

I sat back down in my chair, completely perplexed.

Kara appeared five minutes later with her lunch in hand and two Diet Cokes. She handed one over to me. "What's with you?" she asked.

"Did you know Andre Gonzalez got arrested last night?"

Her eyes flashed with disappointment. "Yeah. It sounds serious. They caught him in possession, selling to minors."

"Oh, my god."

"He's eighteen," she added.

"I heard that."

We were silent for a minute. "Jay Allen might come find you."

"Which one is that?" I was just about to explain what he looked like when she said, "Oh, I know that kid. He was just in my office last week for harassing a teacher."

"Which teacher?"

"Mr. Bunch."

I nearly smiled, but caught myself. "He's going to come talk to you again I think."

"Mr. Bunch?"

I threw a chip at her. "No, Jay. I'm convincing him to go to college."

Her eyebrows drew down and her shoulders sagged. "Do you think he's serious?"

"I don't know. I hope so."

"Me too." She sat down on the edge of my desk and opened her soda with a long, pink fingernail. "How's the divorce?"

My stomach sank. I had just been contemplating texting him about Jay and Andre. Old habits die hard apparently. They die really hard.

"Uh, we're still at a standstill. Neither one of us will budge."

"When's your next mediation?"

"Not until March. I guess I never realized how long this stuff took." I stared down at my desk, cluttered with papers to grade, papers to hand back, pencils, whiteboard markers and other odds and ends. "Do you think I'm making a mistake?" I asked the mess.

Kara was quiet for a long time and when she finally spoke her voice was gentle and reserved. "Do *you* think you're making a mistake?"

I looked up at her and tried to decide. "It's normal to question something like this, right? At least I would think so. Except that I can't stop questioning it. I can't stop going over my marriage and the night we decided to get a divorce. I can't stop thinking that there was more we could have done." I took a deep breath and tried to figure out what I was really trying to say. "I just got finished telling a student that the best things in life are hard work and that he shouldn't stop trying just because they force him to try harder. He should try harder and harder and harder until he gets what he wants. Isn't the same true for me? For Nick and me?"

Kara frowned at me. "This is why I took so long to tell you about my divorce. I *needed* to leave Marcus. He was an awful person. But you... your circumstances are completely different. Neither one of you are bad people, you just... I don't know, you fell out of love. That happens too. There are all kinds of reasons people get divorced. No reason is right or wrong, just different."

But mine felt wrong. All of my reasons felt wrong.

I kept a running tally of them in my head. I always had. Everything he did wrong, everything I did wrong, everything that we did wrong together

I tallied it up in my mind like the worst kind of scoreboard. And then I'd used that ledger to wage war on him and our divorce. I'd used it to attack him, to show him that we needed to separate and I'd held it over his head ever since.

Did that mean we shouldn't get a divorce, though?

Maybe he wasn't as toxic as I'd made him out to be, but there were still facts. We didn't get along. We couldn't stand each other. We were better off apart.

Right?

I met Kara's concerned gaze and told her, "I'm sorry you went through this. I'm sorry that you were hurt so badly."

She waved it off, "It was a long time ago."

"It still cuts deep."

Her gray eyes flashed with proof that divorce cut deep, so deep and jagged it was like death. The death of something sacred... something holy and set apart. Marriage, no matter how short or long, was bound in vows and promises made from our very souls. Severing that tie was like murdering a part of your body.

I felt that daily. I felt it in a way that I knew would never go away.

Kara could talk cavalierly about how she had to go, but she still went through this. She still grieved. She still let those vows wither and die.

"Thank you," she whispered, blinking brightened eyes. "You're a good friend."

"You're a good friend too."

"And thank god we have each other. We can become spinsters together."

"Can we get a cat?"

"Babe, we'll get cats. Dozens of them. So many that our clothes will be covered in cat hair and we'll have to pick it off our food before we can eat."

"That's disgusting." But I smiled because I really did like that picture. I liked the idea that I would never be completely alone. I could always become a crazy cat lady with Kara and carpool with her to work daily.

My future wasn't as bleak as I once thought it would be.

She sighed. "Okay, I have to get back to work. I think I was supposed to be in a meeting five minutes ago."

"With who?"

"Kellar and that kid that flooded the boy's locker room."

I snorted a laugh. "Good luck with that."

"I don't need luck," she mumbled on her way out the door. "I need someone else to flood a locker room so I don't have to go."

I watched her leave and waited another minute before I pulled my phone from my purse. I opened my text messages with every intention to text Nick. I had to tell him...

Something.

I didn't know what, I just... what? I needed to hear from him?

But why?

My fingers hovered over the screen. I didn't have anything to say to him. I was supposed to be furious with him for causing so much trouble during mediation. I should have wanted nothing to do with him.

And yet I couldn't stop myself. It was like my body was possessed by the ghost of Christmas past.

Or a demon.

A demon that couldn't get over her ex-husband.

Cheese and rice, there was something wrong with me.

I tossed my phone on the desk and crossed my arms. And my legs. And tapped my foot.

When I couldn't stand it anymore, I picked it up again and scrolled through old messages. Finally, I settled on texting my mother. That was safe.

Need me to bring anything for dinner on Sunday?

Three minutes later, she texted back: *Just be on time.*

Oh, my god. *Mom.* I needed boundaries with my family. They were literally going to drive me over the edge if I didn't put a stop to this.

The bell rang and I breathed a sigh of relief. I could lock my phone away now and I wouldn't be tempted. At least not very much.

I bent over and unlocked my bottom drawer. But then, as if I was actually possessed, I pulled up Nick's number and texted: *Do you think there was more we could have done?*

I pushed send and my heart stopped beating. I lost all my breath and I wanted to immediately take it back. I wanted to delete it and unsend it and erase this moment from time completely.

I needed a time machine or the Doctor or freaking Michael J. Fox and the DeLorean.

I dropped my phone into my purse and slammed my drawer shut. *Idiot.* I was such an idiot.

I didn't look at my phone until the end of the day. Until I'd gotten into my car and turned it on.

Then finally I allowed myself to see if he'd texted me back.

He had.

Of course, he had. I had never doubted that he wouldn't.

Yes.

That was all he wrote. A simple, world-changing, confusing, mind-boggling, frustrating *Yes*.

Chapter Twenty-One

28. I **can't** do this **on my own**.

Spring came overnight. One day I thought my toes would fall off if I stepped outside my house and the very next day the sun rose warm, bright and ready to melt every ounce of snow from Illinois.

It was amazing.

I had never been more ready for a change of seasons. This winter had been the darkest, gloomiest yet and I didn't think I could survive much more of it.

Thank god, I didn't have to.

The beginning of March brought all kinds of hope and anticipation for what was to come. I felt my heart swell in my chest and my spirits pick themselves up off the filthy ground. It was a new day, a new dawn and if I had the voice of an angel like Michael Bublé, I would have sung the shit out of it.

Instead, I decided to take Annie for a walk after school. I wore rain boots so we could stomp through melting piles of snow. She loved every second of it. I knew I would have to bathe her as soon as we got home, but we'd been cooped up in the house for so long that I didn't care.

We just needed to breathe freely and move our winter-atrophied appendages.

Walking was beyond therapeutic. I didn't just have cabin fever from being indoors for months; I had it from being in my own skin... in my own head. I was exhausted from myself.

But today felt different. The end of the school year was in sight, the end of my divorce was too. Maybe.

Hopefully.

And tomorrow was my birthday. Thirty-one.

I nearly had a meltdown when I turned thirty. I couldn't stand the idea of aging into a new decade. I wasn't ready to let go of my twenties and the youthfulness they represented. Thirties seemed too mature for me. Too grown up.

But Nick had been the one that made it amazing. He'd given me bouquets of thirty things all day long. He kept having them delivered to my classroom until my desk had overflowed and I had to set things along the windowsill.

Thirty pink roses. Thirty cans of Diet Coke. Thirty Snickers Bars. Thirty brand new red Sharpies. Thirty dollars for my Kindle. Thirty dollars to Garmans Deli. Thirty packs of my favorite gum.

I had to make three trips out to the car to carry it all, but he was at home to help me haul it all inside. Then he'd taken me to a bar called Thirty and Clover. The food had been awful and we'd laughed about it all night. He had leaned over the table at the end of the night and said, "See? Thirty isn't so bad."

The next day we'd fought about something stupid. I couldn't remember what it was now. But I knew we didn't speak to each other for four days.

Two months later I demanded a divorce.

Annie and I walked around the corner of our block. I could see our cute house, up a little hill. The grass had started to peak out from beneath the melting piles of snow. It was still dead and brown, but at least I could see it.

It felt like hope.

It felt like change.

Mrs. Dunn was outside getting her mail and I stopped to talk to her. I hadn't seen her in months. She was an elderly woman. Most of the people on our street were elderly or young parents with wild kids running everywhere. There wasn't much in between.

"Hi, Mrs. Dunn." I smiled at her and paused on the sidewalk. The leash hung loosely in my fingertips while Annie skipped around Mrs. Dunn's pink velour jogging suit.

"Hi, Kate." She bent over to pat Annie on the head. "Hi, pretty girl. Out for a walk?"

"It's so nice today. We couldn't resist." Across the street, young kids bounded into their driveway with a basketball.

"Seems like everybody needs to get out of the house today," Mrs. Dunn smiled across the street at the children playing. "Do you know the Jacksons? Nice family. The kids are sweet." She gave me a sideways glance, "Loud, but sweet."

I couldn't help but smile. Mrs. Dunn thought the mailman was too loud.

I looked across the street as the basketball hit the rim of the hoop and bounced backward. It rolled off the end of the driveway and into the street. I watched in horror as the littlest girl ran for the ball just as a car came zooming down the street, way too fast for a neighborhood.

I threw my hands up to warn her to stop, but her older brother grabbed the back of her shirt just in time. I sucked in a gasping breath because my nightmare wasn't over.

When I'd panicked about the little girl, I dropped the leash. Annie had raced into the street to get the ball. The car saw her, but couldn't stop soon enough and my poor little Annie girl was caught under the tire.

I watched it all in a slow-motion nightmare. The car couldn't get out of the way fast enough. I heard her pained yelp and leaped into motion. I followed her into the street, scooping her up in my arms as I sunk to my knees on the damp, cold pavement. She was filthy from our walk and soaking wet. Blood mingled with her wet, dirty fur, turning it a sickly brown color.

I sunk my fingers into her sticky coat, beyond terrified that she had died, that the monster in the car had killed her. Her little lungs trembled with the effort to breath. They shook in her small chest while her head rolled listlessly in my arms.

I ripped off her leash and the new collar Nick had bought her. I couldn't figure out where she was bleeding from or what exactly was wrong with her. My mind spun and spun and spun and all I could do was panic. I was useless. Stupid. Completely hysterical. Nothing but terror and dread.

I could barely see her through my tears. I didn't know what to do. I knew I needed to do something. I *had* to do something. *But what?* Not my Annie.

Please, not my Annie.

Please please please please.

I needed Nick. Oh, god. *Nick would know what to do.*

The driver got out of his murder machine and tried to talk to me, but I was too frantic to make sense of anything he said. Mrs. Dunn tried to intervene, but even she couldn't translate my panic-stricken sobs.

Poor Annie just kept whimpering and twitching in my arms as I held her tightly to my chest.

I rocked her as gently as I could. I couldn't let her die. The rational part of my brain told me to move, told me to get up and do something. But the fear of losing the one thing left that loved me so completely was too heavy. Too consuming.

"Kate, who can I call?" Mrs. Dunn's voice slowly penetrated through my haze of panic. "Kate, we need to call someone."

"Nick," I gasped. "I need to call Nick." I reached into the pocket of my coat with my clean hand and with shaking fingers I punched the right buttons.

I cooed to Annie as I waited for him to answer. Please pick up. *Please, please, please* pick up.

Finally, on the second try, he answered. "Hello?"

"Nick," I cried. "It's Annie!"

"Kate?" He sounded so confused, but I needed him to get this. Now.

"She's been hit by a car," I sobbed.

"Wait, what? Annie's been hit by a car?"

"Yes!" My voice was a wretched sob from my chest. Annie winced again and my tears fell faster.

"Is she alive?"

"Barely."

"Where are you?" His tone changed from fear to decision in a second. I closed my eyes against a fresh wave of tears. These ones were relief. I knew he would take charge. I knew he would know what to do.

"I'm in front of our house. It just happened. I don't... I don't know what to do."

He cursed under his breath. "It's five-thirty, it will take me forty-five minutes to get to you with traffic. Is there someone there that can drive you? I can meet you at the vet."

I looked up at Mrs. Dunn. "Can you drive me to the veterinarian? It's only ten minutes away. Nick can meet me there."

"Of course, I can," she said quickly. I noticed her exchanging information with the stranger, but I couldn't even look at him.

He'd nearly killed Annie. I hated him. I didn't care that it was an accident. I couldn't stand the sight of him.

I knew I would eventually calm down, but I couldn't right now. I needed to know she would be okay first.

"Mrs. Dunn's going to take me," I told Nick with a more level voice. But then it broke when I asked in a ragged whisper, "Promise you'll come?"

"I'll be there as soon as I can, Katie. I swear."

"Thank you."

"Go," he ordered. "Get her some help."

"Tell me it's going to be okay," I cried. "Tell me she's going to be okay."

His voice pitched low with sincerity and promise. "Kate, everything is going to be okay."

I stood up and followed Mrs. Dunn because I believed him.

An hour later I had been banished to the vet waiting room and my tears had turned into sickening panic that crushed my insides and turned everything into mucky goo.

God, I was a mess.

But I could not lose Annie. I *could not*.

The vet hadn't given me good news, but he hadn't given bad either. I looked around the bright waiting room and blinked against the utter whiteness of it.

We had been coming here since we first got Annie. A buddy of Nick's from his work told us about it. The Animal Doctor was run by a gray-haired man in his late sixties. Dr. Miller had the kind of smile that reminded me of a horse, all big teeth and long face. But he had always done a phenomenal job with our puppy. His daughter worked here too, the second-generation veterinarian that would presumably take over the practice. She soothed my frayed nerves when I couldn't stop staring at her dad's shaking hands.

She'd wrapped her ice-cold fingers around my forearm and smiled patiently. "Annie's in good hands," she promised. "We'll take care of her."

She had walked me to the receptionist who had asked if there was someone she could call for me.

"My husband's on his way," I had explained. It hadn't felt like a lie. It hadn't even felt weird. Nick was still my husband. Maybe not for much longer. But today I needed him in his husband role.

Besides, I wasn't sure if there was a family only policy. I didn't want him to be banned from seeing Annie.

Did they do that here?

My head swam and I plunked down on the white plastic waiting room chair. White had always seemed like a bizarre choice for a place animals trotted into on a daily basis. And this wasn't just any white. It wasn't off-white or dull-white or faded-white. This was *white* white. The kind of white that reminded me of bleached teeth and black lights.

How did they get it this white?

How did they *keep* it this white?

"Kate?" Nick was suddenly kneeling in front of me, his warm hands gentle and comforting on my thighs. "How are you holding up?"

I swallowed roughly and stared into his ocean blue eyes. I couldn't speak. I couldn't say the words. I shook my head in a frightened way and a few more fresh tears slipped out.

"Come here," he murmured, pulling me against his solid chest.

I threw my arms around his neck and didn't let go, even when he wobbled unsteadily. He caught us, pulling me to my feet so we could press against each other.

One of his arms wrapped around my waist and held me tightly to him, while his other hand palmed my nape, his fingers trailing through my hair. I buried my face against his neck and trembled against him.

"Can you tell me what happened?" His voice was a low rumble that cascaded over my skin like a warm caress. I felt his chest vibrate with his words and the flex of his fingertips against my side.

Pieces of me that had started to fragment, to break off and float away like I was some kind of shipwrecked rocket in space, found purchase in the gravity of Nick's presence. All of these scarred, jagged splinters returned to their home and I became whole once more.

"We went for a walk," I sniffled. "I stopped to talk to Mrs. Dunn and wasn't paying attention. There was a basketball and she ran out to chase it, but... but there was a car... and-" My explanation died on a hiccupped sob.

Nick understood the gist of it anyway. He squeezed me tighter. His strong arms encased me in a protective shield that promised everything would be all right. We fit so perfectly together. His body was just tall enough to tower over mine in just the right way. I could tuck my arms under his or reach up and wrap them around his neck and either way was comfortable. When we lay in bed, his body could cover my back perfectly. His legs were just long enough to entwine with mine and make me feel tiny. His arms were the perfect length to hold me against him.

I had never really noticed before, at least not in this complete, awestruck way.

If I left this man, would I ever find another body so suited to mine? We were like puzzle pieces in the way we came together. And I didn't know if I would ever fit into another puzzle.

Maybe I didn't want to.

"Has the doctor said anything?"

I closed my eyes at the sound of his voice. It was as anguished as I felt. I knew he had stopped by to walk Annie whenever he could since we broke up. I knew he wanted to take her from me in the divorce settlement. But I had never really believed how attached to the dog he'd gotten.

I always thought he was trying to torture me.

"No. Nothing."

"But she wasn't already dead, right? They're trying to save her."

I nodded. "They're trying. She was so weak, though. God, Nick, she seemed to be barely hanging on. You should have heard her. She could barely breathe and her little body was just limp."

We stood there silently for a long time. Neither of us was willing to let the other go. I didn't know what would have happened to me if Nick hadn't been there to hold me together. I would have completely fallen apart. I would not have been able to survive the interminable waiting and minutes that stretched on like hours.

The waiting room became too bright so I closed my eyes, knowing I was safe in Nick's arms... knowing he would keep me in one piece.

After a long time of silence, I pulled back from Nick. I wanted his comfort still, but my arms had started to fall asleep and my legs were tired. My hands trailed down his chest and he caught them by the wrists over his heart. His blue eyes pierced mine, searching for something or maybe just making sure I was okay to stand on my own.

He leaned forward and I inhaled him again, breathing in his skin. He pressed a delicate kiss to the corner of my eye and then as if he couldn't help himself, to the corner of my lips.

When he released me, I felt like I'd cut off my arm. I wanted to throw myself on top of him. I wanted to weep in his arms, make him promise to never let go of me again.

Annie, my rational mind whispered. *You're just worried about Annie*.

The dog had me too emotional. I felt like I was losing every single thing I had ever loved or cared about. I felt like it was my fault she was here and that Nick and I were in the place we were. I felt like I poisoned anything I touched, destroyed it with a look, killed it just by caring for it.

I argued with my emotions. They were overly sensitive because of the crisis. These things were not true. They couldn't be.

I pulled back completely and slunk back into one of the waiting room chairs. The hard plastic dug into my spine and the backs of my thighs. I shifted, frustrated with the discomfort. "Did you come from work?"

Nick took the seat next to me and turned his whole body to face me. "Yeah."

"I'm sorry I made you leave."

"You didn't," he said immediately. "I wanted to come."

"Can you leave whenever you want? Or, uh, um, tell me about your new job."

His stare unsettled me, it was too intense, too absorbed in me. When his tongue dragged over his lower lip in concentration, I had to remind myself to swallow.

"I have set office hours, but if I need to leave, like today, I can. My boss is pretty cool with stuff like this."

"And the scouting stuff? Is that part of your office hours?"

His smile was brief, but for a second it was there. "Yes, in a way. They're considered mandatory, but nobody at the studio would turn them down. The shows I check out are in addition to what we do during the day, though."

"That sounds busy. Does it ever get exhausting? Do you get tired of music?"

He leaned forward. "Come on, you know me better than that."

I felt my lips tip up in a small smile. "Yeah, but how many shows do you have to go to a week? They can't all be ready to sign."

This time he chuckled and the waiting room suddenly seemed yellowed and dingy compared to his blinding brightness. "They're not. So far I've only brought one band into the studio that I've thought could have some potential. And I've seen a *lot* of bands over the last few months. But we try not to do more than two shows a week. There's a handful of scouts so we try to spread it around some. We have bands that we track down ourselves, but then there are some that request for us to come out and some that are brought to us through recommendation. Those we can pick and choose from."

"Very cool."

His eyes narrowed and his smile disappeared. "You don't sound convinced."

"I am! Really. I'm just tired from..." I gestured at the waiting room. "Seriously, Nick, I'm so happy for you. This sounds like the coolest job for you."

"It is." His palms spread out on his thighs and he pushed them down his jeans, reaching his knees with nervous energy. "It's like a dream job, seriously."

"Really? But what happened to the band?"

He canted his head thoughtfully. "I'm too old, I think."

"You are not. Oh, my god. You're thirty. That's hardly ancient."

"Thirty-one," he corrected.

I swallowed, remembering his birthday too late. It had been last month. Valentine's Day. I had never had a problem remembering in the past, but this year I had been too wrapped up in feeling alone and pathetic to think of anyone else.

Did it matter that I forgot his birthday? Was I supposed to remember? No, right?

We weren't together anymore. His birthday happiness wasn't one of my obligations anymore.

I glanced at the door that led back to the operating room and wondered what was taking them so long. *Fix her, damn it.*

Nick's voice pulled me back to our conversation. "I just think... I honestly think I'm better at this. It's like I found myself. I thought I knew who I was or what I wanted before, but it wasn't until I stepped into the studio that I really figured it all out. I belong there. I've always belonged with music, but this is the how and why of it."

"Nick, that's amazing." My words came out in a breathless whisper and I knew I was close to crying again. I blinked away hot tears and struggled to hold myself together. I hated that this bothered me, that he'd found this huge thing, discovered parts of him he hadn't known, while he was away from me. I hated that I had nothing to do with it. "I'm so happy for you."

His smile was small, nervous. His thumb and first finger tugged on his earlobe. "Kate, I-"

But I would never know what he wanted to say. Dr. Miller, the second, younger, female Dr. Miller, pushed through the swinging door and stepped into the waiting room. "She's going to be okay," she announced and I nearly crumpled to the floor after just standing to hear the news.

Nick caught me by the waist and anchored me in place. Dr. Miller smiled sympathetically at me and gestured for us to sit down again.

She walked over to us, her stubby heels clicking against the tiled floor. "She has two broken ribs and a broken toe. We had to give her stitches over her eye and on her side, but she's going to make it."

I mumbled something unintelligible so Nick took over and thanked her for us.

"We'll need to keep her overnight for observation, but we might be able to send her home tomorrow. We'll call you in the morning after we know more."

Nick's hand landed on my shoulder, squeezing it. "Can we see her?" he asked. "Just for a minute?"

"She's still asleep from surgery," Dr. Miller warned. "But you can see for yourself that she's still alive. I know how scary losing a loved one is."

I was sure she did. But the possibility of losing Annie felt like the absolute worst kind of pain. I couldn't believe that anyone loved his or her pet as much as I did. Nobody else would feel it this acutely.

Nick grabbed my hand and pulled me after Dr. Miller. We followed her back to the post-op room where Annie was laid out on a metal table. Her fur had been cleaned everywhere and shaved where she needed stitches. Her middle was wrapped tightly. Her rounded chest moved up and down, stuttering a little in between her shallow breaths.

"It's hard for her to breathe right now," Dr. Miller explained. "But that will heal."

Nick asked some logistical questions about home care while I walked to her side and gently trailed my fingertips over her plush ear. "Hi, baby girl," I whispered. Tears sprang up in my eyes and fell before I could stop them. "I'm so sorry." She made a whimpering noise and lifted her nose as if she could smell me. I spread my fingers out on her back and buried them in the thick softness of her fur.

Nick sidled up to me, pressing his chest into my side. He reached out and covered my hand with his. "You're a tough one, Annie girl," he murmured. "Small but fierce."

The sincerity in his voice did something inside me. It felt like a wrecking ball as it crashed through my system, upheaving everything I thought I knew about life, love and living.

"You didn't drive here, did you?" he asked me. His fingers moved over mine, stroking gently. I didn't know if he was caressing Annie or me.

"Mrs. Dunn dropped me off."

"Come on, then," he murmured. His lips were right at my ear when he said, "I'll give you a ride home."

He took my hand and led me to the receptionist desk. I stood there dumbly while he filled out some paperwork and handed over his credit card. There was some small part of me that suggested I object to this. I should pay for this, right? I wasn't even sure what exactly he was paying for.

I realized I didn't have my wallet, though. I only had my cellphone and house keys. My purse was still at home.

Nick finished up with the receptionist and led me outside. The late afternoon had turned to dusky evening. The breeze had chilled again and the wet puddles of melted snow were starting to freeze.

I shivered against the change of weather. My jacket wasn't enough to keep out the chill.

Nick noticed immediately, wrapping his arm around my shoulders and pulling me against his body. I loved the feel of his skin through his cotton shirt. I loved the hardness to his body, the lean muscle he worked so hard to keep. I loved that this was so familiar, that this was what I needed.

We reached his old Subaru Forester and I couldn't help but smile. His car was even older than mine and had a bajillion miles on it. It was actually a decently reliable car, but it was just so old. He had always threatened that once it died for good, he was going to buy an old conversion van for the band.

Thank God it had never come to that while we were still together.

He opened the door for me and I climbed into the achingly familiar cab. I settled back in my seat and inhaled the scent that was his car, that was him, that was him in his car and years and years of memories.

He walked around the front and climbed in next to me. With a sly grin, he asked, "Did you miss her?"

I found myself smiling back. "I think I did."

He looked forward again and started the car. The radio was on softly and he pointed to it, "This is a band I'm thinking about going to listen to."

I sat quietly while the haunting sound filled the car. The girl had one of those instantly memorable voices, smoky, sexy and ethereal all at the same time. The instrumentation was incredibly good as well. There was something missing, though.

Nick noticed and said, "They need drums. And they need to grow up a little. But they're good."

"They are good," I agreed.

I felt his eyes on me, but I couldn't look at him. A sudden strong punch of sorrow hit my gut and I didn't know how to recover from it.

I realized this was the only glimpse of Nick's new life I would get. I gave him up. I gave this up. We would never talk music again. I wouldn't get to go to shows with him anymore or listen to bands he wanted to go see. I wouldn't get to hear him play his guitar or make up new lyrics to songs on the radio- usually about something dirty.

I wouldn't get to see him live out this new leg of his life. I wouldn't see him in his dream job or where it would take him. I would miss it all.

I was choosing to miss it all.

He pulled into the driveway and I couldn't let the night end. I couldn't let him leave me. I wasn't ready for it yet. The car idled quietly. He was waiting for me to get out.

"Have you eaten anything?"

He turned to face me. I couldn't look at him, but I felt the intensity of his expression, the raw concentration in his gaze. "I haven't."

I tilted my head and my gaze fell on his long fingers wrapped around the bottom of the steering wheel. "Do you want to come in? The least I could do is feed you."

His voice dropped low and rough. "I'm not hungry."

I licked my dry lips. "Come in anyway."

Chapter Twenty-Two

29. I don't know **how to stop** loving him.

I jumped out of the car, too nervous to hear him tell me no. I fumbled for the keys in my pocket and exhaled a whoosh of breath when I heard the car shut off and his door open and shut.

My fingers were still trying to work the keys in the lock when his body heat warmed my back and his hand settled low on my hip. His other hand covered mine with the keys and made them work for me, shoving the key into the lock and turning it.

We stumbled into the dark house, my feet causing the problems when they tripped on the rug. Nick caught me by squeezing my waist, yanking me back against his chest. My heart kicked into a gallop and my breath hitched in my chest.

His palm slid forward and splayed over my stomach, pressing hotly even through the layers of my jacket and long-sleeve tee beneath.

I could feel the hammering of his heart against my back, his ragged breath as it flowed in and out of him unevenly.

His head dipped until I felt his lips against my neck. "Kate," he whispered and I shivered from the tickle of his mouth.

There was a pause between us as if the world stopped turning and time froze. I took in a breath and held it while I waited... waited for him to do something, to not do something, to turn around and escape.

That waited pause lasted an eternity. My fingers tingled from the fierce silence, the utter stillness. I thought I would die from anticipation.

Then everything burst into motion at once.

The keys jingled as he ripped them from the deadbolt and threw them on the ground. He slammed the door next, shaking the walls with his intention. I stood motionless, too afraid to move, too much of a coward to take what I wanted.

In the end, I didn't need to take anything. Nick did the taking for the both of us.

His hand wrapped around my bicep and turned me to face him. My eyes were adjusting to the dark, but I didn't get a chance to take him in before his mouth descended on mine, consuming me with his dizzying kiss.

His mouth moved against mine with a hunger that made me weak. I responded immediately, as desperate and greedy for him as he was for me.

He tasted me with his tongue, his teeth, his entire body. Everything about this kiss was designed to bring me to my knees with the weakness I still had for this man... the weakness I would always have for him.

His fingers fumbled with the zipper on my jacket, desperate to tear it off. I couldn't form rational, cognizant thoughts through my haze of lust and exhausted emotions. I couldn't do anything but feel and touch and give Nick exactly what he wanted.

But I also knew *I* wanted this.

Him.

I wanted him.

It had been so long. It had been too long.

Despite our separation, my body was used to having this man whenever I wanted. There was a sharp familiarity between us, an aching intimacy that could not be denied. I knew every angle of this man; I knew how his hipbones felt in my hands, the press of his naked thighs against the inside of mine. I could close my eyes and conjure him in seven years of intimate nights, lust in his eyes and perfect knowledge in his hands... in his body.

I couldn't say no to this.

I couldn't deny him tonight.

I needed him too much.

He succeeded with the zipper, growling in victory. He pushed it off my shoulders, turning it inside out in his fury to get it off me. Butterflies erupted in my stomach, flapping their huge wings with ravenous anticipation.

He kicked my jacket out of the way as he pushed me back against the door. I hit it with a thud, clutching his shirt for support.

He was too impatient for that. He didn't care if I was settled or not. And I loved it. I loved his greedy hurry... his intense need.

"This," he rasped, tugging at my shirt.

224

I helped him this time. We yanked it off together. My fingers went to the hem of his t-shirt. "This," I mimicked. He ripped it off with one hand.

We collided again, both of us frantic to feel the other. My body pressed into his naked chest and I moaned from the feel of it. My arms wound around his neck and I plunged my fingers into the soft tendrils of hair at his nape.

"Nick, I can't stop," I whimpered.

"Don't," he ordered coarsely. "Don't stop. Don't you dare fucking stop." But then he did.

He pulled back and stared down at me. Even in the darkness, I could see the hunger in his eyes. He looked ready to consume me, to pull me completely into his body until we were one without question. Until I could never separate myself from him again.

I tilted my chin, knowing he would meet me, knowing he couldn't help himself. Except he didn't. I tugged on his neck, hoping to bring his mouth to mine, but he kept his distance.

"No." I sucked in a breath as disappointment ripped through me. I abruptly wanted to cry. But then he said, "Not like this. Not here again."

In the next second, he swept me into his arms, cradling me against him. I let out a squeak of surprise, grabbing for his neck again as he turned suddenly and headed for the stairs.

"Where are we going?"

"Bed," he grunted as he took the stairs two at a time. "Our bed."

My eyes bulged. I didn't know what to think about that. I felt like I should protest. Hot sex in our entryway, against the wall, that was one thing. We'd done that already. There hadn't been any consequences.

Er, not many anyway.

But the bed. *Our* bed? That meant something different... something more.

I was just about to protest or suggest someplace else- like the kitchen table- when his head dipped down and he bit my nipple. I squeaked again, completely taken off guard.

His answering growl did something to my insides. Like melted them completely. His head dropped again and he licked me through my bra, soothing the small sting of pain.

He tripped on the last couple steps and nearly dropped me. He caught me just in time and steadied out, laughing at his clumsiness.

I found myself smiling when he tossed me on our unmade bed. I landed in a tangle of sheets and blankets, bouncing once.

He didn't waste any time getting back to business. He tugged on my rain boots, throwing them over his shoulders. His palms rubbed a hot path up my thighs and flicked the button of my jeans off.

I watched him in complete fascination. He watched me just as closely. His eyes roamed over my body, eating up every inch of exposed skin. His searing gaze lit me on fire, turned my body into a panting, wanting mess.

I pulled the straps of my bra off myself. I couldn't wait for him. I wanted him to see me like this. I wanted him to admire all of me. I wanted him to touch me… taste me… and never ever stop.

When I reached around and unclasped my bra, then pulled it from my chest, his breath caught in his chest and he stared at my breasts as if he couldn't look away, as if he would die if he did.

His mouth descended on my nipple and the moan I let out when his tongue came into contact with my skin was a sound I had never made before. I was sure of it. I had never been this desperate… this needy. I had never needed him so badly before. Needed him like I needed to breathe.

Needed him like I couldn't live without him or his touch.

Or at least not in a very long time.

After he'd spent equal time with each breast, he stood up slowly, reluctantly. His eyes never left me, even while his hands had to. He worked his jeans off, then his boxer briefs.

He stood before me for a few heart-stopping seconds and it was my turn to take my fill of him. My heart stuttered in my chest and my fingers tingled with anticipation.

Had there ever been a more beautiful man?

I scooted back on the bed as he crawled over me, covering me completely with his length. He kissed my hip and I jerked from the sensation. His chuckle sent warm breath floating over me and I shivered again.

"So ticklish," he murmured. His lips trailed over my abdomen and I tried not to wiggle. He kissed the place just below my belly button and then again before moving on.

His body hovered over mine like a feral animal, like some primal creature from a different world. He was so sexy, so incredibly enticing and oh so dangerous.

I couldn't help but feel threatened by his power, his utter dominance of me. I couldn't help but acknowledge that he was about to ruin me completely.

That I would never recover.

His mouth moved to my breasts again and I wiggled beneath him, suddenly hating the slow build. I needed this now. I needed him *now*.

I settled my hands on the sides of his face and begged, "Nick, please."

He looked up at me, lust, hunger and something so much deeper reflecting in his darkened gaze. "Do you need me?" His fingers settled on the inside of my thigh, pushing it to the side.

His words made me breathless, left me gasping for some purchase on reality. I held his face in my hands and nodded, unable to speak the words.

He kissed my neck, my jaw, my lips. Then he pulled back so he could watch me while he pushed into my core, filling me completely with him.

My back arched off the bed and I wrapped my arms around his neck again, pulling his face to mine.

He took me wildly; he took me with savage need and unrelenting power. He took me in a way that proved he was just as desperate as I was. I could do nothing but wrap my legs around his hips and hold on.

Just when I thought we were nearly finished, just as I started to reach for that tingling cliff of perfect insanity, he slowed down. The abrupt change of pace surprised me and I tilted my hips, telling him what I wanted.

I needed him to finish. I needed him to keep his pace and never stop.

"Nick," I whimpered.

"Kate," he growled against my sweat-dotted neck. "Like this." He took my arms and stretched them over my head. He held them there with one hand while he found leverage with the other. I could do nothing but hug my thighs tighter around his waist and offer up my control. "I need you like this."

I thought he had been amazing seconds before, but this was something else entirely. I sighed in pleasure, my eyes fluttering closed, unable to stay open against the intensity of this moment.

He turned something desperate and greedy into something so achingly sweet I felt branded by it. He was leaving his mark, his name tattooed on my soul.

I gasped for breath as he worked us closer. He drew out each moment, making them all memorable, promising nothing else would feel this good or be this complete.

Nobody else would ever make me feel like this.

Nothing else could reach this absolute height of ecstasy.

When he finally pushed me over the edge, my entire body trembled from the force of it. He followed after me, chasing the same blissful blindness I still quivered with.

He collapsed on top of me, his skin heated and slick with sweat. We were stretched out on our bed diagonally in a sleepy tumble of limbs. His hand settled on my bare abdomen and his nose trailed up the line of my jaw, teeth nipping playfully, lips kissing, tongue tasting.

"God, we're good at that," I teased.

He replied with a drowsy, "Mmm…"

I snuggled closer to him. He shifted back and I missed the touch of his body immediately. The emptiness between us was too big, too cold. His arms wrapped around me and pulled me to him before I could panic.

We adjusted on the bed until his chest nestled against my back and his arms hugged my middle, holding me to him with a tightness that made me feel safe and satisfied. My eyelids drifted close and the exhaustion from the day, from Annie's accident and from the most mind-blowing sex of my life caught up to me all at once. I couldn't fight it anymore.

I knew there were things to talk about. I knew doubt would find me in the morning, quickly followed by regret and probably fresh heartbreak. But I physically couldn't make my mind worry about that right now. I couldn't make myself care.

Sensing I was slipping, he leaned over me and rubbed his roughened scruff against my check. I felt myself smile, but I couldn't make my eyes open.

"Kate," he coaxed in a tone that dripped with contentment and amusement. "Katie," he whispered. "We need to talk."

"Mmm," I agreed. "In the morning." I wouldn't ruin this. Not tonight. This had been too perfect… beyond perfect. This had redefined the entire meaning of perfect for me and I refused to give that up tonight.

"Katie," he murmured. "This changes things."

I yawned. I was past the ability to speak. Sleep took hold and pulled me under, sending me into the peaceful slumber of relaxed dreams and the wonderful feeling of the most beautiful man's body entwined with mine.

I woke up once during the night. I blinked awake on the wrong side of the bed with Nick's arms still holding me to him and his legs, hot and heavy, slotted between mine. His head had pulled back from mine, presumably so he could breathe without my hair suffocating him in his sleep, but I could still feel the steady beat of his heart on my back and his hips tucked against mine, fitting exactly right.

228

I had a sharp, concentrated moment of panic as the reality of our actions set in. Ice cold lucid thought jerked me awake and kept me there. I felt hysterical laughter bubble in my chest, but I swallowed it down.

How did this keep happening to us?

And why had I ever thought it was a good idea for him to sleep over? *There might actually be something wrong with me.*

I lay as still as possible, terrified of waking him. I tried to talk myself through my meltdown, tried to rationalize and reason my way out of it. But I couldn't.

What we did was going to permanently screw things up between us.

We had mediation in three days.

Oh, my god, he was going to bring up the possibility of being pregnant again.

I thought I would be sick.

I focused on the night sky. I hadn't closed my blinds tonight because Nick and I hadn't really been thinking about those things. The stars spread from one side of my vantage to the other, glittering like diamonds on a background of onyx and indigo. The crescent moon hung like a pendant in the middle. Its milky glow stretched and spun in the tranquil sky, turning wispy clouds to gold. I concentrated on those things.

I steadied out my breathing, letting the calming rhythm of Nick's heart soothe me back to sleep. His body was deliciously warm. He'd covered us with the comforter after I fell asleep and our mingled body heat had become something extreme, but it felt amazing.

He felt amazing.

Choosing to put off my panic till morning, I closed my eyes once again and drifted off.

By the time I woke the second time, he was awake behind me. I could feel his body twitching, his general awakeness intruding on my slumber.

I blinked at the same sky that had sung me to sleep the night before, but the moon and stars were gone, replaced by a soft violet and dusky gray. The sun hadn't risen yet. It was still very early. But Nick was awake and I knew, before I'd even opened my eyes, that our night was over... that it was time to face our actions.

I let myself stir and stretch lazily against him. I couldn't quite give this up yet. Just a few more minutes, I promised myself.

"Happy birthday, Kate," he said with his sleep-roughened voice. His fingers surprised me by lightly running down my hip. "How did you sleep?"

How did I sleep? It was probably better if I didn't answer that question. It would only confuse both of us. Instead, I dropped my hand over my mouth and mumbled, "I need to brush my teeth."

"Me too," I could hear the grin in his voice. "But we've been married for almost eight years, Katie. Can't it wait another minute?"

Still hiding my mouth, I narrowed my eyes and demanded, "Why?"

"We should talk."

"Why?"

His low laugh vibrated in his chest. "Last night…"

"Was a mis-"

The tension that rocketed through his body was so strong that I fell silent before he could cut me off. "Don't say it."

"Nick-"

"*Goddamn, Kate*" he muttered. "Are you kidding me?"

I scrambled to sitting, yanking the covers with me. We were both starkly naked and I flushed from head to toe, realizing I was about to launch into an argument with him while I wasn't even wearing underwear.

There was something wrong with my mouth that it just couldn't shut up and be quiet.

But I couldn't listen to what he had to say either. I couldn't go through that just because my boobs were everywhere.

"We're in the middle of a divorce!" I pointed out. "We have mediation in three days, Nick! What were we thinking?"

"Maybe we thought the divorce was a stupid idea. Maybe we thought we couldn't keep our hands off each other!"

I sucked in a gasping breath and swayed with dizziness. I couldn't… I couldn't grasp his words. I couldn't make them concrete thoughts and ideas in my head. They danced in the air outside of my reach, taunting me… laughing at me.

"Is that what you think?" I asked breathlessly. For a second I thought I might faint. I shook my head, desperate to find my senses. "Do you think the divorce is a stupid idea?"

His shoulders fell with defeat. "It was your idea, I… I just…"

My emotions took a sickening twist and my head spun again. "You're blaming me?" Hot tears pushed against my lashes. "This is *my* fault?"

"I'm not blaming you," he stated firmly. "I'm just trying to think. God, Kate, there are times when I think you hate me. When I think you would do *anything* to get rid of me. And then… then there's last night. And all of the other times like it. I have never been more alive than when I'm with you."

I sat up straighter. "Nick, you're still blaming me. I'm the reason we're getting a divorce. I'm the reason we don't work! I'm the reason your life is miserable or not miserable or I don't know what! Was last night all my fault too?"

He abruptly sat up. The blanket fell to his lap, hiding his important bits but exposing inches of smooth, muscled skin. His tousled chestnut hair fell over his forehead as he leaned into me. He had never been more beautiful, an angry Adonis rampaging for vengeance.

"I'm not blaming you for everything. I'm… I'm trying to make sense of this. And I need you to figure out what the hell you want. Is it me, Kate? Or is it this?" His arm flung wide, gesturing at the room. "Without me?"

"We're in the middle of a divorce," I repeated, but this time it was broken. This time it held the years of pain and hurt and heartache. "We're in the middle of a divorce."

He jumped from the bed as if it burned him to share the same space as me. "You've made that abundantly clear." He gave me his back and naked bum and tore into the closet. I watched in horror as he opened drawers, then slammed them closed.

Tears streaked down my face, wetting the sheets I held tightly around my torso. "What are you doing?"

"Going home," he growled. "Then I'm going to shower. Then I'm going to work." His eyes flashed to mine, searing me from where he yanked on old running shorts. "What are *you* doing?"

"Nick," I sobbed. He waited. He stood there in his shorts and tousled hair, his jaw ticking with anger and pain and scars that I gave him, scars that I ripped open, and he waited for me to say what it was I wanted to say. "I'm sorry."

"For what?"

I winced with frustration. "For this." I waved at the room. "For the divorce." I sniffled back a flood of tears. "For last night."

He stalked into the room, his feet moving with determination and his body so filled with tension I felt it vibrating off him in waves. He hovered over the edge of the bed. I could smell him. I could almost touch him. His voice pitched low and serious. "I'm not sorry," he declared. "Not for any of it."

He gave me one more scorching glare, then turned around and left. His loud footsteps took the stairs at a clipped pace. There was silence for a minute and I could picture him yanking on the rest of his clothes. Then the door opened and slammed behind him.

I was alone- truly alone. And all I wanted to do was chase him down and drag him back to my room. I wanted to lock him in here until these feelings went away, until this fissure in my heart stopped tearing me apart.

I broke down and cried after that. I cried for a very long time. Then I called into work, explaining about my dog, but not about my husband.

Then I lay down again and cried all the way through my birthday.

Eventually, the vet called. Annie made it through the night. She was going to be okay.

But even Annie's good news couldn't soften the blow to my heart or the eclipsing truth that I'd made a very big mistake.

If only I could figure out which of my mistakes was the right one to regret.

Last night?

Or the divorce…?

Chapter Twenty-Three

30. I **can't** let him **go**.

Three days later, on the morning of our next mediation, I prayed for the flu.

When I did not immediately start puking, I prayed for an earthquake. When that didn't work, I prayed for a tornado. Then an alien invasion.

And finally, a zombie plague.

Then I decided I should probably stop wishing thousands of people had to die just so I could skip seeing Nick again.

It wasn't that I *wanted* thousands of people to die or a zombie pandemic to sweep the globe. Not really. I just thought, maybe it was more favorable than coming face-to-face with a man that was so pissed off at me, I felt like my entire house needed cleansing.

I pulled up Google on my phone. Was it possible to hire a witch doctor to hoodoo the shit out of my house and at the same time give me a non-life-threatening trip to the emergency room?

Chicago area witch doctors.

My phone rang, changing the screen to Kara's name. I answered with a sigh. "Hey."

"You sound glum."

I decided it was better to go with the truth. "The only witch doctors Google pulled up are on LinkedIn. I swore to myself I would never get a LinkedIn profile. I don't care how many emails they send me a day."

"You've lost your mind," she laughed. "You're officially crazy."

"I'm not crazy," I argued. "I just want the flu or maybe malaria. Typhoid would be fine."

There were thirty seconds of complete silence before Kara recovered. "Please don't bring typhoid to school with you. I'm not sure if our health plan covers typhoid."

"If I find the right witch doctor, you're not going to have to worry about a thing. It will be an isolated incident. I just decided that I don't really want to kill thousands of people."

"Kate?"

"Yeah?"

"As your therapist, I'm going to need you to separate yourself from your delusions and tell me five real things that happened in your life this morning."

Surprised laughter bubbled up inside me and I started to feel just the tiniest bit better. "Unfortunately you're not my therapist. Also, does that work with your students?"

"How should I know? I just made that shit up."

"I'm impressed."

"Thanks! But if we're honest, most of what I use is made up."

"Wow, K. Summa cum laude from Northwestern is really coming in handy, huh?"

She let out a dramatic sigh, "I do what I can." With a delicate throat clear she added, "And it was magna cum laude. I was off by three-tenths of a point."

"My apologies."

"You are forgiven." Another pause. "Are you coming to school today?"

"No."

"Mediation?"

"Yes."

"This is your second sick day this week."

"This one was planned."

She made a tsking sound with her tongue and then said, "Give him hell."

It was my turn to fidget nervously. I hadn't told Kara any of the drama with Nick other than he had come to the vet when Annie got hit and taken me home. But I could tell she knew something went down. She had been giving me funny looks all week. I also knew she was holding her tongue for my sake, but part of me had wanted her to demand to know what went on.

I was dying to tell someone. I wanted to hear an outside opinion. I wanted her advice, her perspective, her curse words.

But I couldn't bring myself to say anything. Instead of blurting out what had happened, I kept it locked tightly inside of me. I felt like I had to protect it... protect Nick. Even if Kara would have ended up on his side of the argument, I was reluctant to put our marriage, or what was left of it, on trial.

I was tired of other people's opinions. I was tired of looking elsewhere for answers and ignoring the strong, still voice inside me.

I was sick and tired of dissecting every single thing that Nick did wrong and giving it to a jury of my peers to decide how to feel for me.

I needed to figure this out for myself. And fast.

When I didn't respond to Kara, she backed off and said, "Or give him really polite, pleasant discussion."

I laughed, despite the seriousness of my thoughts. "I'm honestly not sure what he's going to get out of me today. I guess I'll decide when I get there."

She gasped, "You don't mean the house? Not Annie. You really have lost your mind. Oh, my god, did you already call the witch doctor?"

"Stop," I laughed. "You're the crazy one. Not me."

"I trust you, Kate. You know that I do. But this year has been emotionally draining for you. I just don't want to see you get hurt because you're tired. Promise me, you'll be careful today... that you'll think everything through? Even if it's hard and you don't feel up to it?"

Now those were some words I could live by. "I promise." And I meant it. I would do exactly as she asked. "Thanks for being such a good friend."

"Mwah! Love you. Good luck today."

"Thanks. Love you too."

We disconnected and I felt marginally better.

Marginally.

As in just barely.

Most of me was still a pile of nerves and sweating pits.

I had taken the day off because I was tired of rushing into mediation after school and I was tired of mediation affecting my teaching and thoughts and general motor functions all day long.

So today I took it easy. Annie still needed twenty-four-hour care, so she had spent the last couple days with my parents while I taught. I was going to pick her up after mediation today and keep her for the weekend.

For all of their faults, my parents were really good with her. I knew she was in good hands and they were surprisingly good-willed about keeping her for me.

I hadn't told Nick about it because I wasn't quite sure what he would have said.

Just kidding, I was terrified he would demand to keep her.

And also, I was just terrified of talking to him.

So I didn't.

And he hadn't tried to reach out to me.

It stung a little that he hadn't called or stopped by. Okay, more than a little. It hurt deeply. I was embarrassed and heartbroken and a million other things I didn't even want to name. But I also knew that it wasn't his responsibility to forever chase after me.

As much as I wanted to be chased.

He was right; I had to figure this out.

I had to decide what I wanted. And in the meantime I had to go to mediation and fight with him over who gets the dog.

What had I done to my life?

Mediation was scheduled for early afternoon, so I took the morning to laze around the house. I ate breakfast, an actual breakfast. Not just coffee. I actually made myself a peanut butter and jelly sandwich.

I took my time getting ready, dressed carefully, paid attention to my makeup and hair. It wasn't that I was trying to impress Nick more than usual; I just never had this much time in the morning.

Usually I was a whirlwind of the fastest blow dry in the history of hair, a quick brush of foundation and some swipes of mascara before I jabbed earrings in, slipped on work-appropriate clothes and grabbed coffee on my sprint through the door.

This morning I sipped coffee on my couch while watching the *Today Show* and got ready without stress. I made sure all of my hair dried and I added bronzer and blush to my makeup routine.

So basically I was almost late for mediation because it took so long to get ready.

My official prognosis? Being a woman was officially the worst.

There were way too many steps to just looking halfway decent. Men had it so easy.

Mediation was back at Ryan Templeton's office. Mr. Cavanaugh had hosted the last failed session in his smaller office tucked away on the outskirts of the city proper. It had been a stark deviation from the expensive, swanky suites in the heart of downtown, but I had felt more at ease there. I hadn't minded the faded furniture or scuffed conference table.

Mr. Cavanaugh had offered coffee and pastries. I'd had two. Ryan Templeton offered expensive bottled water and no snacks. These offices were meant to impress... meant to intimidate.

And they did that in spades.

I checked in with the security guard and walked slowly to the elevator. I felt nervous energy gaining momentum and I wasn't quite sure what would come of it. I had no idea what I was thinking or what I would say upstairs. My mind was a tornado of confusion. Spinning and spinning and spinning.

To add paranoia to my already agitated nerves, this session felt final for some reason. I couldn't shake the feeling that whatever we decided or said here would be permanent and lasting.

I felt equal parts sick to my stomach and anxious. I leaned against the back wall of the empty elevator and closed my eyes. My arms were crossed over my chest, holding my body in a tightened cocoon of protection. I couldn't relax or I would fall apart. I had to physically hold myself together or I would splinter into a thousand unfixable pieces.

Someone else entered the elevator before the doors could shut and my eyes popped open, surprised and not surprised at the same time.

Nick.

I could sense his presence before I saw him. It was something in his energy that was inexplicably tied to mine. I felt him in the atmosphere, in the very atoms dancing in the air around us. I could smell him. Feel the heat of his body even from several feet apart.

Okay, maybe not in the real sense of the word, but I knew the feel so intimately that I could easily imagine the sensation of his body heat warming me, pressing into my skin, turning everything inside me into molten lava.

"Nick," I whispered, unable to stop myself.

He didn't turn around. He didn't acknowledge me. He stood near the doors, his finger retracting from the buttons. "You forgot to push for the floor."

I nibbled my bottom lip and shook myself. I was a mess.

"Thanks," I mumbled weakly.

The elevator started with a jerk and began the ascent to the eleventh floor. I held my breath for as long as I could, then let it out with a forced puff of air.

I watched Nick's back with fascinated awe, wondering how to engage him. His spine was absolutely straight. His shoulders were taut with tension and from the view of his profile that he gave me I could see his jaw flex and release.

He was dressed nicely again, gray slacks and a light blue oxford with a stylish gray vest that made the outfit look expensive and tailored. Maybe it *was* expensive and tailored. His hair had been styled back from his face.

He wore the watch I bought him two Christmases ago. His shoes were shiny.

Oh, my god, who was this man?

My heart thumped painfully.

"Annie's better," I blurted.

He turned his head slightly, still not looking at me. "Your dad called me."

"Oh." My parents were traitors. So was my dog.

So was my heart.

The elevator stopped and the doors slid open. Gripped by fear and doubt, I grabbed Nick's wrist and pulled him to a stop.

"Wait," I pleaded.

He didn't look at me. He didn't even turn his head. "I want this over, Kate. I want it finished."

I let go of his wrist and he shifted his shoulders, adjusting his shirt without physically tugging it into place. He walked out of the elevator with purpose, striding straight for the conference room.

Mr. Cavanaugh waited for me in the greeting area again. His expression read concern and maybe something else... maybe something like pity.

"Ms. Carter," he nodded when I finally found the courage to step out of the elevator.

"Hi, Mr. Cavanaugh."

His voice gentled and he asked, "Are you all right?"

I swallowed thickly and looked at the hallway where Nick had disappeared, "Is anyone ever all right during these things?"

He chuckled at my candor. "No, Ms. Carter. They are not." We had stood there for another moment before he gestured toward the conference room. "Should we go get settled?"

I didn't verbally respond, but I did follow after him- a feat I didn't think I was capable of.

Nick stood in the corner of the cool room, in a quiet discussion with his lawyer. They both flicked glances our way when we entered the room, but that was it. Just a glance of bitter acknowledgment that I had entered into his space. That was all I got.

I sat down in one of the rolling leather chairs and tried not to let self-pity swallow me whole. I straightened my spine and masked my expression with false bravado. I would not let him see me ruffled.

This man had been in my bed three nights ago. This man had held me all night long. He had wrapped his arms around me like he never wanted to let go and fought with me the next morning when I suggested that what we did was a mistake.

He wasn't indifferent to me. He was the opposite of that.

I held on to that small portion of hope. I clung to it. I couldn't sit here and enter into this discussion if I really thought Nick hated me.

When had that changed?

I reached for the cold bottle of water that had been set out for me and took a shaking sip.

Nick took a seat across from me and his lawyer followed. Marty Furbish walked into the room and took a seat at the head of the table. Ryan made an announcement reminding us where the restrooms were and that we should ask if we needed anything, but I barely heard anything he said.

When we were finally settled, Nick leveled me with a steely gaze and said with finality, "I want this finished today. Whatever it takes... however long it takes... I want this to be done."

The lawyers looked at me next. I forced words from my lips. Words I wasn't sure I felt. "Me, too."

Marty let out a pleased sigh. Mr. Cavanaugh relaxed just barely, but I felt it next to me. He wanted this over as much as I did.

"Good," Ryan Templeton nodded. "Now, if we can all apply a little give and take, we can finish this part and move on to the next. You'll be divorced before you know it." His smile was meant to ease the tension in the room. But it did the opposite.

I felt a panic attack slide over my skin, squeezing my lungs and blurring my vision.

I thought we were here because we couldn't stand each other? I thought that was the whole point of it?

So why did it feel like my heart had been shredded? Why couldn't I breathe? This wasn't like before when the sorrow of our failed marriage had weighed so heavily on me. This new pain pressed me into the earth... threatened to bury me alive.

This was worse somehow. This felt like I would never be able to catch my breath again. This felt like endless drowning and an emptiness so vast I would be forever lost in it.

Somehow I had stopped worrying about how much we'd hurt each other in the past and started worrying about how much we would hurt without each other in the future.

A few months ago, I couldn't imagine living my life in the same pattern of crazy we had been stuck in. And now I couldn't imagine my life without this man in it.

What was I doing?

Was I making the biggest mistake of my life?

Yes.

Yes.

I had asked myself that question countless times over the last several months, but I finally had an answer.

Yes.

A loud, resounding yes.

This *was* the biggest mistake of my life.

My lips were too dry. My mouth felt like someone had stuffed it with cotton balls. My throat was prickly and sore. But I couldn't drink enough water.

I couldn't quench this thirst.

My hands trembled badly, but there was nothing to calm my nerves.

I finally realized that I wanted to fight for my marriage and it was too late. I had finally realized that this man was everything to me. Even with his faults and flawed humanity. Even with our rocky history and hurtful past. This man, *my husband*, was my life. He was everything to me. He was my past and present. He was my future. He was my heart. My very soul.

But we had already announced our divorce to every person we knew.

He had moved out.

He'd gotten a new life.

We'd hired lawyers.

We were smack dab in the middle of mediation.

I had to go through with this. I had already made the decision. I just had to buck up and go through with it.

These were my consequences to pay. I had made this bed, now I needed to lay in it.

Forever.

Forever and ever and ever, amen.

Oh, damn.

Oh, shit.

Shit shit shit.

"She can have it all." I heard the words, but they didn't make sense. Nick kept talking. "The house, the dog. Whatever she wants, she can have it."

"Nick," his lawyer spit out. "I would recommend rethinking your position-"

"I don't want it," he growled. "I don't want any of it."

Tears filled my eyes. "But I do."

I made a new decision. I decided it didn't matter what we had done or who knew about the divorce or what anybody else in the entire world thought.

I could not let this man go.

I could not.

"Yeah, we know," Ryan spit out rather unprofessionally. "That's why you're *getting* it."

I jerked my chin and a lone tear escaped, rolling down my cheek. "No, that's not what I mean. I don't just want the house and the dog or the things. I want everything, Nick. I want... I want you."

Looking at him across the table, I realized something so vitally important that it knocked every last breath out of me. I didn't want a divorce because I didn't love him anymore. I had never stopped loving him. Against all reason, against every valid argument I'd made against him and our marriage... I loved him.

His entire body reacted with my words. He sat back in his chair with a swift pull of motion. His head cocked back and his blue eyes flashed with something strong and piercing. "What?"

"I surrender," I whispered raggedly. Whatever courage I had left, I gathered quickly to hold his furious glare.

"*Kate.*" His whisper was agonized, full of conflict and turmoil.

I struggled to swallow and smooth out my trembling voice. It didn't help. "I surrender, Nick. To this." I waved my hand between us. "To us. To *you.*"

Just as abruptly as he had leaned back, he shot forward and placed one palm on the shiny conference table. "You're doing this *now*?"

Fear boiled inside me, superheating my insides, making me feel wobbly and off balance. But I had to get this out. I had to say this or I would hate myself for the rest of my life. "I don't want a divorce."

Mr. Cavanaugh jumped in, hoping to rescue me. "Ms. Carter, I think you should take a minute to think about this."

I shook my head, acknowledging him, but not wanting to waste time to address him. "Nick, I was wrong. I was so wrong."

"You can't do this now." He sounded pained, shocked and beyond confused. "Just the other night-"

"I'm not asking anything from you. I... I don't even really know if I want anything from you. I just... I just can't do this. I can't go through with this. I'm sorry."

"For what?" His words were a punch through the air.

Confusion roiled through me and I thought I would be sick. More tears spilled over and a shuddering sob racked my chest. I fumbled for my purse somewhere on the floor.

"For what?" Nick demanded. He stood up. His voice grew louder, commanding, desperate. "Katie, for what?"

I glanced wildly around the room, my eyes bouncing from his lawyer to mine, then out the window at the traffic far below.

"For this," I whispered. "For all of it. For everything."

Nick fell back in his chair, defeated and out of breath. I was his opposite- like usual. I jumped to my feet and for the second time since we began mediation, I fled the room.

I nodded once to Ryan Templeton, then turned to Mr. Cavanaugh. "I'm sorry for wasting your time, Mr. Cavanaugh."

My feet stumbled over themselves as I raced out of the room. I needed fresh air. I needed to find a dark place so I could curl into the fetal position and rock myself into a stupor.

I needed so much tequila.

Like all the tequila.

A hand caught me just as I reached the elevator. For a fast second, my lungs filled with breath and hope zinged through me. But when I turned around and found that it was Mr. Cavanaugh and not Nick, my entire spirit crumpled.

"Ms. Carter... Kate, are you sure about this? Are you sure this is what you want? Because if you leave today, we are basically giving up our position. It will be much harder to argue in your favor."

"I'm so sorry," I sniffled. "But I'm sure. I'm positive. I can't... I can't do this."

"Well, if you're sure."

"I am."

His expression softened and some of his frightened concern receded. "If it helps any, I don't think he wanted the divorce any more than you did."

I shrugged helplessly. My chin trembled too violently for me to respond. I didn't know if it helped or not. I didn't know if it was true or not. I didn't know what to say.

Seeing that I couldn't speak anymore, he patted my shoulder with his hand and gave me a sad smile. "Good luck, Kate. I hope it works out for you."

"Me too," I whispered, even while I knew I didn't deserve for it to work out. Even while I knew it probably wouldn't.

I stepped into the elevator and he let me go down alone. I was thankful for that. I was thankful for him. As far as divorce lawyers went, he was one of the good ones.

Not that I knew very many.

The elevator doors closed behind me and took me to the ground floor. I left the building, walked to my car and got inside.

I drove home. I walked inside my house. I collapsed on my couch and I started to cry.

I didn't stop for a very long time.

Nick never came after me.

Chapter Twenty-Four

31. I **love** him.

My mom called later in the day. She wanted to know how mediation went. She wanted me to get the dog.

I didn't want to move for the next forty years.

"How did it go?" she asked impatiently.

"Not well."

"Are you divorced?" Her tone was panicked and concerned. She rarely sounded panicked or concerned. "Is it final?"

I sniffled. "No. No, it's not final." I didn't explain to her that we couldn't have finalized it in mediation. That there were more steps to it than this. It didn't matter now because if I had any say about it, I would never take those steps. Nick would have to go on living his life forever anchored to me. I would be the ball and chain that never let him move on.

He'd have to become a polygamist if he wanted to get married again.

Oh, god, what if he wanted to get married again?

I collapsed back to my side and let out a high-pitched whimper. "Kate? Katherine? What's wrong? What happened?"

"I couldn't go through with it," I cried.

"Go through with what?" Her patience had run out. She had started shrieking.

"The divorce, Mom! I couldn't go through with the divorce!"

"Oh." Her tone evened out and she sounded obnoxiously pleased. "Well, that's a good thing."

I started crying harder. It wasn't a good thing if Nick still wanted one.

"Oh, Kate," she sighed. "It's going to be okay. Everything is going to work out."

She had never said that before. Not once since I told her Nick and I were going to end things.

"How do you know?" I croaked.

"Because you love each other. Because you went through some hard times, but you've never stopped loving each other."

Ladies and gentlemen, my mother, the closet romantic.

I propped myself up on my elbow. Some of my tears dried and I took a steadying breath. "He didn't say he didn't want to end the divorce. He might still want one."

"He doesn't," she said confidently.

"How do you know?"

She sighed again, only this time I could hear the smile in her voice. "Because he's a good man, honey. He's a good man that loves you."

"I thought you hated him?"

"Katherine Claire, I am your mother. I always want what's best for you. I suppose we were a little harsh with Nick because... well, because I didn't think he was giving you the life you deserved. But when you left him, I realized I was wrong." She cleared her throat while my entire world tipped on its axis. Did my mother just say she was wrong? Had I prayed a little too hard for that zombie apocalypse? "In comparison to your life of loneliness, he was the best thing for you. No matter what his profession."

I let the passive aggressive digs slide and said honestly, "Thanks, mom."

"I love you, Kate."

"I love you too." I sat up fully and added, "I can't come to dinner every Sunday though. It's too much. I love you and dad, but I can only make it once a month."

"Twice."

"What?"

"Come twice a month and I won't bug you about it again."

"Okay," I laughed. "I'll come twice."

"We can keep the dog another night, too. Your father has grown really attached. I think I'm going to have to buy him one by the end of it."

I blamed my heartbroken exhaustion, but nothing she was saying was making sense. "Buy him what?"

"A dog," she muttered. "Like this one. I might have to hit it with my car too just so he can feel needed."

"Who?"

"Your father, Kate. Keep up! He won't watch TV anymore unless the dog is curled up on his lap. It's ridiculous. You should see the way he babies it! You'll help me find the right breed, won't you?"

246

Feeling sufficiently exhausted and completely weirded out, I nodded. Then I realized she couldn't see me and so I said, "Oh, okay. If you think he really wants one."

My dad had never loved anything in his life. Not even me! Okay, that wasn't true. But small animals were definitely not on his short list. They ranked right under traffic for things he could not tolerate.

I couldn't picture him cuddled up with Annie.

I wasn't sure I wanted to picture him cuddled up with Annie.

"Alright, get some sleep. Your dad will bring the dog back to you tomorrow."

"Thanks, mom."

She clicked off and I dropped my phone on the cushion beside me. That was the most bizarre conversation I had ever had with my mother.

It beat the birds and the bees talk she tried to have with me when I was fourteen.

It had been too late by that point. I went to public school and there was this thing called TV.

I knew everything I needed to know.

I figured the logistics out later. As God and my sanity intended.

I felt oddly at peace then. Everything wasn't quite so dismal. My mom believed Nick still loved me, so that had to mean something, right?

That peace carried me through the rest of the day and eventually I was able to get up off the couch and at least change clothes.

I stripped off my pencil skirt and blouse and replaced it with yoga pants and a racerback tank. They were workout clothes, but I was not planning on working out.

Unless one considered inhaling a couple gallons of ice cream working out.

But mostly I needed the clothes for their stretchiness.

I walked down the stairs, anxious to get started on my ice cream marathon when I saw him. The sight of him there, in the entryway, standing so tall and looking so beautiful, nearly made me face plant down the remaining four stairs.

I caught myself on the railing, but my stomach took the tumble anyway.

"What are you doing here?"

He stood there out of breath with his shoulders heaving, as if he'd run all the way here. His mouth was set with determined lines. His eyes were so intent, so intimately focused... but maybe a little lost too. Or maybe it was something deeper than lost. Something profound and permanent that reflected in my eyes too. Something like finally being found. "You still don't know?"

I shook my head and tried to swallow. "No."

"You, Kate. I'm here for you."

I carefully made my way down the rest of the stairs and took a step toward him. It was strange being in this place. I felt like my emotions had taken steroids. There were too many of them. And they were at war with each other.

The man that I wanted, the marriage that I wanted, stood right in front of me and still I had to fight my pride and swallow humility. I had to choose to let go of our past and hold onto the hope that we had a future. I had so many things I wanted to say to him, but I needed to choose the best things... the things that would move us forward and give us healing.

It wasn't easy. It was the opposite. It was traumatizing and against my nature. I knew I was stubborn. I knew I was a control freak. I knew I had a thousand faults that only this man could love.

We were so broken. *I* was so broken.

Yet I wanted this more than anything in the world. More than I had ever wanted anything else in my entire life.

And I knew, without any doubts or misgivings, that if I let him go... if I gave up on our marriage and walked away, I would regret it every single day for the rest of my life.

More than that, I would be giving up a quality of life. I would be letting the best thing in my life go. I would have to resign myself to a secondhand citizenship *in my own life* and I could not do that.

I didn't deserve it.

He didn't deserve it.

We didn't deserve it.

Before I could create words and explanations and apologies out of all of that, he stepped forward again, closing the distance between us and said, "I'm sorry, Katie. I'm sorry for everything." When I saw real tears reflected in his deep blue eyes, I immediately burst into tears. I couldn't help it. I had never seen him like this before.

"Nick, you don't have to-"

"I do. I need to say all of this. It's stuff I should have said years ago. I should never have let us get this far. I should never have let you go. Not once." More hot tears spilled down my cheeks and I nodded, letting him go on. "I'm sorry that I couldn't let go of the band. It was stupid. It was stupid of me to hold onto it for so long. I haven't wanted it, not really anyway, for a long time. But I hated the taste of failure and disappointment and when I looked at you, with this career that you loved and all of your success, I just couldn't... I couldn't deal with that. I was stubborn in a way that deeply hurt us... hurt *you* and I'm sorry I did that to us." I opened my mouth to answer him, but he held up his hand and with a small smile said, "Please wait. There's more."

"Okay," I whispered.

"I'm sorry I didn't take the burden off you financially. I know you will teach no matter what I do, but I shouldn't have put you in that position. I will never do it again. And it's not because I don't think you're capable or that you weren't handling it. I know you are and I know you did. But we are in this together. We *have* to be in this together. We're a partnership. One-half isn't greater or less than the other. We are two halves that make one whole. I'm sorry I stopped us from being equals."

He took another step toward me and we were only an inch apart. I felt him this time and it was real. I felt his body heat. I smelled him, the way only he could smell. I could reach out and touch him if I wanted... if I wasn't so afraid he would shatter into glass, proving I had conjured him up in my depression.

"I'm sorry we haven't had a baby yet. I'm sorry I haven't done everything in my power to find out what's wrong and give you the thing you want most. I'm sorry I ignored you and neglected you and treated you cruelly. I'm sorry I let us drift apart while we were together. I'm sorry I left you. And I'm sorry I stayed away for so long.

"There are so many things between us, Kate. I know we can't just fix ourselves overnight. But I want you to know that I'm going to do everything I can to make this work. I am going to work as hard as I can. I am going to think of you first and show you love... show you how *very much* I love you. I can't do this anymore. I can't keep fighting with you and making you miserable. I can't keep making myself miserable. We deserve so much more." His blue eyes speared me with a heated, powerful look. "*You* deserve so much more. Because the truth is, I surrender too. To this. To us. To *you*." He swallowed roughly, then with sincerity that rocked me to the center of my being, asked, "Will you forgive me?"

The words were stuck in my throat, clogged with too much emotion and racing each other to get out. I threw my body at him, wrapping my arms around his neck and flattening myself against his chest. He caught me. I knew he would. "Yes," I whispered. "Yes, I forgive you."

When he tightened his arms around my waist, it was different than before. He held me with promise, with hope. He held me in a way that was so permanent and lasting I felt it to my bones.

249

"I'm sorry, too," I cried against him, wetting his shirt. "I almost don't know where to begin. There are just too many things." His fingers trailed gently through my hair, giving me courage to go on. "I'm sorry I didn't respect you. I'm sorry I didn't support you. I'm sorry I didn't trust you. I'm so sorry this got so convoluted." I took a second to breathe through trembling sobs. "But most of all I'm sorry for leaving you too. I'm sorry I didn't try to do everything I could to fix us first. I'm sorry I was so selfish."

"It's okay," he whispered against my hair. "It's going to be okay." His lips touched my forehead and he said, "I should never have let you get away."

Some of the old fear reared its ugly head and I tilted my face toward his. "Are we going to be okay?"

He pulled back so he could hold me with his gaze again. "We are. We're already on our way to okay." A tremulous smile tilted my lips and he mimicked it. "God, Kate, I have never loved anything or anyone like I love you. I know we're going to make it because you are the most important thing in my life and I am tired of not treating you like that. I can't let you go. I don't want to let you go. I want to fix this, Katie. I want to shed all the bullshit and get to the center of things... the center of us. I love you, Kate. I'm never going to leave you again."

I leaned up on my toes and pressed a kiss to the underside of his jaw. He didn't hesitate to dip his head and meet my mouth. His tongue swept over my bottom lip and then he deepened the kiss into a frenetic free fall of love and passion and apology.

We clung to each other as tightly as we could, as if the smallest space between us was intolerable. His mouth moved over mine greedily, hungrily... adoringly.

This was just a kiss, but so much more than anything we had ever done. This was more than sex, more than fighting, more than any hurt we could have ever caused each other.

We promised something new to each other, saying our vows all over again. This kiss became the beginning of a new life for us, the foundation for which everything else would be built.

This *wasn't* just a kiss. This was forgiveness. This was healing.

This was our future.

When he pulled back, it was to trail sweet kisses along my temple and down my cheek to the line of my jaw. He tasted my tears and I felt cherished.

I felt loved again.

He took my hands and led me to our couch. We sat down, tangled in each other with the words to his song hanging behind us and the home we'd built surrounding us.

"It was all for you," he murmured.

"The job?"

"That was the start of it," he agreed. I had my head on his chest, listening to the beautiful cadence of his heart, but I felt him nod. "The night I left I knew I'd lost the best thing in my life. I knew I'd lost everything. The job was first. I knew I couldn't come back to you without one." He laughed at himself, running a hand through his hair. "God, I sound like a deadbeat."

I sat up quickly, facing him, letting him see the truth in my expression. "You're not one. Nick, I never thought that. No matter what we fought over or how damaged we became, I never thought you were a deadbeat. I wanted to support your dreams. I did for as long as I could, but… but there came a point when I didn't think you wanted it anymore. It felt like you were just hanging on to it because that was all you could think of. I saw so much potential in you, Nick. It destroyed me to see you give up."

His hand, filled with callouses from his guitar, cupped my jaw. "I know that now. I didn't then because I didn't want to see it. I wanted to blame someone. I wanted to hurt someone. I wanted someone else to feel like I did. I'm sorry that was you. I will never let it happen again."

Fresh tears filled my eyes. "I believe you."

He swept the sweetest kiss on my lips and pulled back. We weren't finished talking. "It wasn't just the job. I, the, uh, the mediation was because of you too. I couldn't let you go. Not even after you made it so clear you wanted nothing to do with me. I got the best lawyer I could and I made your life a living hell just to keep you from leaving me. I hired Ryan Templeton to drag out our divorce for as long as he could."

I felt my stomach pick up out of my body and start spinning uncontrollably. I felt like I was on the steepest rollercoaster. I couldn't catch my breath. "You didn't really want the house?"

His voice pitched low, "I wanted the house… with you in it." One corner of his mouth kicked up in a half-smile. "And I wanted the dog as long as you got her too. I wanted the TV and the kitchen table and the bed upstairs and whatever else I made that asshole lawyer fight with you about because they came attached to you. I couldn't let you go, Kate. Until the other morning when I thought you would leave me anyway. I didn't know what else to do besides give you what you wanted. But you should know that if you had gone through with it, I would have still

251

belonged to you. You own me, Kate. You will always own me. You are my wife till death do us part."

My heart swelled in my chest until I was certain it would burst. Until I knew I would die from happiness.

"Thank you," I whispered. "Thank you for fighting for me."

He pulled me against his chest again and I rested there. I gave up everything at that moment and just breathed in my husband.

He was right. He was mine. I was his. He owned me and I owned him. *Till death do us part.*

We stayed there the rest of the afternoon and evening. We stayed there, on our couch and talked and talked and talked. We made more apologies. We made more promises. We decided to find a couple's counselor that could help us through the next part of this journey. And we finally made love.

Right there on the couch.

Afterward, wrapped in the throw blankets from our living room, we ate a meal of cheese and crackers and ice cream. Then we walked hand in hand to our bedroom where we made love all over again.

This time when Nick wrapped me in his arms, I didn't wake in a panic. I fell blissfully asleep in his arms and didn't stir until morning.

And when we woke, we kissed without brushing our teeth. We held each other closely and made promises all over again.

It wouldn't always be like this. Seven years of marriage had taught us that every day would be different, that life would throw us curve balls and we wouldn't always get along. But our eyes were wide open now. We knew what we wanted. And that was each other.

He would drive me crazy and I would inevitably make him furious.

But he would also make me happier than I had ever been. He would also take care of me, adore me, love me. And I would love him in return. I would support him. And I would respect him.

We had a long way to go toward healing, but we were starting in the right place.

We were starting hand-in-hand and together.

And neither one of us would ever let go.

Chapter Twenty-Five

31. He **loves** me.
32. He will **always love** me.

"Are you finished?" Kara's pretty red head poked in my doorway and she took in the room with lightning fast quickness. "You look finished."

I stood up from a box I had been taping closed and stretched my back. "I think I am. Nick is going to pick me up and carry all this."

She grinned at me, "Perks of having a good man." I laughed and waggled my eyebrows at her. She stepped into the room completely. "This year went by so fast. I can't believe it's over."

I smiled wryly, "I can. I'm ready for summer." I sighed. "I'm ready to actually start summer."

She rolled her eyes at me. "Why, Kate? It's not like you have a job in the fall. What does it matter to you?"

I laughed as my hand landed gently on my slightly swollen belly. "I didn't take you for the jealous type. I thought you had a purpose here."

She stuck her tongue out at me. "Well, mostly my purpose is to annoy my parents. These hoodlums are a side effect of bad judgment and stubborn rebellion."

"You're such a liar. You love the kids here. And you're only half serious about annoying your parents."

"I'll give you the kids. I do love the little monsters. But I'm serious about my parents. My life work is to drive them to their early graves and inherit their estate."

I just shook my head. There was no arguing with her. "I *am* coming back," I told her. "Maybe not right away... but I will be back. I can't walk away from teaching forever."

Her gray gaze found mine and glistened with unshed tears. "I know you will. You're too good at what you do to give it up forever. You'll just have to turn that endless inspiration on your own little ones now. They get to keep you for a while. As they should."

Hearing the sorrow in her tone, I had to assure her. "Good thing they have their Auntie Kara to keep it real for them. I've been told I'm a little delusional with my optimism at times."

She let out a bark of laughter, "Who told you that?"

"Mostly my students. The same ones I'm trying to inspire."

She grinned at me. "You know, this is much better than being spinsters together. I probably would have eventually stabbed you with my crochet hook."

"We would have made terrible spinsters," I agreed. "We're way too hot for cats."

She snorted. "Because only ugly people have cats?"

"Oh, no. That's not what I meant."

She waved me off. "I know what you meant. Your secret hate for people with cats is safe with me."

It was my turn to laugh. "Well, I am a dog person you know."

"How could you not be? A dog saved your marriage *and* knocked you up."

"The dog did *not* knock me up."

She winked at me. "Not what I heard."

I shook my head and joined her at the door. "I need to check my mailbox."

She sighed. "I need to go fill out paperwork. Apparently your powers of inspiration worked better than usual. Jay Allen signed up for summer school."

"Why?" I gasped. "His grade in my class was excellent. What classes does he have to retake?"

She leaned in as if she were telling a secret. "He's not retaking anything, Kate. He's taking as many AP classes as I'm going to let him. Apparently, he wants to get into a good school."

"You're kidding."

"I am very serious."

My smile was so big I practically glowed. Tears filled my eyes and I blamed hormones. I rarely cried under normal circumstances.

Just kidding.

"Good." I finally said.

"Thought you'd be happy." We reached the hall where her office was nestled next to the teachers' lounge. "I'll call you later, k? Andrea and I are planning a baby shower for you. I need your input."

"Oh, my god, what is wrong with you?"

"It was her idea."

"Kara, I'm not going through with that. You can't make me. Besides, last I heard everyone thought I was a drama queen for calling off my divorce."

She shot me a mischievous grin. "But now that you're preggers they understand why you called off your divorce. You can't raise a baby alone. Plus he got that nice job. Clearly you're in it for the money."

I groaned. "Do none of them realize there was no possible way for me to know I was pregnant when I called off the divorce? Or that I thought it was literally impossible for me to have a baby? Are they *all* morons?"

Her smile dimmed, "Every last one I'm afraid."

"And these are people in charge of educating the future leaders of America. I'm actually afraid." She laughed at me but didn't argue. I turned to her and said seriously, "I don't want to do the baby shower."

"If only life was all about the things we *want* to do."

"You are the worst guidance counselor ever."

She gave me a quick kiss on the cheek and disappeared into her office, throwing over her shoulder, "You don't mean that. I saved your marriage!"

I couldn't help but laugh. She was absolutely ridiculous.

And I loved her for it.

She might not have saved my marriage, but she definitely saved me when I thought my marriage was over.

Maybe she wasn't the *worst* guidance counselor ever. That might have been a slight exaggeration.

I lifted my head and stumbled to a stop when I saw Eli Cohen watching me intently from the table beside our mailboxes. He was perched on the edge of it, with legs stretched out and ankles crossed. His arms were folded over his chest and his thick-framed glasses in place, hiding his eyes from me.

"Hello, Mr. Cohen," I said, hoping for casual. We had never regained the friendship we'd lost after our inauspicious coffee date. Things had been strained and forced ever since.

It was strange to me because I thought our friendship had been real. But it was hard to sort out now since he had avoided me like the plague ever since he realized I wasn't interested in him romantically.

And I honestly didn't want to dissect it too much.

"Hi, Kate. How are you?" His smile was genuine, even as his gaze drifted to my small, round belly.

At the end of June, I was only three months along, but there was a small enough bump to make it clear that I was pregnant. The kids had been out of school for three weeks, but teachers still hung around, working on their classrooms or teaching summer school.

I was packing up my classroom, as I would be taking a couple years off. I had a baby to raise. A family to focus on.

A husband to let take care of me.

"I'm good," I told him honestly. I allowed a smile and repeated, "I'm really good."

"You look good, Kate." His head tilted to indicate all of me. Just as I started to feel slightly uncomfortable, he added, "I've meant to tell you something, it's just I've always felt a bit awkward about it. But, I wanted to say that I'm happy for you. I really am. I'm glad everything worked out with Nick. It was obvious you were never over him."

My smile stayed in place. I felt his authenticity and I respected it. "Thank you, Eli. I appreciate that."

"Good luck with the baby," he added. "You'll be a great mom."

He stood up and strode from the room before I could say anything else. But I found that I didn't really have anything else to say. It was nice to have that chapter closed, but it hadn't been necessary.

I did hope the best for him, though. I hoped he could one day move on from his own heartbreak and find someone else. I hoped he could find someone that fit him, that loved him as much as he deserved.

My phone buzzed in my pocket. Nick was here. I texted to tell him to meet me in my classroom, then gathered the last papers from my mailbox.

I walked back to my room slowly, savoring the smell of metal lockers and floor polish. There was a mustiness that clung to the building that usually made me wrinkle my nose. But now I realized it smelled like school to me. This was how I would always define Hamilton.

And I knew I would miss it.

I had been here for nine years, just a little longer than I had been married. Unlike my marriage, though, it was time to close this door. It was time to move on.

For now.

I thought about Jay Allen and knew I would eventually be back. I couldn't give this up forever. But for now, it was the right thing to do for my family.

I smiled to myself. God, it felt good to say that.

Nick and I had made so much progress over the last three months. Not because we were forcing it because of the baby, but because we both *wanted* progress. We both wanted to heal and create a safe, comfortable home for our little one.

We both wanted each other and this marriage and real, authentic happiness.

And finally, after everything that had happened, we had it.

In April, we had celebrated our eighth wedding anniversary. We had gone out to a nice dinner and shared a bottle of champagne at home. We had never been happier. Never more content to make something work. Never shared life that was so beautiful.

Two days later we found out I was pregnant.

Nobody had been more surprised than us when we found out about the baby. But nobody had been more overjoyed either.

We were seeing a counselor too. We wanted to heal from our past and move forward with the tools we needed to succeed. I taught my students that knowledge was power. Not because you could rule with it, but because it prepared you for the future and equipped you for whatever was to come.

I had taken that advice to heart and applied it to our marriage. We were growing closer and closer together every day, but there was still a lot of work to be done and neither Nick nor I knew what the future would hold.

We wanted to be prepared.

We wanted to be ready to stand side by side and face whatever the world threw at us together.

Sometimes I wondered if I fell in love with him for all the wrong reasons. But I also knew I had wanted to leave him for all the wrong reasons too.

The only thing that mattered now though was that I wanted to stay with him for the right reasons.

That we used those reasons to choose to love each other and choose to stay together no matter what obstacles we faced.

I loved him.

I would always choose to love him.

And he would do the same for me.

"What are you smiling about?" His voice drifted in from the doorway, where he leaned against the frame watching me.

"You," I told him honestly. "Us."

He walked toward me, a slow, prowling gait that gave me butterflies in all the right places. "Those are good things to smile about." He reached me, swooping down to kiss my hands that rested on my belly. When he stood up again, his eyes shimmered with adoration, "That's a good thing to smile about too."

I leaned into him and wrapped my arms around his waist. His hands held me to him, one of them rubbing a soothing pattern over my back.

"Are you going to miss this place?" he asked gently.

I nodded against his chest. "Yes, eventually. But I'm going to love staying home too. At least for a little while."

"I'm going to love you staying home too," he chuckled. "You can make me lunch every day and iron my clothes."

I pinched his nipple and made him yelp. "You can make your own lunch," I scolded. "I *will* iron your clothes, though. It's cheaper that way."

He let out a bark of laughter. "It's true. I get tired of buying new shirts every time I ruin one."

"You're a smart man, Nicholas. I don't know why you can't figure out an iron."

I felt his smile when he pressed a kiss to the top of my head. "It's just one of the many reasons I need you, Katie. Don't ever leave me."

I lifted my face to meet his gaze. "Never," I promised.

He squeezed me tighter to him. "I love you."

His words were powerful. So powerful I felt them in my very core, in the very heart of me. I felt them as something permanent and lasting. I felt them as an oath, an unerring truth... as the conviction I lived my life with.

He was my husband.

He loved me.

He would always love me.

That was reason enough for me to love him back.

"I love you too."

He kissed me slowly, lazily and so not appropriate for school. Then he helped me pack up nine years of teaching and we drove home to start the next chapter of our lives.

Together.

Look for Rachel's next contemporary romance, The Opposite of You, coming January 26, 2016!

Acknowledgments

To God. For creative words, thoughtful moments and messy females. For loving the broken ones.

And to Zach. You are the greatest thing that has ever happened to me. I respect you. And I surrender. Every single day.

Mom, for the example you set. For being the wife that you were. For being the mom, the grandmother and the friend that you will always be.

To Carolyn, thank you for your endless work. Thank you for being unfathomably strong. For editing through cancer. For not hating me for asking you to. You are my hero.

To Caedus Design Co., you did more than create a cover. You molded a story. Thank you for always knowing what I need.

To Candice, Leigh, Miriah and Lenore. You girls. Seriously. *You girls*. I love you more than words. I love you more than confusing plot points and missing moments and all of the things that you catch and share and give. And on top of everything you are so careful with me. Me, the fragile, insecure artist. You are champions in my corner and I am so blessed to have you in my life. Thank you for your honesty. But most of all, thank you for believing in characters that are underdeveloped and words that are wrong, misplaced and grammatically incorrect. You believe in my stories before they're anything. And you fall in love with characters before they are what they're supposed to be. Thank you.

To my peers and my friends, Samantha Young, Shelly Crane, Lila Felix, Amy Bartol, Georgia Cates, and Heather Lyons, thank you for being people I can count on. Thank you for understanding my fears and insecurities. For listening to me while I talk about them. For believing in me. And for supporting me. You ladies are the very best that there is. I would be nothing but a hunchback hermit without you.

To Mark My Words Book Publicity, thank you for being the best. Thank you for believing in me enough to work hard for me. Thank you for being so incredibly cool.

Rachel Marks, my agent, you are awesome. I am so lucky to know you and work with you. Thank you for putting in all of these hours and phone calls and emails. Thank you for wanting the best for me.

To my Rebel Panel. I started a group to support my career, but instead I found support for my life. I could never have predicted the kind of community we've formed together. But I am constantly thankful for it. And for all of you. Thank you for always being there to answer my quirky questions and for loving me even when I disappear for way too long. Thank you for loving these words and these characters and for treating them like they are your own. I love each of you.

Reckless Rebels. Girls. You are the very best of the best. Thank you so much for treating me like a rock star and always showing up when I need you. Thank you for just being there and listening to me and encouraging me. You humble me. And you make me so endlessly grateful. Thank you so much.

And now, thank you dear Readers. Thank you for taking this journey with me. Thank you for spending your time with my words. That is the greatest gift you could ever give me and I am so, beyond blessed that you chose this book to read. You have changed my life. And with every single download of something I've written, you continue to change it. And me. And I can never thank you enough for that.

About the Author

Rachel Higginson was born and raised in Nebraska, but spent her college years traveling the world. She fell in love with Eastern Europe, Paris, Indian Food and the beautiful beaches of Sri Lanka, but came back home to marry her high school sweetheart. Now she spends her days raising their growing family. She is obsessed with bad reality TV and any and all Young Adult Fiction.

Please look for Rachel's next contemporary romance, The Opposite of You, coming January 26th, 2016.

Other Books Out Now by Rachel Higginson:

Love and Decay, Season One
Love and Decay, Volume One (Episodes One-Six, Season One)
Love and Decay, Volume Two (Episodes Seven-Twelve, Season One)
Love and Decay, Season Two
Love and Decay, Volume Three (Episodes One-Four, Season Two)
Love and Decay, Volume Four (Episodes Five-Eight, Season Two)
Love and Decay, Volume Five (Episodes Nine-Twelve, Season Two)
Love and Decay, Season Three
Love and Decay, Volume Six (Episodes One-Four, Season Three)
Love and Decay, Volume Seven (Episodes Five-Eight, Season Three)
Love and Decay, Volume Eight (Episodes Nine-Twelve, Season Three)

Reckless Magic (The Star-Crossed Series, Book 1)
Hopeless Magic (The Star-Crossed Series, Book 2)
Fearless Magic (The Star-Crossed Series, Book 3)
Endless Magic (The Star-Crossed Series, Book 4)
The Reluctant King (The Star-Crossed Series, Book 5)
The Relentless Warrior (The Star-Crossed Series, Book 6)
Breathless Magic (The Star-Crossed Series, Book 6.5)
Fateful Magic (The Star-Crossed Series, Book 6.75)
The Redeemable Prince (The Star-Crossed Series, Book 7)

Heir of Skies (The Starbright Series, Book 1)
Heir of Darkness (The Starbright Series, Book 2)

Heir of Secrets (The Starbright Series, Book 3)

The Rush (The Siren Series, Book 1)
The Fall (The Siren Series, Book 2)
The Heart (The Siren Series, Book 3)

Bet on Us (An NA Contemporary Romance)
Bet on Me (An NA Contemporary Romance) coming fall 2016

The Opposite of You coming January 2016

Connect with Rachel on her blog at:
http://www.rachelhigginson.com/

Or on Twitter:
@mywritesdntbite

Or on her Facebook page:
Rachel Higginson

Keep reading for an excerpt from The Five Stages of Falling in Love, a
second chance adult contemporary romance and after that, please enjoy
a preview of Rachel's zombie novella series, Love and Decay.

Please enjoy a preview of Rachel's second chance romance, The Five Stages of Falling in Love.

Prologue

"Hey, there she is," Grady looked up at me from his bed, his eyes smiling even while his mouth barely mimicked the emotion.

"Hey, you," I called back. The lights had been dimmed after the last nurse checked his vitals and the TV was on, but muted. "Where are the kiddos? I was only in the cafeteria for ten minutes."

Grady winked at me playfully, "My mother took them." I melted a little at his roguish expression. It was the same look that made me agree to a date with him our junior year of college, it was the same look that made me fall in love with him- the same one that made me agree to have our second baby boy when I would have been just fine to stop after Blake, Abby and Lucy.

"Oh, yeah?" I walked over to the hospital bed and sat down next to him. He immediately reached for me, pulling me against him with weak arms. I snuggled back into his chest, so that my head rested on his thin shoulder and our bodies fit side by side on the narrow bed. One of my legs didn't make it and hung off awkwardly. But I didn't mind. It was just perfect to lie next to the love of my life, my husband.

"Oh, yeah," he growled suggestively. "You know what that means?" He walked his free hand up my arm and gave my breast a wicked squeeze. "When the kids are away, the grownups get to play…"

"You are so bad," I swatted him- or at least made the motion of swatting at him, since I was too afraid to hurt him.

"God, I don't remember the last time I got laid," he groaned next to me and I felt the rumble of his words against my side.

"Tell me about it, sport," I sighed. "I could use a nice, hard-"

"Elizabeth Carlson," he cut in on a surprised laugh. "When did you get such a dirty mouth?"

"I think you've known about my dirty mouth for quite some time, Grady," I flirted back. We'd been serious for so long it was nice to flirt with him, to remember that we didn't just love each other, but we liked each other too.

He grunted in satisfaction. "That I have. I think your dirty mouth had something to do with Lucy's conception."

I blushed. Even after all these years, he knew exactly what to say to me. "Maybe," I conceded.

"Probably," he chuckled, his breath hot on my ear.

We lay there in silence for a while, enjoying the feel of each other, watching the silent TV screen flicker in front of our eyes. It was perfect- or as close to perfect as we had felt in a long time.

"Dance with me, Lizzy," Grady whispered after a while. I'd thought maybe he fell asleep; the drugs were so hard on his system that he was usually in and out of consciousness. This was actually the most coherent he'd been in a month.

"Okay," I agreed. "It's the first thing we'll do when you get out. We'll have your mom come over and babysit, you can take me to dinner at Pazio's and we'll go dancing after."

"Mmm, that sounds nice," he agreed. "You love Pazio's. That's a guaranteed get-lucky night for me."

"Baby," I crooned. "As soon as I get you back home, you're going to have guaranteed get-lucky nights for at least a month, maybe two."

"I don't want to wait. I'm tired of waiting. Dance with me now, Lizzy," Grady pressed, this time sounding serious.

"Babe, after your treatment this morning, you can barely stand up right now. Honestly, how are you going to put all those sweet moves on me?" I wondered where this sudden urge to dance, of all things, was coming from.

"Lizzy, I am a sick man. I haven't slept in my own bed in four months, I haven't seen my wife naked in just as long, and I am tired of lying in this bed. I want to dance with you. Will you please, pretty please, dance with me?"

I nodded at first because I was incapable of speech. He was right. I hated that he was right, but I hated that he was sick even more.

"Alright, Grady, I'll dance with you," I finally whispered.

"I knew I'd get my way," he croaked smugly.

I slipped off the bed and turned around to face my husband and help him to his feet. His once full head of auburn hair was now bald, reflecting the pallid color of his skin. His face was haggard showing dark black circles under his eyes, chapped lips and pale cheeks. He was still as tall as he'd ever been, but instead of the toned muscles and thick frame he once boasted, he was depressingly skinny and weak, his shoulders perpetually slumped.

The only thing that remained the same were his eyes; they were the same dark green eyes I'd fallen in love with ten years ago. They were still full of life, still full of mischief even when his body wasn't. They held life while the rest of him drowned in exhaustion from fighting this stupid sickness.

"You always get your way," I grumbled while I helped him up from the bed.

"Only with you," he shot back on a pant after successfully standing. "And only because you love me."

"That I do," I agreed. Grady's hands slipped around my waist and he clutched my sides in an effort to stay standing.

I wrapped my arms around his neck, but didn't allow any weight to press down on him. We maneuvered our bodies around his IV and monitors. It was awkward, but we managed.

"What should we listen to?" I asked, while I pulled out my cell phone and turned it to my iTunes app.

"You know what song. There is no other song when we're dancing," he reminded me on a faint smile.

"You must be horny," I laughed. "You're getting awfully romantic."

"Just trying to keep this fire alive, Babe," he pulled me closer and I held back the flood of tears that threatened to spill over.

I turned on *The Way You Look Tonight*- the Frank Sinatra version- and we swayed slowly back and forth. Frank sang the soft, beautiful lyrics with the help of a full band, while the music drifted around us over the constant beeping and whirring of medical machines. This was the song we thought of as ours, the first song we'd danced to at our wedding, the song he still made the band at Pazio's play on our anniversary each year.

"This fire is very much alive," I informed him sternly. I lay my forehead against his shoulder and inhaled him. He didn't smell like himself anymore, he was full of chemo drugs and smelled like hospital soap and detergent, but he was still Grady. And even though he barely resembled the man I had fallen so irrevocably in love with, he still *felt* like Grady.

He was still *my* Grady.

"It is, isn't it?" He whispered. I could feel how weak he was growing, how tired this was making him, but still he clung to me and held me close. When my favorite verse came on, he leaned his head down and whispered in a broken voice along with Frank, "There is nothing for me, but to love you. And the way you look tonight."

Silent tears streamed down my face with truths I wasn't ready to admit to myself and fears that were too horrifying to even think. This was the man I loved with every fiber of my being- the only man I'd ever loved. The only man I'd *ever love.*

He'd made me fall in love with him before I was old enough to drink legally, then he'd convinced me to marry him before I even graduated from college. He knocked me up a year later, and didn't stop until we had four wild rug rats that all had his red hair and his emerald green eyes. He'd encouraged me to finish my undergrad degree, and then to continue on to grad school while I was pregnant, nursing and then pregnant again. He went to bed every night with socks on and then took them off sometime in the middle of the night, leaving them obnoxiously tucked in between our sheets. He could never find his wallet, or his keys, and when there was hair to grow he always forgot to shave.

And he drove me crazy most of the time.

But he was mine.

He was my husband.

And now he was sick.

"I do love you, Lizzy," he murmured against my hair. "I'll always love you, even when I'm dead and gone."

"Which won't be for at least fifty more years," I reminded him on a sob.

He ignored me, "You love me back, don't you?"

"Yes, I love you back," I whispered with so much emotion the words stuck in my throat. "But you already knew that."

"Maybe," he conceded gently. "But I will never, ever get tired of hearing it."

I sniffled against him, staining his hospital gown with my mascara and eye liner. "That's a good thing, because you're going to be hearing it for a very long time."

He didn't respond, just kept swaying with me back and forth until the song ended. He asked me to play it again and I did, three more times. By the end of the fourth, he was too tired to stand. I laid him back in bed and helped him adjust the IV and monitor again so that it didn't bother him, then pulled the sheet over his cold toes.

His eyes were closed and I thought he'd fallen asleep, so I bent down to kiss his forehead. He stirred at my touch and reached out to cup my face with his un-needled arm. I looked down into his depthless green eyes and fell in love with him all over again.

It was as simple as that.

It had always been that simple for him to get me to fall in love with him.

"You are the most beautiful thing that ever happened to me, Lizzy." His voice was broken and scratchy and a tear slid out from the corner of each of his eyes.

My chin trembled at his words because I knew what he was doing and I hated it, I hated every part of it. I shook my head, trying to get him to stop but he held my gaze and just kept going.

"You are. And you have made my life good, and worth living. You have made me love more than any man has ever known how to love. I didn't know this kind of happiness existed in real life, Liz, and you're the one that gave it to me. I couldn't be more thankful for the life we've shared together. I couldn't be more thankful for you."

"Oh, Grady, please-"

"Lizzy," he said in his sternest voice that he only used when I'd maxed out a credit card. "Whatever happens, whatever happens to me, I want you to keep giving this gift to other people." I opened my mouth to vehemently object to everything he was saying but he silenced me with a cold finger on my lips. "I didn't say go marry the first man you find. Hell, I'm not even talking about another man. But I don't want this light to die with me. I don't want you to forget how happy you make other people just because you might not feel happy. Even if I don't, Lizzy, I want you to go on living. Promise me that."

But I shook my head, "No." I wasn't going to promise him that. I couldn't make myself. And it was unfair of him to ask me that.

"Please, Sweetheart, for me?" His deep, green eyes glossed over with emotion and I could physically feel how painful this was for him to ask me. He didn't want this anymore than I did.

I found myself nodding, while I sniffled back a stream of tears. "Okay," I whispered. "I promise."

He broke out into a genuine smile then, his thumb rubbing back and forth along my jaw. "Now tell me you love me, one more time."

"I love you, Grady," I murmured, leaning into his touch and savoring this moment with him.

"And I will always, always love you, Lizzy."

His eyes finally fluttered shut and his hand dropped from my face. His vitals remained the same, so I knew he was just sleeping. I crawled into bed with him, gently shifting him so that I could lie on my side, in the nook of his arm and lay my hand on his chest. I did this often; I liked to feel the beat of his heart underneath my hand. It had stopped too many times

269

before, for me to trust its reliability. My husband was a very sick man, and had been for a while now.

Tonight was different though. Tonight, Grady was lucid and coherent, he'd found enough energy to stand up and dance with me, to tell me he loved me. Tonight could have been a turn for the better.

But it wasn't- because only a few hours later, Grady's heart stopped for the third time during his adult life, and this time it never restarted.

Stage One: Denial

Not every story has a happy ending. Some only hold a happy beginning.

This is my story. I'd already met my soul mate, fallen in love with him and lived our happily ever after.

This story is not about me falling in love.

This story is about me learning to live again after love left my life.

Research shows there are five stages of grief. I don't know what this means for me, as I was stuck, nice and hard, in step one.

Denial.

I knew, acutely, that I was still in stage one.

I knew this because every time I walked in the house, I wandered around aimlessly looking for Grady. I still picked up my phone to check if he texted or called throughout the day. I looked for him in a crowded room, got the urge to call him from the grocery store just to make sure I had everything he needed, and reached for him in the middle of the night.

Acceptance- the last stage of grief- was firmly and forever out of my reach, and I often looked forward to it with longing. Why? Because Denial was a *son of a bitch* and it hurt more than *anything* when I realized he wasn't in the house, wouldn't be calling me, wasn't where I wanted him to be, didn't need anything from the store and would never lie next to me in bed again. The grief, fresh and suffocating, would cascade over me and I was forced to suffer through the unbearable pain of losing my husband all over again.

Denial *sucked*.

But it was where I was right now. I was living in Denial.

Chapter One
Six Months after Grady died.

I snuggled back into the cradle of his body while his arms wrapped around me tightly. He buried his scruffy face against the nape of my neck and I sighed contentedly. We fit perfectly together, but then again we always had- his big spoon nestled up against my little spoon.

"It's your turn," he rumbled against my skin with that deep morning voice I would always drink in.

"No," I argued half-heartedly. "It's always my turn."

"But you're so good at it," he teased.

I giggled, "It's one of my many talents, pouring cereal into bowls, making juice cups. I might just take this show on the road."

He laughed behind me and his chest shook with the movement. I pushed back into him, loving the feel of his hard, firm chest against my back. He was so hot first thing in the morning, his whole body radiated warmth.

His hand splayed out across my belly possessively and he pressed a kiss just below my ear. I could feel his lips through my tangle of hair and the tickle of his breath which wasn't all that pleasant first thing in the morning, but it was Grady and it was familiar.

"It's probably time we had another one, don't you think?" His hand rubbed a circle around my stomach and I could feel him vibrating happily with the thought.

"Grady, we already have three," I reminded him on a laugh. "If we have another one, people are going to start thinking we're weird."

"No, they won't," he soothed. "They might get an idea of how fertile you are, but they won't think we're weird."

I snorted a laugh. "They already think we're weird."

"Then we don't want to disappoint them," he murmured. His hand slid up my chest and cupped my breast, giving it a gentle squeeze.

"You are obsessed with those things," I grinned.

"Definitely," he agreed quickly, while continuing to fondle me. "What do you think, Lizzy? Will you give me another baby?"

I was getting wrapped up in the way he was touching me, the way he was caressing me with so much love I thought I would burst. "I'll think about it," I finally conceded, knowing he would get his way- knowing I always let him have his way.

"While you're mulling it over, we should probably practice. I mean, we want to get this right when the time comes." Grady trailed kisses down the column of my throat and I moaned my consent.

I rolled over to kiss him on the mouth.

But he wasn't there.

My arm swung wide and hit cold, empty mattress.

I opened my eyes and stared at the slow moving ceiling fan over my head. The early morning light streamed in through cracks in my closed blinds and I let the silent tears fall.

I hated waking up like this; thinking he was there, next to me, still able to support me, love me and hold me. And unfortunately it happened more often than it didn't.

The fresh pain clawed and cut at my heart and I thought I would die just from sheer heartbreak. My chin quivered and I sniffled, trying desperately to wrestle my emotions under control. But the pain was too much, too consuming.

"Mom!" Blake called from the kitchen, ripping me away from my peaceful grief. "Moooooom!"

That was a distressed cry, and I was up out of my bed and racing downstairs immediately. I grabbed my silk robe on the way and threw it over my black cami and plaid pajama bottoms. When the kids were younger I wouldn't have bothered, but Blake was eight now and he'd been traumatized enough in life. I wasn't going to add to that by walking around bra-less first thing in the morning.

He continued to yell at me, while I barreled into the kitchen still wiping at the fresh tears. I found him at the bay windows, staring out in horror.

"Mom, Abby went swimming," he explained in a rush of words.

A sick feeling knotted my stomach and I looked around wild-eyed at what his words could possibly mean. "What do you mean, Abby *went swimming*?" I gasped, a little out of breath.

"There," he pointed to the neighbor's backyard with a shaky finger.

I followed the direction of his outstretched hand and from the elevated vantage point of our kitchen I could see that the neighbor's pool was filled with water, and my six-year-old daughter was swimming morning laps like she was on a regulated workout routine.

"What the f-" I started and then stopped, shooting a glance down at Blake who looked up at me with more exaggerated shock than he'd given his sister.

I watched her for point one more second and sprinted for the front door. "Keep an eye on the other ones," I shouted at Blake as I pushed open our heavy red door.

It was just early fall in rural Connecticut. The grass was still green; the mornings were foggy but mostly still warm. The house next to us had been empty for almost a year. The owner had been asking too much for it in this economy, but I understood why. It was beautiful, clean-lined and modern with cream stucco siding and black decorative shutters. Big oak trees offered shade and character in the sprawling front yard and in the back, an in-ground pool was the drool-worthy envy of my children.

I raced down my yard and into my new neighbor's. I hadn't noticed the house had sold, but that didn't surprise me. I wasn't the most observant person these days. Vaguely I noted a moving truck parked in the long drive.

The backyard gate must have been left open. Even though Abby had taught herself how to swim at the age of four- the end result gave me several gray hairs- there was no way she could reach the flip lock at the top of the tall, white fence.

I rounded the corner and hopped/ran to the edge of the pool, the gravel of the patio cutting into my bare feet. I took a steadying breath and focused my panic-flooded mind long enough to assess whether Abby was still breathing or not.

She was, and happily swimming in circles *in the deep end*.

Fear and dread quickly turned to blinding anger and I took a step closer to the edge of the pool while I threw my silk robe on the ground.

"Abigail Elizabeth, you get out of there right this minute!" I shouted loud enough to wake up the entire neighborhood.

She popped her head up out of the water, acknowledged me by sticking out her tongue, and promptly went back to swimming. *That little brat.*

"Abigail, I am *not* joking. Get out of the pool. *Now!*" I hollered again. And was ignored- again. "Abby, if I have to come in there and get you, you will rue the day you were born!"

She poked her head back up out of the water, shooting me a confused look. Her light brown eyebrows drew together, just like her father's used to, and her little freckled nose wrinkled at something I said. I was smart enough or experienced enough to know that she was not on the verge of obeying, just because I'd threatened her.

"Mommy?" she asked, somehow making her little body tread water in a red polka dot bikini my sister picked up from Gap last summer. It was too small, which for some reason infuriated me even more. "What does *rue* mean?"

"It means you're grounded from the iPad, your Leapster and the Wii for the next two years of your life," I threatened. "Now get out of that pool right now before I come in there and get you myself."

She giggled in reply, not believing me for one second, and resumed her play.

"Damn it, Abigail," I growled under my breath but was not surprised by her behavior. She was naturally an adventurous child. Since she could walk, she'd been climbing to the highest point of anything she could, swinging precariously from branches, light fixtures and tall displays at the grocery store. She was a daredevil and there were moments when I absolutely adored her "the world is my playground" attitude about life. But then there were moments like this, when every mom instinct in me screamed she was in danger and her little, rotten life flashed before my eyes.

Those moments happened more and more often. She tested me, pushing every limit and boundary I'd set. She had been reckless before Grady died, now she was just wild. And I didn't know what to do about it.

I didn't know how to tame my uncontrollable child or how to be both parents to a little girl who desperately missed her daddy.

I focused on my outrage, pushing those tragic thoughts down, into the abyss of my soul. I was pissed; I didn't have time for this first thing in the morning and no doubt we were going to be late for school- again.

I slipped off my pajama pants, hoping whomever had moved into the house, if they were watching, would be more concerned with the little girl on the verge of drowning than me flashing my black, bikini briefs at them over morning coffee. I said a few more choice curses and dove into the barely warm water after my second born.

I surfaced, sputtering water and shivering from the cool morning air pebbling my skin. "Abigail, when I get you out of this pool, you are going to be in *so* much trouble."

"Okay," she agreed happily. "But first you have to catch me."

She proceeded to swim around in circles while I reached out helplessly for her. First thing I would do when I got out of this pool was throw away every electronic device in our house just to teach her a lesson. Then I was going to sign her up for a swim team because the little hellion was too fast for her own good.

We struggled like this for a few more minutes. Well, I struggled. She splashed at me and laughed at my efforts to wrangle her.

I was aware of a presence hovering by the edge of the pool, but I was equally too embarrassed and too preoccupied to acknowledge it. Images of walking my children into school late *again*, kept looping through my head and I cringed at the dirty looks I was bound to get from teachers and other parents alike.

"You look hungry," a deep masculine voice announced from above me.

I whipped my head around to find an incredibly tall man standing by my discarded pajama pants holding two beach towels and a box of Pop-Tarts in one arm, while he munched casually on said Pop-Tarts with the other.

"I look hungry?" I screeched in hysterical anger.

His eyes flickered down at me for just a second, "No, you look mad." He pointed at Abby, who had come to a stop next to me, treading water again with her short child-sized limbs waving wildly in the water. "*She* looks hungry." With a mouth full of food he grinned at me, and looked back at Abby. "Want a Pop-Tart? They're brown sugar."

Abby nodded excitedly and swam to the edge of the pool. Not even using the ladder, she heaved herself out of the water and ran over to the stranger holding out his breakfast to her. He handed her a towel and she hastily draped it around her shoulders and took the offered Pop-Tart.

A million warnings about taking food from strangers ran through my head, but in the end I decided getting us out of his pool was probably more important to him than offering his brand new neighbors poisoned Pop-Tarts.

With a defeated sigh, I swam over to the ladder closest to my pants and robe, and pulled myself up. I was a dripping, limp mess and frozen to the bone after my body adjusted to the temperature of the water.

277

Abby took her Pop-Tart and plopped down on one of the loungers that were still stacked on top of two others and wrapped in plastic. She began munching on it happily, grinning at me like she'd just won the lottery.

She was in *so* much trouble.

I walked over to the stranger, eying him skeptically. He held out his remaining beach towel to me and after realizing I stood before him in only a soaking wet tank top and bikini briefs, I took it quickly and wrapped it around my body. I shivered violently with my dark blonde hair dripping down my face and back. But I didn't dare adjust the towel, afraid I'd give him more of a show than he'd paid for.

"Good morning," he laughed at me.

"Good morning," I replied slowly, carefully.

Up close, he wasn't the giant I'd originally thought. Now that we were both ground level, I could see that while he was tall, at least six inches taller than me, he wasn't freakishly tall, which relieved some of my concerns. He still wore his pajamas: blue cotton pants and a white t-shirt that had been stretched out from sleep. His almost black hair appeared still mussed and disheveled, but swept over to the side in what could be a trendy style if he brushed it. He seemed to be a few years older than me, if I had to guess thirty-five or thirty-six, and he had dark, intelligent eyes that crinkled in the corners with amusement. He was tanned, and muscular, and imposing. And I hated that he was laughing at me.

"Sorry about the gate," he shrugged. "I didn't realize there were kids around."

"You moved into a neighborhood," I pointed out dryly. "There're bound to be kids around."

His eyes narrowed at the insult, but he swallowed his Pop-Tart and agreed, "Fair enough. I'll keep it locked from now on."

I wasn't finished with berating him though. His pool caused all kinds of problems for me this morning and since I could only take out so much anger on my six-year-old, I had to vent the rest somewhere. "Who fills their pool the first week of September anyway? You've been to New England in the winter, haven't you?"

He cleared his throat and the last laugh lines around his eyes disappeared. "My real estate agent," he explained. "It was kind of like a 'thank you' present for buying the house. He thought he was doing something nice for me."

I snorted at that, thinking how my little girl could have... No, I couldn't go there; I was not emotionally capable of thinking that thought through.

"I really am sorry," he offered genuinely, his dark eyes flashing with true emotion. "I got in late last night, and passed out on the couch. I didn't even know the pool was full or the gate was open until I heard you screaming out here."

Guilt settled in my stomach like acid, and I regretted my harsh tone with him. This wasn't his fault. I just wanted to blame someone besides myself.

"Look, I'm sorry I was snappish about the pool. I just... I was just worried about Abby. I took it out on you," I relented, but wouldn't look him in the eye. I'd always been terrible at apologies. When Grady and I would fight, I could never bring myself to tell him I felt sorry. Eventually, he'd just look at me and say, "I forgive you, Lizzy. Now come here and make it up to me." With anyone else my pride would have refused to let me give in, but with Grady, the way he smoothed over my stubbornness and let me get away with keeping my dignity worked every single time.

"It's alright, I can understand that," my new neighbor agreed.

We stood there awkwardly for a few more moments, before I swooped down to pick up my plaid pants and discarded robe. "Alright, well I need to go get the kids ready for school. Thanks for convincing her to get out. Who knows how long we would have been stuck there playing *Finding Nemo*."

He chuckled but his eyes were confused. "Is that like Marco Polo?"

I shot him a questioning glance, wondering if he was serious or not. "No kids?" I asked.

He laughed again. "Nope, life-long bachelor." He waved the box of Pop-Tarts and realization dawned on me. He hadn't really seemed like a father before now, but in my world- my four kids, soccer mom, neighborhood watch secretary, active member of the PTO world- it was almost unfathomable to me that someone his age could not have kids.

I cleared my throat, "It's uh, a little kid movie. Disney," I explained and understanding lit his expression. "Um, thanks again." I turned to Abby who was finishing up her breakfast, "Let's go, Abs, you're making us late for school."

"I'm Ben by the way," he called out to my back. "Ben Tyler."

I snorted to myself at the two first names; it somehow seemed appropriate for the handsome life-long bachelor, but ridiculous all the same.

"Liz Carlson," I called over my shoulder. "Welcome to the neighborhood."

"Uh, the towels?" he shouted after me when we'd reached the gate.

I turned around with a dropped mouth, thinking a hundred different vile things about my new neighbor. "Can't we... I..." I glanced down helplessly at my bare legs poking out of the bottom of the towel he'd just lent me.

"Liz," he laughed familiarly, and I tried not to resent him. "I'm just teasing. Bring them back whenever."

I growled something unintelligible that I hope sounded like "thank you" and spun on my heel, shooing Abby onto the lawn between our houses.

"Nice to meet you, neighbor," he called out over the fence.

"You too," I mumbled, not even turning my head to look back at him.

Obviously he was single and unattached. He was way too smug for his own good. I just hoped he would keep his gate locked and loud parties few and far between. He seemed like the type to throw frat party-like keggers and hire strippers for the weekend. I had a family to raise, a family that was quickly falling apart while I floundered to hold us together with tired arms and a broken spirit. I didn't need a nosy neighbor handing out Pop-Tarts and sarcasm interfering with my life.

Please enjoy an excerpt from Rachel's zombie novella series, Love and Decay!

Chapter One
647 days after initial infection

Oh, god.

The smell was the worst. *The absolute worst.*

It wasn't enough that I had to pick my way through dismembered and half-eaten bodies, or that at any moment one of them could spring up from the ground and make an afternoon snack out of me.

It wasn't enough that I hadn't had a shower in over a year and a half, hadn't worn eye liner in even longer than that and my hair was somehow simultaneously disgustingly greasy while frizzing into a perpetual fluff ball.

Oh no, that would never be enough. My ugly tan work boots were a size and a half too small, I ripped my too big Grateful Dead t-shirt off a very, very dead man, and my jeans…. or what was left of my jeans was the last of my stash from my once excessive closet.

After all of that- and I mean, the shower alone should have been enough suffering for any living being to suffer through- it was the smell that got to me.

Putrid, rotting flesh from both the dead that littered the ground around me and the remnants of stench that lingered in the air when the Feeders were finished was what triggered my gag reflex and watered my eyes. There weren't enough words in the English dictionary to describe my revulsion, or the way my empty stomach flipped with every breath.

I probably would have puked if I had eaten anything in the last two days.

The best thing about the Zombie Apocalypse? I was no longer addicted to sugar and caffeinated beverages.

I wiped my forearm across my sweaty forehead and re-aimed my handgun in the general area in front of me. This is the point of the story where I'm supposed to tell you what kind of gun I'm carrying, but let's be real…. Before the end of the world I was a cheerleader at a small town school, where I was the debate team captain and student council secretary. I lived for throwing parties when my parents went out of town, making out with my football captain boyfriend and doing the occasional trip to the homeless shelter where I would put in my monthly two hours of good deeds.

I'd never even held a gun-- scratch that-- I'd never even been in the same room as a gun until the world went to shit. Who knew the cure for herpes would turn all those sexual deviants into people-eating, brain-dead, infection-giving assholes?

Not me.

The whole phenomenon gave a girl a serious complex about safe sex.

Not that I was having sex. Or would be any time soon.

I hadn't even seen an eligible bachelor in a good six months and it wasn't like I had exactly been interested when we passed each other with guns raised and a suspicious glint in our eyes. Although there was a sort of mutual give and take between us that could have been considered an instant connection, possibly love at first sight. I let him loot the dead gentleman that had his head literally severed from his body by Feeders, and he let me raid the vending machine offering one bag of Funions that had been smashed into pathetic crumbs.

But then we both went our separate ways and I will never know if he got eaten, turned or found the promised land of Zombie-free showers and espresso machines.

Plus, I was still pining over poor, deceased, Quarterback-Chris.

Just kidding! Quarterback-Chris had apparently been less than faithful to me during our two year relationship and after things with the government, army and general world went to hell, Quarterback-Chris tried to eat me!

So I did what any loving, devoted girlfriend that just found out she had been serially cheated on by her now zombie boyfriend would do. I plunged a butcher knife into his eye socket and when that didn't effectively do the job, I drove over him with my mom's Escalade until his head detached from his body.

God, I was glad I held onto my v-card.

Could you imagine me as a zombie?

Ugh, it made me shudder just thinking about it.

A rustling to my left had my gun up, pointed and steady at whatever was stupid enough to make noise in a regular Feeder playground. I only had three bullets left, so this kill would have to be spot on.

That was the thing about living in a world in which it was a very likely possibility that you could end up as someone else's meal before lunchtime, you've got to be very good at shooting. Very quickly.

So even though the most I knew about my gun was that it was a Beretta from the label on the handle, and the exact kind of bullets it took, .40 S&W- because those were an absolute necessity and I was always on the lookout- I knew exactly how to use it. I knew exactly how to get my bullet from my gun to the perfect dead zone right between the eyes.

In fact, it was kind of freaky how good I was at killing things.

Well, killing already dead things.

It was like I was born for the Apocalypse. No, I couldn't find a hot shower, figure out how to make food last longer than twenty-four hours and effectively loot a Walgreens that still had hair products available. But I could stay alive.

I had an innate ability to stay alive.

And in this day and age, ninety-two weeks after the first recovering STD victim bit his doctor and the world fell apart, staying alive was very important.

Back to the rustling….

I slowed my breathing, stopped moving completely and waited for the sound to come to me.

One of the first things I learned about survival was that there was absolutely no need to go hunting down trouble. In the world I lived in, trouble would find you soon enough. It was better to cover your back, stay calm and have a loaded weapon ready and waiting.

"Reagan, check this out!" Haley squealed in a loud whisper.

"Holy hell, Hales!" I whisper-shouted back, "I almost shot you in the f-ing head!"

She made a resigned grunting noise and I heard her mumble, "Too bad, I bet they have showers in heaven."

"We are so not convinced you're going to heaven," I whispered back while stepping over a particularly decayed body.

Did I say the smell was the worst? I meant maggots.

The maggots were definitely the worst.

"It wouldn't matter," she countered with that distraught, depressed tone even the best of us were known to fall into. "This might as well be hell."

We were still whispering, there was no other option, since Feeders were drawn by sound. And sight, and smell, and light and movement.... But since we were rummaging around a dilapidated department store somewhere in what used to be southern Missouri, we had a little bit of cover.

The floor was covered with dirt and grime; metal racks that had been looted a long time ago were scattered and broken across the floor and we've already discussed the body count problem. We were using what was left of the evening light streaming through the broken window fronts to see and from the sounds of things we were alone, at least on the first floor.

One of the best things about Feeders was their incapability for stealth. They were heavy mouth breathers and tended to stumble over anything in their way. It was like they had their own warning bells.

Well, if you stayed alert, kept yourself surrounded by noisy debris and never fell asleep, you could sense their presence.

"What is it?" I asked; at the exact same moment my stomach growled.

Haley shot me a sympathetic look and shook her head, sending her dark blonde hair bouncing around her shoulders. "Not that."

I sighed, but continued to follow her down a dark hallway. Track lighting hung at awkward angles, the glass long shattered, the bulbs broken since the beginning. The once white walls were smeared with streaks of what I had to assume was blood and dirt. But the stench was less overwhelming here, the air easier to breath.

"I hit the jackpot," Haley said excitedly in almost a full-volume voice. We rarely spoke above a whisper so I was taken aback at first. I had almost forgotten what her real voice sounded like.

"In?"

"Jeans!" She turned back to look at me over her shoulder, giving me a goofy smile and waggling her eyebrows.

Now this *was* a jackpot.

We exited the hallway straight into the Junior's section. The racks were less knocked-over in this part of the store and still stocked with clothes. Racks and racks of fall fashions from almost two years ago filled the floor. A discount shoe rack with boxes of clearance items sat in one corner and in the middle of the department was a makeup counter.

An f-ing makeup counter.

Eyeliner!!!

At this point, you might be wondering who I could possibly want to look good for. And that is a valid question. But it wasn't like that.

In the last two years, I had been forced to live as a homeless, basically-starving person, with shredded, usually-covered-in-blood clothes, no shampoo, let alone conditioner and perpetually covered in dirt. I was tired of looking ugly.

Tired of it!

I just wanted a little bit of makeup, just something to make me feel like the world hadn't completely blown apart in the prime of my life and left me a wandering vagabond.

I had given up on finishing my education. I had given up on feeling guilty for killing what used to be human beings. I had given up on being happy again, living in a house, having a hot shower and whatever dream I had imagined myself living out. I had even given up on finding love.

Hell, I had given up on finding *sex*.

I just wanted to look anything but tired, weary and worn out.

Was that so much to ask?

"Welcome to the promised land, my friend," Haley whispered proudly before turning to a rack of longs-sleeve tee's.

I had a theory about why this section of the department store was untouched and it went something like this. In the beginning of the end, families protected their young. If you were a teenager, you were home, holding down the fort. Especially if you were a girl. The whole raping and pillaging thing didn't apply to most kids that still had parents around. And if you were young and stupid enough to try to make it in a world where sane people spent their time looting, overthrowing local government and shooting at any and every potential threat, chances were your inexperience and still rose-colored-glasses-of-the-world made sure you ended up dead.

How Haley and I survived living on the street and dodging not only the Feeders, but the crazed militia, and all the old man creepers that thought we would make fantastic sister wives was a straight up miracle. We got lucky in the beginning by sheer location. Small town, middle-of-nowhere Iowa finally paid off.

Well, except for the whole Quarterback-Chris thing.

But it wasn't like we didn't get Feeders in Atlantic, Iowa. Of course we did. Herpes was a worldwide disease. *Everybody* got Feeders, even remote islands in the middle of Oceans. If there were people there, then there were people having sex. And that meant STDs. Why? Because men would always be sluts. Always.

Was I a little bitter about Quarterback-Chris? Hell, yes.

Did I not mention he tried to *eat* me?

285

My parents were killed by Feeders. Haley's dad was killed by a Feeder. I was almost killed by a Feeder.

They were everywhere.

What we did have was an absence of a lot of people and an abundance of guns. Thank you, farmer Fred, for your once unnecessary stash of ex-military contraband.

I hopped over the counter, sliding my butt across the filthy glass. My already-grimy jeans smeared a dust-coated path the size of my hips. I landed on the pads of my feet and my toes were smashed even worse in my small hiking boots, but it was a soundless landing I was kind of proud of.

I had the reflexes of a cat, thanks to living every minute of my life expecting an attack. If the world ever got its f-ing act together and cleaned up this mess, I imagined they would make a movie of my life about the whole Zombie thing. I'd obviously be played by that hot brunette from the Vampire Diaries in which I would run around in a sexy Cat Woman suit, totally playing the super hero.

I opened the cabinets behind the makeup counter and slipped my backpack off my shoulder. Inside my hiking pack everything was orderly and neatly packed for maximum space and easy access. But I didn't have time for that now. I would reorganize everything later.

I started swiping handfuls of products into my bag, not caring about color or usefulness. This was what Haley and I called the Grab and Go- get as many supplies as we could now, as fast as we could, then leave the scene before either Feeders or protective townsfolk happened upon us. We could sort it out later. Without even having to discuss it with Haley, I knew she was picking out shirts and jeans for me and she knew I would cover her with whatever I could find.

After makeup, I hit up the clearance shoes, except there wasn't anything hiking, nature resilient or weather-proofed. Haley's shoes were in good condition actually, so I didn't bother debating over her. She was tiny by nature, not just because we only ate every three days and probably had scurvy since we were lacking serious vitamin C. She barely cleared 5'3, and her feet were average size enough that she could double up on socks and fit almost any pair we found.

I had clown feet even for my 5'8 frame and most the time found myself searching the small-feeted men. There were plenty of feet to choose from, but we didn't run across the right kind of shoe very often.

Like right now. There were a pair of tennis shoes that I could upgrade to, and they were my size. Or should I stick with the weather-proofed boots that would protect my feet from the elements?

The other part of the debate- tennis shoes were much lighter than these things, easier to walk across country in and much, much nicer to run in.

Still, I had to protect my feet. And I definitely didn't want trench foot. Not that I knew what trench foot was…. but I knew it was a big deal for everyone on Band of Brothers- my go to reference for everything survival.

"Get the shoes that fit," Haley said from across the room while digging through every style of jeans.

"You're right," I agreed. A shoe that fit had to be infinitely better than what I was wearing now. I toed off my boots and ripped off my socks. There was a whole rack of socks near the checkout counter, so I grabbed handfuls of them and stuffed them in the bag, saving a crazy-patterned neon pair for now.

"Sweatpants?" Haley asked from a new rack.

Moving quickly was essential to our survival, and we had honed this skill in order to stay alive. "Absolutely," I agreed. Jeans were practical and resilient, but there was nothing better than a pair of yoga pants when running for your life.

As I moved on to underwear-which might as well have been gold at this point- the light grew dimmer in this department. We were already squinting and stumbling around in the dark, and I knew we had been here too long. I had a flashlight that hadn't run out of battery yet, but I really didn't want to use it if it meant drawing the attention of wandering Feeders.

"Haley, we need to go," I whispered harshly.

I heard her zip up her pack and shoulder it, but I could barely make out her form anymore. We'd learned to act as soon as a command was given between us. There was no time to hesitate anymore, so by the time I'd slipped my heavy backpack on again, she was already moving toward the exit.

One of the weirdest parts of the Apocalypse was the quiet. I couldn't get used to it. Back in my old life, before the infection, there seemed to always be noise around. Cars on the highway, music from my iPod, airplanes overhead, my parents talking at me; there was always something in my ear. Now, there was nothing, no background elevator jazz to soothe us while we shopped, no other shoppers bustling around and bumping into us. The only sound to break up the silence was our careful footsteps and the heavy mouth-breathing from a Feeder in the next room.

Oh shit!

I grabbed the handle on Haley's backpack and tugged her backward. Her head whipped around and she opened her mouth to probably ask *what the hell*, but I held my finger to my lips and motioned with my head toward the way we just came from. It took her a second, but as soon as she heard the panting and wheezing in the next room she was instantly game for my plan of retracing our steps.

There was plenty of food for the bastard in the room he was in now, but I knew he would be able to sniff out our live, fresh flesh in the next two minutes and that was like the difference between prime rib and an old, moldy hot dog.

Best case scenario, he was going to lick the hot dog first, and come back for it later, after he ate his prime rib.

Which was me.

I stepped carefully until we were back in the Junior's Department, always keeping my gun trained on the direction of the Feeder. Haley stood a little bit behind me, her gun aimed to the left where this area opened up to the children's section.

"Son of a bitch," she breathed on a strangled whisper.

A quick glance toward the direction of her pointed gun, showed the glowing red eyes of two different Feeders. That was the signature of the last stage of their digression into Zombie-hood: first came the cravings for flesh, then the heart stopping in a semi-death, the disgusting process in which their brain still worked, but their bodies started to decay and then the tell-tale red eyes, showing basically that all humanity was lost. By then, they were stronger, didn't feel pain and only craved brains.

Basically, this *sucked*.

They could smell us, but couldn't see us yet, and so they were still trying to pinpoint us before they attacked. Unfortunately, we could also smell them. What really sucked was that there were at least three of them, these two and the one munching away on all that delicious dead flesh.

They weren't exactly pack animals, and usually they traveled- wandered aimlessly- alone; but if they ever found themselves together it was like they shared a hive brain or something. They acted as a team, without speaking or seemingly communicating, and once their eyes were red they were a hundred times harder to take down.

Our backs were against the wall, literally, and I wasn't exactly sure how we were going to get out of this one.

I glanced over my shoulder again and noticed for the first time an exit toward the corner of the room. A discounted clothing rack had been pushed up against it, and it was barely visible in the almost completely-dark room, but a reflected Exit sign was still pasted on the top.

As quietly as I could, I whispered, "Behind us, Hale. An exit. Lead or Cover?"

Haley let my noise settle before she answered. The Feeders had already started moving toward us. Despite every Zombie movie I had ever seen, the real life versions were not exactly the dumb and easy to kill version of walking corpses. They were hunters, fast and intuitive. While humanity still had the advantage of a rationalizing, fully functioning, not-addicted-to-living-flesh advantage, they weren't exactly a helpless opponent.

"Cover," Haley finally whispered back.

And with her blessing I turned on my heel and sprinted for the door. I could feel her behind me, but out of experience, I knew she was keeping her gun trained on the Zombies that were now chasing us down to make snacks out of our innards. I gave up on being quiet and threw anything that stood in my way.

The trip across the room took maybe five seconds, but it felt like the longest run of my life. I could already hear the Zombie from the other room tearing his way to join his friends. My heart was hammering in my chest, my vision focused only on the exit and my ears trained to listen for any surprises.

As soon as they were in my reach, I grabbed onto the tightly-packed, discounted clothes and went to toss the rack, but it only swayed. Something was holding it to the ground.

Pure panic prickled my blood and my eyes watered immediately from the stress of the situation. I heard Haley's gun go off behind me, but because the mouth-breathing was so loud I knew she had missed.

That meant she had four bullets left in her magazine.

Shit. Shit. Shit.

I pulled again on the rack of clothes and this time it moved an inch. I realized then that it was tethered by something on the ground. While Haley shot off another bullet, I dropped to my hands and knees and felt blindly for whatever was holding onto the base of the rack. Once I found the thick rope that was tied to the base, I whipped out my pocket knife I kept in the pocket of my pants and began cutting at the rope frantically.

Another shot from behind me and one of the Feeders dropped to the ground. *Good shot, Hales.* There were still at least two more Feeders left, and I could hear more commotion from the front entrance. All these shots were probably drawing everything out there in here.

I finally got through the rope, but as soon as the slack was gone, something huge and clanging crashed to the ground just on the other side of the door. It sounded like pots or pans and a whole bunch of breaking glass.

Shit!!!

I didn't have time to process that right now, so I stood up, effectively shoved the rack out of the way and went for the door handle. Another gun shot behind me and another Feeder dropped to the ground.

I lunged for the door handle, and turned it desperately. And nothing. It was locked.

"No!" I screamed, not caring about the noise level at this point.

Haley's last bullet exited her gun and the last Feeder felt the hit and fell to the ground directly behind me. These guys were dead, but there were who knew how many now headed toward us. Haley was out of bullets, and I had three left.

And our only exit was locked.

"What are you waiting for, Reagan. Let's get the *hell* out of here!" Haley's back was still to me as she faced her now empty gun at the hallway, just waiting for the rest of the Feeders to follow the sounds and find us.

"It's locked! *Damn it!*"

Completely panicked, I yanked on the handled and kicked it with my new shoe. Nothing happened. The door stayed firmly locked, stubbornly unmoving. This was definitely worst case scenario.

And not ten minutes ago I had been really excited about all that eye liner and a new pair of jeans.

This was so not how I was going out. I'd survived Quarterback-Chris, the death of my parents and almost two freaking years of living as the most depressing version of Mila Jovovich in *Resident Evil* ever.

"Open, damn it!" I screamed at the door, giving it another kick with my foot.

Only this time, my foot didn't connect with anything. The door wrenched open and my body flew, following my foot, through the empty space I wasn't expecting. I fell straight to my hands and knees in a huge pile of glass shards and broken ceramic. I felt the thick chunks of debris dig and slice through my skin immediately. My jeans would be completely irreparable after this and, with my luck, as soon as I was able to stop bleeding; I was for sure going to get gangrene.

What the hell?

"What the hell, Reagan?" Haley practically screamed at me as soon as she was through the doorway. She slammed the door behind her and braced her body against it; meanwhile, I was still doggy style in a pile of glass I was too afraid to stand up from.

The damage was going to be annoyingly excessive.

Before I could answer her though, I heard the signature click of a bullet being loaded into the chamber. More dread slithered through my body; other humans were just as deadly and dangerous as Zombies these days. And apparently we were trespassing.

"Don't move," a deep, masculine voice ordered in a quiet, steely tone.

"Out of the frying pan," Haley mumbled resignedly.

"And into the fire," I finished for her.

I would never complain about eyeliner again.

Every Wrong Reason

Rachel Higginson